Never-ending hatred . . .

Shaking from the pain of the wounds, Falon shifted back into her human form.

"Rafa," she pleaded, touching his bloody muzzle as he came around to her, "don't do this. I could not bear losing you."

He snarled and shook his great golden-furred body, blood stinging her skin. She looked past him to the great black wolf that was Lucien, the brother whose own chosen one, a forbidden Slayer, died by Rafael's righteous hand almost sixteen years ago. And today, Rafael paid the price of the Blood Law for his deed. Falon's life had been spared, but in sparing it, the counsel gave her to the prodigal son as payment for what his brother had so viciously taken from him.

It was fair in all eyes but hers and Rafael's. She would never lay with his brother, not when she loved Rafael and not after the pain and suffering she had endured by Lucien's hand. She would kill him first . . .

D0772066

Titles by Karin Tabke

BLOOD LAW

BLOODRIGHT

Anthologies

MEN OUT OF UNIFORM

(with Maya Banks and Sylvia Day)

BLOODRIGHT

KARIN TABKE

HEAT
NEW YORK

THE BERKLEY PUBLISHING GROUP
Published by the Penguin Group
Penguin Group (USA) Inc.
375 Hudson Street, New York, New York 10014, USA
Penguin Group (Canada), 90 Eglinton Avenue East, Suite 700, Toronto, Ontario M4P 2Y3, Canada
(a division of Pearson Penguin Canada Inc.) • Penguin Books Ltd., 80 Strand, London WC2R 0RL,
England • Penguin Group Ireland, 25 St. Stephen's Green, Dublin 2, Ireland (a division of Penguin
Books Ltd.) • Penguin Group (Australia), 250 Camberwell Road, Camberwell, Victoria 3124, Australia
(a division of Pearson Australia Group Pty. Ltd.) • Penguin Books India Pvt. Ltd., 11 Community
Centre, Panchsheel Park, New Delhi—110 017, India • Penguin Group (NZ), 67 Apollo Drive,
Rosedale, Auckland 0632, New Zealand (a division of Pearson New Zealand Ltd.) • Penguin Books
(South Africa) (Pty.) Ltd., 24 Sturdee Avenue, Rosebank, Johannesburg 2196, South Africa

Penguin Books Ltd., Registered Offices: 80 Strand, London WC2R 0RL, England

This book is an original publication of The Berkley Publishing Group.

Copyright © 2012 by Karin Tabke.
Cover photograph by Claudio Marinesco.
Cover design by Rita Frangie.
Text design by Laura K. Corless.

PUBLISHING HISTORY
Heat trade paperback edition / April 2012

Library of Congress Cataloging-in-Publication Data

Tabke, Karin.
Bloodright / Karin Tabke.—Heat trade pbk. ed.
p. cm.—(A blood moon rising novel; 2)
ISBN 978-0-425-24301-5 (pbk.)
I. Title.
PS3620.A255B58 2012
813'.6—dc23
2011046414

PRINTED IN THE UNITED STATES OF AMERICA

10 9 8 7 6 5 4 3 2 1

PEARSON

To Steven

Vulkasin Compound, Sierras, California

THE BLOOD LAW *is avenged.*

Years after alpha Rafael Vulkasin kills his brother Lucien's chosen one, the ancient council of the Lycan, the omnipotent Amorak, demands that Rafael honor the Blood Law. The Blood Law can only be avenged with an even exchange. An eye for an eye. The life of Rafael's chosen one in exchange for the life he took from Lucien.

But Rafael refuses to give his beloved Falon to his vengeful brother, who will destroy her. Rafael pleads to the Amorak to spare Falon's life.

After a great debate, the council reaches a verdict both brothers as well as Falon agreed in advance to honor. The council could have demanded Falon's life for the one Rafael took, but because doubt is cast on both brothers' claims, the council gives Lucien the choice: accept Falon as his own chosen one and treat her with the respect and honor due an alpha's mate, or surrender Falon to his brother, alive. Revenge never tasted sweeter to Lucien. Lucien chooses to keep

Falon as his own. And with his choice, the Lycan nation plummets into chaos.

"I WILL NOT join with him!" Falon shouted, pointing a finger at Lucien, the dark and dangerous brother the council had just given her to. The brother she despised. The brother she would never lay with!

Lucien's brilliant golden eyes sparked furiously. Hand extended, he strode toward her with the confidence of a man who knew he had won the prize fair and square. "You are mine now. Come to your master."

Rafael, Lucien's twin brother, the man Falon loved, snarled as he shifted to wolf and lunged. Lucien shifted and met him in the air, his black wolf snarling just as ferociously as Rafael's golden wolf. Their two bodies clashed and, as they had years ago, they tore at each other with one purpose: to kill. Only this time, it was Rafael who fought his brother for the life of his mate.

Still shocked at the verdict, Falon's brain sputtered, unable to react.

Never in her wildest dreams had she expected the verdict that had just been handed down. *Never* would she have agreed to abide by it. This could not be happening! She was supposed to stay with her beloved Rafael. Did the council not hear his truth? Lucien's mate was a Slayer! It was every Lycan's bloodright to kill *any* Slayer. And so Rafael had. But they believed Lucien's lies that she was not, and for his deceit, Falon was being torn from her true love's arms and forced into his brother's.

Just as stupefied, her pack, Vulkasin, and Lucien's pack, Mondragon, stood in dumbfounded silence. Unmoving, Falon stared as the twin wolves viciously tore into each other. Warm blood sprayed across her face and chest. Chunks of fur and flesh flew around her. The cracking sound of breaking bones, punctuated by terrifying snarls. Dear God, they were really going to kill each other!

Falon shifted into a ferocious she-wolf. She would defend her mate to the death. She would *not* live without him. Falon leapt into the vicious fray. She yelped as fangs sunk into her flesh and bones, tearing her apart. Despite their blood frenzy to destroy the other, the brothers broke apart when they realized Falon had entered the fray. Neither wanting to harm her, they backed away. Heads down, ears pinned low, with wary eyes on the other, they circled her maimed body.

Shaking from the pain of the wounds, Falon shifted back into her human form.

"Rafa," she pleaded, touching his bloody muzzle as he came around to her, "don't do this. I could not bear losing you."

He snarled and shook his great golden-furred body, blood stinging her skin. She looked past him to the great black wolf that was Lucien. The brother whose own chosen one, a forbidden Slayer, died by Rafael's righteous hand almost sixteen years ago. And today, Rafael paid the price of the Blood Law for his deed. Falon's life had been spared, but in sparing it, the counsel gave her to the prodigal son as payment for what his brother had so viciously taken from him.

It was fair in all eyes but hers and Rafael's. She would never lay with his brother, not when she loved Rafael and not after the pain and suffering she had endured by Lucien's hand. She would kill him first.

Falon swallowed hard and looked at the two packs that had drawn into a tight circle around them, and then behind them the other packs that had come in support of each brother. Past them on a raised dais stood the council of the Amorak, the keeper of the wolves. Their grave faces stared unblinking as the blood feud that had been building for over fifteen years played out.

Falon's heart ached with such pain she could scarce draw a breath. Her lover's blood smeared her bare chest, mingling with her own, dripping onto her feet, pooling around her toes. Rafael's great body heaved as he drew ragged breaths. Lucien was in no better shape. If she did not intervene, they would kill each other. For Rafael's life, she accepted what she must do. Inhaling deeply, Falon held her breath for long seconds, then exhaled.

Rafa, my love, my heart, my soul. Your life is more important to me than all the lives in this world combined. Please, stop this. Let me go. We will be together again. I promise.

He will kill you, Falon, if I do not kill him first!

Rafael leapt over Falon, tackling his brother. And the fight was on again.

Frantic, and desperate for them to stop, naked and bloody, Falon stumbled into Rafael's office where she knew he kept a loaded handgun in his desk. She grabbed it. She would not stand by and watch her beloved be destroyed. Running back into the great room, Falon shot several rounds into the ceiling.

The shots had no effect on either brother. They continued to fight. Time stopped. In slow motion, Falon watched the wolves tear each other apart, their fangs dripping red with blood, their great chests heaving as they sucked in air.

"You must stop this!" Sharia, the elder Amorak, shrilled, pushing past the council into the crowded floor. Falon shot off another round. When the brothers continued to fight, she put the barrel of the gun to her chest and screamed, "Stop now or there will be nothing to fight over!"

Simultaneously, Rafael and Lucien shifted into their human forms and turned to face her. Falon cried out at Rafael's condition.

Large gaping gashes filleted his chest, thighs, and arms. His golden skin glittered crimson.

He reached out to her, taking an unsteady step toward her. "No, Falon," he said hoarsely.

"The Blood Law has been avenged!" Sharia cried, stepping toward the alpha brothers. "You both know to kill an alpha is a death sentence!"

The grizzled old woman tottered toward Lucien and grabbed his bloody hand. "Kill your brother this day and lose your life before the sun sets." She took Rafael's hand and placed it over his brother's. "Swear before the packs you will not break our covenant."

Rafael yanked his hand from Sharia's and spit on the floor. "The Blood Law has forsaken me! Only Lucien's death will atone for it!"

Lucien stepped snarling toward Rafael. "The Blood Law has betrayed me *twice*! Only your chosen one's death will redeem it!"

"No," Falon whispered. "I do not want to die."

Lucien turned and faced her. "You will not die by my hand. I swore to accept the verdict and so I shall." He extended his hand, motioning her to him. "You belong to me now."

"I don't." Desperately Falon looked past Lucien to Rafael, who stepped toward her. His ocean-colored eyes cried out with pain, longing, and a love for her so profound she felt it to her marrow. But shining just as passionately, she beheld his honor, his pride, his love for his people. And most heartbreaking of all, the truth of what she must do. Go with Lucien or refuse; either way, the outcome would destroy Rafael. She could not live with that guilt. She straightened and faced Sharia. "I reject both alphas. I choose to remain unmated."

"You gave up that choice when you exchanged marks with Rafael," Sharia said evenly. Her tobacco brown eyes glittered furiously. Her gnarled hands fisted at her sides. "See it done!"

Falon shook her head and stepped back. This was barbaric! She was not a commodity to be traded because of a law she did not live by. And she would not be a slave to any man *or* nation.

"Come with me now," Lucien said softly.

She looked at him through blurry eyes. Lucien: the dark, mysterious, misunderstood alpha who maybe, in a different place and a different time, she could accept. But not now. Not when that choice would destroy Rafael. "No," she whispered and pulled the trigger.

Pain exploded in her chest. Her heart shuddered from the percussion. Falon knew her body was shaking, but she felt only the profound loss of the life she had prayed for with Rafa. Barely able to stand, she blinked back the blood and tears as every eye in the great room stared dumbfounded at her. The only eyes she met were Rafael's stunned aqua-colored ones. "Noooo!" he cried, running toward her.

The gun slipped from her bloody fingers. The pain mushroomed throughout her body. "I love you," Falon said as she crumpled to the floor.

It was not Rafael's arms that caught her but those of his brother. Lucien's horrified golden eyes were the last thing she saw before she gave up her life for the man she loved.

One

LUCIEN GRABBED FALON to his chest before Rafael could touch her and whirled away from him deep into the safety of his pack.

Rafael lunged after him, but pack Vulkasin had the wherewithal to swarm around their alpha, as much for his protection as theirs. They understood what had to happen next.

Rafael snarled, wildly lunging, his powerful arms and legs held back only by the combined effort of a dozen of his men.

"I will give this warning only once," Lucien growled from the security of his pack, speaking not only to his brother but to the council. "If Rafael or *any* of pack Vulkasin, including the Berserkers, make any attempt to take what is mine by bloodright, by the Blood Law, I will destroy them and in so doing be justified!"

He sneered at the assembled council of Amorak elders. "You are weak. By your failure to enforce the Blood Law as it is written, I will no longer live by it."

"You would have her death?" Sharia demanded, pointing at Falon's broken body in his arms.

"I would have the right to choose my own mate!" Lucien shouted.

"Then return her to Rafael and choose," Sharia said sharply.

And what penalty would his brother have paid for destroying the woman Lucien chose to stand beside him? None. And that he would never accept!

Shaking his head, Lucien looked down at Falon's naked bleeding body. An emotion he could not put a name to tugged at him. This half-Lycan, half-human female represented many things to many of his people. Whoever possessed her possessed her unusual powers. And through that connection they would gain untold power. But for Lucien personally, the true power Falon gave him was the power to destroy his brother. And for that alone, he would not allow her to die.

"You cannot have it both ways, Lucien," Sharia said. "Live by the Blood Law, or refute it and return her to Rafael."

Pride aside, Lucien was a fool if he returned her to his brother. From the moment he laid eyes on the sultry beauty, she became the one thing he must possess. And possess her he would.

He looked back at Sharia and nodded. "So be it. She belongs to me now by bloodright." His eyes narrowed as he turned to face his brother. "As mine, *I* will choose if she lives or dies," Lucien taunted. For sixteen years, he had waited for the day he would hold his brother's chosen one's life in his hands. That day had come. But instead of taking her life, he had been given it. Part of him resented it, part of him reveled in it, but another part of him feared it would blow up in his face. Her love for his brother would never die. And he would never share any part of her.

"You agreed not to take her life," Maleek, an elder from the north, said, stepping around Sharia's shriveled frame.

"It is my choice to allow nature to take its course or to redirect it,"

Lucien defended. Now Rafe would finally know what it felt like to have the woman he loved ripped from his arms.

"Give her to me!" Rafael shouted, fighting against his men. "I can heal her!"

"As can I, Brother. If *I* choose."

"You would not dare allow her to die!" Sharia screeched.

Lucien glared at the assembled packs. "I would dare, and more! I will kill any human or Lycan who dares to challenge my right to decide if she lives or dies!"

Lucien turned with Falon in his arms. Her pulse had weakened and her heartbeat had slowed to a death knell. Her lifeblood covered his body. Never more furious than at that moment, Lucien looked down at the woman who had driven the wedge deeper between the packs. His brother's chosen one. The woman Rafael loved and who loved him equally in return. Why had she been given a second chance when his own chosen one had not been given even one? His heart still ached over the loss.

As would his brother's for Falon. Because now she was Lucien's. And though his vengeance burned white hot in his heart, there was the slightest sliver of it left untainted by the ugliness his world had become. That tiny piece of him cried out to Falon to love him as she loved his brother.

He looked over his shoulder to his frantic twin. It took the combined effort of pack Vulkasin and those of pack Ruiz's alpha and sergeant at arms to hold Rafael back. "Take your honor and your Blood Law and find another mate, Brother." Lucien raised the dying Falon in his arms. "This one is mine." Rafael's eyes blazed bloodred, froth covered his mouth, and the muscles in his body strained so tightly against his skin it looked as if his body would split at the seams. "Come near her, Brother, and I will kill her *after* I kill you."

Rafael snarled and shifted. As he lunged at Lucien, a shot rang out. Rafael's big body hit the floor with a heavy thud.

Stunned, Lucien looked past his brother to Sharia, who stood with the handgun Falon had used on herself, pointed at Rafa's now-human body. A profound sense of loss he could not explain filled Lucien's heart.

"My gods! What have you done!" Lucien railed at the old medicine woman stepping toward his brother's still body.

She raised furious brown eyes to him and levelly said, "Leave here before he shakes off the wound and kills you, or I will kill you myself."

Lucien stepped back, unsure how to interpret the emotions crashing inside him. So he did not try. "If he dies from the wound, you will answer to me."

"What do you care?" the old woman scoffed.

"He is my brother! When his time comes, it will be by my hand alone!"

With Falon hanging unconscious in his arms, Lucien strode bloody and naked from the Vulkasin compound building to his waiting motorcycle. His pack swarmed behind him. Talia, his cousin and Mondragon spirit healer, shoved her way through the bodies to Lucien, her big purple eyes wide with concern. She pressed her hand to Falon's heart. "She does not have much time left, Lucien."

"I know." He whirled away. Holding Falon to his chest, he mounted his chopper. Moments later, they roared out of the compound.

Luca.

Lucien ignored his brother's desperate call.

Luca, please, I beg you, if you have any love for me left in your heart, heal Falon.

Rafael's words tore at him. The devil that drove Lucien wanted

Falon to die, to punish Rafael for what he had done to him. An eye for an eye; Rafael would finally live Lucien's pain. But that barely perceptible part of the human that was left, stayed his revenge.

Save her.

Lucien ground his jaw, shutting off his mind to his brother's pleas. The beast in him wanted to save Falon, because for selfish reasons, for noble reasons, for purely primal reasons, he wanted her for himself.

Save her, Luca. She is powerful and strong. Save her and you save yourself.

"What payment do you offer for her life?" he shouted to the wind.

As Lucien made the demand, he steered his chopper to the shoulder of the road where he abruptly stopped. He growled and looked down at the pale face. The face that had pitted Lycan against Lycan. The face Rafael had fallen in love with. The face Lucien dreamed would one day be his to kill. The face that could end the Lycan nation as a people. Because there was no chance for the packs to reunite now. Not as long as one of the brothers lived. Or, if she died.

Save her life and I swear on our mother's heart, I will not come for her.

But she will come for you.

I will shun her.

And she will know it is a ploy.

I will make her think I love another.

Then swear to take another mate before the next full moon.

You will save her, then?

I will save her. But that decision was made the minute she pulled the trigger.

I swear it.

That Rafael did not hesitate to give up the one thing he loved most in the world to save it was not lost on Lucien. He hated his brother for his honor. But despised himself more because he loved nothing enough to make any sacrifice.

Then it will be done. Because honor was Rafael's Achilles' heel. Not only would he abide by the council's decision, Rafael would keep his word and stay away from Falon. The cards could not have been dealt more favorably to Lucien had he handpicked them himself.

As Lucien laid Falon's still body down on the side of the road, her heart arrested. Quickly, Lucien bit his wrist until his blood flowed in a thick, steady stream and then pressed it to Falon's pale lips. He pressed his other hand to the gunshot wound in her chest. Closing his eyes, he called upon the Great Spirit Mother to spare her life, just as she had spared his and Rafael's lives all those years ago.

Talia came up behind him and pressed her hands to his shoulders and began an ancient healing chant. Her hands infused him with a warm heat. It traveled from his shoulders to his arms to his hands, and into Falon's body. His blood thrummed hot in his veins.

Iridescent energy flickered along Lucien's skin to Falon's. Her heart lurched against his hand, and in a slow, unsteady cadence, it began to beat. Lucien's own heart beat with it, urging hers into a steadier rhythm. Falon choked as his blood drenched her lips. He pressed his wrist more firmly to her lips.

"Take it, Falon," he commanded.

She moaned.

"Yes," he whispered. "Take more."

Her lips tightened around him, her tongue slid across the bite wounds, her lips pulled, sucking hard. A desire like no other thrummed through him, slamming into his defenses before filling every inch of him with a wild, possessive greed.

Lucien closed his eyes, fighting the call of the wild. But once he wrangled the beast to submission, he heard it again. Stronger this time: the inarguable call of her blood to his.

Like a lightning bolt striking a mountaintop, it struck Lucien that Falon was meant to be his. He believed strongly in fate, fate he directed, not fate directing him. He forced a tight smile and smoothed away a hank of blood-soaked hair from her cheek. She would be his now, and with her by his side, they would lead the nation against the Slayers and destroy each and every one of those murderous miscreants.

Lucien lowered his lips to the bullet wound that still seeped blood and licked it, sealing it enough to buy him some time to get to his own compound in the flatlands.

Falon's body had stilled, but the strong beat of her heart told him she would live.

He looked up to Talia, who stood by silently. "She's strong enough to make it to the compound."

"I'll go ahead and prepare your room."

Lucien nodded. Falon's other wounds could wait. He pulled out the spare clothing he always carried from one of the saddlebags. He wrapped one of his shirts around Falon's shoulders, and quickly dressed himself. Carefully he picked her up and mounted his chopper.

Readjusting Falon's limp body in his arms, Lucien gave the go-ahead signal to his pack, and they carefully continued down the steep mountain road to his own compound nestled in the flatlands at the base of Sierras.

His mind swirled with what it would mean to finally have a mate, and how she would affect his future. Lucien glanced down at Falon's pale face. His chest tightened. He would not love her. Could not. Not when she loved his brother. He trusted Rafael would not come for her, and he believed Rafael would do all in his power to convince Falon he loved another, but Falon's heart would never beat for Lucien. She would never share her heart with him, but more than that, he would not share what was left of his with her.

He was incapable of loving.

The day he watched his parents die the most heinous of deaths at the hands of Thomas Corbet and his brothers Balor and Edward had jackhammered away a chunk of Lucien's heart. The day his chosen one died in his arms by the brother he loved as much as he loved himself, what little part of his heart was left disintegrated into dust. While his vengeance against Rafael had eaten at him for years, his true driving passion since he was ten years old was to destroy every drop of the Corbet bloodline. Destroy the blood, destroy the threat.

The rising was two months away. His mother was Mondragon of the greatest European pack. They would follow him. But Rafael had the support of the Russian and northern packs.

Lucien sneered. That loyalty would not last once they heard how the great golden alpha had softened because of a female, and one not even full Lycan.

Falon stirred in his arms as if she knew he thought of her with disdain. Even if every pack on the planet served Lucien, Rafael held the trump card: the Eye of Fenrir. The ancient ruby ring that housed the powerful but traitorous wolf, Fenrir. The power the ring held was untold. The soul who possessed it, and understood the power within and how to wield that power, was untouchable.

Throwing his head back, Lucien howled at the waning moon. "Oh, Rafael, had you not been blinded by your honor, you could have used the power of the ring to destroy me and have your woman. No one would dare challenge you!"

But Rafael played by the honor code. Using the ring would have disrespected the council's decision and in so doing disrespected the Blood Law. What did it get him? Nothing but a ring with the promise of power that would never be used and the loss of his chosen one.

If Lucien possessed the ring there would be no doubt what he would do with it. He would exploit every facet of it. He would not wait for the rising. Single-handedly he would go on a rampage destroying every descendant of Peter "the Wolf" Corbet. There would be no place any of them could hide. None with the power to stop him, and once he had eradicated the world of that bloodline, he would go after the rest of them. One by one, they would die a slow, miserable death by his hand alone. And when the world was free of every last Slayer, he would call the packs together and they would unite and rebuild as one.

What had Rafael done with the ring? Nothing proactive that Lucien could see. It was wasted on a man who was so blinded by his honor, he could not see that to survive, he must use the power *now* and strike before the rising.

Lucien glanced down at Falon. Mauled and bloody as she was, her unusual beauty shown through. But there was more than that holding Lucien's attention. Her mystical essence was strong. Magic swirled around her bright aura. He knew firsthand she had a temper. Knew she was a fighter, too. He inhaled her rich, musky scent. Carnally, she would be unpredictable and insatiable. She was a worthy mate. That he would not deny. He looked ahead at the dark ribbon of road. To be loved by this woman as she loved his brother would be as powerful in itself as the Eye of Fenrir.

Even his own chosen one had not loved him the way Falon loved Rafael. Was he not worthy of such love? Snarling, Lucien dug his fingers into Falon's waist. He *was* worthy! More than worthy. He was alpha! He deserved all that Rafael possessed, including being loved by his chosen one. But to receive love, one must give it, and Lucien had none to spare.

His lips pulled back from his teeth. Yeah, she may never love him, but the silver lining was that *he* would have her. She would bear *his* children. And long after they triumphed over the rising, Rafael would roam aimlessly among the mountains craving the one true mate he could never have.

Lucien leashed his anger before it took control of him. Even if he were to die an untimely death, once he took Falon and marked her as his, Rafael would never take her back. His honor would never allow it, much less his pride. Lucien scoffed. He got the pride thing. Had Falon lain with any other man than his brother, and if his revenge would not live on in his possession of Falon, even with all her powers combined, Lucien would have refused her as his chosen one.

Lucien smiled. She had a few other assets that swayed him. His gaze swept her full breasts. She was a prize. And naive. She had unknowingly been lured last month into trading blood with him. Small though it was, it took only a drop from each of them for the exchange to manifest into the power to slip into her subconscious and not only speak to her but—touch her. He suspected Falon didn't realize she possessed the same power. The sensations were real. All senses firing when the bloods recognized their counterpart. And for all that she had belonged to Rafael, she belonged to him now.

His skin warmed as he remembered how, like a mist, he had gone into her dreams and intimately touched her. Heat sluiced through his veins straight to his dick. He could not remember ever feeling so sexual as when she responded to his touch in her dreams, and it had been just an illusion. She had been delectably innocent to his power over her then, now—his arm tightened around her waist drawing her closer to his chest. Once she healed, he would come to her in full flesh and bone. He would fuck her until she howled herself hoarse and every Lycan for three hundred miles would know what he was doing to her. It would drive Rafael mad.

Keeping Falon alive had been a score on more than one count.

*   *   *

FALON WRITHED IN pain on the damp sheets. Her body sizzled with fever. Feeling like lead, her limbs weighed her down. Every joint ached. Her swollen eyes pounded like wrecking balls against her eyelids.

She had been slogging through crowds of aimless souls for days, weeks, months, fighting her way toward the sliver of light that beckoned in the distance, just beyond the souls who slogged as she toward the light. Each time she got close enough to feel the warmth of the light across her cheeks, thick fog sucked her back into the gray purgatory of nothingness. Far below her feet, the churning black abyss of hell waited for souls to fall into its hungry jaws.

Strong hands caught her each time she slipped through the fog toward the violent vortex beneath her. If the whirlpool caught hold of her, it would suck her down, and even the strong hands that had repeatedly pulled her from it would not be able to save her. It had been what she wanted: that black numbness of death. But when faced with the reality of death, she fought to live.

Rafa! Come for me!

Each time she called out to him, her voice echoed back. Unanswered.

A choked cry caught in her throat. *Rafa, why do you ignore me?*

Her heart shuddered to a halt with grim realization. There was only one reason Rafa would not return her call. He was dead.

I'm so sorry! she sobbed.

Why had she sworn to abide by the council's decision?

Because the verdict could be only one of two. Either they would believe Rafael was justified to kill Lucien's chosen one because she was a Slayer, and with that belief allow her to stay with Rafael, or they would not believe him and hand her over to Lucien to destroy. The word of the Blood Law was painfully clear: an eye for an eye.

Had they given Lucien license to kill her, she would have killed him in self-defense and lived with the consequences. She would have hidden until the rising when she would reveal herself to stand beside Rafa and fight for their lives. With the dawn of a new world, new laws would be written. New laws that would make it possible for her to be with her true love.

Never had she imagined that the council would allow her to live. A twist on an eye for an eye. Her living, breathing life for the one Rafael took from Lucien. Why didn't they condemn her to death? She had the power to destroy Lucien when he took his revenge. Now, as much as she longed to be with Rafa, she could not, would not, kill Lucien in cold blood.

Why was this happening? Who did she piss off? And how the hell was she supposed to get out of this mess?

The fog began to clear as the same powerful hands that guided her through her perilous journey slid possessively along her arms, to her shoulders. Warm lips pressed against the pain in her chest. A thick tongue swathed a warm, moist trail across a sensitive nipple. Arching into the soothing cadence, Falon moaned.

A deep growl reverberated from the sensuous lips pressed to her. Sensitive waves of desire shimmered across her chest, down her belly to settle in her womb. A keen sense of safety encompassed her like a warm fluffy blanket just out of the dryer. Thick emotion clogged her chest. "Rafa," she whispered, "you came for me."

Deep laughter vibrated around her. "Not Rafa, love. Lucien, your alpha."

Falon's eyes flew open. Lucien's dark head hovered above her breast as his lips suckled her nipple, sending harsh flashes of fire to her loins. "No," she cried. *Not Lucien.*

He smiled against her nipple and tugged at it with his teeth. "Yesss," he hissed. "In the flesh."

Falon swallowed hard. Trying to raise a hand against him was impossible. Her limbs would not respond to her command to move. The ache in her joints radiated to other parts of her body. Squeezing her eyes shut, Falon inhaled deeply, then exhaled. This was a dream. A *nightmare*. She would wake up next to Rafael. But instead of falling back into the safety of unconsciousness, her body responded to the sensuous pull of the man above her.

It terrified her.

Not his touch. No, his touch—she moaned and arched into his hand when he cupped her other breast—thrilled her. What terrified her was how much it thrilled her.

He plucked her sensitive nipple with his fingers as he licked and suckled the other. "Lucien—" She gasped. *Stop.*

"Falon," he roughly responded. *Make me.*

How could she make him stop when she could not raise a hand? And did she want to? She felt tipsy as if she had drunk too much wine. The sizzling wake of her blood as it raced to her womb felt like tiny hot champagne bubbles. Tempting and teasing her sensitive places.

She climbed a slippery slope. By rights, she had sworn to go with Lucien as his chosen one, as well as all that went with that title. But—if she gave into the temptation of Lucien, if Rafael lived, he would turn his back on her for all time. That she could not bear. Ever.

Falon screamed her frustration, and arched weakly against the strong arms pinning her down. Lucien's laughter reverberated across her hot skin. In a slow, languorous trail, his lips and tongue swept across her aching body.

As his touch extracted one pain from her, it infused her with a different pain. Even if she could fight it, she wouldn't. After the trauma her body had just been through, what he did to her now felt too damn good. Intuitively she knew she had lost a substantial amount of blood, and that despite Lucien's healing powers, her body would need more time to rejuvenate. Her strength was nothing compared to what it would be if she were healthy. If it were, Lucien would be part of the wall right now.

"Don't fight me, Falon, not now when you are no match for me."

She fought to open her eyes again, but they were so heavy. "Take advantage of my weakened state, Lucien, and it will be the last thing you do."

His tongue slid across a deep bite on the inside of her thigh perilously close to her mons. Falon bit back a deep moan, trying unsuccessfully to stay the slow undulation of her hips.

"Oh, God," she gasped when his tongue slid along the wet seam of her soft, fleshy nether lips. Her fingers dug into the linen beneath her. His audacity should not shock her. When they had bitten each other in Rafael's room less than a month ago, she had unwittingly made a blood bond with him. He had come uninvited into her thoughts more than once, and more than once had touched her in a most salacious way. That it was all in her head made it no less real.

Dear God, stop him, before I cannot stop myself. She hated him. He was ruthless, cruel, and sinister. Yet, from their first meeting, he fascinated her on a dark and dangerous level . . . Whereas Rafael was all that was golden and honorable, Lucien was all that was dark and decadent. His emotions ran as deep as his brother's, maybe deeper. It made him all the more dangerous. All the more of an enigma. All the more unpredictable. The ultimate challenge to any woman to tame the tortured beast within him.

"I would never take advantage of you in such an unseemly way, Falon."

"Liar," she moaned as his tongue sluiced down the inside of her thigh. Her hands fisted the linens tighter. Her wounds throbbed with each heartbeat; his tongue soothed them in long, languid strokes. The intoxicating blend of pain and pleasure drove her mad. Falon steeled her muscles to resist him but the effort painfully torqued her mauled body. Loosening her muscles, she stopped fighting.

"I have never forced you."

"You have—" She moaned when his tongue slid down her calf to her ankle and licked a deep bite there, then along her instep to her toes. "Stop—that."

"If I stop, you will not heal."

"I'll take my chances."

"It is not your decision to make."

"You are not the boss of me!"

He laughed low. Taking her foot into his big hands, Falon hissed as the pain shot through her. "The bones in your foot have been crushed." Gently he began to massage her foot.

Heat emanated from his fingertips into her skin, through the tendons and muscles to her bones. God, it felt so soothing, so— "Ahh, Lucien, that feels so"—she bit back a moan of pleasure as it tangoed with the pain of the fractures—"good."

He lowered his lips to just above her mons and whispered, "When I take you, Falon—and mark my words, I will—you will want as badly as me."

Falon swallowed hard, pressing her bottom firmly into the mattress, away from Lucien's decadent lips. "Never!" She would never willingly lay with anyone, except Rafa.

Releasing her foot none too gently, he rolled her over onto her belly. Trailing a finger along the curve of her back, she flinched. "You have a nasty bite here. My apologies if I was the culprit." Falon opened her mouth to tell him to go to hell when his tongue slid along the deep bite. She squeezed her eyes shut and moaned, pressing her hips into the mattress. God, that felt good. "Never say never, Falon."

When she tried to squirm away from him, her pain-laden limbs barely moved. His grip tightened. Each time she fought him, her energy ebbed a little more. Her eyelids felt like concrete slabs on her face. Like a drug, lethargy stole through her. "Stop fighting me."

"Only when you stop breathing," she mumbled as she gave up to blissful unconsciousness.

Lucien's laughter was the last thing she heard before her ravaged body succumbed to the trauma inflicted upon it.

SHE DREAMED OF Rafael, of running wild and free with him as wolves deep into the Sierra timberline, not once looking back, only forward to their future together. Her chest constricted in realized heartache when Rafael ran ahead of her to be met by a beautiful, snowy white she-wolf. "She is Lycan, Falon," Rafa gently explained as he took his place beside her. "My true mate, and the future of Vulkasin."

"No, Rafa! I am your true mate!"

He looked sadly at her, as if she were something to be pitied. "You belong to Lucien now."

"No!" she screamed when he turned from her and with his mate at his side, leapt into the swirling mist. "No! Rafa!" She leapt after him but fell through the mist down the mountainside. She screamed, clawing at the rocky edge not wanting to die but not wanting to live without Rafa.

"Rafa!"

"He is gone to you, Falon," a soft soothing voice said beside her. It was vaguely familiar.

"You cannot hide in your dreams. Open your eyes and face your reality," the voice commanded.

Falon shook her head. She had no heart to live in a reality that did not include Rafa.

Fingers dug into her tender shoulders and shook her. Falon flinched, her wounds still tender, and flung the hands from her. She sat up, opening her eyes. Where was she? Who was the woman? Blinking rapidly, Falon shook the cobwebs from her head and looked at the woman staring at her.

Her ugly reality came flooding back to her. The council hearing, their unbelievable verdict, her life sentence with Lucien. As his chosen one!

And the woman standing so close. Talia! Rafael's cousin and healer. She had been kidnapped by Lucien and forced to stay in his compound just as Falon was being forced! Would Talia become her ally or her foe? Wide-eyed, Falon looked around the room and absorbed her surroundings.

If she didn't instinctively know where she was, she would know by the heavy dark furniture and the rich earthy scent swirling around her like a possessive cloak. She was chin deep in Lucien's lair. The room was larger than the one she shared with Rafa. Deep blood colors mixed with the earth tones of the rich textured fabrics. Brocade, satin, smooth linen. Despite the richness of the adornments, the room was distinctly male. Distinctly sensual. Distinctly—dangerous.

A gnarled black oak armoire and dresser unit that took up an entire wall faced the bed next to the door. Two distressed pale leather chairs sat opposite each other with a table made of the same leather between them. On the wall above the grouping was a wicked ebony-handled sword, the metal polished to a high shine. It appeared well used. On the other side of the room, a large gnarled wood desk dominated with several computers and neat stacks of paper piled atop.

Above the desk on the wall a large red, black, and gold painting of a fire-breathing dragon with a wolf head. Lucien bore the same dragon tattoo on his chest, back, and abdomen.

Instead of lamps, groupings of thick beeswax candles with rivulets of wax running down them and pooling onto the nightstands flanking the huge four-poster bed she lay upon appeared to be the only source of light with the exception of one window in the corner adjacent to the bed. The computers were the only modern amenity. If she didn't know better, she'd think she was locked in a Gothic castle.

Falon looked directly at Talia's stormy face. The Lycan healer was pretty. No, more than pretty. Talia's earthy sensuality punctuated by large, vibrant violet-colored eyes was no less than stunning. Rafael spoke of his cousin often and with love.

"I will not stay here as Lucien's slave."

Talia snorted and moved from the edge of the bed. She was petite to Falon's statuesque. The sultry Lycan tossed her long, sable-colored hair over her shoulders and said, "I didn't peg you for a drama queen, Falon," Talia said.

Falon stiffened.

"If you renege on your sworn oath to abide by the council's verdict, that you accept Lucien as your true mate and he you, you will create such chaos among the packs they will not survive the rising."

"Don't try to lay that on me! What if I weren't here? What if I had never met Rafael?"

"Fate intended you to meet Rafael. You were meant to break this insufferable sixteen-year stalemate!" Talia moved closer. "You have powers no Lycan possesses. You are at the middle of something that is bigger than all of us. Bigger than your wants and desires. Bigger than your heart, your life, *and* your soul!"

Falon shook her head. She was not the key to anything!

"It doesn't matter whether you understand or not. I don't know that *I* understand what our future holds. What I do know in my heart is what matters now: you must exchange marks with Lucien. Become his true mate in every sense. United, the two of you will have more power than ten packs! And we need all the power we can muster for the rising."

"My destiny is not with Lucien."

"Your destiny is to listen to your calling, Falon."

"My calling and my heart belong to Rafael."

Talia contemplated Falon's answer, then said, "Our hearts have the capacity to love many."

How could she love another when her heart was so filled with love for Rafael? How could anyone love Lucien? He was dark, moody, and unpredictable. He was her beloved's sworn enemy! It would kill Rafa if she loved Lucien. She would never hurt him that way.

Vigorously, Falon shook her head. "I could never love Lucien." Falon leapt from the bed but caught the thick poster, as her world tilted right then left. She slowly shook the clouds from her head, still feeling as if she were going to faint. Looking down at her naked body, her vision blurred, then focused. Her eyes widened in shock. There was no trace of even the slightest wound. Her skin was as smooth and unblemished as a baby's. *All* of her skin! Her mons was shaved smooth, no vestige of the downy shield that used to be there. Heat rose in her cheeks. She was going to kill Lucien!

The heat intensified in her cheeks as her gaze locked with Talia's. The Lycan smiled sheepishly and shrugged. "Lucien likes his women unfettered."

"How dare he touch me! How dare he—" Falon's knees wobbled. Her blood loss would take time to regenerate, but her temper was as volatile as ever. She scooted back onto the bed before she fell to the floor.

Talia shrugged. "The sooner you accept Lucien as lord and master over everything you see here, the sooner you will find peace."

"I will never accept him! I cannot!" Rafael would never forgive her. "If he touches me, I will kill him."

Talia tsked, shaking her head. "To kill an alpha is punishable by death."

"They'd have to catch me first."

"Lucien is many things, some of which I strongly disapprove of, but he is alpha. His word is law. That he accepted you as his true mate was not a decision he made lightly. In accepting you, he forfeited his right to pick the mate of his choice. Instead of sullen, you should feel honored."

"Honored? How can I feel honored when the man I have unwillingly been given to does not know the meaning of the word *honor*?"

"There is honor in the simple fact he is alpha."

"Lucien has taken his title through force and coercion. He will never be half the alpha Rafael is. He is a joke among the Lycan nation."

Talia's eyes flashed angrily. She stepped to the edge of the bed and leaned into Falon. Chin to chin she spoke slowly but concisely. "Do not *ever* say such things about Lucien. Until you have walked a mile in his shoes, keep your judgments to yourself."

"He has brainwashed you. You are obviously a victim of his coercion tactics."

"I have been free to leave here from the moment I arrived."

Falon's brows wrinkled in confusion. It was common knowledge Lucien had kidnapped Talia and forced her to stay here. "But—"

"It's true," Talia reiterated.

"Then why have you allowed Rafa to think you were being forced to stay here?"

"He never asked, he, as the rest of the Lycan nation, assumed the worst of Lucien."

"Yet you did nothing to school them?"

"Lucien forbade it. He stands by his actions. He does not require anyone to champion his cause."

"If Lucien was such a noble alpha, he would have long ago made peace with his brother."

"Peace between the brothers can only come when there is peace with their true mate."

"But I am *Rafa's* true mate! We *are* at peace!" Or at least they were.

"You belong to Lucien now."

"I am not his true mate!"

"You are because you both accepted the council's judgment. Be glad your life was spared."

"Lucien would have preferred they signed my death warrant."

"He would not have done it."

"The hell he wouldn't have! He despises his brother. He despises me." Falon swallowed and wondered had she known what her other options were when she agreed to abide by the council's verdict if she would have agreed or run. She rubbed her throbbing temples. How could she have agreed to such a ridiculous verdict?

"If he despised you, when your heart stopped beating after you shot yourself, he would have laid you down on the road and walked away." Talia's voice lowered dangerously. "Make no mistake; *Lucien* saved your life because *he* chose to. The Blood Law had no hand in it, not even fate. It was Lucien's decision alone to make—be grateful for your second chance."

Falon shook her head, refusing to believe Lucien saved her at all, much less for noble reasons. "Lucien's hatred for his brother overrides his hatred for me. I live, Lucien rubs the fact that I am here in Rafael's nose. I die, Lucien's revenge dies with me."

"You are wrong about Lucien."

"There will never be love lost between us."

"Only you can change that."

"My heart aside, Talia, I would never betray Rafa by loving his brother."

"Would you betray the pack by refusing your chosen one?"

"Mondragon is not my pack! Lucien is not my chosen one!" Falon denied knowing as she said the words they were a lie.

"Both are now! Whether or not you understood the options the council had to work with, *you agreed to accept their decision.* The Blood Moon is on the rise. The packs converge. The battle for our existence will be fought in less than two months' time. Accept that you are here. Accept that this is not about you but about the survival of a nation. Have you no honor? Does your word mean nothing? Would you disrespect Rafael's honor by refusing the council's decision?" Talia leaned in close. "If you refuse to accept Lucien as a mate, he will lose face not only with Mondragon but with the other alphas. Become a laughingstock. We must all unite! It is imperative he be at his strongest, most deadly now in the shadow of the rising. And Falon, you can give that to him by accepting him and by marking him." Talia stood. "If you refuse, Mondragon will tear you apart and seek a more worthy alpha. And what, pray tell, Falon, do you think your beloved Rafa would do then?"

Falon swallowed hard and shook her head. But she knew the answer.

"He would destroy all of them and in so doing sign his death warrant." And the honor Rafael lived and died by would die with him. She could not do that to him. Not for her own pride, not for anything.

Talia grabbed her by the shoulders and shook Falon so hard her teeth rattled. "You are a selfish, stupid woman if you do not realize that the survival of the Lycan nation is bigger than your longing for another. A thousand lives are dependent on the packs uniting. It is the only way we can defeat the Slayers. Without Mondragon and Vulkasin to lead the nation, there will be no Lycan nation left to fight for."

"I did not ask for any of this!"

"You may not have asked for it, but when you marked Rafael, you accepted all that went with him. Including accepting the code of honor he lives by."

Falon shook her head, not wanting to hear the truth. "I cannot accept Lucien as my mate."

"There is a difference between cannot and will not. Either way, you are a fool, Falon. A fool who cannot see past her own human weakness."

Falon opened her mouth to school the little Lycan on just how dastardly her alpha really was but instead clamped her mouth shut. There would be no good in making an enemy out of Talia.

"Where is your almighty alpha now? Licking his wounds in a hole somewhere as he plots more ways to destroy his brother?"

Talia smiled tolerantly and stepped back. "I am a healer; I took care of Lucien."

"I would have given you the moon to let him die." Falon slipped from the bed, carefully standing on the floor before she took another step. "I need clothes."

"Lucien has given strict orders you are to walk among the pack as you were born."

"Lucien can go to hell! I'm not his sex slave, and I'll be damned if he's going to humiliate me by refusing me clothing."

Talia stood for a long, contemplative moment before she said, "I don't agree with his tactics . . ."

"Why did you choose to stay with him when you could have gone back to Rafa?"

"I love Lucien as I love Rafael. The blood of both packs runs through my veins. Lucien needs me."

Falon swept past her to the window and said over her shoulder, "Lucien needs no one."

"Ah, there, my lovely, you are wrong," the devil in wolf's clothing said from the doorway.

Falon slowly turned to face him as Talia hurried from the room. Back straight, chin high, chest out, she glared at him. As his brother had the first morning after he had marked her, Lucien leaned casually against the doorjamb, his arms crossed over his wide chest, his golden eyes glittering with unabashed desire.

"You cannot force me to love you," Falon stated and realized as she said the words, Talia was right. This, whatever *this* was, was bigger than her.

"Love?" Lucien scoffed. "Love has no place in what we are to become, Falon."

"Then what? I am simply a tool for repeated revenge?"

He unwound his long arms and stalked toward her. Lucien Mondragon was many things, but one thing he was not was unattractive. His dark sensuality aside, he moved with the controlled stealth of a predator. He did not have to prove to any man or beast that he was in charge; it was understood. "Oh, no, you are much more than that. You are half Lycan with immeasurable power." He stopped a foot away from her. He reached out a hand to her cheek and traced his index finger along the high curve, then down to her jawline. Falon steeled herself. His touch was not violent, nor, she swallowed, was it unpleasant. In another place, in another time, while she may not love him or trust him, she could want him. "Despite the tragic events that forced us together, I have chosen *you* above all other females, human and Lycan, to bear my children. It will drive my brother mad when he sees your belly ripe with my child."

Falon slapped his hand away. "Do you think, Lucien, that I would allow that to happen just so that you can torture Rafael?"

"Rafael's torture is simply an added benefit. You, my love, are the real prize."

Lightning quick, he cupped his big hand around the back of her head and pulled her to him. He lowered his lips to hover above hers. "You will come to me willing, Falon. You will beg me to take you. You will beg me not to stop. You will scream *my* name, *not* my brother's, when you come."

Falon shook her head, refusing to see herself as the wanton he foretold. "I despise you."

"Really?" He pulled her hard against his chest. His eyes glittering passionately, his nostrils flared as a small twitch of a smile twisted his full lips. He sniffed the air. "Your heart may belong to my brother, but—" His free hand swept down her back to the rise of her bottom, then between them to her belly, to the smooth rise of her mons. Her body jerked against his when he slid a finger along her slick seam.

"There will be no space between us, Falon." He slid his finger into her. Her muscles gripped him. "No secrets," he breathed, pressing deeper into her.

Falon's breath hitched as her body caught fire. He cupped her warmth. Her lips parted and she felt the pull of him.

His eyes flared in triumph. "No shame."

She licked her dry lips, forcing her heart to slow its erratic beat and her skin to cool. Falon didn't trust her human body. Their blood bond was too strong. Stronger now since he had saved her life. And her human will too weak to fight it. She shifted. As she hit the floor on all fours, she turned snarling at him.

Lucien threw his head back and laughed, then shifted himself.

Falon leapt onto the bed. Lucien leapt up after her. The mattress dipped with his weight as his big wolf body pushed her against the headboard. Falon snarled and bit his snout, drawing blood. He growled and snapped back at her though he did not break the skin as she had.

As a wolf, her honed senses were at their apex. So were Lucien's. His nostrils flared, smelling her fear. And her excitement.

His long tongue lapped the side of her face, followed by a nuzzling wet nose. Falon whimpered. Her wolf recognized his dominance even if her human did not. He nipped at her neck, growling low. His hips pressed against her flanks. Placing a big paw on her back, holding her immobile, he licked her face. She wasn't going anywhere. If she bolted, he would hunt her down. Wear her down until she surrendered to him. What she refused to admit was that she wanted to surrender.

Panic rumbled along her spine. The she-wolf in Falon drove her now. Her tail swept up and away from her flanks. Her heady scent swirled between them. Lucien growled possessively and nipped her neck again, but this time, the sting of pain as his teeth sunk into the thick fur protecting her vital vein did not frighten her. No, his bite provoked an already heightened sexual awareness. Falon closed her eyes, wishing with everything she possessed that her she-wolf didn't respond the way it did to his alpha. But nature would not be denied. His teeth sunk deeper into her fur, holding her immobile.

Keeping his big paw on her back, Lucien growled low, releasing his bite. He sniffed her face, then her neck where his mark drew blood. He licked it away, the deep lapping of his tongue an unnerving combination of highly charged sensuality and a soothing cadence that lulled her into a sublime sense of tranquillity. His nose sniffed along her back, along her flanks. Falon stood rigid, her muscles so tight they trembled. He moved his big body into her, pushing her down to a prone position on the big bed. Falon didn't move, barely breathed, not wanting to incite his wolf. He could shred her to pieces in a heartbeat. He was twice her size, and more powerful. She had more of a chance against him in her human form, but felt more sexually vulnerable to him in that state. As a wolf, she could blame her weakness on the primal part of her. As a human, she would have to face the reality of her human behavior.

Lucien nudged her to her side. Falon rolled onto her back, submitting to his dominance. She closed her eyes, barring her teeth as his nose sniffed down her soft vulnerable belly to her— His tongue slid along her underbelly. Falon growled, snapping at the air, not in anger but in sexual aggression. The beast had taken over, and try as she may to fight it, she could not quell its primal nature.

Tense, panting, and wanting him to mount her more than she would admit, Falon waited. His nose sniffed her sex. His warm breath rushed against her. He placed a big paw on her belly staying her. He didn't have to. She was supine and submissive. And she hated herself for it.

When his tongue lapped against her sensitive female spot, Falon snarled. Snapping at the air, she struggled for control. He licked her again. She whimpered. When he licked her again, she growled low, the sound more like a purr, her paws digging at the air. Humiliation shivered through her. How could she submit so easily to him? Had she no pride? No honor? No self-control? Sex with Lucien, no matter how much her primal self desired it, would be the ultimate betrayal to Rafa.

Falon shifted, and nearly died when Lucien's wolf tongue lapped between her human thighs. Her entire body shook with outrageous pleasure. The eroticism of the sensation was overridden only by its taboo connotations. Rafa had been a bold, lusty lover, but never so shameless as Lucien was now. Her body flamed in embarrassment at her shameless response. He licked her again. Longer. Deeper. Salaciously. "Lucien!" she gasped, fighting the wrongness and the wantonness of what he did to her.

He raised his head and snarled. She pushed away from him, but his big paws dug into her thighs, immobilizing her. Falon looked down her belly, past the smooth swell of her mons to his blazing golden eyes. His brilliant white fangs glittered dangerously. He looked every bit the big bad wolf of every little girl's nightmares.

But at that moment, Falon realized Lucien despised the situation as much as she. Even though he accepted her as his true mate, she was not his choice. She had been thrust upon him, and he had taken her, and while he had done it only to piss Rafael off, at the end of each day, he was stuck with her. And he resented her for it.

And she couldn't blame him for that. It stung her more than she cared to admit that she was nothing more to this complex alpha than a means to torture his brother.

Lucien snarled and dropped his head, flattening his ears. His resentment fueled his lust to breed. Because though he may resent her, Falon was certain, he would not throw away an opportunity to continue his line.

Not understanding what drove her, Falon reached out a compassionate hand to him. "Lucien—"

He snarled and bit her. Falon screamed, jerking her hand away. Lucien shifted to human and pushed her thighs farther apart. Falon moved to sit up, to hurt him as he had just hurt her. But he licked a long, bawdy swath from her anus to her clit, then caught the sensitive hooded core of her between his lips.

The contact was electrifying. Explosions went off in her head, short-circuiting her denial. He licked her again, his thick, warm tongue driving deeply between her swollen folds. "God, Lucien, stop," she begged, pushing back into the damp sheets. She meant it as a command, but her body was not nearly as adamant.

To her amazement he stopped. Panting heavily, she looked down her belly to his glittering gold eyes between her trembling thighs. His sensuous lips glistened with her moistness. Catching her breath, Falon bit her bottom lip. One thing she could never deny about Lucien Mondragon: sensuality oozed off him in wild erotic waves. He was carnally driven and capable of wicked things. Very wicked things she knew if she succumbed to would rule her.

His lips twisted into a knowing smile. He rose up on all fours and climbed above her. The length of his heavy cock dragged across her thigh. He was blistering hot. She held her breath, causing her breasts to rise and scrape against his hot skin. They both hissed at the contact.

"Give yourself to me, Falon," Lucien said huskily. "I can make you forget Rafa ever existed."

Rafa.

She choked back a sob, squeezing her eyes shut when he did not return her call.

Rafa! Do not forsake me now!

"He will not answer you, Falon."

Her eyes flashed open, meeting Lucien's burnished ones. "How did you know I called to him?"

"We share blood. I have heard your desperate calls to him in your sleep. He will not answer."

Terrified to ask but forcing herself to, she asked, "Is he—hurt?"

Lucien shook his head; his eyes glittered like polished gold. "He is well and seeks another mate."

Falon shoved Lucien from her and rolled to the edge of the bed. "A lie!"

Shaking violently, she hugged herself, wishing Lucien lied, but knowing in her gut Rafael had no choice but to seek another mate. His love for her would never die, but for his pack, he would take another mate. And she could not stomach it.

"I lie only to my enemies."

"I am on top of that list!"

Lucien smiled wickedly. "Would it make it easier for you if I said I hated you? That the only reason I wanted you was to hurt my brother?"

"I know what is in your heart, Lucien. I know you resent me and despise your brother. I know that you would lie, cheat, and steal to hurt him. You would do the same to me!"

"You underestimate my affection for you, Falon."

"Your only affection is for yourself!"

Lucien's eyes narrowed dangerously. "Regardless, Rafe has no choice but to move on, and so he has. The sooner you accept that, the sooner you will understand your destiny is here."

Rafa! Please, answer me!

Desperately, Falon waited for him to answer, to tell her he would be there, that he would never desert her.

Her heart cracked and crumbled as the long minutes dragged by. But Rafael did not respond. She could not even feel his presence. It was as if he did not exist. How could he reject her so easily? So thoroughly?

Raking her fingers through her hair, Falon stood on shaky legs and faced Lucien, who lay on his side, not the faintest hint of modesty anywhere near him. Or a care given to the fact her heart was breaking for the hundredth time that day. Lucien was callous, insensitive, and just plain mean. And a liar!

"How long have I been here?"

"Five days."

"Five days!" She swallowed hard. "Has—has Rafael even asked about me?"

Lucien shook his head. "In exchange for your life, he vowed he would not interfere."

Her world went black. Falon grabbed ahold of a thick wooden bedpost to steady herself, not wanting to believe it. He sacrificed their love so that she could live? Live to lay with his brother? *How could he?* Falon rubbed her forehead against the bedpost. He could because he loved her that much. Because he was honorable. Because unlike her, Rafael would honor the Blood Law to his dying breath. It made accepting Lucien that much harder.

Cold emptiness filled her. She was beaten. Without Rafael, she had no reason to live. Slowly she drew herself up and looked at Lucien. "Release me and I will give you anything you ask for."

Lucien rose up on an elbow and smiled wickedly, not caring that her heart was in a million pieces. "I have everything I want."

Falon shook her head. "I will not submit to you!"

"You just did."

"I cannot control that beast. It recognizes you as the dominant one, but know that if you force yourself on me as a wolf, it will be only because I cannot control nature. My human does not recognize you as anything but exactly what you are: a man forced upon me!"

He moved swiftly from the bed and stood beside her. He wiped the drop of blood on his chin where she had nipped his wolf. He pressed the bloody finger to her lips and smeared it across her bottom lip. "I was not forced on you any more than you were forced on me! We both, of our own accord, agreed to the council's verdict! Stop this. What is done is done. By bloodright you belong to me now. I protect what is mine."

"I belong to Rafael even if he chooses another."

He yanked her hard against his chest, his straining erection thrust high between them. "He swore on your life he would walk away. You are nothing but a memory to him now! He prepares to go north as we speak to meet the northern packs. From there he will choose a mate."

"No! He loves *me!*" *He will fight for me!*

Rafael! Lucien bitterly called to his brother. *Tell her!*

Falon stilled. *Rafa?*

Falon, Rafael's deep voice reverberated in her mind, *the Blood Law has been avenged, it cannot be undone.*

I would not have agreed had I known!

There was no choice, it is our law. For your life, I swore to release you, Falon. You belong to Lucien now.

You should have let me die!

I could not live if you had died.

Rafa! Don't leave me.

Good-bye, Falon.

Lucien cupped the back of her head in his big palm and sneered, "Do you want me to prove to you right now who you belong to?"

Anger flared through her despair. "You would not dare!"

"I would dare the devil if it meant proving to you I keep what is mine!"

Falon licked her dry lips. "Forcing me will prove nothing."

"It will prove that despite your feelings for my brother, your body recognizes me as your mate." He lowered his lips to hers. "And that is enough for me."

"It isn't for me," she said breathlessly, turning her face so that he could not kiss her.

He threw his head back and laughed at her. Then released her and stepped away. "Where is the fiery she-wolf who fought me tooth and nail?"

"She is with her true mate."

Lucien snarled and grabbed her to him again. "*I am your true* mate!" He shook her. "You chose me when you agreed to abide by the council's decision."

"You will never have my heart or my soul!"

"I can live without your heart and your soul. I don't have to love you to fuck you." He ran a hand down her back to her bottom and dug his fingers into her skin. "But your body I will have. And you will freely give it to me."

"Or else you will bully it from me!"

He laughed softly and whispered against her ear. "The only thing I will bully from you, angel face, is that denial of yours that keeps getting in the way."

"Don't call me that!"

He licked the shell of her ear. "I'm going to fuck you before I leave this room." Shivers shimmered down her back straight to her nipples. "And you're going to come for me."

Terrified that she would if she did not do something drastic, Falon closed her eyes and as she had the first time he threatened her at his brother's compound the previous month, she gathered what strength she had now and mentally thrust him from her with enough power that he flew across the room and crashed into the armoire.

He was up in the blink of her eyes and lunged at her. She thrust her hands toward him again, but he kept coming. His eyes glittered furiously as he grabbed her hands, crushing her fingers.

Falon screamed in pain. He lifted her and tossed her onto the bed. He followed, covering her with his big body. Molten gold, his eyes blazed furiously. She had pushed him too far. He snarled and shoved her thighs apart with his knee, digging his fingers into her hair as his hips pressed her thighs into the mattress. His wide cock head pressed against the tender flesh of her inner thigh.

"Say you accept me," Lucien said roughly.

"I will never accept you!"

His lips dropped to a hard nipple and sucked. Falon screamed, masking the cry of pleasure that swept through her. Dear God, why did her body yearn for his when her heart cried out for another?

"Say, it." Shaking her head, afraid her body would force her to admit what it wanted, Falon scratched his arms, his shoulders. She dug her nails into his back. He snarled again. But instead of returning the favor, his lips took hers in a brutal kiss. Falon flailed. She shook her head trying to unlock her lips from his, but his big hands kept her head steady. Her only weapon was her nails. She shredded his back to bloody ribbons. His blood scent wafted around them. His kiss deepened, forcing a response from her.

Falon's head swam with sensory overload. Fear and fury swept with the force of a category five tornado within her.

The wide head of his cock pressed against her slick lips. Tearing her lips from his, Falon gasped for air. He clasped her head tighter and kissed her again. Her head reeled with conflicting emotions. His kiss deepened. His tongue slid in and around her mouth in a languorous swirl, coaxing her to taste him.

She bit his tongue. He growled but did not release her as she expected. The warm coppery taste of his blood flooded her senses. Like a shot of adrenaline, as if she needed it, bloodlust infused her. Her lips stopped fighting; her bloody hands clasped his head. She pulled him tighter to her, licking his wound, savoring the taste of him, drawing more of his blood into her. It infused her with power. She opened her eyes to his penetrating gold ones staring at her. "I accept you," she moaned and bit him again as a ravenous hunger for him overtook her.

"Falon," he said roughly, pulling away from her.

"This is what you want, is it not?" she demanded. What had taken hold of her made the very bed she lay upon shake, but more than that, it ate away at her resolve. The only emotion she felt for

Lucien Mondragon was lust. Lust she could not shake. Her attraction to him confused her. Terrified her. How could it be when her heart belonged to a man who, even now, sought another?

Was she destined to love one man but lust for his brother?

She looked the cunning dark brother in the eye. Yeah, Lucien was an alpha to be reckoned with. He was powerful. He had a way of making a woman forget things. If his blood did not race through her veins, maybe she could ignore him as she so desperately wanted to. But that was not the case.

"You give yourself to me freely?"

Yes, she'd give herself to him. God help her, but she would honor the Blood Law as well as Rafael's sacrifice for her life. Falon threw his words back in his face. "I don't have to love you to fuck you."

His full lips tightened into a grim smile, but he nodded. "That is good enough for me." He pushed her back onto the bed, covering her body with his. He was beyond warm. His skin burned hers on contact. "Though love does not bind us, make no mistake, Falon, you are my true mate now. My seed will take root inside your womb, and once it does, even if my brother comes crawling back to you on his hands and knees, you will remain mine."

Hot tears stung her eyes. How could Rafael release her?

"Because his duty lies with his pack first," Lucien answered.

Falon gasped. How had he—

"You died in my arms, Falon. To restore your life, I gave you my blood to replace what you had lost. There are no secrets between us."

Was there more to his desire for her than revenge? Would it make a difference? She needed to know. She searched his deep golden eyes for the truth. "Why me?"

"Because you were my brother's."

Lucien's honesty cut like a knife. She respected him for the truth, but the truth that she was simply a means of revenge gave her no hope for any reasonable future with him. Why did that hurt more than his words?

Lucien lowered his lips to hers. "And because you are beautiful and strong." He kissed her. Falon closed her eyes, trying to hold back the tears. She didn't want his last words to mean something to her. But in the tumult that was her world, they did.

Even if they were lies.

Lucien broke the kiss to look hard at Falon. "I will never lie to you, Falon, even if you will not like the truth."

Falon stretched out against Lucien's long body, liking the hard warmth of him, despite her dislike of him. "Here is my truth, Lucien: You may be able to force my body to desire yours, but you will never be able to force my heart to love you. Because every time I give myself to you, I'm doing it for Rafael and the promise he made to save my life."

She slid her hands down his back and pressed his ass to her hips. "Now show me just how much of an alpha you really are."

Lucien snarled and grasped her hands. His fingers entwined with hers as he raised her arms over her head. The heat of his breath singed her cheeks. His teeth scraped along her jugular, the wide head of his cock pressed arrogantly against the inside of her thigh. "You want truth?" he demanded.

"Yes," she gasped.

"Here is your truth," he breathed and slid into her. Falon screamed, the feral sound as terrifying as it was mournful. In that inscrutable instant, her body no longer belonged to her. It belonged not only to Lucien, but by accepting Lucien into her, she let go of pack Vulkasin and accepted Mondragon. Shame that she had succumbed to Lucien and disrespected her true love was overridden only by a longing so deep for the man inside of her, she could not deny its existence.

In the distance, the long, sorrowful howl of a lone wolf filled the night. "Rafa." Falon sobbed.

"Say his name again, and I will cut your tongue out of your mouth," Lucien growled as his hips slammed into hers. The violence of his action took her by surprise. His hatred and jealousy was monumental in its depth. Falon cried out as he pushed deeper into her. His body filled her, and hers, God help her, accepted his violence with a violence of its own.

It was manic, fierce, macabre, and in a way she refused to admit, the most earth-shattering experience of her life. Lucien's golden eyes glowed in satisfaction when she squeezed her fingers around his. He threw his head back and roared with triumph when her body, traitor that it was, unraveled.

Falon bit her bottom lip to keep from crying out as the orgasm blindsided her. She would never give Lucien that satisfaction.

"You belong to me now, Falon," he said roughly. His body tightened. His fingers dug into hers. He sank his teeth into her neck as he came in a torrential frenzy. Falon's body answered. Her vaginal walls fisted around his cock and milked him dry. Sobs tore from her chest, knowing, now that he had taken her and marked her, despite Rafa's promise to his brother, he would never take her back.

"You bear my mark and now my seed, Falon," Lucien said against her breast. He rose and looked down at her, his laconic golden eyes mesmerizing in their intensity. "I will kill any man who so much as looks at you with desire." He pushed his hips against hers. His thick cock swelled possessively inside of her. And God help her, her muscles just as possessively embraced him. He nipped at her bottom lip and held it between his teeth. "If you look at another man, I will make you regret the day you were born."

Falon shoved his body from hers and rolled off the bed and turned on him. Never in her life had she met such an arrogant man. "You are

the biggest asshole on earth! How dare you threaten me like that?"
She moved to the edge of the bed and shoved him. "Do not dare follow through on your words or mark *my* words. I will walk away from
you, your pack, the rising, and every other damn thing remotely
related to you!" She shoved him again. "Do you understand *me*?"

His lips twisted into a wry smile. "Do you threaten your alpha?"

"Oh, fuck you, Lucien, and the high horse you rode in on." She
leaned into him and poked him in the chest. "It's the twenty-first
goddamn century. Get with the program."

"I am alpha; you will abide by my rules!"

"'*I am alpha*,'" she mocked, shaking her head. "Well, guess what,
almighty alpha, so am I! Oh, and guess what else? I have powers you
don't, so go to hell!"

He reached out to grab her. She smacked his hands away. It was
all she could do not to laugh at his shocked expression. Lucien Mondragon had met his match. "Touch me again, and I'll shred you."

Lucien stared at her for a long, drawn-out minute before he stood
and began to dress. As he zipped up his jeans, he shook his head and
raked his long fingers through his hair. "I made my mark. Until you
are willing to return it, we will have no more intimate contact." He
shrugged on his shirt and began to slowly button it. "Not even a kiss."

"We'll both see hell before that happens."

Lucien's eyes glowed as a smug smile tugged at the corner of his
mouth. "We'll see." He pulled on his leather boots, then strode from
the room, leaving the door wide open in his wake. Falon slammed it
shut and flung herself against it. Crossing her arms over her chest,
she narrowed her eyes.

"Lucien Mondragon, I'm going to make your life so miserable,
you'll wish you had let me die."

Two

LUCIEN STRODE DOWN the steep metal stairway from his rooms on the third floor of the large warehouse that served as the pack's lair, down to the ground floor and into the large common room. Anger eroded his triumph. She had accepted his mark but it meant nothing when she longed for his brother!

Damn, Rafael! Damn it all to hell! Since he could remember, Rafael had been the golden son. Firstborn, Rafael was the heir apparent, the one their father groomed for alpha. The fair-haired son their mother found no fault with. While Lucien never had trouble finding a warm body at night, Rafael was the one surrounded by females. Lycan and human.

Rafael always got what he wanted. Most of it handed to him. It was why Lucien could not, *would* not accept Rafael's slaying of his chosen one. She had been his. She had loved *him*! And Rafael destroyed her for that transgression. The golden son would pay as long as Lucien drew breath.

What better revenge than to take the one thing his brother loved above all others?

Lucien laughed bitterly. But revenge was a double-edged sword. While he could force Falon into his bed, he could not force Rafael from her heart.

As much as he did not want to admit that he wanted the woman upstairs for himself more than as a means for revenge, he would not deny it. From the first time he touched her in his brother's bedroom on that fateful day last month, his desire for her had become as addictive as his thirst for vengeance against the man who possessed her. Falon's blood flowed in his veins. Like cocaine, the feeling was euphoric; he wanted more. Needed more. Would *have* more. He would have it all.

"I don't like to be kept waiting," Sledge, the new Viper leader, said.

Lucien scoffed at the outlaw biker and the handful of his men that flanked him. Like all Vipers, Sledge defined skinhead. Tatted, shaved head, and Aryan, he was a bloodthirsty bastard that would kill his own mother for a ten-dollar rock. If Lucien was mortal, he would be afraid, but he was neither. "The day I care about keeping you waiting, Viper, is the day the world ends." Lucien strode past him and his thugs to the large open kitchen and snatched a beer from the fridge. He did not offer the biker one. He never entertained pleasantries with Vipers. While the Slayers had their own purpose for the miscreants, Lucien had his as well. They served one purpose for him and one purpose only, a means to keeping his brother entertained.

"You owe me for a dozen men," the Viper said, striding toward him.

Lucien twisted off the bottle cap and tossed it into a nearby trash can. "I don't owe you for shit."

For a human, Sledge had the balls of a Brahma. He moved into

Lucien's space posturing like a damn ape. Lucien's lips twisted in a contemptuous sneer as he drew a mental line that if Sledge stepped over it, the biker would be eating worms with Gordo, the previous leader. A few weeks ago, in a throw down, Lucien and Rafael had taken care of Gordo, along with a dozen other Vipers. It had been like old times when as brothers they fought side by side. For a few minutes as they kicked Viper ass, Lucien forgot they were sworn enemies. But unlike the old times when he would have come to his brother's aide regardless of the odds, Lucien told himself at the time, he only intervened with Gordo to preserve one of his prized possessions: his tricked-out chopper, the same one his brother had taken without asking. But in truth, the real reason he came to his brother's aide was to keep him alive so that when his turn came for revenge, Rafael would have the physical and mental wherewithal to be destroyed by it.

"After what happened on the mountain road and the warehouse with your brother, my numbers are down. I can't hurt a fucking fly with what I got right now."

Lucien shrugged. "Not my problem."

"The fuck it ain't!" The biker sneered. Flexing his burly arms, he stepped over Lucien's line.

Lucien shoved the six foot four, 270-pound biker so hard, his heels dug into the wooden floor, leaving sawdust in their wake as he flew backward into the wall. Lucien took a long swig of his beer and calmly looked across the room at the downed biker. "We have no business, Sledge. If I see you anywhere near here again, I'm going to rip your throat out."

"I came with an offer from Corbet."

Lucien's head snapped back. He knew the Vipers did business with the Slayers, but messenger? Corbet must be getting desperate. "I wasn't aware you and Balor Corbet were so chatty."

"Our relationship with Corbet's people is no secret."

"Indeed." Lucien took another long swig of his beer. "Corbet funds your meth labs and keeps the cops off your back; in exchange, you run his dirty errands so he can keep his hands clean."

"Look, dude, he's been gone for a while, he's back and wants to talk."

"About what? In less than two months he will be dead."

Sledge shook his skinned head as he stood. "Your arrogance is going to get you all killed."

Lucien laughed and took a long pull from his beer, then leveled his glare at the tall biker. "My 'arrogance' is fueled by what I know as fact: Corbet can hire every mercenary on the planet and he will still lose the war."

"You're the only one of your kind to believe your bullshit. No fucking way will you survive the rising."

Lucien did not acknowledge the biker's comment about the rising. He wasn't going to bullshit the biker that Lycan were a figment of his imagination, but that Corbet would divulge such proprietary information as the rising to a mere mortal infuriated him. But he kept his cool and said, "That's because I am the only one of *my kind* that understands the power I hold."

"I don't give a shit what you think. I'm here to relay a message: Corbet wants to meet and discuss an arrangement."

"What kind of arrangement?"

"Something to do with positioning you as the leader of all the packs."

Lucien snorted his contempt. "I don't need Corbet for that."

"Why not hear him out?" Falon's husky voice said from behind him.

Lucien stiffened and slowly turned around. His eyes widened, then narrowed as his blood pressure shot up one hundred points. He swiped his hand across his chin. Jesus Christ! The woman had bigger balls than he did.

Lucien glanced at Sledge and his temper spiked dangerously. He could deal with Falon butting in on a subject she had no understanding of, but what he refused to accept was the reason for the biker's hungry, slack-jawed look. Fury exploded inside of Lucien, not for Sledge's reaction but because of Falon brazenly calling his bluff. If he challenged her here and now, he would look the fool. If he— Lucien's blood shot straight to his dick. Holy mother of Jesus, she was going to pay for this.

Butt-ass naked, Falon strode past Lucien to the fridge. She tossed her long hair over her shoulders and yanked open the door. He watched helplessly as the frosty air swirled around her nipples and the way they pebbled in reaction. Sledge choked back a strangled sound. The rutting sounds of Vipers spurred Lucien's pack into action. They growled low, pressing closer around the bikers.

Lucien knew his pack smelled his mark. But more potent than that was the sex scent clinging like a heady aphrodisiac to Falon. Tonight would be a wild lusty orgy the pack had not seen in over fifteen years. When—not *if*, he told himself—Falon marked him, her womb would be ripe for his seed and then, his line would be born. His cock thickened at the thought. She was a magnificent specimen of woman and Lycan. Their children would be strong, lusty hybrids, capable of leading the pack into the next millennia.

The cloying scent of their lust swirled around the room. The urge to push her to the floor on all fours and take her from behind as his pack witnessed his dominance over her was overpowering. But Lucien tempered it with his promise that he would not touch her again. He also tempered it with his silent vow to respect her wishes that he not eviscerate any man who looked at her like Sledge and his dirty pack of jackals did at that moment. It took every ounce of self-control Lucien possessed not to rip out the biker's throat.

Lucien's face tightened. How had she turned this around on him? He had vowed not to touch her when touching her was all he wanted. He swore to kill any man who looked at her with lust. And yet, there Sledge stood drooling onto the floor like a starving dog over a bone, and Lucien did nothing to stop it.

He realized in the unlikely circumstances that he could seduce Falon without touching her, without her even knowing what he was about. But it would be an empty victory because fucking her was easy. Winning her trust and respect was the true challenge. In another place and another time, he would woo her relentlessly.

He sneered. And would that not be the ultimate revenge? More than possessing Falon's body, but possessing her heart? That victory would be worth all of his defeats combined.

Lucien shook his head. Falon had cast some kind of spell on him, because he was thinking crazy. What did he care about love? He cared about two things: destroying Slayers and rubbing salt into his brother's wounded heart.

His eyes narrowed to slits. She was a witch. She'd tempted and beguiled his brother to distraction, and now she was doing her damnedest to do the same to him. He opened his mouth to tell her to return to his room but when Falon grabbed a beer and twisted the top off, Lucien's vigilant gaze raked her from the top of her dark head to her face, then down the long graceful column of her neck. She stood straight and proud, her tits sitting up firm and high. The pebbled pink tips strained toward him. She put her lips to the bottle and tipped her head back and drank. In silent awe, every man in the room stood rooted to the floor and beheld the spectacular sight. His hot gaze swept the long length of her. Yeah, she was worthy of any alpha. Of a king. And she was his. In body only, but that was enough—for now.

"Fuck me," Sledge whispered, taking a step toward Falon.

Lucien flung his fist backward into the biker's chest, the force sending him crashing to the floor. His patience gone, Lucien grabbed Falon by the arms, her beer flying out of her hand as he flung her over his shoulder and stormed upstairs to his room. Angrily he tossed her onto the bed. She popped up snarling, tossing her wild mane over her shoulders ready to fight.

"Do not ever interfere in my business," he commanded.

Falon threw her head back and laughed. Then narrowed her eyes at him and demanded, "Am I not your chosen one? As such, I demand to stand beside my almighty alpha." She bowed to him as if he were King Shit. "By rights, I am entitled to not only interfere in pack business but to be a part of the process."

Lucien refused to answer her. As his chosen one, she was entitled to everything he had. And by agreeing to the council's terms, she was in every way his chosen one. But that was not what spurned his anger. Her wanton behavior in front of the biker disrespected not only his pack but Lucien personally. "I warned you what would happen if you tempted another man!" Lucien knew how ridiculous he sounded, but jealousy gnawed viciously at him.

Falon slid from the bed and sauntered toward him. "Did the big bad wolf get burned by his own huffing and puffing?" She traced a fingertip along the width of his chest and up and over his shoulder. As she rounded behind him, she traced her fingertip along the rigid line of his shoulders. "Perhaps you should rescind your spiteful orders." She rose up on her toes and whispered against his ear. "Be careful what you ask for, Lucien, you might get it." She strode past him into the bathroom and slammed the door shut.

He stood for long, furious minutes fighting down the violent reaction she evoked from him. Never had a female infuriated him the way this one did. Never had he wanted to bend one to his will as he did this one. Never had he wanted to sink to his knees and beg a female to let him in as he did this one.

And never had he lost control and composure with one as he did Falon.

Be careful what you wish for, indeed. She would be the death of him!

In slow, measured steps, Lucien returned to the common room. Sledge had not moved from where he hit the floor. Lucien waved him away. "Go. We have no business."

"Will you meet with Corbet?" the biker asked, slowly standing up.

"No."

"Not even hear him out?"

Lucien growled. Humans were the most insipid beings on earth. "Leave here!"

When the heavy metal doors closed soundly behind the Viper leader and his ragtag men, Lucien looked at the haggard faces of his pack. There were less than seventy of them now. Each and every one deserved more than what they had endured these last sixteen years.

"Our time is at hand, Mondragon. I have marked my mate. Soon she will return the mark and then—" Emotion filled Lucien's chest. "Then there will be such a rise of the Lycan nation, no man, Slayer, or beast will deny our right to live freely and without persecution!"

Three

FOR THE FIRST time in nearly sixteen years, Lucien watched hope spring into the eyes of his pack. It warmed his heart to see them smile. And for the first time since he was ten years old, he felt that same warmth swell inside himself. Not even when he was about to mark his first chosen one had he felt such optimism for the future. Perhaps it was because he never actually marked her. Perhaps had he, he would have felt the same sense of euphoria he now felt having marked Falon.

He smiled and gathered them close. "We are on the precipice of something great, Mondragon," he said softly, as if saying it too loud would jinx it. As they huddled around him, their excited anticipation for the coming night was palpable. It was good, their lust. As was customary when an alpha marked his mate, the pack celebrated by playing the field to narrow down their chosen ones for the day the mark was reciprocated. By the time Falon marked him, his pack would have decided on mating pairs and when Falon became pregnant, it would signal a wild tidal wave of fertility for the pack. Within the year, an entire generation would be born and for as many years as he and Falon were together, his pack would regenerate their bloodlines.

And, gods willing, he and Falon would set the bar high and have more than a single child. A profound sense of what he must do swelled within Lucien. For the first time in his life, Lucien looked ahead and saw the faces of his children before him. Strong, lusty children full of fire like their mother and passion like their sire.

He wanted that. Strength, power, a family bound not only by blood but by love. It was the family his mother and father had built for their children. It was a family, though imperfect, he had thrived in.

But before he could begin, there was the rising. To destroy the Slayers, every pack must focus solely on that end and be proactive.

"In less than two months' time, the Blood Moon will rise. Between now and then, it is imperative we hunt daily. Each Slayer we destroy now is one less to rise against us later."

Cheers rose up around him. Lucien waited for his pack to settle down. "I have met with each California pack leader over the last month, even those who do not approve of Mondragon, and all have agreed we must be proactive now. To that end, at first light tomorrow, we will hunt daily." Aggressive growls of approval rose around him. "My promise to you is that before the next full moon, I will cut Balor Corbet down, strip him bare, and—" Lucien caught Falon's scent. He raised his head and looked past his gathered pack to see her standing on the last step of the metal stairway. She stood tall and proud, and shock of shocks, clothed in one of his black T-shirts and a pair of black sweats. Collectively his pack turned and followed his eyes. He felt their anxiety rise. They were unsure how to feel about this female they were supposed to accept as their alpha when she made it clear she did not want to be a part of Mondragon. Lucien understood. But he was determined to change both Falon's and his pack's feelings toward the other.

He nodded. *Thank you.*

Falon leaned against the wall and crossed her arms over her chest. *I didn't dress for you.*

Of course you didn't.

He dragged his eyes from her and turned back to his pack that was now focused solely on Falon. In a drastic shift, their mood went from excited and hopeful to agitated and wary. Not anxiousness for the coming matings or for the hunt, this anxiety was altogether different. What had just happened?

"What is it?" he asked no one specifically.

He was met with downcast eyes and shaking heads. Something was wrong. He looked back at Falon, who had not moved, but knew by the rigid set of her spine she detected the change as well.

There was no love lost between Falon and his pack. Though they had been loyal once to Rafael, their loyalty now lay firmly with Lucien. That Falon was the marked chosen one of his enemy did not sit well with the pack. It was something Lucien had not considered when he had agreed to accept Falon as his chosen one.

"There have never been secrets here," Lucien said, angry his pack refused to look at him with Falon in the room. "Speak!"

When they remained silent, he looked to Talia, who stood off to the side. "What are they afraid to say to me?"

Talia looked over at Falon, then moved into the gathered pack to stand in front of Lucien. "They fear she may carry Rafael's child."

Talia's words stunned Lucien. He felt as if he had been a mule kicked in the gut. He had never considered since Falon and Rafael had traded marks that she could indeed be pregnant with Rafael's child. He snarled and turned to Falon, who stood proud and defiant before them all.

"Do you?" Lucien demanded, striding toward her but stopping before he came too close. He was afraid of her answer and what he might do.

Her cheeks pinkened. Her body trembled. "I am not pregnant."

"How sure are you?"

"Sure enough that I would have killed you or any Lycan who tried to keep my child from his father."

"Always standing up for my brother. How do you expect Mondragon to accept you as their alpha when you cannot even look at them?"

"I did not choose to be here, Lucien." Falon looked at the gathered pack. "Any more than they chose to have me here."

She stepped down off the last step and strode toward him. "In fact, Lucien, you have been the one who has fueled the blood feud for the last sixteen years. You have refused all attempts by your brother and the council to breech the divide. You have held both packs hostage to your bloodlust for vengeance." She stopped several feet from him and demanded, "Is it even remotely possible, Lucien, that your beloved chosen one *was* a Slayer? Is it even remotely possible that your brother who loved you above all others acted not only to protect the pack but to protect you?"

"She was *not* a Slayer," he defended. "I would have known it. Sensed it, felt it every time I fucked her! What she *was*, was the one thing that belonged to *me*." Lucien jabbed his index finger into his chest. "The one thing Rafael could not have! So he took her from me! Just as he took everything else."

The pack stirred, Lucien's righteous anger transferring to them.

Falon looked around to them as they tightened around her and Lucien. "Why didn't you take another mate before now? You still would have had the satisfaction of revenge by destroying Rafael's mate that you so desperately wanted."

"Because until you, there were none worthy enough to stand beside me."

Falon's eyes widened, the golden flecks in them pulsing. Lucien smiled a bitter smile and ran his knuckles across her bottom lip. "And now that I have you, I will not let you go."

"So I am your prisoner."

"You are my chosen one."

"There is no difference."

"One day you will see that there is."

You will force yourself on me again?

I did not force you. You wanted what I wanted.

Not with my heart, Lucien. There is a difference!

I have said I will not touch you again unless you ask it of me.

Let me go.

I cannot.

You will not.

Emotion roiled in Lucien's chest. He could not, *would* not let her go. She would run to his brother, and he would be left with nothing. His heart thudded like an engine against his chest. If he had to have her unwilling as opposed to gone from him forever he would insist she stay.

And she would grow to hate him more than she already did. Could he live with that? Could his pack? Hatred and distrust was not a foundation on which to build a dynasty. But he could not stomach her with his brother or any other man, when he wanted her for himself.

He stared at Falon's beautiful, defiant face. Could she come to care for him enough to accept him and his pack? The answer became painfully clear. Not if he forced her to stay.

Swiping his hand across his chin, Lucien looked at his pack. They regarded him as they always had, with complete trust. A trust he did not altogether deserve. Falon was right; he should have taken a mate long before now. Just as his brother refused for his own reasons, and Lucien his, they had both let the packs down in the most basic of ways. To thrive they needed to reproduce. The blood feud had prevented it.

Keeping Falon here against her will with the rising just two months away would cause discord with his pack. Having her here against her will would distract Lucien from what he needed to do: destroy Slayers. Keeping her here against her will was not the act of a true alpha. It was the act of a coward. In that instant of clarity, the hope for his future that had swelled only moments before crashed down around him.

As pack leader, it was expected he do what was best for the pack, not for himself. And what was best for his pack was an alpha whose chosen one was in for the count.

Lucien took a leap of faith and threw the dice. He pointed to the large double metal doors leading to the enclosed yard and beyond. "You are not a prisoner here." He stood still, staring at the door. If she chose to walk past him and out the door, he would not go after her. His pride would never allow it. But nor would he allow her to go to his brother.

Her eyes widened. "I am free to go? And never return?"

"Go anywhere, except to my brother, and I will not stand in your way."

You are bluffing.

Lucien shook his head. *I will not force you to stay.*

What game do you play, Lucien?

No games. If I force you to stay here, you will grow to hate me more than you do now. But more important, Mondragon cannot thrive under an alpha who does not place their well-being above his or her own.

Falon gasped at his honest words. He watched the wheels turn in her head. His vengeance aside, he wanted her to stay because he wanted her for himself. He wanted—argh! He would not make a spectacle of himself. He would not force her to stay here, any more than he would force her to mark him. She was a wild and free spirit, one that would dry up and die if corralled. Giving her her head was key to lassoing her power. It was also crucial to the survival of his pack.

Lucien strode to the heavy metal doors and yanked them open. Sunlight flooded the large room. It was imperative to his pack that if Falon chose to stay, they understood she stayed of her own choice, not because she was being forced. Otherwise, they would have no confidence in her and would always question her loyalty as well as her authority. And that was not something Lucien could allow. Either she was in or she was out.

Falon took a step toward Lucien. His heart thudded dully in his chest. She took another step and another, her focus on the open doors. The pack parted as she passed through them. She kept her chin high, refusing to look at them almost as if she saw the want in their eyes for her to choose them, because if she chose to stay with Lucien, she also chose them. And they desperately wanted to unite, as a true pack should. She stopped at the door and looked out. She looked up at Lucien, then looked back to his pack and stepped through the threshold.

The pack moved in behind him, straining to watch her next move.

"Open the gates," she commanded.

Lucien pressed the main switch to the left of the doors. The tall metal gates jolted, then rolled back. Falon strode toward them, not once looking back. When she cleared the gates to the outside world, she stopped.

Lucien's stomach did a slow, aching roll. He and the pack held their breaths. When she took another step away from them, Lucien's stomach dropped. She took several more steps away from the compound.

"Lucien," Talia whispered. "Bring her back."

He shook his head. "No."

"You must! If the Slayers or the Vipers get ahold of her, we are doomed."

"I will kill any man who lays one finger on her."

Falon turned then. Almost fifty yards separated them, but Lucien could see the flare of her nostrils, hear the thud of her heart against her chest, see the indecision in her eyes. It was clear she was torn. But why? There was no love between them or her and his pack. Why did she hesitate? Was it because she still mourned the loss of his brother? In his own way, Lucien mourned as she. He mourned the loss of the love and closeness they shared despite the constant rivalry. They shared the same blood, the same womb, the love of the same mother and father, and yet they were bitter enemies. He wanted to ease the ache in her heart but could not bring himself to give her the one thing she wanted most.

FALON TURNED AWAY from Mondragon. Inhaling deeply she beheld what lay before her. Freedom. Civilization. Unlike Vulkasin, whose compound was a hidden fortress buried deep in the depths of the Sierras, Mondragon hid in plain sight. The compound was a warehouse nestled against the beginning swell of the Sierras at the edge of a bustling town. Probably Folsom. To the north was Rafael. Here Mondragon. And all around her, Vipers and Slayers.

Fear of the unknown skittered along her spine. What would happen to Lucien if she continued to walk away? To Mondragon? To the brothers? One night, not so very long ago, when she was just as confused and afraid as she was now, she had come to the realization that if there was ever going to be peace between the brothers, she would be the only one to broker it. She felt that now, stronger than ever. Lucien was the key. It was reason enough for someone else to stay, but for Falon, what stayed her step was Rafael. How ironic, that for him she would choose to stay for Mondragon. Rafa had sacrificed their love for her life. The noblest of all sacrifices. She would not desecrate such an honorable act by walking away.

The sound of the metal gates jerking to life pulled her out of her thoughts. Her stomach lurched against her rib cage. She turned to the closing gates and Lucien standing stalwart behind them at the doors to the clubhouse.

Never had a man infuriated her as he did. She wanted to slap him for his insensitiveness. He was his own worst enemy. Stubborn, vindictive, and in pain. She could see it in his eyes every time he spoke of his brother. She shivered as she remembered his passionate taking of her just an hour before. Her body warmed, wanting more of him. She hated herself for it, but—at least they had that.

As the gates clanked shut, Falon's closed heart did the opposite. It cracked open. She would not abandon Lucien. Nor would she abandon Mondragon. She cracked a smile as she envisioned throwing herself on the sword, the martyr of all martyrs. But there was honor in that. And it was what Rafael would want her to do.

"I have no choice but to stay," Falon softly said, stepping toward the closed gates.

"So I am your default?" Anger flickered through Lucien's words.

She understood it. Her own anger that fate had torn her from the arms of the man she loved and set her down here was no less than Lucien's feeling that he was sloppy seconds.

"I will honor Rafael's sacrifice with my own."

Angrily Lucien strode toward her; he pulled the gates apart just enough for her to step through. "So now you are a martyr?"

"You gave me a choice, Lucien. Stay or go. I choose to stay here. Isn't that what you want?"

"Not because you're throwing yourself on a sword!"

"You expect too much from me! I cannot just turn my feelings off and on!"

He shoved his hands into his pockets and paced in front of her, then abruptly stopped and stared hard at her. The turmoil in his eyes was devastating. He was a proud man desperate to put his pack back together. He wanted her to stay for more than his pack; she could see it in his eyes. Vengeance or not, he wanted her for himself. Falon shivered at the realization that she, too, despite her love for Rafael, wanted a part of Lucien for herself. What part she did not know. If she stayed, it would reveal itself. And that terrified her. She was emotional ground beef as it was. She could not take much more. "I'll give you a week to sift through your emotions, Falon," Lucien said softly. Falon nodded and slipped through the gates. Then he said, "The seven days are conditional."

Her head snapped back and she looked up into his blazing eyes. Angry, angry Lucien. Would he ever smile?

"Of course there are conditions, Lucien; there always are with you."

"During your seven days, so as not to alarm the pack, you will stay by my side and retire with me each night and at least act like you are content to be my chosen one."

Frustrated she put her hands on her hips. How could she sort her feelings if she was stuck to him like glue? And was she expected to have sex with him? Sex muddied the water. "I will not lay with you."

"You *will* lie beside me each night *in my bed*; what happens between us will be up to you."

"And then what? At the end of the week if I don't throw myself at you, you kick me out?" She blinked back the sudden sting of tears. Dear God, this man could make her so angry and feel so vulnerable in one single breath. And vulnerable she felt. She had nowhere to go. No one to talk to. No friends, no family. Before she discovered what she was, it wasn't a big deal, but becoming a part of Vulkasin had been the first time in her life she had a sense of family. It had been ripped from her arms. And while she didn't feel that same sense of family with Mondragon, for all his anger and hatred for the man she loved, she understood what drove Lucien and did not fear him. Outside of these gates, despite her powers, she would wander aimlessly like the gray souls in her dreams. Her desire to belong was too strong for that. She wanted to be with her kind.

Lucien reached out and swiped a tear from her cheek with his thumb. "That will be up to you."

She slapped his hand away. "No matter how I feel, you will ultimately find a way to force me to stay; why act like you are giving me a choice?"

"Seven days, Falon." He turned and walked away from her, back to his pack that waited expectantly.

"She chooses Mondragon!" Lucien shouted triumphantly, more Falon was sure than he really felt. But she understood what he was doing. The pack had been bouncing between hope and despair. Their mood was literally tied to Lucien's. If he doubted her, so then would the pack.

Loud cheers and wide smiles erupted from the watchful pack. Their profound sense of relief was palpable.

"Tonight we will celebrate the marking as planned," Lucien said excitedly. "At first light we hunt!"

The forty or so men and twenty-odd women who made up Mondragon nodded, but looked past Lucien to where she stood by the gate. As wolves in the wild, they could detect something was not quite right with the alpha pair. Falon's heart went out to them. Here in the comfort of their home they were not the vicious rebel pack they were made out to be. Lucien for all his anger and kicking up dirt had not only their love but their respect. They trusted him. And as they stared at her, she wanted them to trust her, too.

But a part of her held back earning that trust. Because if she had her happily ever after, it would not be with Mondragon's alpha, but Vulkasin's.

F o u r

LIVID THAT HE had given Falon an out when she had chosen to stay, Lucien fought to mask his anger as he strode through his pack. He grit his jaw so hard he almost cracked it. He was a fool!

Falon was headstrong and passionate. If she could find a way back to Rafe, she would promise her soul to the devil to have it. She stayed because of Rafael! Not for him, not for the pack. He should just tell her to go now. What difference would seven days make?

But he couldn't. Her decision to stay, regardless of why, infused the pack with joy. He would not take that away from them. Not until he had to.

Cold resignation settled in Lucien's heart. What would be would be. If Falon left at the end of the week, he would mark another, more willing mate within hours. The time had come for Mondragon to rise above the ashes.

"Lucien?" Talia said, coming toward him.

She sensed his anger and knowing Talia, she knew nothing was set in stone. He did not want to talk about it. Lucien shook her off. "Leave it alone."

"Why did you give her an out? We need her to stay."

"I will not force her to stay!" he bit off, turning away from her. He turned back to the pack and singled out Joachim, his sergant at arms. "I have a need for sport, brother. Bring me Wrath." Lucien called to him as he strode toward the back of the warehouse. "Then armor yourself and three others of your choosing."

He needed to fight. Too much roiled inside of him. Anger, vengeance, frustration, fear Falon would walk out the front door, and an ache in his loins that no amount of fighting would relieve.

Lucien rarely lost control, but in the last several days, he had been pushed beyond his level of tolerance. He had nearly killed his brother, had a mate forced upon him, then because the thought was abhorrent to her, she tried to kill herself rather than be with him. And he had saved her! Then all but forced his mark on her. Never mind her body called to his: her mind did not. And her heart? Her heart was locked against him. He scoffed. Her heart did not matter to him; he'd long ago stopped caring about feelings. Not heartfelt ones. He had loved and lost once. Vengeance drove him every second of every day since. But now that that vengeance was his, why did his anger still roil? And why had he challenged Falon to leave a second time?

"Fuck!" he yelled, punching the air. Was it because his pride could not handle the fact that Falon did not want him? That despite his possession of her body, her heart cried out for his brother?

And what had he done to warm her to him? Pushed her until she could no longer resist. He was not an animal. Lycan, yes, but he had supreme control of his beast. Never had he forced a woman in his bed. Never had a woman denied him, until today. Lucien grabbed one of the wooden dummies his pack regularly practiced maneuvers

on and hurled it across the wide concrete yard. He grabbed the one
next to it and chucked it against the warehouse wall.

Falon had capitulated. Just as wolves did in the wild, once the
alpha chose his mate, she surrendered. She was his for the taking. It
was understood, damn it! For the greater good of the pack, she
answered to the alpha!

But not Falon! Oh, no, she had taunted him, had demanded he
prove to her he was worthy enough to be alpha. He'd shown her he was,
then she scorned him!

He swiped his hand across his chin and turned as the metal doors
opened and slammed shut. Joachim strode confidently into the yard
followed by three of pack Mondragon's strongest Lycan. They were
in for an ass-kicking. "Send for Talia," Lucien called to Joachim.
"You will need her when I am done." As the words left his mouth, the
metal doors opened again and Talia stepped into the sunlight.

"You are my sergeant at arms for a reason, Joachim," Lucien said
as his man tossed his broadsword, Wrath, to him. Lucien caught it
and expertly wielded it in a complex combination of slices, thrusts,
and dices.

He gave no warning; he lunged, catching Joachim off guard. The
hefty Lycan went down with a heavy thud on the ground. The three
men flanking him, pack Mondragon's premier night guard, Darius,
Barron, and Dax, hesitated. Lucien snarled, furious they showed
hesitation. "Fight me for your lives, lads. If you don't, I will kill you."

They returned his snarl with one of their own. Joachim stood,
shaking the dirt from himself and raised his sword. Four on one, they
circled Lucien.

He lunged into the air and kicked Darius in the chest as he swung
at Barron. Darius flew backward, Barron caught Lucien's blade across
his thick leather chest armor. Joachim and Dax rushed him. Lucien
gave no quarter. He rushed them both, sideswiping Joachim with his

broadsword, and leveling Dax with his fist. He turned to find all four of his men standing together. In a wall of flesh and bones and steel, they rushed him.

Subconsciously, Lucien knew he would not mortally wound any of his own, and he knew they knew it. But that didn't mean he wouldn't push them as far as his temper would allow.

One after the other, Lucien pushed his men to their limits, until one by one they submitted to his greater strength and the fury that drove it. Long moments later, breathing heavily, he stood in the middle of his downed men. They were done. He had just begun. His anger at himself, at Falon, and at the whole fucking world raged inside of him. He looked up at the window to his room and caught sight of Falon's flushed face. His gaze locked with hers. Regret for his earlier actions aside, the emotions she elicited from him enraged him more than his anger at the world.

He did not want to feel anything but indifference toward her. But he felt the opposite. He wanted her attention. Her trust. He wanted her a willing partner in bed. He completely understood his brother's attraction to her. She was beautiful, proud, and strong. There was a time when he wanted to break her spirit, but he realized now that would be akin to a sin against nature. She was too special to damage. Yeah, she was something special, and he was a fool to treat her so callously. Some of his anger left him. And as much as he didn't want her to go, he knew in his heart, dead as it was, he could not, would not smother that wild spirit of hers by forcing her to stay. He had done the right thing in giving her the choice. Now, would she stay? And if she stayed, would she understand what that meant? All or nothing, he would accept nothing less.

He crossed his sword across his chest and bowed. "I am an ass, Falon. My apologies," he softly said but knew she could hear. She could hear him anywhere. They were blood bound.

Her eyes widened in shock. His men's jaws dropped. Talia smiled and said, "Mark the calendar, Joachim. The day Lucien Mondragon apologized will go down in the Lycan annals as the day hell froze over."

"I am not above apologizing when I am wrong," Lucien said, scowling at his cousin. He swiped the sword blade across his right thigh, removing some of the dirt and grime.

"Are you implying that today is the first time you made a mistake?"

He looked up at Falon, who still stared at him as if he were mad, then sheathed his sword and looked back at Talia. "Yes." He strode toward his men, who were still lying on the ground rubbing their battered bodies, and extended a hand to one after the other, helping them up.

"Take the night off," he said to his guard. "You deserve it."

The five pair of eyes surrounding him opened wider in shock. Lucien strode past them and said over his shoulder to Talia, "Take the black duffel bag of clothes in my downstairs office up to Falon." He yanked open the metal door and walked into the building.

"What clothes?" Talia said, hurrying up behind him.

Without looking at his cousin, Lucien said, "The ones I purchased for her."

"When did you have time to go shopping?"

Lucien stopped and turned around so fast, Talia bumped into his chest. He set her away from him and scowled. "Last week." From the moment he tricked Falon into trading blood with him in his brother's bedroom last month, Lucien knew come hell, high water, and the Blood Law, he would have her. He had been patient and played his hand, and for his cunning, had won the prize.

"You were that sure of yourself?"

"When am I not?"

Talia shook her head, smiling. "Never. But? How did you know what to get? When have you ever shopped for a woman?"

Lucien snorted and turned toward the metal stairway leading to his rooms. "I'm not a caveman, Talia. Now, please, just do it, and don't tell her they're from me. Tell her you sent the betas out this morning for the clothing."

FALON STOOD IN shocked silence and watched Lucien help his men up, and then Talia followed him into the building. What had just happened? First Lucien tells her she can leave; next he almost kills four of his men in a fit of fury when she chooses to stay. And then he apologizes to her? For what? The rough sex? For turning her life upside down and inside out? Shaking her head, she moved away from the window. Was it a backdoor ploy to get her to stay, or did he truly regret marking her?

She rubbed her fingertips across the tender spot on her neck. She could have done without the mark, but the sex? It had been— Her blood pressure shot up a dozen points. Hell, it had been crazy. He had not taken what she was not willing to give. Dear Lord, what was she going to do? Guilt flooded her. Rafael knew the second Lucien entered her. Did he know she enjoyed it? Her cheeks flamed hot. He must hate her right now.

She could walk out that door, and Rafael would sleep better knowing she was no longer with Lucien. But what about her? By accepting Lucien's mark, she accepted him and his pack. Despite the feud, Mondragon was family now. She was safe here. And, she had a place here if she wanted it. All she had to do was assume it. That meant rising above her own wants and desires, and acting like the alpha she was. Her feelings for Lucien aside, Falon had no desire to live in the human world again. Slayers were everywhere, and even if they were not, she identified with the Lycan part of her. It was who she was, what she was, and it was where she wanted to stay.

If she were completely honest with herself, she could make a list of reasons why, even had Lucien not marked her, why she should stay. She understood the fine line between love and hate. Lucien could not hate his brother so viciously if he had not loved him so deeply. And buried beneath all of his smoke and fire, there was no doubt in Falon's mind that Lucien still loved Rafael. With each step Falon had taken away from Lucien earlier, it became clearer and clearer to her: while Lucien was the key, she was the lock that would once again bind the brothers. If she did not believe it before, she believed with all her heart that the entire Lycan nation would succumb to the Slayers if the two strongest alphas, the alpha twins, Mondragon and Vulkasin, were not united in heart, blood, and soul as they led the charge.

Letting out a long breath, Falon sat on the bed. It would be easier in the long run for Rafa if he thought she had completely accepted Lucien. Her heart clenched painfully in her chest. No, she didn't want Rafa to think she thought so little of their love that she would jump right into a relationship with the brother he despised. But, as Lucien proved so profoundly a half hour ago, being alpha was not about doing what you wanted for yourself; it was about doing what was right for the pack. For nearly sixteen years Rafael had done what was right for himself. Now it was time he do what he was born to do: produce the next generation.

A lump clogged her throat at the thought of Rafa making love to another woman as he had made love to her. She squeezed her eyes shut blocking out the vision of Rafa marking his next mate as he thrust into her.

Shaking the visions from her mind, Falon stood and peered in the mirror above the low dresser attached to the armoire. "Pack first," she whispered. She would stay here regardless of her feelings. Was she alpha enough to do it?

The door abruptly jerked open and Lucien strode in. His golden eyes glowed furiously.

Her mood shifted seamlessly into provoke mode. "So much for the contrite Lucien," she taunted.

Lucien strode past her and placed his sword back on its wrought-iron hanger above the table grouping. As he turned, he unbuttoned his shirt with short angry motions. Falon's eyes widened. Blood and sweat glistened on his chest, obliterating his unusual tattoo from view.

"You were cut?" she asked surprised. She had watched the entire fight and not once had Lucien been touched.

He dragged the shirt from his torn torso. The muscles in his arm flexed and bulged as he rolled up the dirty shirt. He tossed it into a small trash can by his desk. "Not by a blade." He turned and Falon gasped. Thick rivulets of damp blood ran like tributaries down his back. From the base of his neck and arms all of the way down to the dip at the small of his back and, she was sure, farther down, his skin was ripped to shreds.

Falon looked down at her bloodstained hands, then back to Lucien, wanting to apologize for shredding him to ribbons but unable to utter the words because she really wasn't sorry.

His lips quirked before he strode past her into the huge bathroom she had taken a peek at earlier and shut the door behind him.

As one door shut, another opened. Falon started as Talia walked into the bedroom lugging a thick black duffel bag behind her.

"It's called knocking," Falon said.

Talia's cheeks pinkened. "Sorry, I—"

Falon waved her off. "No big deal, but when you're sitting around half naked it's nice to have a little warning."

Talia smiled and lifted the bag that was almost as big as she was. "This is going to change all of that."

Falon helped her lift the bag onto the high bed. Talia unzipped the cumbersome thing and smiled looking up at Falon. "Your new wardrobe."

"But Lucien said no clothes." As if that had stopped her.

"Amazingly, he changed his mind," Talia said, digging into the bag and pulling out a handful of clothing.

As she set them on the bed, Falon dug out several pair of designer jeans. "You say that like it doesn't happen often."

"Trust me, it doesn't."

Talia reached in and pulled out half a dozen lacy thong panties, several microscopic tops, more pants, and a pair of UGGs. As she set them out on the bed, Falon pulled out a pair of pink suede cowboy boots, several concho-type leather belts, a black leather vest, a doe-skin vest, several fitted long-sleeved shirts, and two cute little dresses. All of the colors rich gem tones. Every one of the blues matched her eyes.

She stood back from the bounty and put her hands on her hips. "I suppose I shouldn't be surprised there are no bras or pajamas. Everything here screams sex." Even if it was tasteful, each article of clothing was sensual in fabric, color, and design. Classic Lucien.

"I guess the betas forgot."

"Lucien didn't buy these?"

"He paid for them, but the betas did the shopping."

Falon set aside a pair of sleek black jeans and a black-leather, sapphire-satin-lined vest. "Really? I'd think they would have shopped at Walmart in the burlap sack section, not at Victoria's Secret."

"I'm sure Lucien told them what he wanted."

Falon moved a stack of clothing and sat on the edge of the bed and stared at Talia. "Why did he change his mind?"

The Lycan healer looked down at the cache of clothing and shrugged. "You'll have to ask him that." Talia strode to the door and stopped. "Falon, what are you going to do?"

She shrugged.

"Mondragon is a powerful pack. Lucien is a strong leader. They both need you."

"Lucien needs a kick in the ass."

"That, too. But—" Talia's violet eyes implored her. "For the sake of Mondragon, it is imperative you stand united with Lucien. If you don't, the pack will lose their confidence in him as alpha, and that cannot happen under any circumstance."

"Where is your loyalty to Rafael?"

"My loyalty is to the Lycan nation first, Lucien and Rafael second."

"If I leave here, Lucien cannot force me to stay away from Rafa."

"You are wrong, because until he releases you completely, you belong to him. He will never release you if he thinks you will return to Rafa."

"Then I am still a prisoner, am I not?"

"Choose to stay and your prison will be a happier place." She opened the door and said over her shoulder, "Dinner is about to be served. Come down as soon as you're dressed."

"I need to wash Lucien off me first," Falon yelled at the closed door.

Grabbing the clothes she wanted to wear, Falon yanked open the bathroom door and strode in. She stopped half a step in. Lucien stood with his back to her under one of the two showerheads in the walk-in shower stall. No door for privacy. Not that she minded the sight. He was something to behold.

The muscles in his back rippled beneath the red-and-black tattoo. It was unusual in that it was a hybrid of a wolf and a dragon. The main body of a wolf wrapped around his torso with a howling dragon-head up his shoulder and the fire-breathing snout halfway around his neck. Lucien raised his arms above his shoulders and rubbed shampoo into his thick black hair. When wet, his hair reached just past his wide shoulders. Falon swallowed as her gaze swept down the corded muscles of his back to his tight ass. His legs were long, straight, and muscled. As her gaze rose, he turned. She gasped. He was erect, and she swallowed again. The tail of the wolf had a dragon spear-tip tail. The wolf head wrapped around his neck but the dragon tail wrapped around his narrow waist to his belly and straight down to his— She'd never seen a tattoo on a man's private parts or a cock piercing. Heat rose in her cheeks. When he was inside of her, that metal ball on the underside of his shaft that protruded just to the edge of his cock head had stimulated her to crazy. Maybe that was why she had come so hard and so fast . . .

Her gaze traveled up from his arrogant erection to his taut belly to his wide, defined chest. Soapy suds slid lazily down the hard, defined planes to his belly, sluicing around his erection in slow, foamy waves. His hand slid down his chest to the root of his penis. Lucien grabbed himself and slowly stroked his erection until it turned angry and red.

Look at me, he commanded.

Falon's chest rose and fell in quick harsh puffs. She shook her head, afraid he would mesmerize her with his eyes and make her do something her heart did not want her to do.

Chicken.

Refusing to be sucked in by him, Falon set her clothing on the long slate vanity, then stripped his clothes from her body. She turned toward Lucien, who stood unmoving in the middle of the large stall, watching her. She would prove to them both that she could resist his carnal call.

Chin high, she stepped into the shower. She heard his hiss of breath as she stepped past him, her thigh brushing against his. Falon steeled herself. The contact was like an electrical shock. Turning her back on him, she stood beneath the other showerhead and drenched herself. She reached past Lucien, who had not moved, and grabbed the shampoo from the slate inset. Her left breast brushed against his chest.

"Play with fire, Falon, and you will go up in flames," he warned.

She smiled, liking the control she had over him. She pushed the envelope more. Turning around, she faced him, catching and holding his hot gaze. Lifting her hands, she squeezed the shampoo onto her head. Back arched she closed her eyes, dug her fingers into her scalp, and scrubbed.

Furnace-grade heat radiated off Lucien. She felt his desire, his want, his battle not to press her against the shower wall and take her. Then visualized him doing just that. She tried to think of Rafael, but she could not quite conjure his image. Not with his brother so close.

Lucien snarled beside her. Her eyes flew open.

Eyes blazing furiously, he moved within inches of her. Falon stepped back, he stepped forward until her back hit the wall.

Whatever it was between them was strong. Because despite her love for Rafael, and her powers, powers she would not hesitate to use, she felt every bit the submissive female to Lucien's dominant male.

"You cannot will me to want you," she said, pressing her palms against the slate wall behind her.

Lucien put his hands on either side of her head and leaned into her until she felt the throb of his body heat. "I don't have to."

"You swore you would not touch me—"

"I swear a lot of things." He stepped back from her, then rinsed off. He strode from the shower and grabbed a towel from the rack and said over his shoulder, "I'm hungry; hurry up so we can eat."

The dining area just off the common room was comprised of two long, heavy, wooden, granite-topped tables. The aromas wafting from the covered dishes lining the middle of both were mouthwatering. Lucien led her to the larger of the two tables where there were two large chairs seated next to each other at the head of the table. He pulled out one of the chairs and sat her, then took his place beside her.

As soon as Lucien sat, two women heaped their plates with rare roast beef, roasted chicken, and savory lamb chops. Bowls of stir-fried vegetables and mounds of steaming pastas were set down around their laden plates.

She looked to Lucien, who cut his meat. "This is too much food, Lucien."

"Eat all that you can, Falon, you're too thin."

That she could not argue with. She had not had a period for almost two years, and knew it was because her body fat was nonexistent. She had just started to put a little weight on with regular meals when all hell broke lose. With sudden realization, Falon realized she was famished. She dug in. Halfway through her plate, Falon looked up to find the eyes of the entire pack on her. Not one of them ate. In fact, not one of them had food on their plate.

She set her fork down and looked at Lucien. "Why don't they eat?"

"It is customary they wait until the alpha has had his fill."

Flabbergasted, Falon laughed. "Are you serious?"

Lucien scowled. "It is our way."

She shook her head and sat back. "That's ridiculous. A pack is a family, as a family, the pack should eat together." She did not say that Vulkasin did not adhere to such archaic rules.

Do not undermine my authority, Falon.

Authority has nothing to do with this. Families *eat* to-ge-ther.

She pushed her plate away and said, "I eat when Mondragon eats."

Lucien set his fork down and stared at her. *Do you purposely look for ways to thwart me?*

Falon smiled and shook her head. *I live to thwart you, but on this I feel strongly. How can you not? By eating first, you do not show them the respect they are due.*

My eating first is symbolic of who I am.

No one here questions your leadership, Lucien. Don't rub it in their faces. By all means, be served first but share the meal with them.

He shook his head and stood. "Mondragon, while I am your alpha, we are a family first. From this meal forward we *all* eat at the same time and we will also share so that all the way down to the omegas, no one leaves the table hungry."

Almost eighty pairs of eyes turned on Falon. In some she saw uncertainty, in some of the females open hostility, but in most—even the big sergeant at arms, Joachim—she saw quiet gratitude.

"Eat, Mondragon!" Lucien bellowed. "You will need your strength for the pairings!"

With a gusto she had never witnessed, the pack dug in. Their bawdy talk and laughter punctuated with the noises of happy eating.

Lucien pushed his plate away from him and sat back in his chair. He set his right arm on the back of Falon's chair and watched the beer and wine flow and his pack grow louder and bawdier by the minute.

One of the men Lucien fought earlier reached across the table to a young woman and pulled her toward him. She screamed, pretending to fight him. He tore her shirt off and captured a nipple in his mouth. Moaning, she arched into him. His actions set off a chain reaction.

Falon was not unaffected by the pheromones swirling around her. Lucien's body tightened beside her. Hers answered with its own tension. She dared to look up to find his golden eyes blazing brightly.

Falon swallowed and turned away just as Joachim bent one of the girls across the table next to her, flung her skirt up, and then thrust into her. The woman howled as she pushed back against him. The air warmed exponentially. The thick musk of sex rose around them, hanging like a storm cloud above them. Lucien had not moved. Falon dared not to.

Dishes crashed to the floor, chairs were knocked over, the table-top vibrated as the wild wantonness of the rutting pack jostled for position. The females moved from one male to another, some returning to the first one. From what Falon could see, there was no ejaculation, just wild, crazy fucking.

"Why do the women take more than one man?"

"There are more males than females, but only two can pair."

"How will they choose?"

"They will see which one fits best."

Heat stung Falon's cheeks. "That sounds so barbaric."

Lucien shrugged. "It happens in most civilized human societies. In Lycan land it's just concentrated and accelerated. But unlike the human world, once the marks are exchanged, the bond cannot be broken. Not by man, by beast, nor by any act of Congress."

Not wanting to mention Rafael but wanting to know why the same did not apply to her and Rafael, Falon asked, "Then how do you expect me to act as if my bond to your brother does not exist?"

Instead of anger, Lucien looked at her with laconic eyes. The pheromones excited him on one level but drew his anger, for the moment, from him. "There are several factors involved Falon. One, Rafael is alpha as are you and as am I. But more defining is the Blood Law." Lucien's jaw tightened when he said, "You will always feel what you feel for my brother. That will not change even when he chooses another mate. He will always feel your bond to him, but survival trumps pheromones and love. The packs must reproduce or die. Love is a weakness we can ill afford. Rafael knows that. So do I."

"Is that why you allowed me to leave today?"

He inhaled sharply, then exhaled. "I gave you the choice to leave today to show the pack you were either in or out. I cannot ask for their trust and confidence if they think my chosen one does not trust me. It will weaken the pack. A weak pack is a dead pack."

"So, you would have let me go and then what?"

He exhaled in a long breath. "Then I would have done what I should have done a decade ago, chosen a mate and got on with pack business."

"So any female will do?"

"No, Falon, not any female would do!" he hissed, looking hotly at her. "I have waited sixteen years for you!"

"You do not live by your credo, Lucien."

"I always act with my pack's best interests first."

"Then you would have forgiven Rafael, and moved on."

"You have yet to understand that strength and respect rules a pack. Though we walk the earth most of the time as humans, we are wolves first. In the wild, an alpha strives for peace in his pack. He does this by being just, confident, and strong. He does not hesitate to fight for his pack or clean house within his pack if there are those who would challenge him on even the simplest level. If I had publicly or privately said, 'Hey, Rafe, even though I know you thought my chosen one was a Slayer even though she wasn't, and killed her, I'll forgive you.' Do you know how that would have been perceived? Weak. Just a hint of blood and the sharks would circle before they would have torn me apart. There can be no show of indecision, weakness, *or* hesitation."

Lucien's golden eyes blazed. "Pack first, Falon. A strong pack led by a strong alpha is life. A weak alpha is a pack's death warrant. There is no in between."

Falon nodded, trying to understand more of what survival for the Lycan nation entailed. It wasn't as easy as just staying alive, it was about dominance. And to dominate, one had to be strong, cunning, focused, and when the situation warranted: ruthless.

A naked body slid across the tabletop in front of Falon and Lucien. Perky pink nipples glistened from a suitor's kiss. Joachim claimed the owner of those breasts. Right beneath Falon's and Lucien's noses, Joachim's big tan hands grasped the woman's thighs and pulled her onto his glistening erection.

Falon's cheeks flamed with heat. She stood so fast she knocked the wooden chair she was sitting in over, afraid if she stayed another minute, she would turn to Lucien for succor.

She was beyond hot and bothered. She needed air. Abruptly she hurried to the front of the building. Yanking the heavy metal door open, Falon stepped out into the cool night air.

She knew Lucien followed. His warmth wrapped protectively around her. She shivered because it was him, the big bad wolf she needed protection from.

"Afraid I'm going to skulk out while you're not looking?" she asked him.

She felt him raise his hand to touch her, but he lowered it. She wished he hadn't.

"The door remains open, Falon."

His words stung. Was it that cut and dry for him? She wanted to hurt him back. She turned around to do just that, but he was so close to her, her breasts scraped across his chest, radically changing the trajectory of her intentions. She swallowed back a moan. The thin leather of her vest not only offered her heavy breasts in a most seductive pose, but the satin lining rubbing against her nipples did not help her cause.

Lucien's nostrils flared as he moved into her. "Did I tell you how fuckable you look in that leather?"

Heat speared straight to her womb. "No," she breathed, backing up.

Lucien lowered his head to hers. "Did I tell you it took every goddamn shred of willpower I had not to touch you in the shower?"

"No," she squeaked.

"Did I tell you I love your tits?"

She swallowed. "Don't be crude."

He lowered his lips to her ear and whispered, "Or how sweet your pussy is?"

Her pussy clenched as if his words had caressed it. Maybe they had. Lucien's voice on a normal day was deep and rough, as if he had spent the night before drinking and smoking, but the primal tenor of it now stirred her up in ways she did not know she could be stirred up.

Falon licked her dry lips. "How s-sweet?" She squeezed her eyes shut. She did not just say that!

His warm breath caressed her neck. "It's so sweet that if I only had one meal to eat before I met my maker, it would be eating that sweet pussy of yours."

"Shut up," she hissed, as tiny prickles of heat spread across her chest.

He trailed his nose along the length of her neck to where it met her shoulder. "Falon, you are so fucking hot, I melt every time I think about fucking you." He withdrew just enough so that she knew if she opened her eyes she would be staring straight into his soul.

"Lucien," she breathed, forcing herself to open her eyes and confront this crazy attraction between them. She caught her breath. His eyes burned with the brightness of a dozen torches. In their fiery depths his desire raged so hot, she felt the warmth of it against her own eyes. She blinked, sure it was just an illusion, but when she looked at him again the fire still raged.

He backed her up against the warehouse wall. And just as he did in the shower, he braced his hands on either side of her head. Her breasts heaved against his chest as she sucked in giant gulps of air. "Unbutton the vest," he quietly commanded.

"No—"

"I just want to see, Falon. I promise I won't touch you."

"Lucien . . ." She unbuttoned the top three buttons just before her nipples were exposed.

"That's it." His warm breath caressed her skin.

Falon caught another moan before it escaped. Her body was on fire and he had not touched her.

"One more button, Falon."

"No," she said, closing her eyes and resting her head against the wall.

"Please," he begged.

She sucked in a breath and unbuttoned the rest of the vest. His long fingers pulled it away from her sultry skin. Air swept across her turgid nipples. Oh, God, a flood of warm moisture soaked her thighs. Her sex scent was so strong it left no doubt about what her body wanted.

"Beautiful," he whispered, blowing his hot breath against her nipples.

Falon made a funny noise arching against him.

Lucien laughed and traced a finger along the buttons. The pressure against her skin was excruciatingly delicious. "You are so tempting right now. If I were less of a gentleman, I would have my way with you right here, Falon."

"You are no gentleman."

He moved into her and against her ear, he asked, "Are you giving me permission not to be?"

She closed her eyes and let her imagination run wild with the wicked things he could do to her—if she let him. "I'm just saying . . ."

He growled low, his beast surfacing. It thrilled her. "Falon," he breathed along her nipples. "I want you like I have never wanted another woman." He nipped at her chin, just barely missing. "Don't make me beg."

"Lucien . . ." she breathed. "Sex will complicate things between us."

"We are already beyond complicated."

She opened her eyes and smiled and felt no guilt about it. His eyes sparked brightly under the floodlights. "Complicated is an understatement."

He returned her smile and she nearly swooned. His smile widened. The gesture changed everything about him. It was like a beautiful solar eclipse, the sun lighting up the night.

She reached up and traced her fingertip along the curve of his lips. "You should smile more often."

He nipped at her finger, then sucked it into his mouth. Heat shot straight to her womb. He sucked her finger deeper into his mouth, swirling his tongue around it. Falon squeezed her eyes shut and fought the intense sensations crashing through her body. Every cell in her had lit up like a freakin' Roman candle.

With her free hand she dug her fingers into his thick hair, amazed how soft it was. Lucien pulled her finger from his mouth and placed her hand on the other side of his head. She dug her fingers in. He pressed his forehead to hers and looked down at her swollen breasts. His fingers tightened around her arms.

What he did next stunned her. Carefully, he buttoned up her vest and then stood back from her. He held out his hand to her. Dumbfounded, she took it. He led her through the heaving, gasping, humping pack up the metal stairway to his room.

Quietly, he shut the door behind them. "Get some sleep, Falon. Your body isn't as strong as you think it is."

He walked past her into the bathroom.

Speechless, she stood there in the middle of the bedroom, her body on fire while he—he did what? Brushed his teeth?

Five

AFTER WHAT SEEMED an eternity, Lucien exited the bath-room. The low glow of the candlelight flickered across the smooth skin of his broad chest and defined belly. Falon's eyes dipped lower to the thick ridge tenting his black boxer briefs. Swallowing hard she looked up into two blazing eyes above his set jaw. "Do what you need to do, Falon. I have an early day tomorrow."

She moved past him into the bathroom and closed the door softly behind her. For a long minute, Falon stood flat against the door, slowly inhaled, then more slowly exhaled as she tried to calm the electrical storm in her body and the turbulence in her heart.

She missed Rafa. At one time, she had thought she would give anything to be with him, but yet here she was. Yes, mostly she was here for the benefit of Rafa and the Lycan she'd come to love. But part of her knew she was also here because of Lucien. He had a crazy chemical combustive hold on her. Was it simply a Lycan thing? Lord knew it was as basic as basic could be. She wanted to mate. With

Lucien. Like down and dirty, crazy animal mating. She felt like a damn bitch in heat around him. And if he wasn't snubbing her, he was telling her how much he wanted to fuck her. Not make love. Fuck. Fuck, she strongly suspected like she wanted to be fucked. Gloves off, no holds barred. And what made it all worse was that the embarrassment that usually followed such lurid Lucien thoughts were barely a blimp on her propriety radar. Not that she was a prude. But what Lucien promised was miles outside of her comfort zone. What next? She'd beg him for it?

He drove her crazy! He pushed and pulled her into his seductive web, only to let her free-fall to the ground.

Rafa would never treat her so . . . haphazardly. Rafael was direct. He treated her as the equal she was. Lucien was a puppeteer. One minute yanking one string, the next minute pulling another string until she was all twisted and caught up in them. Was this his way of teasing and tempting her to the point of capitulation? Did he think if he could work her up into a sexual frenzy, she would throw herself at him for succor?

Falon bit her bottom lip. He had come perilously close to doing just that tonight. She should be thanking him for saving her from herself instead of damning him for it. Falon took another deep breath and slowly exhaled. She could do this. She could resist Lucien Mondragon's sensual sway. Her beast did not rule her; she ruled her beast. She stripped down to her panties and blushed. She could not wear them now, they were so damp. She tossed them into the large laundry hamper. What did he think of her? Because she knew what she thought of herself. And she didn't like how it made her feel as if she were being unfaithful to Rafa.

She washed her face, brushed her teeth, and grabbed a big fluffy bath towel. Wrapping it around her naked body, Falon inhaled deeply then slowly exhaled. Back straight, chin up, she strode confidently into the bedroom. Expecting to go a few verbal rounds with Lucien, she was disappointed to find him lying in bed with his back to her. Falon dropped the towel and grabbed a pair of panties from the stack on the table along with a skimpy camisole, quickly dressed, and then slid into the big bed beside Lucien.

On her back, she stared at the ceiling. Her mind ran rampant with wild thoughts and roller-coaster emotions. All of them centered around one complex man she could not quite get out of her thoughts. She rolled over, back to back with Lucien.

"Good night," she said softly.

Good night.

"LUCIEN!" TALIA SHOUTED, bursting into the bedroom. "Hurry before they kill each other!"

Lucien shot out of bed and went flying down to the common room. He felt more than saw Falon behind him.

The sight that greeted him sent every hair on his body straight up. Joachim, his second in command, and Darius, his third in command and captain of his night guard, had shifted and were literally tearing each other apart. He looked past their snarling to Lisette, a pretty, young thing wringing her hands with worry, and understood immediately what the cause of the friction was.

Darius was challenging Joachim for second seat. If he prevailed, he would have first pick. If Joachim set the youngster on his ass, Joachim would walk away not only with the continued respect of the pack but the girl, too.

"Make them stop!" Falon screamed, grabbing his arm.

Lucien whistled sharply and strode toward their heaving bodies. "Shift!" he commanded.

Both men shifted to human form but remained on all fours. "Fight as you are now or end it," Lucien said.

Joachim swept his leg around, dumping Darius on his back and dove onto him. The pack widened around the two warriors, giving them room. Brutally they punched and kicked each other. Just as one got the advantage, the other took control.

After what seemed a brutally long time but was less than ten minutes, Joachim finally got the edge over Darius. The younger man stumbled backward as Joachim drilled him with one vicious punch to the face after another. He landed on his back, and Joachim went for the knockout punch. As his brawny arm flew into Darius's face, the younger man shifted and bit Joachim's arm at the elbow, crushing his bones, snapping it in half. The pack growled at the cowardly act.

Lucien did not hesitate to stop the mauling and mete out the stiff punishment for Darius's blatant disobedience. He jumped in and grabbed the snarling Darius by the scruff of his neck. "Release him!" Lucien roared.

Darius's eyes blazed defiantly; he growled viciously at Lucien and savagely sunk his fangs deeper into Joachim's arm. Shaking his head, Darius severed the arm at the elbow.

"You will not defy me again," Lucien thundered.

The pack snarled, closing in. Lucien threw his head back and roared his rage. Violently, he shook Darius, and then shifted himself. In less than a minute, it was over. Darius lay dead on the floor, his tattered human body replacing that of his dead wolf.

Lucien shifted, pulling his shorts on. "Talia!" he shouted. "See to Joachim!"

But she was already applying pressure to the bloody wound. The big sergeant at arms listed on his feet as he stared at his bloody stump as if it did not belong to him.

As second, this was a devastating blow to the proud warrior. Lucien was sick to his stomach, not by the sight, but because his friend's life would never be the same. The damage to Joachim's arm was extensive. He doubted even the most skilled surgeon could save it.

"The damage is too severe to your severed arm for any hope of reattaching it, Joachim," Talia said softly, visually inspecting the limb. She looked up at the big Lycan. "I can triage you here to get you to the hospital where they will sew you up, or I can do what needs to be done. It's your call."

"I don't trust those quacks," Joachim muttered, the color leeching from his face. "Do what you need to do here."

Talia ripped off the sleeve of her shirt, hastily making a tourniquet above Joachim's elbow. She guided the giant of a man to an overturned chair. Falon hurried to turn it upright. Then, gently, she helped Talia seat him. Lise pushed her way through the crowd to his side.

"I'm so sorry, *precioso*. I told Darius I wanted only the sergeant at arms. I did not mean the *position*, I meant I wanted *you*!"

Joachim raised his glazed eyes to the girl and tried to smile. It came across as a grimace. "Do you still want me? A three-legged wolf?"

With a sob, she dropped to her knees before him and grabbed his only hand. "I want whatever part you are willing to share." She touched his cheek and smiled. "It's always been you, all of you, part of you, I don't care. Just don't change."

A week ago, Lucien would not have understood such unconditional love between a man and a woman. A mother and child, yes. But this? If Joachim could not find a way to use his disability to his advantage, he would be ostracized and relegated to socialize with the omegas of the pack. Would Lise want him then?

Lucien's gaze rose past Joachim to Falon, who stood quietly

watching him. The tightness in his gut intensified. He would give his own right arm to have Falon show the kind of affection for him that Lise showed Joachim.

"Don't move, Joachim," Talia said, breaking Lucien's spell. "The tourniquet isn't working; you're still losing blood too fast. I'm going to have to cauterize the main artery before I can heal you." Talia hurried from the room to the kitchen where the hearth fire burned hot.

Joachim's face paled considerably, not, Lucien knew, from what Talia said she must do, but because of the blood loss. Lucien gently nudged Lise to the side and picked up Joachim's stump, raising it above the man's head. "Steady, brother. The tourniquet is helping. Stay calm and breathe evenly or you're going to bleed out and poor little Lise is going to cry."

The pack chuckled but there was no mirth behind it.

Losing Darius was going to hurt. He was one of the strongest men Lucien had the pleasure of knowing, a proud Mondragon. His Slayer kill count was nearly as high as Lucien's. He had not intended to kill him, punish him for his initial defiance, yes, but when Darius purposely, after being commanded to release Joachim, maimed him, Lucien knew if he allowed Darius to live, he would become a cancer in the pack.

But losing Joachim would have been devastating. His sergeant at arms had been with him since the day the pack split, never once wavering in his allegiance to Lucien.

Joachim grimaced through his pain and held up his good arm. "At least it wasn't my right arm." He reached out with it and swept the startled Lisette into his embrace. "And I still have my most important arm!" He pulled her down onto his bare lap and forced a lopsided grin. "I won't let you down, Lise, I promise."

She cupped his face in her hands and kissed him. "Trust me, I will never let you *go* down!"

Lucien smiled. Perhaps with the love of this woman, the one-armed Joachim would surprise them all and retain his position within the pack. For the sake of the pack, Lucien would do everything possible to make that happen.

His grip on Joachim's stump tightened as Talia hurried back into the room holding a glowing red-hot knife in the air. "Look at me, *precioso*," Lise whispered against Joachim's lips. She kissed him just as Talia inserted the blade an inch into the bloody stump, then withdrew it, and as if she were icing a cupcake, she cauterized every millimeter of his exposed flesh. Sweat poured off Joachim's face, down his chest to his thighs. His lips were white tight, his hand fisted at Lisette's back, but he did not move. Not even when Talia stood back and the scent of burned flesh thickened putridly around them. Joachim did not so much as flinch a muscle. Falon put her hand delicately to her face and coughed behind him, but the pack stood rigid and watchful. Joachim was a pack favorite. Like Lucien, he did not command anything he was not willing to do himself.

Lucien clasped him on the shoulder with his free hand, but his words were directed at Talia. "Have one of the betas prepare one of the guest rooms."

"They are always ready, Lucien," Talia said, not looking up as she inspected her handiwork.

Lucien looked down at his friend's strained brown eyes. "Once you're healed, we'll have Hector make you the mother of all prosthetic hands."

Joachim nodded, his skin fish-belly white and just as clammy. Lucien squatted down beside him, carefully continuing to hold up the stump, then gently put his shoulder beneath Joachim's armpit and helped him to rise. Falon sprang into action and came around to Joachim's good side, and wrapped his beefy arm around her shoulder. Lise placed a calming hand on his chest. Carefully they lifted him to standing, and moved him out of the great room, and then down the hall to one of the comfortable guest rooms. Here Joachim would be under Talia's watchful eye, not stuck in the barracks.

As the big Lycan was laid back onto the mattress, he let out a long groaning breath and closed his eyes.

Lucien raised worried eyes to his cousin. "He'll be fine," she said. "The bleeding has slowed enough that I can work on him without fear he'll bleed out."

Boulder-sized relief rolled off Lucien's shoulders. Fatigue replaced it. He was physically and emotionally wiped out. But he kept his mask of strength firmly in place. If he exuded anything less than total confidence, his pack would run in circles chasing their tails.

"Take care of him, Talia," Lucien said. "If you need *anything*, do not hesitate to wake me."

He grabbed Falon's hand and withdrew from the room, quietly closing the door behind them.

He stopped just inside the hallway and looked down at her pale face. "You okay?"

She let out a long breath and nodded. "That was terrifying and amazing, Lucien. It all happened so fast, and you just—handled it."

He smiled slowly not feeling any joy in destroying not only a formidable soldier but also a friend. "I had no other choice."

She squeezed his hand. "I understand why you did what you had to do."

"Do you?"

Vigorously she nodded. "Had you not acted when and how you did, you would have sent the message it was okay to ignore your command."

"The price came too high tonight, Falon. Darius was a good man. But tonight, he could not control his beast. Lose control once, it becomes a habit."

He tugged her arm and walked back to the common room where the scent of sex, blood, and burned flesh infused the heavy air. The pack moved restlessly about.

"I want your attention," Lucien said quietly. The pack responded as if he had blasted it over a bullhorn. All movement stopped, every eye in the room, riveted on him. "You saw what happened to Darius. His beast got the better of him tonight. Either control your beast or the same will happen to any one of you who defies me or attacks another, regardless of reason, in wolf form. Am I clear?"

"Yes, Lucien," the pack said as one.

He nodded and looked at Dax. "You will assume all of Darius's duties and pick up the slack for Joachim until he is healed."

Dax nodded, stepping forward. "I will not let you down, Lucien."

"I don't expect that you will, Dax. Joachim was to leave on an errand for me early tomorrow morning, but he cannot and since Darius is unavailable, I'm putting the chore in your hands."

"I am ready," the anxious Lycan said.

Lucien gauged the mood of the pack before he proceeded, looking for the slightest hint of negativity. There was none. Mondragon trusted their alpha and in so doing trusted his choices.

"Put together a hunting and gathering party." Lucien smiled; the women were going to love this. "Eight male, two female." His smile widened as the women swarmed Dax as if he were a rock star, begging to be chosen.

What the females lacked in strength they made up for in ferocity. It had been too long since he had allowed any of them to hunt. They were too valuable to the pack to risk in battle. But they had become restless and bored. It was time to let the girls out.

Dax all but wagged his tail, he was so excited. "The black van is loaded with the tools and weapons you'll need, but take your swords; you're going to need them," Lucien said. "Prepare to depart by three a.m.

You're going shopping in Lodi. Balor has a new munitions supplier. A 'Nam vet by the name of Skeet Yoder. The old man fronts his arms business with a junkyard just on the Highway 99 edge of town. He has a dozen rotties and pits running the yard after hours. While they are a nonissue for us, he does have cameras everywhere. Via my computer, I've scheduled them to disarm at four a.m. You'll be clear to access the rear of the property via the back gates. Once in, you'll have plenty of time to get the lay of the land and take position. There are detailed maps and schematics of the property in the van."

"Does he sleep on the property?" Dax asked.

"No, he usually comes in around nine, doesn't open to the public until ten. But as a precaution, shift first and check it out. I know he has a big morning planned."

Lucien smiled down at Falon, who raised questioning eyes to his. He turned back to Dax. "I hacked into Skeet's computer last week and discovered there's a scheduled pickup at eight tomorrow morning. Corbet is stocking up arms. You need to be set up no later than six. I want the guns, the cash, and the Slayers who show up put out of their misery. Tie the old man up until it's all over, then let him go."

Dax nodded.

"Any questions?" Lucien asked.

Dax looked behind him to the gauntlet of females who were just waiting to pounce, then back at Lucien. "How do I choose?"

Despite the pall that hung around them, Lucien laughed, shaking his head. Taking Falon's hand into his, he started for the stairway. "That will be your first official act as captain of the night guard."

The females squealed. "Ladies!" Dax shouted.

Lucien laughed louder, as Dax's voice was drowned out by those of the demanding females.

As they slowly walked up the three flights of stairs, Lucien felt Falon's desire to talk more about what just happened, but there was nothing to be said. What could be said that wasn't already said? He opened the door and allowed her to walk through first. He followed her in and shut the door closed behind them.

"I'm going to jump in the shower, then I have some computer work to do," Lucien said as he strode toward the bathroom door. He left her on the bed and went into the bathroom and took his second shower of the night. When he emerged a few minutes later, Falon lay feigning sleep. He smiled to himself and chucked the damp towel across the room and grabbed a fresh pair of shorts from his armoire, then settled at his desk.

Falon's restless movements in bed distracted Lucien. His work was not progressing as it should. He was tired, horny, pissed off over the night's events, and fighting a losing battle with the green-horned monster: jealousy. He wanted the kind of devotion from Falon that Lise had for Joachim. Like Falon had for his brother, damn it! The emotions made no logical sense to him. He did not care about love and devotion. He cared about loyalty and courage, strength and intelligence.

"Lucien?"

Her soft voice startled him from his thoughts. He stiffened, refusing to turn around and look at her. He knew what he would see, and he knew what the sight of her would do to his semi-erection.

"What?"

"Is it hard?"

He grinned. "It's getting there."

A pillow smacked him in the back of the head. He focused on the computer screen in front of him. He'd double- and triple-checked the camera shutdown at four a.m. He'd peeked back into Skeet's computer to confirm the appointment with "Longshanks," his code name for the Slayers. Lucien could be done for the night—if he wanted.

"I wasn't finished with my question."

He clicked open a spreadsheet to take his mind off the stiffness in his shorts. Hundreds of numbers popped up on the screen. He did not see any one of them. "I'm listening."

"Being alpha, is it hard? Do you ever want to just walk away from it?"

Though there was no doubt to his answer, it took him a long minute to respond. "It's challenging at times. *Most* of the time. But I have never regretted my position." He turned and looked at her. He about came in his chair. She was all long and golden, stretched out like the queen of Sheba on his bed. He swallowed hard. She had changed while he was in the shower. The sexy little thong panties that accentuated the soft curve of her hips and the formfitting spaghetti-strap half tee that hugged her lush tits like an offering should be arrested for the lewd and lascivious acts he wanted to perform on the body they adorned.

"I—" He forgot the rest of the question.

Falon smiled and brushed her dark hair off her left shoulder, exposing the hollow of her collarbone. It was sexy as hell. He loved dipping his tongue into and then across that silky spot. "Do you ever want to walk away from it?"

"No." He exhaled. He wanted to plow right into it. "Never."

"Not even a little?"

Lucien shook his head, his gaze holding hers. "Not even a little." He would never abandon his pack.

She pulled the blanket over and across her body. "I'm glad." She closed her eyes and turned on her side away from him.

Lucien blinked, ignoring the ache in his loins and his urge to demand from Falon what she freely gave his brother. He swiped his hand across his chin as the anger returned.

"Damn it," he cursed softly. One way or another Falon was going to get so deep under his skin he'd either have to cut her out or let her take over his body. He wasn't sure which would hurt less.

Damn it all to hell! He shut down his computer and blew out all but two candles, then slid into his big, comfortable bed that had become a torture chamber.

AFTER WHAT SEEMED like hours of tossing and turning, reliving frame by frame the horrible fight between the two Lycans, and Joachim's terrible injury, it was Lucien who was predominant in Falon's mind. Specifically his swift punitive damage followed by the gentle handling of his man. The first action she accepted, hell, expected no less from Lucien. But the latter threw her for a loop.

Just when she thought she knew what drove the complex alpha, he showed a side of himself that made her rethink her judgment. Falon mentally threw her hands up in the air deciding she would never understand Lucien Mondragon, and with that conclusion, she was finally able to fall asleep. It was short-lived. She was being chased through the timberline, running toward the safety of Vulkasin. The deep rumble of motorcycle engines closing in fast behind her. She looked over her shoulder and screamed. Dozens of armless Vipers, no more than three feet away, gunning straight for her.

Rafa! she screamed. He materialized out of the mist, his arms extended, running toward her.

Falon!

Her relief was so overwhelming she lost her footing and fell. She screamed as the burn of a hot engine seared her bare legs. Strong arms grabbed her. She looked up into golden eyes.

Lucien.

He pulled her out of the fire and into the safety of his arms.

With a start, Falon woke to a darkened room. It took her a moment to realize where she was. Who lay beside her in the big bed. Why she was with Lucien and not with Rafael.

Her heart tightened. *Rafa.* He was gone to her. Would she ever feel that wild sense of wonder at the world again? The way she'd felt with her true love by her side? Falon let out a long, exhausted breath. Would her heart ever recover? She shivered and knew she would never stop loving Rafael. Not as long as she drew breath.

Falon raked her fingers through her tangled hair. Resignation forced its way in. She may no longer have that vital part of her, but she was not dead, and despite her loss, she did not want to die.

She wanted peace if she could not have love. She wanted to belong if she could not have the arms of the man she loved around her every night. She wanted to make a difference, not fade into the woodwork.

In that glaring instant, Falon realized her chance was here. With Mondragon. Peace if Lucien could find a way to shelf his perpetual anger. She could belong to Mondragon if she simply allowed them to belong to her. And to that end she could make a difference because she was alpha. She had power, not just Lycan power but other powers she had no clue as to where they originated. But she could use them. She *would* use them!

It would not be handed to her. She would have to dig deep and work tirelessly to establish her place in this new world of Mondragon. And that work began with accepting the man whose bed she shared. And he was not making it easy.

"Lucien?"

I'm here.

She turned to find him lying on his side, calmly watching her. The weak candlelight flickered across his dark features, making him appear more dangerous than she knew he was.

"I—I had a nightmare."

"I know."

She lay back down on the bed. Her heart still thud against her chest, her skin was damp, her breaths shallow. The worst part of the dream had been Lucien's part in it—that he had been her savior rather than Rafael. What did it mean? She turned her head and stared at Lucien, who returned her stare.

"I was being chased by dozens of Vipers. They had no arms; they were bleeding." She squeezed her eyes shut, wanting to erase the gruesome vision in her mind's eye. "I couldn't stop them. My powers didn't work, I had no way to defend myself—" Her eyes fluttered open to his deep golden gaze. "You saved me," she whispered.

"Even in your dreams, I will protect you, Falon."

His words melted through her like warm chocolate syrup over vanilla ice cream. Never did she expect that such a simple declaration could mean so much to her. Perhaps it was because it came from a man who spit nails for breakfast and ate fire for dinner.

She resisted the urge to reach out and touch him. Not in a sexual way, but with a simple, reassuring, thank-you type of touch. "Tell me about your chosen one." Her question surprised her. It had been in the back of her mind to ask him, but he was always so damn angry she'd resisted.

The gold in his eyes snapped and crackled. He rolled onto his back and locked his hands behind his head. "There is nothing to tell."

Falon scooted closer to him and poked him in the rib. "You said you would never lie to me. There is plenty to tell. Now tell me."

"If I asked you to tell me about Rafe, how would you feel discussing him with me?"

"I would tell you whatever you wanted to know."

He cracked a smile. "Now who is the liar?"

She moved closer to him, folded her arms across his chest and set her head down on them to look him straight in the eye. His body stiffened beneath her arms. She ignored the warning and pushed a little harder. "I want you to tell me about her so that I have a better understanding of you."

A small muscle flickered along his left jawline. "What do you want to know?"

Falon almost jumped for joy. "How did you meet? What was her name? What did she look like?"

He cocked a dark brow at all of her questions.

"You asked me what I wanted to know, so I'm telling you."

He let out a long breath and clamped a hand across his forehead and closed his eyes. "I met her at a bar in Oakland."

"Really? A *bar* bar? How unromantic."

He opened his eyes, though he did not remove his hand. "A bar where you drink alcohol and pick up women."

"But you were underage—"

"I am Lycan; I go wherever I choose."

An arrogant Lycan. "Is that why you were at the bar? To pick up a woman?"

"Yes, Falon, it's what men do."

He stared at the ceiling. "We had just come off a killer hunt. We'd hit the jackpot that night. Balor and his brother Edward had just left the premises when we blew in, but we hit the extended family jackpot. We were the last thing they were expecting that night. We were the last thing they saw before we sent them to hell."

Lucien glanced at Falon and reached out to touch her hair, but withdrew his hand. "Me and the boys were looking to celebrate. We cruised the streets of Oakland until we found an out-of-the-way bar. A place we could tear up. We started drinking and we were feeling damn good. Then *she* walked in. The minute I saw her, I knew I was going to take her home. But she wasn't as easy of a target as I usually encountered." He smiled. "She made me work for it. Had me jumping through hoops. At seventeen, I was doing backflips to get into her pants." He grinned. Falon pursed her lips, not caring at all for his fond memories of this ghost that hung between two brothers. "And when I did, that was all she wrote."

"Did you love her?" she stiffly asked.

"I loved her as much as a lusty seventeen-year-old male could love." He scowled as if he remembered something vital.

"What?"

"Rafa was up north on his spirit journey. The pack was in my hands. They became restless each time she came to the compound. When I moved her in, they began to fight."

"Don't you think it's odd that when she was around, the pack was so restless? Before she came to the compound, was there ever infighting?" They obviously did not care for his choice. Neither, Falon decided, did she. But lust was blind.

"None to speak of. We were young for alphas, and with just one of us in residence, I think they were nervous with Rafael away. And the females of the pack were resentful I didn't choose a Lycan mate."

That made sense. "What was her name?"

"Mara."

"Hmm . . ."

He looked at her. "What is that supposed to mean?"

Falon played off her unexpected irritation. "In several cultures, Mara is equated with death. In some lore she is literally the goddess of death."

"She was beautiful. Like a vibrant flame. Full of life. Until Rafael destroyed her." Lucien did not say it with anger, just matter-of-factly, as if he were reading off a laundry list. She understood his pain, what little he was showing of it. It was hard to believe Mara was the cause of the strife between him and his brother. Had Lucien ever truly mourned her or had he just jumped headfirst into his blood feud?

"You never had a chance to mourn her death, did you?"

"I didn't need to."

"Lucien, to heal we all need to go through the stages of loss. You have been stuck in the anger stage for almost sixteen years. It's time to let it go."

He turned blazing eyes on her. "It's not something I can just get over. I was inside of her! She was in my arms when Rafael ripped her heart out of her chest!" He swiped his hand across his forehead again and rubbed his temples. "She died in my arms. She didn't deserve to die that way. So excuse me if I'm still a little pissed off about it."

"Lucien, I understand the trauma of having your love ripped from your arms."

He snarled.

But she would not back down. He needed to heal even if she had to force it down his throat. "Listen to me!" She pushed off his chest to give him space. "I understand the pain that goes with it. I understand the denial, the anger, the depression, the *everything*! I'm living it! But is there any way you can find it in your heart to at least *try* to accept the fact that your brother, the brother who loved and *still* loves you, did what he did because *he* believed she was a Slayer who had smitten you with her black magic?"

"He never gave her a chance to disprove his suspicions!"

"He didn't give her a chance because there was no question in his mind. By the Blood Law he had no choice but to slay her."

"She was not a Slayer! I would have seen it in her eyes, but more than that, I would have sensed it when I was inside her. Rafael slew her because he wanted the pack for himself."

Falon inhaled a deep gulp of air and then slowly exhaled. Getting angry and raising her voice was not the way to get through to Lucien.

Calmly she said, "Rafael is ruled by honor, not by greed. You know that better than anyone, Lucien. You call him out on it every chance you get. You use his code of honor against him. And knowing that about your brother, you know he would have challenged you fair and square for alpha rights if he believed you were not worthy of the position. He didn't have to kill your chosen one, Slayer or not, to achieve that."

When Lucien did not immediately counter her words, she lowered her voice and said, "And Lucien, did Rafa ever say to you or any one else in the pack he wanted to do anything but share alpha rights with you?"

"Rafael wanted everything."

Falon shook her head not buying it. She knew Rafael Vulkasin. He was not a greedy man, except when it came to her. "Perhaps you mistook his concern and sense of responsibility for the pack for greed. Maybe when word got to him how you were acting with Mara and how she made the pack uncomfortable, Rafael felt he had to make a stand. Maybe he was right about her being a Slayer, maybe he was not, but, Lucien, I swear on my own life, your brother will go to his grave believing he killed a Slayer that day. In that, can you at least *try* to put this behind you?" Falon watched Lucien for any sign of softening. His jaw remained clenched, his muscles tense. "The rising is imminent; Mondragon and Vulkasin are the two most powerful packs in the world. United they will infuse all the packs with hope!"

"The packs will fight for their lives. That is enough motivation."

"You are a hypocrite."

"There is nothing hypocritical about my hatred for my brother."

"What did you say to me earlier tonight, Lucien? Pack first. Not only are you *not* putting Mondragon first, but by holding on to your hatred, you are condemning them to death."

"Let me worry about my pack."

"They are my pack, too!"

He rolled over and faced her. "Since when?"

"Since I chose to stay."

"For the next week?"

"Why do you purposefully make it more difficult for me to stay than it has to be? I told you, *I was staying*. You threw the seven days on the table, not me, so don't even pretend that it was my idea."

"Regardless of what you do, I will never reconcile with Rafael."

"Pride is the devil's handmaiden, Lucien. It will kill you and every Lycan that follows you into battle." Falon shook her head, desperately wanting to get through to him. This was not about her and Rafael; this was about the survival of the nation. A nation she was part of. A nation that had taken her in when the world at large would not. "Lucien, your hatred is eating you from the inside out. Let it go or it will kill you."

"What do you care if it does?"

She cared. God help her, but she cared. She still did not understand fully why, but . . .

She scooted closer to Lucien, wanting to soothe away his hurt. She touched his shoulder. His skin was smooth and warm. He flinched and shrugged her hand off. "I can't touch you now?" she demanded.

He rolled over and faced her, so close their breaths mingled. "I'm pulled about as tight as I can be pulled, Falon. The slightest touch from you and I'll snap." He rolled over onto his back and dug his fingers into his hair. "And when I snap, there will be nothing you can do to stop me from taking what I want."

His words sent heat straight to her womb. "What if it's what I want, too?" she said huskily.

He looked hotly at her. His lips slid into a sly smile. He moved over her, pinning her to the mattress. His erection was hard and warm against her belly.

Falon swallowed hard. He was in a deadly mood. And damn if it didn't turn her on. He lowered his lips to hers, his hair brushing along her cheeks. "Do you think you can fuck your way out of here?"

"Argh!" Falon screamed and shoved him so hard, he flew from the bed and crashed into his desk. She jumped to the floor and came around the foot of the bed. "You are by far *the* most colossal ass to walk this earth, Lucien Mondragon! You can go fuck yourself! Because I'll be damned if you're ever going to fuck me again!"

She grabbed his pillows from the bed and threw them at him. "Go sleep with your horny pack. You are no longer welcome in my bed."

Lucien grinned up at her and raked his fingers through his hair.

"Get out, Lucien!"

His grin widening, he shook his head no. Falon snapped. And when she did, she unloaded.

Lucien caught her before she drilled him deeper into his desk and destroyed his expensive equipment. The beast in her was out of control. If it was anyone but her, his beast would meet hers head-on and fight until she submitted. But he would not hurt Falon like that. Not when he did not have to hurt her to get her to submit. Not when he had more enjoyable ways to do it.

He grabbed her snarling body tighter to him and tried to stand. But she was having none of it. Her nails sunk into his biceps, her teeth into his shoulder. She ripped and tore his flesh. She kicked and kneed his thighs, trying to get him in the balls. He deflected each kick. His blood slickened his skin, and his hold on her slipped.

"Falon! Stop before you get hurt."

"You're the one getting hurt!" she snarled and laid into him again. Each time he tried to stand with her, she managed to force him back to the floor. "I hate you!" she spat, tearing at him. "I hate you!"

He rolled over with her against his chest, then rolled over again until he pinned her to the floor. He grabbed her hands, his blood making it difficult to get traction. Her knee came up between his thighs and she caught him. He grunted in pain.

"That's it!" he snarled. He shoved his knee between her legs and grabbed her hands. With one hand, he yanked her arms above her head. With his other hand, he shoved the leg she was trying to gouge him with to the floor. "Stop it right now, Falon."

She arched and wiggled, trying to get out of his hold. "When you're dead, I'll stop!"

He laughed at her threats. It only infuriated her. She screamed her frustration and arched her back into a perfect C to get him off her. But he was too strong. Even that mental power trick she had could not free her.

He looked at her furious blue eyes and could not help himself. He grinned again. She was a magnificent sight. Her wild black hair was everywhere, her furious blue eyes never sparked so brightly, her nostrils flared, the slightest trickle of blood ran from her nose. The full, succulent lips he dreamed about were parted in a most fuckable way.

He could not help but be aroused by her. Not just the physical aspects of her, but the complexity of her. Mara had been beautiful and sexy as hell, but she had not had the depth of character or the fight in her that Falon had. In fact, Mara hadn't come close to Falon. No woman could.

Falon's eyes widened as his cock thickened against her belly. "Don't you dare, Lucien!"

His grin widened to the point of pain. "Falon," he said huskily, "I would dare anything to make love to you right now." He dropped his head to hover just above hers. "Anything except fuel your hatred." His lips swept across hers in a slow sensuous slide. "Please don't hate me."

Her body trembled beneath his. Warm salty tears touched his lips.

He raised his lips from hers and cupped her face in his hands. "Don't cry."

She squeezed her eyes shut and shook her head. He kissed the tear streaks away. It only made her cry harder. What the hell had he done to cause this emotional tidal wave? He would much rather deal with the spitfire than the waterfalls.

"Falon, talk to me."

She opened her watery eyes and shook her head. "I don't hate you, Lucien." She grabbed his hair. "I *want* to hate you! I *should* hate you!" She released his hair and lay back onto the floor. "But I don't. I don't know why. I wish I could."

He dropped his lips to the pulse beat at the base of her neck. "You want to hate me because you love Rafa?"

She swallowed against his lips. "If I hated you—then I would not want you."

He lifted his head. His eyes quietly held hers.

"And because I want you, I feel as if I have betrayed Rafa. And that I truly hate." She choked back a sob. "He knows I have lain with you. He knows you have marked me, and I know it has broken his heart one hundred times over. I can barely stand the pain of it." She choked back another heart-wrenching sob. "But, you and me, because we share blood or just because we share chemistry, or something else we don't know about, whatever this physical thing is between us . . . I don't want to stop it. And I hate myself for that."

"Falon, we are blood bound. I cannot fight what is between us any more than you can. Even if I were on good terms with Rafa, I could not stop this thing between us. Fight it, yes. I have fought it every second of every minute of every day since we traded blood at Vulkasin. It's stronger now that more blood has been exchanged. But even with the blood bond, Falon, there is a natural attraction between us that defies all logic." He kissed the tender spot on her neck. "And you bear my mark. Gods willing, one day soon you will bear my child."

"It will destroy Rafael."

Lucien tempered his jealousy. "Hearts are meant to be broken, Falon, just as they are meant to heal and love again." His words stunned him, especially when he realized that somewhere in the deepest, darkest, coldest depths of his heart, he might yet love again.

He dug his hands into her hair, smoothing it away from her face. "My brother and I have been witness to the most traumatic pain a child could be exposed to, and yet, we endured. By my brother's hand, my chosen one was destroyed while in my arms, and I endured. Rafael had his chosen one ripped from his arms, and he will endure. We are Lycan, Falon. Our entire existence has been an endurance test. And we are still standing, despite eight hundred years of being hunted."

"I'm afraid, Lucien."

"I will protect you." He lowered his lips to her salty lips and nudged them apart. Her body trembled beneath his. "I love when your body does that," he said against her lips.

"Does what?"

"Trembles when it realizes it cannot fight this thing between us."

His hands swept down her face to her neck and shoulders. His thumbs slid across her tight nipples. Falon moaned, arching into his hands.

His kiss deepened. Desire caught fire in his loins and spread like a wildfire through his body. When she did not rebuff him, his fire flared out of control. His cupped her breasts, his lips trailing down her neck to each sweet peak. Falon arched and grabbed his shoulders.

He slipped an arm around her waist and pulled her to him.

To his surprise and fascination, he felt the warm wetness of her tongue slide across the bite on his shoulder. His entire body wracked with pleasure. The sensation of her healing tongue was unlike anything he had ever felt. His cock thickened and his balls swelled.

"Falon," he breathed and ripped her tiny top from her body. Her hot tits speared his chest. He pulled the flimsy panties from her bottom, and then pulled off his boxer briefs.

She slurped and moaned with pleasure as she tended his wounds, tugging him down to his balls. His fingers dug into her ass. The beast in him snarled and began to rise. His hips thrust against her. He wanted Falon with such urgency; he feared he might hurt her.

She moved behind him to heal the bite wounds on the back of his shoulder. Her long hair swept across his hot skin, her breasts pressed into his back. Her hands slid down his taut belly, brushing the dewy head of his cock, then along his cock piercing.

He hissed in a sharp breath. Closing his eyes, Lucien tilted his head back and grabbed her hand, guiding it to his shaft, then wrapped her fingers around him. He hissed in another breath when she squeezed. Placing his hand around hers, he slowly began to pump as her wicked tongue licked and sucked his wounds. The cadence of both strokes stiffened him to the consistency of granite.

Reaching his free hand behind his back, Lucien slid his hand down her taut belly, across her smooth mons to her slick little clit. She moaned pressing into him. When she did, her teeth scraped a bite on his shoulder, drawing fresh blood. Lucien grit his teeth, reveling in the mixture of pain and pleasure. Oh, the things he could do to her. *Would* do to her.

He dipped a finger into her steamy pussy. She hissed and bit him harder. His cock jerked in response. Pressing his finger deeper into her, Lucien squeezed her hand tighter around his hungry cock. And set a slow, measured rhythm. She pumped him from root to head in agonizing slowness, as his finger thrust in and out of her liquid heat. Her lips followed the same slow, sensual grind.

It was all he could do not to come. He wanted this to last. He wanted it to last because he knew she was doing it because *she* wanted to, not for Rafael.

HEALING LUCIEN INFUSED Falon with supercharged pheromones. His blood inspired wantonness. Her beast demanded his meet her halfway. Her entire body thrummed with sensation. It took everything Falon had in her not to shove him onto his back on the floor and ride him off into the sunset. This thing between them defied reason. His blood was a potent sexual stimulant she could not resist even if she wanted to.

"Lucien," she cried. The orgasm came out of nowhere and slammed into her. His thick fingertip tapped that sweet spot high inside her. "Oh—" He swirled his finger inside her, sweeping back and forth across that sensitive spot, then vibrated against it. "Oh, God." She clamped down around his finger and rode the intense orgasm out. It left her breathless and panting for more.

"I'm going to fuck you like an animal, Falon," Lucien said as he turned around and forced her on all fours.

Wild wanton abandon caught fire in her. She wanted feral, wicked, decadent sex. Sex that would make her forget the pain. Sex that would blow her mind. She wanted to ride, be ridden, and—

"Make me forget everything but you," she begged.

"I'm shameless, Falon," he whispered against her ear. "Do you want to be shameless with me?"

She did not hesitate. "Yes."

She felt him shift behind her.

"Lucien!" she gasped, turning around. His fierce black wolf growled low, his golden eyes glittering in the low glow of the room. He nudged her back onto all fours. Unsure, Falon waited, afraid, excited—his nose sniffed along the smooth dip of her back, toward her shoulders. He nuzzled her neck, licking her. Goose bumps shivered across her skin. His tongue was warm and moist. Long and strong. It felt good . . .

He licked her shoulder and her arm, then ducked his head and licked the side of her right breast. Falon hissed in a long breath, fighting her sense of propriety and the fact that it felt so good. He licked her again, catching her sensitive nipple. She swallowed hard, swaying away from him.

He growled low and nudged her until she moved back into him. His fur was silky soft, sensuality against her skin. He licked her nipple again. Shamelessly, her breasts swelled. She closed her eyes and let herself enjoy the sensations. In long, slow swaths, he licked her breasts, her nipples, her back, and her belly. When he moved behind her, Falon stiffened in anticipation. It mortified her, but she was too far gone to stop him. Her beast wanted his beast. Demanded it. And it didn't matter how.

His nose tracked along the swell of her bottom, stopping just above her anus. Her body trembled when he dipped his nose lower to her pussy and sniffed. Her muscles clenched and unclenched, like a red flag to a bull, her female taunting his male. She was so wet, her scent so strong, she was sure the pack could smell it three floors below. Her arms and legs shook violently.

Lucien was wicked. She'd known he would have no boundaries when it came to sex. He was wild, willful, and—

"Oh!"

His tongue lapped between her thighs, just barely grazing her swollen lips. Her pussy pulsed. Her beast snarled. Lucien licked her again, this time with a long deep swath from her clit to her anus. Hot shards of sensation prickled along her nerve endings. He did it again. "Lu-ci-en." God, it felt so good. Wantonly she spread her thighs, and her creamy wetness trickled down the inside of her legs. She was so hot, so turned on, so hungry for him, she could come with just a breeze.

He licked her lush honey from the inside of her thighs. It drove her crazy.

She dug her nails into the carpet, shredding it. She tilted her hips upward wanting him there at the very core of her. Lucien put a big paw on her behind, and turning his head sideways, he licked her again. His long, powerful tongue slipped between her labia and into her, swirling around the soft, sensitive pink inner parts of her. She sobbed with pleasure, the sensation so fiercely hot, she could scarcely breathe.

Each time he licked her, his salacious tongue swathed around her straining clitoris, hugging it, sliding against it, releasing it, pushing her further and further to the edge. She wanted penetration. Violation. Obliteration. Needed it like a drug. When he mounted her, she cried out. She could stand it no more. She spread her thighs farther, tilting her hips down and back, offering her sweltering pussy to him.

Shift, Lucien.

He shifted just as he slid his cock balls-deep into her. Falon screamed, the sensation so sublime her sensors could barely process the overload. Her muscles clamped possessively around him as his hands grasped the cradle of her hips.

"Falon," he growled. "I just want to tear you up inside."

The tension in his body was so tight she feared he would snap in half. She felt it in the stutter of his heartbeat. The way he pressed deeper into her, the force of his hands on her. His power and energy throbbed like a lightning rod inside of her. He pulled out, and her awareness of him was so acute, she could feel the thick vein running the length of his cock as it slid along her vaginal walls. When he thrust back into her, she could feel the wide fleshy head of his cock and the smooth ball of his cock ring as it sluiced along the sensitive flesh inside, stimulating her to higher heights. He ground against her hips, the hot weight of his balls slapping her sensitive pussy lips and caressing her hard clit, driving her mad.

"You make me forget who I am." He thrust into her again. "Jesus, you feel so right."

Hot moisture stung her eyes. This was a Lucien she had never known existed, let alone believed she'd ever witness. Each time he withdrew, then thrust deeply into her, Falon lost a little piece of herself to him. She had allowed him to do what she had never allowed Rafael to do, though he had tried.

The taboo of Lucien's beast and her human joining as it did should have mortified her, but she felt the complete opposite. They were Lycan. Human and wolf. Why could not both meet? Lycan did not follow the same rules as polite society. They were supernatural creatures of the night. Driven by their primal fire.

But still, what did that say about her, that she allowed his wolf that human part of her?

Stop analyzing, Falon, he said roughly. *Let go.*

He crashed into her, yanking her from the cerebral part of their joining, bringing her back to the primal physicality of it.

Because he had no shame, Falon could lose hers, running brazenly with him on this wild, indecent romp. And ride her hard he did. He took her to a place she had never been.

S i x

THE BEAST IN Falon snarled, fighting for release. She cried out as its claws scraped her belly and its fangs gnashed at her womb, jerking her from the pleasure of Lucien's touch with its own. *What does it want, Lucien?*

Freedom.

How do I free it? she cried as panic gripped her.

Just let it go, Falon.

Lucien's body filled her with such urgency she was afraid if she let go she would never come back.

Let it go.

Arching, she flung her head back. Lucien pulled out of her. She snarled, rearing up, her slick back sluiced against his sweltering chest. He grabbed her up and tighter to his chest and impaled her from behind, his thrusts never missing a beat. Drawn wire tight, she snaked her arms up and around his neck, digging her fingers into his thick hair, and spreading her thighs to give him better access. She was as connected to him as two beings could be. Perspiration soaked her skin, a red haze of blood blurred her vision, and her pussy clutched his cock like a fist refusing to let it go.

"Christ," he called out hoarsely.

She ground her ass against him, burying him deeper into her. Falon could not breathe past the sensations of him inside of her and the wild, wanton demands of her beast.

She dug her nails into his thighs, leaving bloody furrows in their wake. The heady scent of his blood drove the furious beast inside her insane.

Lucien wrapped his arm around her waist to keep her steady. With his other hand he swept her hair up away from her neck. He licked the mark he had made. Moaning, Falon pressed her head back into the crook of his neck, straining against him. His hands slid to her breasts, cupping them roughly together just as he scraped his sharp teeth along the vital vein in her neck. His hot breath and primal growl was so much like his wolf's that Falon half wondered if he had shifted.

Her beast answered with a long, pealing cry as she came in a violent maelstrom of erotic overload. Her muscles clenched tightly around him, giving him no quarter. Impaled upon him, her body jerked and bucked in a wild fit of debauched bliss. And the entire time, Lucien held her steady, never letting her fall.

It took a long time for her muscles to stop clamping spasmodically around Lucien. Only God knew how he maintained the control not to move inside her when her muscles finally released him. She could not catch her breath no matter how many gulps she blew in and out.

She turned slightly to look up at him. His eyes blazed like beacons in a turbulent sea. Once again, she raised her arms up and dug her fingers into his damp hair, pulling his lips to hers. If it were possible, he swelled fuller inside of her.

She moaned and clenched him deeper into her. She was so wet and still so hot for him the intensity of it scared her.

His tongue slid across her tongue, deepening the kiss. She turned more fully into him. He slipped out of her and pressed her gently back onto the carpet. Before her back hit the floor, he filled her again.

She closed her eyes, reveling in the slick, hard feel of his body inside her. Every inch of her body throbbed. Every pore in her skin was sweat soaked. And every inch of her womb burned like fire. He had torn her up, and she wanted it again.

Suddenly, it was all too much. Not just the closeness of their bodies, but the meeting of their hearts.

"Open your eyes, love," he whispered.

Falon swallowed and opened her eyes. She caught her breath. Lucien's golden eyes had darkened to a deep burnished bronze. His features sharpened to that of a predator. Something had fundamentally changed in him. She was afraid to know what it was. Because here was a man who was not ruled by honor, laws, or a code of ethics. He was ruled by his primordial soul and what his soul craved was *her*.

If she wasn't careful, he would become an obsession that could destroy her.

This thing between them, it was too much too soon. She wasn't ready—

Shhhh.

He pushed her arms over her head, then slid his hands along them in a slow caress. When his fingers entwined with hers, he softly said, "I want to watch you come this time."

"I can't—" Her body was over capacity.

"I'll help you," he said against her lips.

And he did. She could not deny him. Did not want to.

Slow and unhurried, he let her body settle down and made love to her mouth with his lips and tongue. He did not move inside her, he just filled her. Her swollen vagina cradled him as it recovered from the shock and awe of his insurgence. When his lips meandered down her throat to her breasts, she loosened. He nipped at one sensitive nipple, then another. Her breasts swelled, and her pussy clenched.

He nuzzled her breasts, licking them, kissing them, sucking them. The heat that had never left her body flared. Just as he moved inside of her, he looked up at her, catching her watching his assault on her breasts. He smiled a wolf grin. "That didn't take long."

Her lips parted and he captured them. His body swelled above hers. And then, in an unhurried give and take, he made love to her as if she were the most delicate creature on earth.

He made love to her as if . . . he loved her.

And because of that, Falon's heavy broken heart trembled, and opened just enough to take a chance that Lucien might one day be allowed inside.

LUCIEN HAD NEVER been so tender with a woman. Nor felt as possessive. He fully understood his brother's willingness to fight to the death for the woman in his arms. He would do the same, even if it meant the death of his own blood.

Even as he felt a twinge of pain and loss, his beast snarled. Lucien soothed it. He and Rafael were enemies and it would always be so. But here, now . . . He did not want to ruin this.

He traced his fingers down the inside of her arms to her face and slid his fingers into her damp hair. She arched into him, moaning against his lips. Lucien drew back to look into her deep blue eyes.

They truly were the windows to her soul. He saw everything in them as he slowly moved in and out of her. Arousal, fear, and the shadow of the she-wolf that—hell, he could barely admit it to himself—scared him as much as it intrigued him.

Wolf to wolf, he wanted to fight beside her.

Alpha to alpha, he wanted to lead beside her.

Lover to lover, he wanted to mark every inch of her body.

She was a worthy partner.

His cock thickened painfully. His balls hurt. He needed to come. Then he wanted to do it again. His rhythm picked up. "Falon," he breathed against her lips, "come with me now."

She trembled in his arms and met him thrust for thrust. Grinding her hips into him. He held her gaze as his balls tightened, preparing for release. She pushed her head back and her full lips, swollen from his assault, parted. The pink tip of her tongue darted out. She strained against him as he pressed her back. Her heavy lids drooped over her eyes. Her nostrils flared as a dewy sheen of perspiration erupted along her skin. God, she was beautiful.

"Luca—" she gasped. "I—"

"Now, Falon," he hissed and came in a wild, reckless explosion. His body jerked hard against her, but he did not pull his eyes from hers. She stared at him as if she had seen God, and then followed with such a powerful orgasm, it rocked straight down his cock to his balls.

It rocked more than his cock, it rocked the world he knew, the world he had control of, the world that had tilted on its side and would never be balanced again.

Their passion was epic, and it was dangerous.

And so was Falon. She meant something to him now, something more than an instrument of revenge, and because she was more, he was vulnerable.

Rolling onto his back, Lucien brought Falon into the fold of his arms. Her body tensed, but he refused to let her go. When she realized it, her body loosened. His arms tightened in acknowledgment, then loosened as well, a silent indicator he would not force her to stay.

But she did not go. His chest tightened painfully.

There was nothing to say. No words to describe what just happened. So he said nothing. He closed his eyes, as fatigue settled into his bones. It had been a hell of a month. The last few days, brutal. Physically he was spent. Emotionally . . . he was sucked dry.

Falon's warm breath teased his neck. When she readjusted herself, and her hand slid down his belly, Lucien hissed. Damn if his dragon did not raise its tail.

Falon's body stilled. But the flutter of her heart against his belied her hesitancy. He squeezed his eyes shut, fighting that part of him that wanted to sink into her again but knew her tender parts needed time to recover from his lovemaking. He slid his hand down his belly to hers. Entwining their fingers, he slowly exhaled and opened his eyes.

"I'm scared, Lucien," she whispered against his neck.

She was not talking about the rising that would take place two months from now. She was talking about the rising between his thighs. This thing between them was powerful; so powerful if it was not managed, it would burn out of control and kill someone. "So am I."

He pulled their entwined hands up to his chest and fought for sleep.

IN THE HUGE four-poster bed, Falon slowly came awake to sun streaming through the window. She stretched and whimpered. Every muscle in her body ached. "Ugh." She slid her hand between her tender thighs and touched her swollen tissue. Her eyes flew open as every detail of what she and Lucien had done came back in vivid Technicolor. Heat flamed her cheeks. Closing her eyes, she lay back into the pillows and exhaled. What *had* happened? And why? *How? How could she* lose herself so wantonly when she loved Rafael?

Guilt, shame, and recrimination swept through her in droves. How could she betray Rafa by—by allowing Lucien to do to her what he had done? She rolled over and buried her face in the pillows, mortified by the debauchery of it all. Even with Rafa, even though he had tried, she had not allowed him to touch her so wickedly.

But even as she tried to pretend she had not enjoyed it, her body loosened in remembrance. It had been wild. Lucien was—well, he was just wicked. She craved that part of him. But he had also been tender, caring. Loving. A side of Lucien she never expected existed. A part she cherished. A part that made her more uncomfortable than the wicked part.

She rolled over and cried out in alarm. Lucien stood at the foot of the bed, staring hotly at her.

"You startled me," she said, not wanting to acknowledge the white elephant in the room.

"I did a lot more than that last night," he said arrogantly.

So much for the tender Lucien.

"You don't have to be so smug about it." She pulled the sheet around her and slid off the edge of the bed.

"Don't you think we're a little beyond that?" he asked, indicating the sheet.

"I—don't know what's going on inside of me." She let out a long breath and looked straight at him. "We need to talk about what happened last night."

"What is there to discuss?"

"I'd like to get a shower and get dressed first."

"I'd like to discuss it now."

Falon nodded. Fine. No time like the present. "Okay. First of all, you caught me at a weak moment."

A devilish smile twisted Lucien's full lips. "I caught you at several weak moments."

"Stop it! I'm trying to be serious here. I— Last night should not have happened."

"Why?"

"Because, Lucien, you cannot try to control me through sex! That's why."

He nodded and crossed his arms. "Okay."

"That's it?"

"Yes."

"So no more sex like last night?" Yes, no more *emotional* sex. Last night had been incredible on so many levels, but the most incredible part was Lucien allowing her into his heart. She did not know what to do with that. Until she did, there could be no more repeats of last night. But how to make it seem like something else entirely . . .

"No more sex like last night."

Falon narrowed her eyes. "Okay, Lucien, let's stop the games. Because I *am* your chosen one, we'll—we'll occasionally have to have sex. But *normal* sex."

"What exactly is your version of *normal* sex?"

"Well, I can tell you what is *not* normal. None of that shifting while I'm still like this," she said, sweeping her arm down her body.

His lips lifted into a knowing smile. "Oh, but you liked my wolf and what he did to you."

If it was possible to blush and cream yourself at the same time, Falon just did. "That's irrelevant. It can't happen again."

"I'm beginning to understand why you're saying that. It's because you liked it a little too much and are afraid you'll want more. That maybe"—he uncrossed his long arms and moved slowly into her space—"maybe next time you'll want my wolf's cock inside you?"

"Never!" But she was lying. And she was dying to know if he had ever done it that way.

His smile widened. "No, Falon, my wolf has never completely taken a human woman." He pulled the sheet from her and yanked her naked body to his. Heat shimmered through her. "But I'm not going to lie—with you, the idea intrigues me." He nipped at her bare shoulder. "A lot."

She ignored the heat his body stoked in hers. "That's against the law in most states!"

"So is what we did last night." Embarrassment colored her pink. He titled her chin up with his hand, and then threaded his fingers through her unruly hair. "We are Lycan. Mortal laws do not apply to us. And, I'm discovering, with you, Falon, most rules don't apply, period."

"There has to be rules. Rules keep order. Rules—"

He shushed her with his lips. "No rules."

Falon twisted away from his lips, afraid she would end up on her back, and Lucien would reveal yet another amazing facet of himself that would suck her in deeper still. "Speaking of rules, we need to set some ground rules. I—"

"*You* need to set rules, and be my guest to set them for yourself. But understand this—rules do not govern me."

"That's your problem! You do as you damn well please and the rest of the world be damned." Including turning my world upside down for your revenge! Oh, she wanted to scream it loud and clear, but they would end up rehashing the same thing again. The brothers would never budge on their stance until there was irrefutable proof to knock one of them down.

Lucien scowled. "As alpha, I must do what is best for my pack. Rules get in the way of that."

"But rules prevent anarchy."

A knock on the door abruptly halted their conversation.

Lucien wrapped Falon back in the sheet, then said, "Come in."

Janice, one of the younger females, came in, eyes downcast, and said, "The Amorak elder, Sharia, is here."

Lucien stiffened. "She has nothing to say that I wish to hear. Tell her to go."

Of course, Janice did not question Lucien's authority. But as the woman turned to close the door behind her, Falon did.

"Why do you refuse to see Sharia? She gave me to you; the least you could do is thank her."

Lucien's head snapped back. "Her ancient ways have no place in my modern world. I no longer give the Amorak authority over my life."

Falon threw a hand up in the air. "Then why am I here?"

His head snapped back and he looked at her with possessive eyes. "Because you are mine."

Falon laughed at the absurdity of what he just said. "But if you no longer honor the Blood Law, I'm free to go back to Rafael."

"You are mine."

"I am yours *only* if you respect the Blood Law, Lucien. There is no Lucien's Law! There is only the Blood Law." She moved closer to him. "You cannot have it both ways. Which is it?"

"Regardless, it changes nothing between us."

"The hell it doesn't! Are you purposely being obtuse? Because, I'm not a slave. I have free will. Only because Rafael lives and breathes honor did I agree to abide by the council's decision. You chose to respect it because you knew it would deliver your vengeance. Now if you choose to reject what the Lycan nation has lived and died by the last three hundred years, you are no more fit to be alpha than Janice!"

"What do you care about the nation?"

"In case you haven't noticed, dumbass, I might not know who my parents are, but I *am* Lycan! A Lycan who wants to live past the rising. A Lycan who wants a family. A Lycan who does not want to live in fear, cooped up in a damn compound because there are Slayers hunting outside her door."

"You walk freely among humans."

"Not while there is one Slayer alive."

"Why are you talking me into the Blood Law when doing the opposite could conceivably return you to your *beloved Rafa?*"

"What has everyone—including you—been shoving down my throat? *The rising is coming,* Lucien, in case you forgot. I want to survive it and live to be an old woman. To that end, we need Rafael alive and healthy. He possesses the ring. We need you alive and healthy. You possess a cunning and strength that is unequaled. Mondragon is strong and with you and Rafael leading the packs, they will come together and fight as one. Between you two, the ring, and my powers, the united packs will go into battle, knowing they can win the day! What happens after will be determined by everything leading up to it."

"What are you saying?"

"I'm saying, with the world free of Slayers, we will no longer walk in fear and the Blood Law will have to be redrafted to reflect the new beginning."

"It will not change that you are mine."

Startled by his words, Falon suddenly understood the battle Lucien fought. "Are you afraid that if you unite with Rafael to defeat the Slayers, you will lose me to him?"

"He will have another mate by the rising."

By not answering her question, Falon knew what it was. "As I already do, but a lot can happen between now and then."

"That is what I am afraid of."

Ah, and the cat was finally out of the bag.

"The future is full of promise, Lucien. It will be all that we make of it." She dropped the sheet to the floor and walked to the bathroom door. "Give me fifteen minutes and we'll go to Sharia together."

She shut the door behind her and let out a long breath when he did not challenge her.

Seven

AFTER SHE DRESSED and returned to him, Lucien's anger was palpable. Falon did not understand it. He had what he wanted. Revenge. The Blood Law had not forsaken him as it had his brother. If anyone had a right to be furious, it was Rafael.

Her mood softened at just the thought of Rafa. He had a way of calming her, making her look at things more clearly. Rationally. In her gut, she knew Rafael was not the greedy power monger Lucien made him out to be. Mara had been a Slayer. Rafael had done exactly what Lucien would have done if their positions had been reversed. Because, while one brother honored the Blood Law to the letter and the other in spirit, the result was the same.

There had to be a way to prove to Lucien that Mara was a Slayer. It would be the only way the brothers could reconcile. And if they reconciled? She would be caught right in the middle of them. There was something to be said for the nonexistent life she had been living just a couple of months ago. It had been hard but uncomplicated. Now she was living in a blender on puree.

As she and Lucien walked down the metal stairway to the common room, he said, "Once this conversation with Sharia is concluded, we're going to visit Hector, my armorer, and have you fitted for a sword."

"I would love that!" she said, excited by the prospect of her own sword. Rafael's had been too heavy for her. She looked up at Lucien as he looked down at her and flashed her a dark, sexy smile. *Finally,* a peek at the Lucien who made her feel as if no other women existed for him but her. Oh, God, did she just think that? Because it was not true.

"You are bloodthirsty."

She could not help but mirror his smile. Yes, it *was* true. And she didn't care. She didn't care because she was quickly discovering there were more layers to Lucien Mondragon than a giant onion. Layers that intrigued her. Layers that challenged her. And that most fascinating layer at his core that revealed the true man he fought so hard to mask. She was also learning a few things about herself. She had a feral side. And she liked it. A lot. "You have that effect on me."

He cocked a dark brow. His eyes twinkled mischievously. "I won't forget that."

Playfully, she touched his forearm. "If you want to live, you won't."

He threw his head back and laughed as they descended the last step into the large common room. He abruptly stopped when, Sharia, the gnarled and stooped spirit leader of the Amorak, turned intense brown eyes on them. Several of her people, a few Falon recognized from the council, stood nearby.

Falon felt like she just got caught with her hand in the cookie jar. Not only had Sharia heard Lucien's genuine laughter, but she had also caught Falon's mischievous smile and her playful touch. Sharia was not the only one. A good portion of the pack had gathered. They were quietly alert, but their anxiety since she chose to stay had all but evaporated. Replacing it was excited anticipation for Mondragon's future.

Heat stung Falon's cheeks. Did they know what had happened last night? She wanted to hide in a hole somewhere. Until she realized the pack's demeanor was probably due to their own wild rutting last night. Despite what happened to Joachim.

Joachim? she asked Lucien.

He is healing.

Dax?

Pulled in an hour ago with a load of AKs.

Slayers?

Four less we have to kill tomorrow.

Any of our people hurt or lost?

Lucien squeezed her hand. *All present and accounted for.*

Falon exhaled sharply. Thank God.

"I see the council did not err in their decision," the old woman said, coming toward them, her brown eyes twinkling. She nodded to Lucien. "It's good to see you in such good spirits, Lucien." She looked at Falon and raised a silver brow. "Life with Mondragon seems to agree with you."

"Mondragon and I have come to a mutual understanding," Falon said quietly. Because anything more would seem like a public stab in Rafael's back. Yes, she accepted her place here beside Lucien, but she did not want Rafael or any of Vulkasin to think she was skipping happily through the forest. She missed Rafa. She missed Vulkasin. They had accepted her before she knew what she was, or who she was. They would always have a special place in her heart.

"Why are you here?" Lucien quietly demanded.

Do not be rude, Falon said.

"You forget, Lucien, who it was who nursed you back to health after your parents were slain."

"I forget nothing."

"Your mother would be very unhappy with the disrespect you show me and the council."

"Do not speak of my mother," Lucien growled.

Lucien!

Stay out of this, Falon.

She was your nurse!

She has always favored Rafael. She is here for his benefit, not mine.

How can you say that? She gave me to you!

Be patient, she will reveal her real purpose and it will be about Rafe.

Jealousy does not become you.

Leave it alone.

Sharia nodded, but Falon could see the old woman was hurt.

"Vulkasin prepares to meet the northern packs. I suggest you prepare to meet your European cousins."

"Those plans are in the works as we speak. Is there anything else you want to tell me, an alpha, I have to do?"

Sharia wobbled, as if Lucien's words had hit her, knocking her off balance. Falon rushed to her side just as Lucien did. Gently, they set her down on a nearby chair. Falon glanced at Lucien and caught the flash of concern in his golden eyes when the elder grabbed his forearm for support. Then it was gone. But she had seen it. It proved once again that Lucien's anger was full of hot air, manufactured to protect himself from—what? Being cast in his brother's shadow?

Sharia shooed them away and said, "The Slayers are converging and the vipers are recruiting. We were stopped by two large groups of that scourge on motorcycles coming down the mountain road."

Falon felt Lucien's anger spark. "They are being managed here in the flatlands. Mondragon slew four Slayers in Lodi this morning, stripped them of their weapons, and confiscated the twenty-four AKs they had just taken possession of. We also cut off their major arms supplier. Another hunting party will leave at dusk, followed by another at dawn."

"You will need more than a hunting party."

Lucien swiped his hand across his face, a gesture of irritation. Falon hid a smile since he was so frequently irritated. It must be difficult being so angry at the world *and* dealing with such a subspecies as humans.

"With all due respect, *niña*, I have been killing Slayers and more recently vipers quite expeditiously. While my brother chooses to ride in like the cavalry, Mondragon prefers the more subtle guerilla approach."

Niña?

Must you question everything?

Everything.

Mondragon roots are Basque. Niña *is a Spanish term of endearment for aunt or godmother.*

But you do not believe in God.

Not your Christian God.

I'm glad you showed her respect.

I'm glad you're glad. Now can we get on with it?

Falon smiled but did not hide it this time. Sharia watched in fascinated silence. Apparently, Falon and Lucien had been so engrossed in their little mental convo, their expressions were as plain as if they had said it out loud.

The old woman looked directly at Falon, then at Lucien and frowned. Something ominous lurked behind her eyes. The hair on the back of Falon's neck shot straight up.

"What?" Lucien asked.

Sharia looked behind her to Maleek and the handful of Amorak that had accompanied her. They nodded in unison.

"Now," Sharia said quietly. "The real reason for our visit. Rafael is—not the same."

Falon's heart plummeted. "What do you mean?" she asked, stepping closer to the old woman. Please, God, let him be okay. She could not bear it if he was hurt or ill.

"I fear he is going mad."

Falon gasped.

"Let him," Lucien said flatly.

"No, Lucien!" Falon cried. "No! He is your brother! He is the man I love! Do not be so cruel and cavalier."

Lucien's face reddened furiously. Falon grabbed his hands. When he jerked them away, she grabbed them tighter. "Look at me, damn it!"

When he refused, she grabbed his chin and forced him to. "I know it hurts you that I love him. I'm sorry for that pain. I'm sorry for this whole damn mess! But I have chosen to stay with Mondragon. I will not betray your trust, Luca. I need you to believe that. Now, if you can, I need you to look past your emotions and see the world as it really is. You, me—" She swept her arm out to include Mondragon and Amorak. "Them. The entire nation needs Rafael alive and focused right now."

Sharia nodded. "If Rafael does not recover, his loss will cripple the Lycan nation."

"With the Eye of Fenrir on my hand, there will be no need for Rafael," Lucien said flatly.

Falon was at her emotional edge. He was the most stubborn, prideful man alive. She grabbed his shirt and pleaded. "You're wrong, Lucien! How do you think it will look to the nation if one of the premier alphas goes mad? It will send the message that if *he* cannot handle the pressure of this crisis, no one can!"

Lucien grasped her hands. "Maybe he *can't* handle it." He looked past Falon to the Amorak. "Did it occur to anyone that maybe the mighty golden alpha, Rafael Vulkasin, crashed and burned under the pressure?"

He turned back to Falon. His eyes softened. "I will not crash or burn. With the ring, Falon, and you by my side, we can lead the nation to victory!"

Mondragon nodded, loudly voicing their agreement.

"You are wrong, Lucien. It will take the power of the three," Sharia said, looking directly at Lucien and then Falon. "Mondragon, Vulkasin, and the woman that stands between them. United. As one. It will be the *only* way to survive the wrath of Fenrir."

"But the wolf is harmlessly contained in the ring," Lucien challenged.

"He is now, but he howls to the Gods for release."

"The lore says he can be released only by one pure of heart."

Sharia nodded, and speared Lucien with a knowing stare. "And so he shall be."

"I must go to Rafael," Falon said pulling away from Lucien. "I can pull him back from the darkness."

"No," Lucien said emphatically.

Furious, Falon turned to him. "Why not?"

"*Because you love him!*" Lucien raged.

"Don't be so thickheaded! This is beyond our personal feelings, Lucien! This is about survival," Falon screamed, finally losing her patience. Yes, she would do anything for Rafael out of love. It would tear her apart to see him again, to touch him, to hold him in her arms knowing she could not return to him. But she would do it.

Endure that pain because she did love him and damn it, she cared for Lucien, more than she would admit even to herself.

His vehemence matched hers. "I forbid it."

Falon's fury soared beyond the stratosphere. How dare he tell her what she could and could not do? She was not a prisoner here nor was she a slave! Fighting with Lucien would do no good. It would only force him to dig in deeper. So she forced herself to an emotional place where she could release her frustration and try a different approach. Holding his stare, she blew several short cleansing breaths, then said, "Do the honorable thing, Lucien."

"Honor is for fools!"

Fisting her hands to keep from smacking some sense into him, Falon lowered her voice and pleaded, "Then do it for the love you once had for your brother, your only living blood."

"Love is for the weak," he spat.

She moved into him, fighting her urge to punch him and her need to wrap her arms around him and soothe his wounded heart. "You are wrong."

"Am I?" He grabbed her to him. His anger swirled in red tidal waves around him. "What has love gotten you but heartache?"

Her heart cracked a little more for this tormented man. His heart had been broken just as hers had. Even now, though he pretended not to care about her, he did. She felt it in everything he did, but especially in the way he touched her. And now, in the way he protested—because he feared she would not return to him. "Love has freed me, Lucien."

"It holds you captive! Everything you do is for *him*!"

Falon nodded, admitting the truth. At least part of it. "I am here because of him. I submitted to you because of him. I stayed for—" You.

"You did not submit to me! I forced you the first time. And last night?" He laughed angrily. "Last night was—" He swiped his hand across his face and stared at Falon. "What *was* last night?"

Her heart cracked a little more. The turmoil etched on his face was tragic.

The truth did not lie. Falon's belly quivered. No, the truth did not lie, and if she were honest with herself, last night had nothing to do with Rafael; it had everything to do with Lucien. She had wanted him. For herself. God help her, but she had. She owed Lucien that part of the truth.

"Last night was amazing, Lucien. I would not give it back for anything or anyone." She touched his arm. "Blood does not lie. By bloodright I belong to you."

She saw the hesitation in his eyes, felt it in his body. He wanted her, but would not settle for just a part of her. Deliberately, he removed her hand from his arm as if he could not stand her touch. "But your heart belongs to Rafael."

"I will always love Rafael." It was the simple truth. "But that does not mean I don't care for you."

His anger was terrifying. Falon stepped away from him as his fiery red aura blasted her and everyone around her. He turned from her and stalked to the front door.

"I stayed for *you*, Lucien!" Falon screamed, running after him. "Doesn't that count for something?"

He yanked open the door and slammed it shut loudly behind him.

Stunned by her outburst, Falon stopped in her tracks. What had just happened? Why did she feel as if her heart was going through the shredder again, this time for Lucien? How could she have feelings for him when she loved his brother?

She turned and looked solemnly at Mondragon. She expected to see a refection of Lucien's anger in their eyes, and while there was some, mostly she saw compassion. "I cannot unlove Rafael any more than Lucien could accept me loving them both."

Talia stepped from behind Dax and approached Falon. "Lucien refuses to accept his heart is not as hard as he proclaims it to be."

Falon's anger spiked when she thought how Lucien's anger infected not just his own heart but everyone's. He was going to drive her to drink. Just when she started to believe Lucien had a heart, he shut down. Falon shook her head, wanting desperately to understand him. To comfort him. But she was beginning to wonder if he was capable of love at all. Not the love of lust, but the deep, all-encompassing love she shared with Rafa. The kind of love where if you had to, you would make the ultimate sacrifice. The sacrifice Rafael had made.

Falon looked at Lucien's cousin. A piece of her heart crumbled as she foresaw Lucien's future. "Lucien is filled with too much hatred. His bloodlust for vengeance eats at him like maggots on roadkill. They will devour his soul until there is nothing left." Lucien, not Rafael, would be the lone wolf howling at the moon.

"He needs time to come to the realization that he must make peace with his brother," Talia said softly. "Until he does, he will never accept your feelings for Rafa, because his anger will drive everything he does."

"Lord only knows he won't listen to reason from me," Falon said. But that would not stop her from going after him. She wanted Lucien to know she cared even if he pushed her away again.

"His kind of anger is a by-product of traumatic pain," Talia continued.

"He must have loved Mara very much," Falon reflected aloud. The thought of Lucien loving another woman, Slayer or not, prickled her heart.

"Lucien's pain began the day his parents were slain by Thomas Corbet. It flared out of control the day Rafael slew his chosen one, and then became unbearable when he and his brother fought to the brink of death."

Falon's heart cracked a little more for the troubled brother. She could not imagine the horror of what he had witnessed. His troubled heart cried out for relief. Falon took a step toward the door but stopped when warm hands grasped hers. Falon looked down into Sharia's watery brown eyes. "His anger will destroy him if his pride does not. Only you can soothe his beast, Falon. Go to him and ease his pain before he does something he cannot recover from."

"I will not soothe him with lies." Though part of her wanted to soothe him at any cost. Even lies. She hated seeing Lucien hurt so. But she could not, would not change how she felt about Rafael.

"He was always the stubborn son. He could never see past his brother's glory to recognize his own." She squeezed Falon's hands. "Only in truth is there freedom. Search for the truth in your heart for Lucien. When you discover it, tell him. Show him. Do not let him push you away." She smiled a bittersweet smile. "He will try to push. Each time he does, hold on to him tighter, prove to him you will not abandon him, Falon. In the meantime, go to him, run with him, fight beside him." Sharia gave Falon a little shove. "Hurry, there is no time to waste."

As soon as Falon walked out the front door, she picked up Lucien's wolf scent. He had shifted. She did the same and followed his scent northeast, toward Vulkasin.

Lucien was running hard. Much faster than Falon could run. His stride was longer and more powerful.

Lucien!

Leave me alone.

Talk to me!

Nothing to discuss.

Then slow down so that I can run with you.

I want to be alone.

She continued her reckless pace after him. Though Mondragon was in the middle of civilization, there was a trail through the back fence of the compound against the hill. There was no chance even in broad daylight for a human to be startled by the wolves. Even so, Falon was not familiar with the trail. Which really didn't matter. As long as she had Lucien's scent, she could find him anywhere.

After more than an hour chasing Lucien into the timberline, dodging Viper and Slayer scents, Falon caught up to him. He stood naked in his human form on the edge of a huge granite boulder overlooking the roaring rapids of the American River. Even at a distance, anger radiated off him. But she would have her say, then see her will done.

Falon shifted beside him.

"It's dangerous out here," he said.

"It's dangerous everywhere."

He turned and looked at her. "This area is crawling with Vipers, Falon. You shouldn't have followed me."

"You shouldn't have run."

He smiled tightly.

"Lucien, I need to speak with Rafael."

His lips tightened to a thin line, before he said, "About what?"

Well, that was a little progress, he did not flat-out say no. Falon swallowed hard and picked her words carefully. "I think I can help him through this thing that has ahold of his mind. But I feel as if I have to explain—"

"Explain what?" He grabbed her, digging his fingers into her shoulders. "That you want me? That you want me like a drug?" He shook her. "That you want me so much it scares you?"

Vehemently, Falon shook her head. "I want to reassure him of my love!"

Lucien's eyes darkened dangerously. "So that he can be more miserable?"

"So he will come out of his dark place!"

Lucien nodded setting her from him. "Sure, go tell him how much you like my dick in you, then tell him how much you love him."

Falon slapped him hard across the cheek. "Do not speak so crudely to me."

He grabbed her to him, and again, despite his rage, his wounded pride, and the hour-long sprint, he was rock hard against her belly. "You infuriate me with your declarations of love. When will you get it through your head, you are Mondragon now!"

"I have gotten it through my head! When will you get it through your damn head that while I can love Rafael, I can also have feelings for you?"

He flung his hands from hers and stepped to the edge of the boulder. "Fuck feelings! I have had enough of feelings!" He slowly turned and levelly said, "You are mine, Falon. *Mine!* That is never going to change. *Ever.*"

"Lucien, I accept I am Mondragon now. I am simply saying, for Rafael's sake, and for my peace of mind, I want to go to him. And I'm not asking."

"You would defy me for another man?"

"I would defy you for myself."

For what seemed like an endless hour, Lucien stood ramrod straight and stared at her. The afternoon sunshine speared through the high pine, repelling off his golden skin. A slight film of sweat covered his body, emphasizing the definition of his muscles and the detail of his wolf and dragon tattoo. Falon did not dare look down. She knew his dragon was primed and ready.

She was not unaffected by the magnificent sight of him in all his naked glory standing in a halo of sunshine. Lucien was as male as male could be, and her female was as aware of that fact as it was that the sun rose every day.

He pointed to the smooth granite beneath their feet. "Lay down."

"No," she said defiantly. Her nipples were as equally defiant. They hardened.

"I want to fuck you. Then you can go to my brother."

Her body shook with rage. "So that he can smell your scent all over me?"

"Yes."

"Are you that insecure, Lucien?"

"I am that vengeful."

"You've had your revenge! I am with *you*! Because of your vengeance, your brother, your *only* brother, the only blood relative you have is suffering to the point of madness. I'll be damned if I'm going to be part of that." She moved into him, pressing into his erection. He hissed in a breath. "End it now, or I swear to God, Lucien, you will never touch me again."

"You cannot resist me."

"You are a pompous ass to think so. So let me be crystal clear: I can resist a man who refuses to grow the fuck up! I can resist a man who is so selfish and self-serving he cannot see past his own petty hurt feelings to the greater good of his pack." She looked down at his raging hard-on and grabbed it. He hissed. "I can resist this, Lucien Mondragon, when it is fueled by hatred." She flung herself away from him. "The choice is yours: drop the revenge card or go fuck yourself."

"You have not walked in my shoes, Falon!"

"Don't make this about the Blood Law, Lucien. It has been avenged! What more do you want?"

"I want what Rafe has."

"You have taken me from him, what more is there?"

"I only took from him what he took from me!"

"Then what else is there, Lucien? His motorcycle? His house?"

His eyes flashed. "I want what you gave him!"

He had her stumped there. The only thing she had to give to Rafael was her love. Her eyes widened as his narrowed. "My love?"

Lucien stood stone-faced, refusing to admit that was exactly what he wanted.

"I gave him my love unconditionally."

"Give me the same."

Shocked, Falon stepped back, shaking her head. He didn't understand. Love wasn't something you just handed over like the keys to a car. "You don't know the first thing about love!"

He grabbed her shoulders. "Show me, Falon, teach me!"

She shook her head again and moved his hands from her. "You put conditions on everything, Lucien."

"It is my guarantee."

"But don't you see? Nothing in life is guaranteed except death."

"I'm not as obtuse as I come across, Falon. Give me a chance."

"The first step to unconditional love is forgiveness."

Immediately, Lucien's dark brows slammed together.

She smiled and touched his cheek. "I never said it would be easy."

"I don't know how to forgive."

Her fingers dropped to his petulant lips. Lightly she traced her thumb along his full bottom lip. "Rome was not built in a day."

Lucien's nostrils flared at the exact moment as hers. She raised her nose to the wind that swirled up from the angry river. "Do you smell it, Lucien?"

He turned, catching a strong whiff of the scent. "Lycan."

"Which Lycan?"

He inhaled again and she felt his excitement. "Layla," he breathed. "She has come home."

Eight

"WHO IS LAYLA, and why is that name familiar to me?" Falon asked, intrigued. She was sure she had smelled the Lycan's scent before, near the Amorak camp last month. "I swear I have smelled it before, from my past and just last month near the Amorak camp."

"That's impossible. While Layla is Vulkasin's healer and spirit guide she was kidnapped by Thomas Corbet the day he slew my parents. She has been gone for twenty-four years. We thought she was dead."

"Maybe she has been held captive all this time?" Falon offered, knowing the scent was familiar. Her nose did not lie. She had smelled it the day she ran from Rafael to the Slayer lair in Oakland to find the truth about any connection between her last name and clan Corbet. She had been immeasurably relieved to discover there was no connection. It was while at the Corbet lair in Oakland she discovered she was Lycan, and knew being related to clan Corbet was an impossibility. No Slayer would lay with a Lycan, and a Lycan would rather eat crap and die before laying with a Slayer. Still, when she'd detected the Lycan's scent that night, it was one she'd recognized from childhood. How could that be?

"She would not have survived their torture all this time, Falon. Layla was powerful, but even as gifted a healer as she was, she has her limits."

"Perhaps she escaped before they could harm her and she is just now after all these years come home? Let's track her and ask her."

Lucien's sharp eyes scanned the wooded landscape below. He shook his head. "Corbet would have hunted her down and killed her like he did my parents." The sorrow in Lucien's voice was undeniable. "As much as I want answers, there is a reason Layla has not revealed herself all these years. I would not presume to force myself on her." His golden eyes continued to scan the landscape, as if he hoped to catch a glimpse of his past. "Besides, with Layla come the memories of what happened that day."

Falon moved closer to him and touched his arm. He started and looked down at her. "Sometimes talking about it purges the pain. Can you tell me what happened?"

A flurry of emotions flashed across his face before he masked them in indifference. "You know what happened."

Rafael had told her his side; now she wanted Lucien's. She slid her fingertips down the hard muscles of his arm to his hand, entwining her fingers with his. "Tell me everything, Lucien," she softly urged.

He pulled his hand from hers and shook his head, taking a step away. Completely withdrawing.

"I want to share that burden with you, Luca. Trust me enough to tell me what happened."

He turned on her, his golden eyes blazing coals. "I relive that day every hour of my life. It only serves to galvanize my determination to destroy every drop of Corbet blood on this earth."

"What happened?"

"Those bastards used their black magic to disguise themselves as an Amorak clan from the north. My father's people. He welcomed them with open arms. The minute the gates closed behind them, they revealed themselves. Thomas Corbet, his brothers, Edward and Balor, and their henchmen." Lucien fisted his hands and moved to the edge of the boulder. The muscles along his back corded in tension as he stared out at the raging river.

"My mother grabbed me and Rafe, forcing us into the bunker beneath the main building. She made us swear, no matter what, to stay hidden."

He swiped his hand across his face. "Even though I swore to her I would hide from the Slayers, I ran after my mother. I had enough rage inside me that day to destroy them all. But Rafe held me back." Lucien laughed bitterly. "I was smaller than Rafe then, nothing but eighty pounds soaking wet. At ten, Rafe was bigger, stronger. He held me down until the door locked behind Mother. He told me I must honor my promise to her. To hide. Like a coward!" He threw his head back and raised his fists to the sky. "We were fucking ten years old!"

He drew in a deep breath and exhaled. "There were shuttered slats just above the ground. Rafa and me, we— Jesus, we watched as my father took on those bastard brothers, but they were high as kites on something and overpowered him. Their henchmen were brutal, forcing most of the pack to their knees as one by one they were beheaded. Their black magic was powerful that day. More powerful than ever before."

Lucien's voice lowered to such a painful low, Falon could barely hear his words. "Edward and Balor grabbed my mother, stripped her naked, and . . . violated her while my father, who was barbwired to the gates, watched. Thomas demanded she tell him the location of her sons. She spit in his eyes. Then he skinned her alive. One inch at a time."

Lucien pressed his hands to his ears. "I can still hear her screams and my father's pleas for mercy. Rafe and I, we went crazy trying to claw our way out of that bunker, but we couldn't. We saw everything. Heard everything. They nearly broke my father. He must have called to the gods for help, because he went crazy and broke free from the gates. But it was too late—" Lucien choked. "My proud, beautiful mother was dead. The Slayers were too powerful that day and the pack too few. Father was subdued and those bastards did the same thing to him. Then they turned on the remaining pack. The last thing I remember seeing was Thomas throwing Layla over his shoulder as they strutted out of the compound like some damn heroes."

Tears blurred Falon's vision as she moved to Lucien and wrapped her arms around his back. His anguish was so palpable it infused her own heart with sorrow. "I'm so sorry, Lucien."

His body tightened but he covered her clasped hands with his own, squeezing them hard. After several long moments, Lucien softly but dangerously said, "I swear on my mother's soul, Falon, if it is the last thing I do, I will destroy every Corbet that walks this earth."

She swallowed hard. "My last name is Corbet."

He squeezed her hands. "So I heard." He turned and looked down at her, his expression grim. "But you are Lycan, and it's a good thing that it is a coincidence."

"What if it wasn't?" She was afraid of the answer.

He swept her hair from her face and rubbed his knuckles across her cheek. "Though it would kill me to do it, I would destroy you."

Fear skittered across Falon's skin. Her mouth was suddenly dry. She licked her lips. "I'm glad it's just a coincidence, too."

His lips brushed across hers. "You are Lycan, Falon, and Mondragon now."

The howl of a wounded wolf pierced their moment.

"Layla," Lucien whispered, raising his head.

Falon raised her head and sniffed the air. "Vipers."

Lucien smiled dangerously. "Let's go hunting."

Simultaneously, they shifted, and like the raging river below, they followed the death scent.

Several hundred yards down the steep embankment, they slowed at the edge of a thick copse of trees and stared at the scene playing out in the small clearing ahead. A honey brown she-wolf struggled in a steel bear trap. A half dozen Vipers poked and prodded her with short silver-tipped spears.

The wolf snarled and snapped, chewing against the vicious metal jaws clamped around her left hind leg.

Fury clamped just as viciously around Falon's heart. Equal fury reverberated from Lucien.

Circle to the other side, Lucien said. *I'll draw them out. As soon as I have their attention, pull the stake grounding the trap. Then take out the nearest Viper. Rip him apart, but stay clear of his spear. When the others turn on you, retreat. I'll take another one out from behind. We'll go back and forth until each one is dust.*

Be careful.

Falon circled around and, as she crouched, Lucien leapt into the fray.

He snatched a Viper by the neck and shook him viciously, snapping his neck. The remaining Vipers shouted, focusing their attention on him. Falon leapt toward the she-wolf. With her strong jaws, she grasped the eye loop of the spike that anchored the chain to the metal trap and pulled. The she-wolf turned and grabbed the spike below Falon's jaw and together they pulled. Slow and steady, the spike responded.

Heat pierced Falon's flank. She snarled in pain as she was impaled to the ground by a Viper's spear. She snarled and snapped the wooden shaft in half, and then pulled the imbedded part out of her leg with her teeth. She flung it at the Viper where it hit center mass.

She looked over to Lucien, who was in the middle of a Viper pile on. Falon leapt into the air and, like the feral warrior she was, she ripped and shredded flesh and bones until she stood side by side with Lucien. Together they turned on the remaining Vipers and decimated them. The remaining two ran for their lives to their choppers. Falon leapt after one and Lucien the other. In perfect symmetry, as if they had been fighting side by side for years, they landed on the leather-clad backs of the men as they roared off on their bikes. The velocity of their hits knocked each biker off his seat to the ground. Blood blurred Falon's vision as she tore the Viper's chest open. He screamed only once before he lay still on the blood-soaked earth.

LUCIEN STEPPED BACK from the dead biker beneath his bloody paws and shook, his heavy body flinging blood off his fur. Falon did the same. Bloodlust hung like a death knell in the air as he turned and surveyed the carnage. Not one Viper survived. His eyes tracked to the metal trap to find it gone. He shifted to human and strode over to where it had been staked. He lifted the metal stake to his nose and deeply inhaled. There was no doubt in his mind it was Layla. He vividly remembered her honey-colored wolf coat. Not only had she been the most powerful medicine woman in the States but she was a favorite of his mother's, and spent many hours of each day in their private quarters.

Falon shifted beside him. "Why did she run?"

Lucien dropped the stake and looked at Falon's blood-smeared body. Her chest rose and fell as she fought to catch her breath. Her nostrils flared, her eyes dilated with excitement. His body tightened. She was a magnificent sight.

"Because she does not want to be found," he said huskily.

"But we have to go after her!"

"She will run faster then."

"Why? If she's so close, why wouldn't she return to her pack?"

Lucien shook his head. "When she is ready, she will come home."

"But I want to meet her. *I have questions*."

"Haven't you figured it out yet, Falon?"

"What?"

"Lycan are social creatures by nature, but there are a few who choose to remain lone wolves. It's not to be questioned or challenged."

"But she's wounded."

"She is also a renowned healer." He grinned. "Now, I have something altogether different on my mind."

He grabbed Falon by the hand and pulled her toward the swirling riverbank, then into the chilly water.

As they went under, he pulled her warm body to his. His passion for her raged. She had been remarkable beside him, tearing into the Vipers with the same blood rage as he. She was quick and powerful. And deadly. She shared his lusts on every level whether it be carnal or primal.

As they surfaced, he kissed her. She didn't refuse him. Indeed, she met his lips with an equal fervor. His passion soared. He dunked them again, washing the blood from their bodies until hand in hand they ran to the sunny bank. Lucien pushed her to the soft ground, his cock thick and heavy.

"You are as fierce as any of my men, Falon," he breathed, parting her thighs with his knee.

She grabbed his shoulders and rolled him over onto his back. Her ocean blue eyes blazed wild with triumph. She was as caught up in the moment as he. Her musky sex scent permeated the pine and loamy scents of the earth. She covered his body with hers. "I am as fierce as you, Lucien." She nipped at his bottom lip, drawing blood.

He growled as he grew harder and clasped her to him. But she resisted, pulling back. She shook her head and drops of blood tinted river water splattered across his chest. She licked him clean. His body stiffened painfully. "I am in charge of me, Lucien. Not you, not Rafael, not Sharia. Not even the Blood Law." She lowered her lips to his. He swelled against her thigh. "I submitted to you once to honor Rafael's sacrifice but after that . . . I allowed you to touch me because I wanted you to. I want you to now." She brushed her lips across his. He clasped her head to deepen the kiss.

She was having none of it. She pulled away, but slid her slick cunt down his belly. He growled, steeling himself.

Rocking her slick folds along the blunt head of his dick, she toyed with him. The stimulation against his cock ring drove him mad. Her eyes burned hot with lust. Her heavy breasts swayed temptingly, and her pebbled nipples begged for his tongue. It took every bit of self-control Lucien possessed not to impale her from below. She ran her hands up his arms, pushing them above his head. Entwining her fingers in his, she lengthened against him. "I am in control now, Lucien. I say how fast." She slid her slickness up his belly then back down to the tip of his cock. Then, in a painfully slow undulation, she moved against him, twirling her hips so that those sweet lips caught the blunt head of his cock just low enough to tease and manipulate his cock ring. He gritted his teeth, fighting the intensity of the sensation and the awareness that all he had to do was tip his hips into her . . .

"And how slow." She ran her slick folds down the length of his shaft. She strained against him, relishing her power over him.

Never had a woman dared to dominate him. Never would he have allowed it. Never until now. Until Falon.

Her lips captured his in a hard, demanding kiss. Her tongue swirled along his bottom lip, into his mouth, and around his tongue. Her damp hair cascaded around them, a shield against the world. His fingers tightened around hers, his entire being on the brink of snapping in half.

She tore her lips from his and kissed his chin, then licked his neck, scraping her teeth along his jugular. "Falon," he breathed. *Mark me.*

The pressure of her teeth against his skin intensified. But she did not puncture his skin.

Her body slickened, warming to hot. Her hips moved in slow, rhythmic thrusts against him. His control stretched to the breaking point. Lucien arched into her, demanding with his body that she take him.

She flung her head back. Lips parted, breathing heavy, she caught and held his gaze. As she slid down him, her lips twisted into a possessive smile. The head of his cock pushed into her tormenting pussy. Her eyelids fluttered as she caught her breath. But she did not break her stare. Inch by slow inch, she moved onto him, and with each inch, he thought he would come unglued.

"My God," he hissed as she completely sat him. "You are so fucking tight." He flexed inside of her. Her muscles clamped around him like a fist and, painstakingly slow, pumped him. He could feel every liquid inch of her sweet velvet sheath. The contour of her lining, the pulsing soft spot at the tip of her where his cock head tapped and nuzzled.

She hung suspended above him, her body trembling as a thin sheen of sweat glossed her skin. She closed her eyes and released his hands. As she slid her hands down his arms, she moved against him. He rose into her, unable to stop what she had set into motion. Her fingers dug into his hair and her lips slid against his. Digging his fingers into her hair, he held her head and kissed her fervently. He let her set the tauntingly slow pace. God, she felt good. She gasped when he ground up into her special spot. He had his cock pierced for his pleasure, but the Apadravya piercing gave a woman pleasure, too.

"Luca—" she breathed.

His cock swelled at her endearment. He just wanted to plow into her, but he kept his control by giving her control. She arched her back; her nipples swept across his lips. He caught one and suckled it against the roof of his mouth. Falon cried out, digging her nails into his scalp. He growled and nipped her. She cried out, this time in pain.

"Harder," she gasped.

He tugged at the sensitive tip with his teeth. Falon moaned pressing into him. Her sultry body shivered in response. Her hips rocked into his, the pace racing to frantic. She sat up, completely on him. He grasped her breasts. She grabbed his wrists to steady herself so that she could increase the pressure of her thrusts. Her body was liquid heat around him, sucking his cock deep inside only to reluctantly release him, then to grasp him again. In feral abandonment, she fucked him to annihilation.

Locking her thighs around his, she ground her pussy onto his cock, holding him captive in her vise girp. He thrust up into her, her feral moans of pleasure driving him crazy. He wanted to toss her onto her back and fuck her until she screamed her throat raw.

Throwing her head back, Falon screamed. Then, fiercely, just as her orgasm slammed into her, she sank her teeth into his neck, finally marking him as hers. Lucien roared his triumph as her muscles clamped him and like a fist pump, she pulled him with her. Lucien exploded inside her with such violence she toppled. He grabbed her to keep her from falling off him, holding her hips down on his thrusting maddeningly into her.

"Too . . . deep," she cried as her body wracked with another explosive orgasm. "Ah, God, Lucien," she gasped.

He could not stop. His body was out of control. The bloodlust of the fight combined with Falon's mark pushed him over the edge of everything sane.

Their bodies gyrated madly, as one violent wave of passion slammed into another.

In a wild chaotic spiral, they crashed against each other. Falon's hot, slick body fell exhausted against his. Still connected, all he could manage was slipping an arm around her pulsating body to keep her from sliding off his sweaty skin.

He closed his eyes under the warmth of the sun.

"Luca?" Falon softly said, nuzzling against his neck where she had marked him.

"Hmm?"

"You belong to me now."

His heart hit his chest hard, followed by an emotion he could not name. He swallowed down the lump in his throat. "I always have . . ." He let himself float off into a state of perfect euphoria. He must have dozed, because he woke to Falon's warm wet tongue licking the wounds her teeth had left on his neck.

"That feels good," he murmured, tightening his arms around her. His cock stirred. He did not know what it was about her, but he was a walking hard-on whenever he touched her.

"Lucien," she said against his jugular. "I want to do that again."

"Kill Vipers or fuck my brains out?"

She raised her head to gaze at him, her blue eyes all soft and sexy, her hair a wild black halo around her. Her pouty lips glistened with his blood. "Both."

He rose up and licked her bottom lip. "Which one first?"

Her lips parted in a beaming smile. "Hmm." She looked down his belly to his fire-breathing dragon, then back at him. "I want that," she said, turning toward his cock.

He breathed heavily, anticipating those ruby red lips of hers locked around him, but the distant sound of baying hounds abruptly broke their private interlude.

"Falon," he said, sitting up and bringing her up and around to him.

"What's wrong?"

"Slayers. And they're on the hunt."

Instantly on her feet, Falon looked across the swirling river. "For us?"

"I suspect for Layla. We need to get to her before they do."

As one, they shifted and picked up the Lycan's scent. As they raced through the timber, the baying of the hounds grew louder. Layla's scent was strong. They came across the discarded trap. Falon swallowed hard. Layla's freedom came with a price. A wolf paw was clenched between the iron jaws. So desperate for freedom, Layla had bitten her foot off to escape. Falon's growl mirrored Lucien's. They picked up their pace. Layla's fresh blood scent was easy to follow. It would be for the Slayers as well.

They hurried, Lucien racing just ahead of Falon. As they made a sharp turn, there was a loud snapping sound, and Lucien was snatched up into a thick metal net. He roared furiously and shifted to human.

"Lucien!" Falon cried. Shifting to human as well, she climbed high into the tree the net hung from, to the sturdy branch that held the weight of him. "Tell me what to do!"

The net burned his skin. He looked closer. Interwoven through the steel were strands of silver. A Slayer trap. The baying hounds loomed closer.

Lucien calmed so that she would not panic. "Falon, the net is made of steel and silver. See if you can unhook it."

"It's a locked metal strap!" She grabbed it and yanked it hard. Then pulled and shook it viciously. It did not give. She shifted and used her powerful wolf jaws on it, but to no avail. She shifted back to human in full panic mode. "I can't break it! Lucien! What should I do?"

She looked over her shoulder. The braying of the hounds closed in. And mingled with their scent was that of at least a dozen Slayers. Payback for this morning's raid no doubt.

"Run to Mondragon, Falon, get help," Lucien said calmly.

"They're too far! I'm not going to leave you!" She dropped from the branch to the ground and grabbed at him through the netting.

The hounds were closer, maybe three hundred yards out. "Go, damn it! You can't handle the Slayers!" He knew what they would do to her if they caught her. He could not stomach it. "Falon," he said urgently. "Get help. There is time, they won't kill me immediately. They'll want their fun first."

"I won't leave you!" she cried frantically, pulling at the net.

"Go, damn it!"

"No!" she screamed, shaking her head. "I will stand and fight."

For the first time since he'd watched his parents die before his eyes, Lucien panicked. Falon was right, Mondragon was too far to the south. Vulkasin was closer. That meant she would be with Rafe. He swallowed hard. But she would be safe. He could not bear the thought of any part of her touched by a Slayer. Gathering what calm he could, he softly but firmly said, "If you care anything about me, Falon, *I need you to go to Rafe now*. He will protect you."

Falon reached through the steel and silver netting and grasped his fingers. Pressing her lips to the metal she said, "I'll be back with all of Vulkasin!"

"Now!" He shouted as the dogs came snarling around the corner. Lucien shifted into wolf and wondered not if he was going to die, but if the blood bond between he and Falon was strong enough to withstand her love for his brother.

Nine

FALON RAN FOR Lucien's life to the one person that could save him. The brother he had sworn eternal vengeance against. As a wolf, she flew through the forest to Vulkasin. As soon as she picked up Rafael's familiar scent, the desperation in her calmed.

Rafa!

When he refused to answer, her desperation spiked. The high walls of the compound loomed like a fortress before her. As she approached, she called to Rafael again. When he didn't answer, she called for Angor, his Berserker, the huge mutant wolf whose life she had saved. Though the beast answered only to Rafael, he would not harm her. At least, he would not have before she had been given to Lucien.

Angor answered with a low warning growl.

"Angor, you forget who saved your life!"

He whimpered for forgiveness.

Falon leapt high over the compound walls and into the yard.

"Rafael!" she screamed as she shifted to human and continued her mad pace into the clubhouse. Naked and breathing hard she stopped as the congregated pack turned wary eyes on her. "Where is he?" she demanded as she inhaled Rafe's deep woodsy scent. A wave of longing swept through her, but she shook it off. Lucien was in mortal danger.

And Rafe was close. Anton, Rafael's sergeant at arms, inclined his head toward the stairway. Falon ran past them and up the stairs to the bedroom she had shared with her chosen one. Familiar scents collided with heart-wrenching emotions as she raced to the man she loved in order to save the man he despised.

She burst into the bedroom and stopped short. Rafael stood staring out the window. He would have seen her approach. Heard her pleas. Yet he stood as if he were deaf and blind. He didn't turn to face her. Her gaze swept him from head to foot, but paused on his swollen left hand. She gasped. His skin was burned and raw around the Eye of Fenrir, the ring that held untold power.

"Rafa?" she said cautiously as she slowly approached. She wrestled against the need to throw her arms around him and her desperate need to save Lucien.

He turned hard, distant eyes upon her. Falon gasped. "Rafa! What's—happened to you?"

"Do you really expect me to answer that?" he asked, his voice so low and cold she didn't recognize it.

Her heart clenched. She grasped his hands and brought them to her lips. She kissed the rawness on his hand. Where her lips touched, his skin healed before her eyes. She wished she could heal his heart as easily. "I'm so sorry all of this has happened. You can't know how much I've missed you." She looked up into his dispassionate eyes. "But, Rafael, they have Lucien! I need your help to free him."

He regarded her with a coolness she did not deserve. It was not her fault they were not together!

"Please, before they kill him!"

A spark of fire flashed in his eyes. "*Who* has Lucien?"

"Slayers! We were tracking Layla—"

More realization in his expression. His eyes widened but she kept talking.

"The Vipers had her. We fought them, but Layla took off. We went after her, and Lucien was caught in a silver net. I couldn't free him. We could smell Slayers, hear their dogs. They'll kill him!"

When Rafael did not respond, Falon fought back the urge to slap him into action. Though he made no move to help her, she saw the turmoil flash in his beautiful aqua-colored eyes. Eyes that had looked at her with such love and passion it had stirred her soul.

Slowly he shook his head and she felt that same soul shrivel and die.

This was not her Rafael.

The anguish in her heart was unbearable. "We cannot leave him to die!" Her hands tightened on his. He hissed in a breath of pain. The burns were already back! "What happened to your hand?" she demanded. "What's wrong with *you?*"

He pulled his hands from her grasp and turned back to stare out the window.

"What the hell has happened?" she demanded again, stepping up behind him.

Without turning, he said, "Fenrir fights for release."

Falon grabbed him by the arm and spun him around. His eyes widened at her strength.

"Rafa, listen to me, we need to save Lucien. Gather the Berserkers and your men. We need to go *now!*"

His eyes narrowed dangerously. Finally, emotion. "Little more than a week ago you wanted to kill him!"

Falon sucked in a deep breath and found she could not look at him. "Things are— different—"

"Different how?"

Still refusing to meet his eyes, she said, "He is a man in mourning, too, Rafa."

"Do you love him?!" Rafael demanded.

Her head snapped back. "No! I—" She didn't know what she felt. "It's complicated."

"It's *complicated*? What the hell is that supposed to mean?"

Falon shook her head, not understanding what she did or did not feel for Lucien. "I don't know what it means. But even if I did love him, he's your brother! Does that mean nothing to you?"

Rafael's features hardened to stone. "The day he took you from me is the day he died to me."

"He saved my life! For that would you at least repay him?"

He grabbed her to him. "I pay for it every minute of every day you are gone from me." He dropped his forehead to hers. "I love you, Falon. It tears me apart every time I think of you with him."

His pain was so intense, it singed the edges of her heart. Melting it in half. And perhaps it was. Because she loved Rafael with every part of her, but she also cared deeply for his brother. It was an impossible situation. Hot tears blurred her vision.

"Oh, Rafa. If I had known what lay ahead of us, I never would have walked into that deli that night." She would have turned and run as fast and as far as she could. The pain of love lost was unbearable. She touched his cheek. "I am so sorry."

"I would not change a thing. Had I not met you that night, Falon, I would never have known what love is."

Falon swallowed hard. Her broken heart swelled with huge love for this man. "Rafa, if by some crazy stroke of fate, there is another chance for us, would you take me back?"

Fury flashed in his eyes. "I know what you have done. I know that you wanted him. That you begged for his touch." He sneered. "The scent of your sex still clings to you! How could I take you back?"

For the hundredth time since she had laid eyes on him, her heart wrenched painfully. Heat infused her cheeks. She looked down at the ground, thinking she should feel ashamed that she had been so bold with Lucien when his brother's heart broke for her but oddly she did not. Not now. She had been thrown into an impossible situation. And she had made the most of it. What was done was done. If Rafael could not see past her impossible situation, then she could not make him see. Not now anyway. Her head snapped back and she looked him directly in the eye. "You will mark another mate by the next full moon. I am with Lucien. Nothing will change that. Now, Rafael, I am begging you, for the love you once had for me, *help* me save him."

"Because of him, I do not have you! Because of what he did to you, I cannot take you back even if he were dead!"

Desperation had a chokehold on her. "Rafael, I love you! I loved you last week. I loved you when Lucien took me. Because of your sacrifice, I allowed him to mark me!" She grabbed his hands. "I love you now. None of what I feel for you has anything to do with Lucien! What I do or do not feel for him will never change what I feel for you."

"What *do* you feel for him, Falon?"

She shook her head and answered honestly and quickly. They needed to go. "I don't know, but I do know I don't want him to die."

He flung her hands from his. "Then save him yourself."

Dumbfounded by his refusal to do what was right, Falon shook her head. "What happened to the honorable man I fell in love with?"

Rafael's eyes hardened to ice. "He died the minute my brother marked you."

"Oh, Rafa, don't do this. Please, don't do this to yourself. This is not who you are."

"It is who I have become."

Tears blurred her vision as she rose up on her toes and kissed his tight lips and softy said against them, "I will mourn my true love's death until my last days." She turned and strode to the door. With her hand on the handle, she turned and looked back at him. He had not moved. But his eyes mirrored what was truly in his heart. It made walking out of his life that much harder. "Good-bye, Rafa." She shifted and ran to Lucien.

Falon cleared the high compound walls and ran as if hell were on her heels to where she left Lucien. Somehow, she would find a way to free him even if she had to—she didn't want to think of what she might have to sacrifice for his life. But she realized she would do it. Whatever *it* was.

She did not want to think of what Lucien meant to her. All she knew was that what she shared with Lucien she did not share with Rafa. He had brought something to life inside her. Something primal. The sex, the fighting, the killing. It was like a drug. Lucien was dangerously unpredictable. He was volatile, he was ruled by his emotions. Rafael was so different. He was methodical, honorable, and though his emotions ran deep within him, he controlled them. He did not make the emotional mistakes Lucien made.

The brothers were as different as day and night, and she was trapped between dusk and dawn. She knew why Rafe refused to help, but she would not let Lucien die.

Falon picked up Lucien's scent. His blood scent. Her heart hammered in her chest and her rage grew. They'd hurt him. Snarling, she dug deeper and ran faster. They would pay for each drop of his blood.

Lucien's scent stopped at the banks of the churning river. Falon looked across the fifty-yard span. She didn't know how to swim as a human but as a wolf it would come naturally. She waded into the cold water and was immediately swept away by the powerful current. She went under but allowed her body's buoyancy to bring her up. Instead of fighting the current, Falon swam with it while she kept her eye on the opposite bank. As the river swept her farther downstream, the current picked up. Her body slammed into a boulder knocking the wind out of her. She yelped and went under. The current dragged her down. Panicked, she flailed in the water, trying to break the surface. Her lungs ached, her eyes burned. She could see the sunlight from beneath the water. Her back leg hooked on a fallen tree trunk. The velocity of the pull made her yelp; she swallowed water. She could not get the momentum to bring her body to the surface, the current was so strong, pulling her downriver underwater.

The gray fog of unconsciousness blurred her vision.

Luca!

But he didn't answer.

"FALON!"

Her eyes fluttered open. Haloed by the sun, she could not see the face above her, but by his scent she knew it was Rafael. She pushed to sit up. She was naked and dripping wet. Rafael was naked and just as wet above her. Angor and the rest of the Berserkers were dripping wet and strapped down with leather packs and sheathed swords. Scores of Vulkasin wolf stood behind them.

Emotion exploded in her chest.

Rafael's eyes shone brightly with emotion but his words were serious. "I am here because I love you, Falon. When I choose a mate and mark her by the next full moon, she will have no place in my heart. There is no room for her or any woman, because you occupy every part of it."

Tears stung her eyes. She reached up to touch his cheek. He grabbed her hand, preventing it. He swallowed tightly. "You belong to Lucien, Falon. I gave my word and it is my vow; I would not encourage you in any way. So that I don't break that vow, let's just go."

He may have made such a vow, but she did not. She threw her arms around Rafael's neck and hugged him to her. She cried when his strong arms wrapped around her, holding her tightly against him. "Thank you," she choked between her tears. "Thank you."

Moments later, Falon shifted as did Rafael. With Vulkasin behind them, they went after Lucien.

LUCIEN SLOWLY BECAME aware that he was in human form, on his back, shackled at the hands, waist, and knees, in pain, but alive. Hellish heat burned the back of his heels. His blood scent was strong. He hissed in a long breath and groaned painfully when he flexed his feet. Both his Achilles tendons had been severed. He could not walk as a man nor run as a wolf. He was literally grounded. Was Falon?

Had she made it to Rafe?

Falon!

Sweat beaded his forehead and his blood pressure shot sky high when she did not respond.

Falon, answer me. Are you safe?

The fear knotting his gut tightened when she still did not answer. There was only one of two reasons she did not respond: because she was with Rafe and did not want to, or she was incapacitated.

Neither scenario eased his taut nerves. He didn't want to think Falon had skipped back to Rafe, leaving him to die at the hands of the Slayers. But worse, he could not bear the thought that she may lay hurt and vulnerable somewhere. He needed to get out of there and find her. Wherever the hell here was!

Familiarizing himself with the scents and sounds around him, Lucien lay still, barely drawing a breath. Hanging like a toxic pall around him, Slayer stink permeated his nostrils. It combined with the fumes of gasoline and the cloying scent of oil, creating a polluted stench. He opened his eyes to dim light outside filtering through dented metal blinds. It was just around twilight. He was chained inside of a large metal cage, securely locked by a cereal bowl–sized cast-iron lock hanging on the outside of the door, tall enough for an average human to walk through. Lucien looked up at the pitched wood ceiling then around what he guessed was some type of storage shed. Gardening type tools hung haphazardly on three walls. Several bales of hay were stacked up across from the wood slat door with a wheelbarrow and several shovels casually propped against it.

Past the shed, the distinct sound of revelry filtered back to him. No doubt Slayers celebrating the fact they finally had him. Lucien sneered. It wasn't over until the fat Slayer screamed.

He shifted. The shackles magically readjusted to wolf size.

Fucking Slayer magic.

Shifting back into his human form Lucien mentally mapped out what he needed to do. First, heal himself. He would need to be in wolf mode to lick his wounds, but the way the shackles were wrapped and locked around his hands, ankles, and body, he could not bend far enough down to do so. So Plan B: get out of the shackles so he could heal himself and get out of there.

He searched the wall for a tool that he could pick the locks with. A long-handled aerator hung next to a long-handled shovel. As he moved to the nearest spot in the cage toward the tools, footsteps hesitantly approached the shed. Not heavy like a man, lighter, like a woman.

He stiffened. Intimately familiar with the scent.

His heart thumped against his chest as the person fumbled with the outside lock. Slowly the door opened.

A small, bare foot followed by a curvaceous body, followed by long red hair he used to wrap around his fists when she— Shocked, his eyes widened as he looked into two familiar cat-shaped, green eyes.

He was dreaming. It couldn't be. Pain, joy, and confusion collided in his chest.

"Mara—"

Her full red lips slid back into a happy smile. She brushed her hair from her eyes.

"Lucien! I had to come when I heard they'd captured you!" she said, flying to her knees outside of his cage. She grabbed the bars, pressing her face to them. Sixteen years separated her death from her resurrection, and she looked as young and beautiful now as she had all those years ago.

"How—"

His heart thudded against his rib cage. *Mara was alive?* He raised a hand to touch her, to feel her flesh and bone, but he hesitated.

She reached through the bars and touched her warm hand to his cheek. She was living, breathing—warm. "I am alive, Lucien."

His brain exploded with the realization that her resurrection, regardless of whether she was a Slayer or a superhuman who had survived a catastrophic injury, changed everything! Not that he wished Mara dead, but alive, Lucien had no right to Falon. His gut fisted.

"How are you here? Alive?"

Her emerald-colored eyes glistened with tears. "I have so much to tell you, Lucien. So much! But first, I need to get you away from those bastard Slayers before they come back for you. What they want to do to you is inhuman." She slipped her hand into her skirt pocket and withdrew several keys.

Too stunned by this crazy turn of events, Lucien lie still on the dirt floor and waited for Mara to unlock the big iron lock. She was having trouble.

"How did you survive Rafael's attack? And what are you doing here with Slayers?" *Was* she in truth a Slayer? He would know it! But as before, whenever Mara was near, he saw only her. Except this time, when he looked into her green eyes, he saw Falon's sapphire blue ones.

A slight frown tweaked her brows, but she quickly hid it. "I thought when we were reunited you would be over-the-moon excited to see me. Instead you ask why I'm not dead."

Guilt pricked him, but not enough to set aside pleasantries before facts. "For sixteen years, I thought you were dead. You *were* dead! How did you survive? Why didn't you return to me?"

The lock popped open. She smiled triumphantly and lifted it off. When she swept her hand down her chest to wipe a smear of dirt from her finger, Lucien's body stirred. She used to do the same thing with his fingers, except naked. The snug translucent top hugged her ripe curves. Her stiff nipples pointed straight at him. She was not wearing a bra. She never needed one. His gaze traveled down her narrow waist to the short black skirt that barely covered her creamy thighs. He raised his gaze back to hers for explanation.

"After your brother nearly killed me, I thought I would die there in your bed, Lucien. I was terrified, but somehow, I managed to drag myself from that room as you and your brother lie dying on the floor. That's all I remember. But I have been told a Slayer found me just outside of the compound gate. I woke up weeks later, chained to that bastard's bed. He saved my life, but every time he raped me I wished I was dead."

It made no sense at all. "I'm sorry, Mara. But you died in my arms—"

"A miracle saved me." She opened the cage door, dropped to her knees, and crawled toward him. Her floral perfume was familiar. Belladonna. Talia used the deadly plant to put wounded animals she could not save out of their misery. It was the same perfume Mara wore sixteen years ago.

She sat back on her heels and pouted when he made no move toward her. "I have planned and plotted for this day for sixteen years, Lucien! Aren't you happy to see me?"

"Keep your voice down," he warned.

Despite his tone and lack of affection, she beamed at him. "I may have been enslaved for sixteen years, Lucien, but I did not cry myself to sleep each night. I paid attention to their black arts. I learned how to create spells and elixirs."

She leaned toward him. "When I heard they had you, I insisted I come along for the entertainment. Then I created a little spell to keep them preoccupied until I had you safely back home." She pressed her lips to his. His cool indifference surprised him. He should be sorry for what she had to endure all these years, and thankful that she came to his rescue, but something else niggled at him.

She pulled away from his lips and raked his body with her gaze. She brushed her fingertips across one of his nipples. "I love the tat." Then trailed them down his chest to his belly to his sleeping dragon. She stroked the cock ring. His cock stirred. "Only sinful Lucien would indulge himself in such a way."

"Mara," he hoarsely said, thickening beneath her roaming hand. "I'm stunned to see you. More like in shock." He turned away from her hand, and groaned, rubbing his forehead against his cuffed hands. "For sixteen years I have hated my brother for killing you."

"As far as I'm concerned, you can hate him for the next sixteen years for almost succeeding! When he sees us together again he is going to be more jealous of our love and power than last time." She chuckled. "But this time I can protect myself against him. He will not hurt me again."

Lucien groaned, suddenly feeling suffocated.

"Get me out of these shackles so we can get the hell out of here."

She slipped another smaller key from her skirt waistband and began to unlock each of the shackles. When she came to the ones around his ankles, she touched his foot. "Lucien, I about died when they did that."

"I'll live."

As she bent over him to unlock it, she said, "I know where Balor is."

Excitement sparked him. "Where?"

"I'll tell you when we get home."

Shit.

"We need to hurry, the spell only works for so long."

He grabbed her wrist as she turned to move out of the cage. "Why didn't you come to me before now?"

"I told you, I was a sex slave."

"But you could cast spells and sneak away."

"I was afraid Balor would come after me! He's more powerful than all of them combined. What if I came back to you, and you rejected me or, God forbid, had another woman? What would I have done then?"

Falon.

His heart quickened when she did not respond to his call. Was she dead? Or had she reunited with Rafael? He shook his head refusing to believe either option. She was alive and would find him.

Mara sensed his increasing distance. He could not help it. His heart belonged to another now.

Grabbing his arms, Mara pleaded with him to understand. "Lucien, I know this is crazy and impossible to understand, but *please* trust me. I am alive and well, and once I get us out of here, you can take me home with you where I belong. Not even Rafael can stand between us now."

Lucien shook his head. "I cannot take you to Mondragon."

She dropped to her knees and grabbed his hands. "How can you not? I've bided my time for sixteen years waiting for this day to be reunited with you!"

He shook his head. "I cannot."

When she moved in to kiss him, Lucien pulled back. Despite the love he once had for her and what she sacrificed for him now, he could no more pretend to love her than he could pretend to hate Falon. Tears tracked down her creamy cheeks. "We love each other!"

She pulled off her shirt. Her full breasts glowed in the low light of the room, she grasped them offering them to him. "Don't you remember, Lucien, how it was between us?" Her voice lowered several octaves. "How you could not keep your hands off me?"

Lucien was not a dead man. His cock stirred. She smiled seductively. "You do remember . . ." She purred and moved closer to him. Her hard nipples speared his chest as her hands slid down his belly to his cock. He hissed in a breath as she slowly began to manipulate him. "How your body craved mine."

Her belladonna scent clamped around his head, his chest, his dick, immobilizing him. Lucien closed his eyes as her siren's call beckoned him. Just like old times . . . he was helpless under her spell.

She is a Slayer, Lucien! He heard his brother's voice all those years ago. *I can smell her black magic.*

"You have no scars on your chest from Rafe's attack," he hissed when she flicked the metal bar just under the blunt head of his cock.

"I erased them with a spell," she breathed.

She had a pat answer for every one of his questions. None of them rang true.

Lucien dug his fingers into her thick hair and yanked her head back. Her scent snaked around his head like a deadly sleeping gas. He set his jaw, fighting her seductive pull. "I loved you a long time ago, Mara. I love another now." Saying it made it real. It felt right. Because it was right, and the rightness of it empowered him. He had loved Falon from the moment he laid eyes on her at Vulkasin. He just didn't know it until now.

Mara's deep green eyes clouded. "But you were promised to me!"

He shook his head. The air cleared, dissipating whatever spell she had cast to seduce him. "We never exchanged marks. There are no bloodrights."

Her eyes darkened. "Am I to pay because of what your brother did to me?" She moved into him. "Lucien, we loved each other!" she pleaded. "I gave you everything. Is this how you repay that love?"

"I have howled at the moon for sixteen years mourning your loss. I know how you feel. But I have marked another and she has returned the mark. It cannot be undone."

"I can cast a spell and make her quietly disappear."

The vision of Falon's death played out in his brain. The pain of losing her so unimaginable his heart, body, and soul shuddered. Fury flared at Mara's proposal. And he suddenly understood why it was so difficult to resist her body now as it had been all those years ago. She had not just learned black magic, she had perfected it long ago. He grasped her shoulders and shook her. "Go near her, and I will kill you myself."

Mara's eyes narrowed to slits. When she fully opened them, he saw it. Granite-hard, onyx eyes. The true mark of a Slayer.

T e n

RAFAEL HAD BEEN just when he'd tried to kill Mara. The realization made Lucien sick to his stomach. Sicker still because part of him—some small, hidden, ignored part of him—had always suspected he'd been right. Part of him had known Rafael could not have done what he had if he had not been sure . . .

But Lucien's pride, resentment, and anger had pushed the truth aside.

"I loved you. I thought you loved me—" Lucien said, not understanding why she had given herself to him if she did not love him.

No longer trying to hide what she was, Mara's eyes glittered polished onyx. Her red hair turned blond and her full, voluptuous body morphed into the svelte athletic one reminiscent of many Slayers. But what defined her for what she truly was, was the Slayer stink that permeated the air around her. His grip tightened.

"You fooled me with your black magic. You fooled everyone except Rafael," Lucien accused. "But why?"

She shoved him onto his back and pinned him to the floor. "I am a Corbet! I watched you kill half of my family the night we met! My mother and my two sisters! I followed you into that bar and beguiled you with black magic. You were so easy. So damn arrogant. I wanted to kill you every time you touched me! I almost had you. I would have bred Slayers into your precious Vulkasin pack and destroyed you all from the inside out."

He flung her from him. She hit the metal bars of the cage so hard, she bent them. When she screamed, he flung his hand across her mouth and grabbed the shackle chain she had just freed him from. Unable to get leverage with his feet, Lucien rose on his knees and shoved Mara harder against the cage bars, pinning her by the neck with the chain as he wound the end of it around her neck. "You nearly destroyed me and everyone I loved with your lies!" He twisted the metal around her neck. She grabbed his arms, dug her nails into his skin, and slammed her feet against his severed heels. He grunted in pain when she slammed him again. She was strong, but Lucien's hatred fueled him to greater strength.

She opened her mouth to scream again but only a hoarse plea emerged. Lucien yanked her down to the floor, pinning her with one knee to her chest, moving all of his body weight on top of her. His hatred was so intense her features blurred. He twisted the chain so tight it dug deep into her skin. He twisted until her body went limp beneath him. Breathing heavily, Lucien kept the tension tight until he felt her life force wane. But it would take more than strangulation to kill a Slayer. Keeping one hand on the metal noose, he crawled out of the cage, dragging her behind him. He reached over to the shovel standing up against the wall by the door, grabbed it by the handle, and then straddled her. Keeping her immobile with the one hand, he grabbed the shovel handle just above the metal scoop and in a vicious blow severed her head from her body. Her black eyes flashed her hatred for the last time. And as Slayers do when they die a true death, her body smoldered to ash. Lucien flung the shovel and shackles from him and rolled over onto his back.

Breathing heavily, he clamped his hands over his eyes, hating what he had done. Not the taking of Mara's life—he would do the same thing one hundred times over. He may have loved her once, but the fact that she was a Slayer erased every vestige of that emotion and replaced it with hatred. He hated Slayers with every fiber of his being. Nothing would change that. *Nothing.*

It stung that she never loved him, that she used him, that he was so damn blind to her wiles.

Though deep regret filled him, he could not change the past. What was done, was done. It was the present and the future that mattered now and both looked dark to him. By Blood Law, he was condemned to death for lying with a Slayer. Because he had no claim to Falon now, death would be welcome.

She would return to Rafael, just as he had always feared. How could he make peace with his brother when he possessed the woman Lucien wanted above all others?

He swiped his hand across his chin. She had marked him today. In that one oh-so-meaningful gesture he never thought he would get, she freely gave herself to him. She gave him everything, including a piece of her heart. He felt it in the way she looked at him. Touched him. Made love to him. He had never been happier than he was this afternoon with Falon. He did not want to lose that. But how could he hang on to her?

He looked at the gray ashes on the dirt floor: The only evidence that Mara was a Slayer. And now, a dead Slayer. Lucien inhaled sharply. Only he knew the truth. Only he could set it free. Only he stood between the woman he loved and Rafael, the man who had always stood between Lucien and his own glory.

He sat up and ran his fingers through his hair. Was he willing to forgo all honor—to lie—to keep the woman he loved?

He snarled. Lucien was many things to many people, but he was a man of his word. He had given his word he would never lie to Falon. And since Falon valued honor so highly, would she value him for swallowing his pride and telling the truth? Maybe, but it would not bind her to him. It would drive her away, straight into Rafael's arms, making Lucien hate him even more.

Setting the truth free would also sign Lucien's death warrant. The Blood Law was clear: no Lycan shall lie with a Slayer; the penalty, death. While the Blood Law was black and white, it had been lenient with Falon. Could it be with him? Lucien was not feeling so lucky. Mara had not been a one-night stand. He had not only lain with her repeatedly but would have marked her and bred with her had Rafe not seen through her trickery.

He was screwed.

Except for one unseen benefit: the vengeance that ruled his every action for the last sixteen years began to unravel. Rafe had been just. Rafe had not slain Mara for personal gain but to protect the pack. Rafe lived by the pack-first credo. And while Lucien did the same in his own way, he was not the honorable man his brother was. Or the honorable man Falon deserved.

He raked his fingers through his hair again and sat up. He needed to get the hell out of there before those bloodthirsty bastards came looking for him. He dragged himself to the door and cracked it open. What sounded like a Slayer kegger party echoed from a large building roughly fifty yards from where Lucien hid. The doors were closed and no guards stood sentinel. Was Mara's spell still in effect? Or had she lied? Lucien guessed everyone was in on the joke except him. Those Slayers were deliberately looking the other way. Just like they had deliberately isolated him so that Mara could act as if she were helping him escape. And then what? They'd let him take her back to his pack to finish what she had started sixteen years ago?

He snarled and shifted. He needed to heal himself. As an alpha, he could heal others but not himself to the same degree. In wolf form, however, he could lick his wounds, healing himself enough so that he could at least walk. Once home, Talia would use her power to repair what he could not.

Once he was able to bear weight, Lucien nosed open the door, and like a shadow, he slipped up to the building housing the merry-making Slayers. Though some were clan Corbet by their scent, there were others Lucien did not recognize. Could these be the Slayers Balor had recruited from the east? There were nearly two dozen of them. He moved around the building, absorbing his surroundings. They were close to water. The scent of motorboats and aquatic flora and fauna was strong. But the Slayer stink was stronger.

Facing north, Lucien raised his nose to the air. The breeze came in from the west, a slight salt scent carried all the way in from the bay, heading due east. By the landscape Lucien knew he was south of Mondragon. Probably somewhere due west of Sacramento close to the delta roads.

He moved in closer and, though it hurt, he rose up on his haunches and peered through the closest window to get a head count. Twenty armed Slayers. Not only did they all have snub-nosed automatic machine guns slung across their backs, no doubt with silver rounds, but a short metal scabbard hung from each one of their belts. New-world weapons to stop them, old-world weapons to kill them.

Old farming equipment was neatly pushed to the back of the building with several stacks of round shipping containers lined up on the opposite wall. His nose twitched. Gasoline.

Lucien dropped to all fours and did a slow perimeter check.

Roughly four hundred feet. Two exits, double wooden doors in the front, same type in the back. From the contents, the building was some type of storage barn with high vents on either side of the pitched wood-slat roof. The building was wood. In the heat of the late summer, it was dry. Perfect kindling.

Lucien!

His heart leapt against his chest.

Falon! I have been calling for you! Where are you? Are you safe?

Lucien, we're coming for you!

Who?

Vulkasin. We're close, your scent is strong.

Lucien grit his jaw. He should be ecstatic she had gone to Rafe for help and not left him there to die. But he could not get past the irksome fact that his brother was coming to his rescue. Or at least was. Lucien had procured his own freedom and was free to go. But he was not running, not when he had the opportunity to take out more Slayers. Four this morning, twenty more tonight? No fucking way.

I will meet you, Lucien called to her and leapt into the night.

In just a few short miles, with the southerly shift in the wind, he picked up not only Falon's scent, but his brother's and half of Vulkasin. His pack. The pack that bore his sire's name. The pack he longed to rejoin with Mondragon, although he would never admit that to anyone but himself. It could never happen. He was not sixteen again and not willing to co-alpha with his brother. Rafael would never go for it, either. All of that aside, the one thing standing between the packs uniting was Falon. He could not watch her with Rafael every day. He would go mad with jealousy. He would—

He was struck dumb with awe when he watched Falon break through a copse of trees. Her long, sleek ebony body ran fluidly, gracefully. Powerfully.

To him.

At her side, in perfect synchronicity, the great golden Vulkasin alpha. Lucien growled possessively.

"Lucien!" Falon cried shifting into her human form. Lucien shifted and caught her as she lunged into his arms. "You're alive!"

He smiled through the grimace of pain as his body absorbed her weight. God, she felt good. He just wanted to fold her into his arms and hold her forever. "I'm fine."

Flinging her arms around his neck, Falon pressed her body tightly against his. Lucien tightened his arms around her waist, then closed his eyes, inhaling her unique scent.

I missed you, angel face.

She threw her head back, her eyes glowing happily. Lucien leaned down to kiss her smiling lips. "I am so happy to see you! We picked up your blood scent. I was so afraid we would be too late."

He cocked a brow as his belly did a slow roll. Did she truly care for him? He was afraid to ask. "Did you suddenly discover feelings for me, Falon?"

Her cheeks flushed and he loved her more. "I have suddenly discovered a few things about you, Luca." She rose up on her toes and kissed his chin. "We can discuss that later." Stepping down, Falon inclined her head to Rafe. "Your brother came to your aide when he didn't have to. Please try to find it in your heart to move through your hatred."

Lucien dragged his eyes from Falon's happy ones and stared straight into Rafael's brilliant gold glare. Lucien nodded, understanding his brother's rage. For the first time in many years, he did not revel in it. "We need to talk," he whispered in Falon's ear.

"We can talk later. But please, Luca, acknowledge that Rafael is here."

Lucien squeezed her. "He knows I am grateful."

Tell him. Please.

Lucien sighed and looked over Falon's head to his brother, who had not moved. Jealous rage had a paralyzing hold of him. How Rafe controlled himself was beyond Lucien. Vow or no vow, jealousy's ugly claws scraped along Lucien's own belly. If he was the one standing where his brother stood, he could not bear it. And for the second time in sixteen years, Lucien felt no triumph in his brother's pain.

Lucien cleared his throat and said, "My thanks, Rafe. But as you can see, I am alive and well."

Rafael strode toward them. "How is that, *Luca?*" his brother sneered, deliberately using Falon's term of endearment.

Falon stiffened in Lucien's arms. Giving her a reassuring squeeze Lucien made no defensive move toward Rafe.

It's okay, Falon. For the first time I respect his rage.

Lucien almost laughed when her head jerked back and she looked up at him as if he had grown horns. *Where is angry Lucien?*

Lucien smiled, wishing he did not know what he knew but knew that without the truth, there could never be peace. And there must be peace if there was going to be life after the Blood Moon rising. *He was becoming too much of an ass so I fed him to the Slayers.*

Shocked by his words, Falon's eyes widened in surprise. *My prayers have been answered!*

Lucien's smile waned. *Be careful what you wish for, Falon. You might get it.*

Ignoring the confusion in her gaze, Lucien looked back to his brother, looking past the contempt tightening his lips. "They severed both my Achilles tendons, injected me with something that knocked me out. I woke shackled in a cage in a shed. I managed to free myself and healed my wounds enough that I can walk."

"I sensed you weren't one hundred percent," Falon accused. "Why didn't you tell me?"

Lucien smiled tenderly. "I am now, love."

"Men," she chastised, shaking her head as she knelt down behind him and pressed her soothing hands to his wounds.

Lucien's body jerked as her healing warmth infused him. Gods, he would never tire of it. His blood warmed. His body tightened. The beast raised its head, clawing at his gut for release. Setting his jaw, Lucien wrestled down the desire pounding through him.

"Falon," he said hoarsely. "That's enough."

"But—"

He turned and grabbed her up to him. Her eyes widened as she noticed his erection.

"Oh."

He growled low. *Do you want to start a fight? My brother watches.*

Red blotches spattered her cheeks. "I—" Shamefaced, Falon looked past Lucien to Rafe. "My apologies, Rafael."

Lucien growled, turning to face his brother.

Rafael's eyes blazed molten, but Lucien sensed his brother's own beast was raging as wildly as his own. He was not immune to Falon, either. How could he be? They had exchanged blood and marks. It could not be undone despite the Blood Law. That damned Blood Law with its double-edged sword.

Ignoring what they both wanted to do to the woman standing between them, Lucien looked over his shoulder in the direction of the Slayers, then back to his brother. "The Slayers seemed more bent on celebrating tonight than killing. I doubt they know I'm gone." He smiled savagely. "Are you interested in taking out a handful of East Coast Slayers and a few of clan Corbet tonight?"

"I'm always interested," Rafael said, the vicious glint in his eyes mirroring his brother's.

"Good," Lucien said, looking down at Falon, then back to Rafe. "Because this is going to require the three of us."

*   *   *

A FEW MINUTES later, Rafael handed Falon a T-shirt and a pair of shorts that were too big. He tossed Lucien a pair of jeans and pulled on his own pair. Falon quickly dressed. Not that she was modest, shifting back and forth cured one of that quick, but honestly, being naked with Rafe and Lucien both looking at her as if she were a fresh-cut pork chop was unnerving.

And thrilling. For that one electrifying moment when she stood between both men, their passions raging, her imagination took off with carnal images of her in Lucien's strong arms, then Rafael's, then—both . . .

Falon licked her dry lips and glanced over at Lucien, who had walked over to talk weapons with Anton. He looked so damn sexy in the pair of low-slung jeans. His muscles rippled along his arms as he grasped a sword from Anton's cache, making stabbing and thrusting gestures. Lucien's dark hair framed his fallen-angel face in a wild halo of midnight black. Her body warmed when she thought of them earlier that day on the riverbank. It had been ferocious, frantic, untamed. But then, so was Lucien. He kept her off balance. She never knew what to expect from him except the unexpected.

Lucien's feral nature was the polar opposite of Rafael's civility. Rafael was a sensualist. Slow. Deliberate, and oh so passionate. With Rafael, Falon knew where she stood, and that he would always do the right thing. He was grounded, revered among his people, and highly intelligent. He was her first. She had always thought he would be her last. But fate had a funny way of stepping in and shaking up a person's life.

Falon's chest tightened with longing. She missed waking in Rafa's strong secure arms. Yet her breath hitched high in her throat and her belly did chaotic somersaults when she thought of Lucien's touch. He was instant heat followed by internal combustion.

How was it that each man, in his different way, completed her?

What she needed was an ice-cold shower. Maybe then she would not feel so— She shook her head, forcing herself to focus on the deadly matter of killing Slayers. But each time she looked at Rafe, then Lucien, she got a funny buzz in her belly. Amazingly they were in the same breathing space and not tearing each other apart. Had it really been less than two weeks ago that all hell had broken loose? When she thought death was better than life with Lucien?

Yet here she was, with the man she loved like crazy and thought she could not live without and the man she craved with the urgency of a heroin addict. They were night and day. As different as black and white, and yet one nurtured her heart, the other her soul.

Why could she not have both?

Falon swallowed hard and closed her eyes fighting off the erotic visions of being in both men's arms. Of one kissing her as the other stroked her. Of one inside her as the other—

Warm hands touched her shoulders. Hungry for succor, she moaned and looked up into Rafael's dark eyes. Air rushed from her lungs. Her tight nipples tingled. "Rafa," she said roughly. "Please."

He moved into her, his eyes holding hers. "Please, what?"

She could barely breathe. His fingers tightened on her, his nostrils flared, his clean citrusy scent intensified. She wanted to melt into his arms, to be held by him, to make love. Swallowing hard, Falon croaked, "I would give anything to make things different."

"Really?" His eyes snapped angrily. "You and Lucien didn't waste any time marking each other."

"I meant I would give anything so that none of us had to suffer."

"I appear to be the only one suffering, Falon."

She swallowed hard, wishing his words bore no truth. While she suffered the loss of Rafe, Lucien soothed the pain. She looked past

Rafe to Lucien, who stood beside Anton, slashing his sword angrily through the air. His golden glare locked and fixed on her.

You disrespect me with your public display of lust for my brother, Lucien growled.

Falon's own temper flashed. *I'm not a cyborg! I cannot turn my feelings off and on!*

Lucien stabbed the sword into the ground. *At least pretend.*

"At the very least, I would have thought you respected me enough not to flaunt your lust for my brother in my face, Falon," Rafael said and stalked toward Anton, who was unloading crossbows and swords from the leather packs strapped to the Berserkers.

Shaking with anger, Falon stood slack-jawed as the men moved around her. "How the hell did this get turned around and put on me?!" she demanded, marching behind Rafael. She pointed to Lucien, who angrily strode toward her. "And you! How dare you intrude on my feelings for another?"

Rafael turned around just as Lucien stopped beside him. Both brothers looked so damn righteous, she wanted to slap them. "Do either one of you care what I have been through? Are you both so selfish that all you can think of is your fragile alpha egos? Do either one of you care that I have feelings, too?" Hot tears stung her eyes. "I did not ask to be thrust into the middle of your blood feud. I didn't ask for any of this, yet I am the one most affected by it!"

She placed her hand on Rafael's chest. More calmly, she said, "I love you. With all my heart, I love you. You are the light that has shown me what it is to love selflessly and honorably."

She placed her other hand on Lucien's warm chest. His heart beat like a kettledrum beneath her palm. She smiled softly. "Lucien, you are the dark side of the moon. You have shown me a side of myself I was afraid to acknowledge existed. In your own way, you have shown me that honor has two sides. You are a glorious alpha I am proud to stand beside."

She pressed her hands more firmly to their chests. "If I could go back in time, I would make it so none of us had to endure this heartache." She stood on her toes and brushed her lips across Rafael's. His heart slammed against her hand. Her vision blurred. Her heart broke that his broke. But she could not undo what had been done. She smiled through her tears and kissed Lucien. He placed his hand on hers and squeezed it as if to say, I'm sorry and I understand. Tears swelled to overflowing, but Falon's voice did not waver. "But since that isn't possible, please, I am begging you both"—her voice cracked—"do not hate me for making the best of a terrible situation. Don't hate me for the feelings I have for each of you."

GUILT CARVED CHUNKS out of Lucien's conscience. But more ferocious was his obsession with the woman who loved his brother yet only desired him. It ate at him that there was no time for her to fall in love with him. Maybe then, she would let the sleeping dogs lie. Maybe if she loved him as she loved his brother, she would forsake Rafe for him when he told her the truth.

He should just tell them both now what had happened in that shed.

"Falon," Rafael said softly. "Forgive me. I only thought of myself, and not you." Despite Lucien standing right there, Rafael took her into his arms and kissed her. When he pulled away, tears rolled down Falon's cheeks. Lucien steeled himself, hating that those tears were for his brother. Rafe cleared his throat and continued, "There are two northern packs arriving at Vulkasin by week's end. Pack Kozlow and Ivanov. Both packs distant cousins of Vulkasin." Rafael inhaled, then slowly exhaled. "I have agreed to accept Anja, the daughter of Ivanov's alpha, Sasha, as my chosen one."

"No!" Falon cried.

Rafael stood back, releasing Falon. "In exchange for your life, Falon, I vowed to mark another before the next full moon. You of all people know my word is my honor."

Falon turned desperate eyes to Lucien. "Release him from his vow!"

Lucien's anger swelled. "You would cast me aside?"

"No, I would not! I just—I cannot bear it."

Rafael grabbed her and spun her around to face him. "No more than I can bear seeing you with another! Who is being selfish now, Falon?"

His words struck her with the intensity of a lightning bolt the way her body jerked and her breath expelled in a short rush from her chest. Falon turned to Lucien and grabbed his hand and stepped back from Rafael, taking her place beside her alpha. "I'm sorry, Rafa." She sobbed. "I have no honor when it comes to you."

Had Lucien just been run over by a Mack truck it would have hurt less than Falon's words. What he knew he must do would kill him. "Falon," he slowly said pulling her into his arms. "I have something I need to say." He looked at his brother and saw his entire world slip away. Because in Falon he had found his place and after what he was going to say, she would no longer belong to him. "Rafe, can we speak in private?"

"Make it quick; those Slayers won't party all night."

"It will take only a minute."

With Falon in his arms, knowing what he must do, Lucien turned away from prying eyes and ears. He would tell them only that he released Rafe from his vow and he forgave his brother for his hand in Mara's death. The blood feud would end when he returned Falon to her rightful chosen one. He would leave out the part about killing Mara. He would let that sleeping dog lie, but he would not live the lie with Falon. He could not. It would eat him up and destroy what he held so precious.

Just as they reached the edge of the clearing they had gathered in, Lucien's nostrils twitched. He looked at Rafe and knew he smelled it, too.

Slayers.

The party was over.

Eleven

THE STENCH OF approaching Slayers punctuated the heavy night air.

As they rejoined the pack, nervous excitement riveted through Falon, followed by an infusion of power. Just as it had when she and Lucien had attacked the Vipers. Only this was different. Stronger. *Magical.*

"They're armed with automatic rifles and short swords," Lucien said. "We'll have a better chance if we shift and come up behind them."

With the exception of Anton, who was quickly reloading the Berserkers' packs, they all shifted. The pack split and stealthily fanned out, making a wide half circle on either side of the incoming Slayers. Falon found herself between the brothers, with Lucien leading the way.

Throat first, disarm, then kill, Lucien said.

Anticipating the primal satisfaction of sinking her fangs into a

Slayer's throat, Falon growled low and nudged Lucien. He turned and nipped at her, then licked her nose, his golden eyes sparking like candles in the darkness. The quickening in him matched hers. Singularly, they were formidable. Together, they were unbeatable.

Heads down, ears flicking back and forth to catch the slightest sound, their noses twitching to keep on scent, they closed ranks, tightening their bloodthirsty net. But nothing happened. They came up empty. The scent had evaporated, as if the Slayers were never there. The hair on the back of Falon's neck rose. She sensed they were near. But where?

Where the hell are they? Rafe demanded.

They've hidden their scent with magik, Lucien said.

A branch above Falon's head snapped.

The trees!

Dropping to the ground like ninjas, the Slayers opened fire.

Retreat! Lucien ordered.

Falon snarled furiously, wanting to stand and fight but knowing it was suicide. As she dove into a thicket, the hot sting of a bullet grazed her right flank. She turned with Lucien and Rafe on either side of her and hunkered down into the thick brush. Adrenaline pumped through her. Every sense open, aware—ready.

Stripped down to a one-on-one fight, the true advantage lay with the Lycan. Not only could they see as sharply in the dark as the Slayers saw in the daylight, Lycan were quicker, and despite their lack of firepower, deadlier. But tonight, the automatic weapons held the advantage. For the moment.

Lucien snarled.

What? Falon asked.

Ian Corbet. Balor's eldest son, Rafael answered for both brothers. *The prick was just a kid when his father and uncles murdered our parents. He's followed true in his father's vicious footsteps.*

Ian is mine, Lucien hissed.

"I smell your bitch, Vulkasin!" Corbet taunted as he strode boldly into a shallow clearing.

As his uncle Edward, Ian Corbet sported the same tall, athletic build, blond hair, and intense blue eyes that branded a Corbet a mile away. The same uncle Falon killed last month when Rafael lay at death's door. The threat to Rafael had forced her to shift for the first time. It was only in the moments before she ripped Edward Corbet's heart out that Falon discovered what she was. Lycan. And a bitch of a Lycan.

Falon snarled. Ian Corbet had no idea what a bitch she was.

Though Corbet's men surrounded him in a tight circle, their guns pointed toward them in the darkness, Falon had a clear view of the arrogant Slayer.

"Or should I say, Mondragon?" Corbet threw his head back and laughed. "Let me settle your feud over the bitch! I'll fuck her and make her a true Corbet."

Lucien's anger radiated like fire from him. Beside her, Rafael's flared, equally violent.

Do not fall into his trap, Lucien, Rafe warned.

Lucien answered with a low snarl as he slowly moved in on the tight circle.

Stay with Angor, Lucien directed as she fell in behind him.

I will not! She moved up alongside of him and touched his neck with her nose. *My place is beside you.*

Falon, Rafe growled, *listen to Lucien.*

You forget, Rafael, who killed Edward, Falon snapped, cutting off any further attempts to keep her "safe." As they continued to move forward, Falon asked the brothers, *If Corbet is destroyed, will the remaining Slayers run?*

Normally, yes, but out here they know if they run, they don't stand a chance, Lucien said. *So they will stand and fight.*

We'll use the two crossbows in Angor's leather pack to take out Corbet, Rafael said. *There's a dozen silver-tipped arrows in one of the packs. Between us, we'll get a kill shot. When Corbet goes down the soldiers will panic, and we'll pick them off.*

Lucien nodded, adding, *As they regroup, we'll send in the Berserkers to loosen them up some more, then we go in for the final kills.*

His men have closed ranks around him. He's packed tighter than a sardine. You'll never get the kill shot, Falon said.

Watch, Rafe said, then called to Angor, the mutant wolf that appeared instantly. The three of them simultaneously shifted and got to work. Rafe took the crossbows from the packs, handing one to Lucien; the other he kept for himself.

"You picked a good night to die, Corbet," Lucien shouted.

"That remains to be seen, Mondragon!" Corbet returned.

Fascinated, Falon watched her alphas. In tandem, Lucien and Rafael notched the arrows in their respective bows.

The last time I hunted with one of these, Rafe, was the last time we went north.

You dropped that grizzly with one shot to the heart. It took me three to ground mine.

Lucien grinned. *I was always a better shot than you.*

Simultaneously, they raised the bows. Falon's heart pounded with excitement and something else. Hope? Was it possible for these two proud men to reconcile?

I'll bet you Angor that my arrow hits that prick center mass, Lucien challenged.

Rafe set his face to his sight as Lucien set his to his. *I'd be a fool to take that bet.*

Despite witnessing the bond that had been forged in their mother's womb, a bond that despite everything that had transpired between the brothers still existed, as the brothers took a trip down memory lane, Falon's anxiety rose to a hazardous level. *Hello! There are armed Slayers pointing machine guns at us,* she cried.

Not for long, Lucien and Rafe said at the same time. Then pulled the triggers.

Falon watched in awe as the arrows struck true. Both center mass. Corbet's body flew backward into two of his men. A violent barrage of bullets answered.

Rafe and Lucien shoved Falon to the ground and pulled her backward behind a thick clump of bush. But not fast enough that she didn't catch a bullet in the shoulder. She bit back a hiss of pain.

Once the hail of bullets ended, heavy silence blanketed the clearing.

Then laughter.

"Touché, boys," Corbet taunted.

What the fuck?

Three heads popped up over the thicket.

Corbet held the two arrows in his hand. "I will thank my armorer for a job well done! Now, what else do you have before we mow you down?"

Frustration tore through Falon, and with it, a surge of energy. Her shoulder ached like hell and unless they were going to run like cowards, they were going to lose lives fighting this Mexican standoff. Something drastic needed to happen.

Her blood scent wafted in the air.

You're hit! Lucien said, touching the hole in her shoulder.

Rafe's worried gaze settled on her. She felt his need to comfort her, but he held back.

It's nothing, she assured them both.

But she lied. The silver bullet burned like hell, burrowing deeper into her shoulder like a termite in wood. She gasped in pain, falling backward. Rafael grabbed her right hand, Lucien her left. Her body stiffened as lightning bolts of energy shot from their bodies into hers. Their hands burned hot, their connection unbreakable. Like quicksilver the charge burned through her, infusing her muscles, bones, and veins with power. The heat of the energy stung along her veins, leaving a warm thrum in its wake. Wide-eyed, Falon stared at Lucien's and Rafael's equally shocked expressions.

The Eye of Fenrir on Rafael's hand flared red-hot. Lucien's hand, grasping hers, flared with the same intense heat. Her body convulsed. Her head ached. She could not breathe.

Falon! Lucien called to her as she closed her eyes.

She opened her mouth to answer but could not speak. Like a hurricane building steam over warm waters, energy surged in her chest. Her body thrummed with power, and just as she relived the bullet entering her, she saw it in her mind's eye tearing out of her shoulder.

A man's scream punctuated the still air.

Falon's eyes flashed open. *What happened?*

Still clasping her hand, Rafael peered over the brush to the Slayers. *You dropped one!*

How?

The bullet! It went home. Lucien laughed. *Holy shit. That was amazing.*

Dazed, Falon shrugged the shoulder the bullet had entered and exited. Not an inkling of pain. Stunned she looked from Lucien to Rafe. Still connected with both men, the energy continued to thrum through her. *All I did was wish it back where it came from.*

Lucien kissed her soundly on the lips. *Keep those thoughts, baby!*

Making sure it wasn't some kind of fluke, Falon released Rafael's hand, then Lucien's. The heat subsided, but the energy hummed within her. *Go for Corbet's head this time,* Falon said, standing.

Get down, Rafael hissed, pulling her back to the ground. Instinctively she flung his hand away with more force than she intended. He went flying back several yards, staring dumbfounded up at her from the ground. She offered no apology. Rafe was well aware of the power that surged within her when she was pissed or threatened.

Until she was provoked to use it, it lay dormant. She was not going to question why it surged the way it had when she became aware of the Slayers or why it had exploded when she was connected to both alphas. What she was going to do was take full advantage of it for as long as she had it.

It was her turn to protect the pack, and she would accept no interference from anyone. She was on fire. Her senses clear and honed so sharply she could see the beads of sweat on Corbet's upper lip. Smell the terror on his men. Hear the frantic pump of their hearts forcing more blood into their veins for what they instinctively knew was going to be their last night on earth.

Falon turned to Lucien and said, *I've got this.*

Before her intent registered, she strode fearlessly toward the Slayers. "You want to fuck me, Corbet?" Falon challenged, striding boldly toward the shocked Slayers. "Then come and get me."

Falon! Lucien yelled going after her. She flung her hand back, stopping him.

Damn it, woman! Listen to me.

She shook her head and kept walking. Corbet was hers.

Holy fuck! Rafael hissed. *How can you allow her to do this?* he demanded of his brother.

Have you ever tried to stop her from doing what she's hell-bent on? Fuck!

When Corbet did not respond to her taunt, Falon shouted, "Cowardly, Corbet!" as she emerged from the thick cover of brush and trees.

She approached the tightening circle of battle-ready Slayers surrounding him. As was their custom, they looked like they had just stepped out of thirteenth-century England. Only these boys were armed with automatic weapons instead of swords and arrows. Warily they watched her approach. She smiled when their eyes dipped to her breasts then lower to her hips, and lower still to her smooth mons.

"I am only half Lycan," she purred to Corbet, who ducked behind his men. "There is nothing written that a Slayer cannot lie with a half-Lycan, is there?" She held up her arms in offering. "Come and take me if you are man enough," Falon taunted.

Ten feet separated her from the closest Slayer. When his greedy eyes dropped to her chest, lightning quick, she grabbed him and flung him on his ass with just a flick of her wrist. Placing her bare foot on his chest, she plucked his gun from his hands and tossed it over her shoulder, then kicked him backward into the brush. His screams as Angor tore him apart set the hair on her neck on end. But she didn't let a little thing like that stop her. She was queen bitch, and she was going to wreck shop on these sons of bitches.

She smiled coyly. "Anyone else care to try me?"

Their collective heartbeats rose to a hazardous level.

"You cannot survive all of our bullets," Corbet threatened from the safety of his circle.

"Do you really want to find out?" Falon taunted stepping closer. Just as quickly as she had the first one, Falon grabbed the next closest Slayer and flung him behind her. Like his predecessor, the Slayer became another Berserker chew toy.

Draw Corbet out just another six inches and we'll have a clear shot, Lucien said.

"I don't think you understand who you're dealing with here, Mr.

Corbet," Falon said in a deadly whisper. "I not only have the blood of the two most powerful alphas in the world running through my veins, one of which bears the Eye of Fenrir, but I have powers they do not have." She raised her hands and shoved them toward the Slayers. A sharp gust of wind slammed into them, shoving all of them back several feet. "I have a few more tricks up my sleeve." She laughed. "Well, actually no sleeve at the moment." Falon continued to walk toward them. They continued to back away from her.

"Since I'm feeling a little generous tonight, how about a deal, Mr. Corbet? Come with me, and I'll let your men go."

"Come with me," Corbet countered, "and I will let your paramours go."

"My *paramours* are not negotiable." She raised her hand and pointed to the small part of his head that was visible. "In fact, I've reconsidered. I'm going to kill you and your little friends, too."

"Kill me and my secrets die with me," Corbet taunted.

"I have no interest in your secrets, Corbet."

He laughed. "Not even if it will save the life of your precious Mondragon?"

Falon hesitated a half of a heartbeat. What did he mean?

In that hesitation, Lucien pulled the trigger. His arrow whizzed past her ear and straight into Corbet's throat. The Slayer screamed, grabbing the feathered end. Falon lunged, shifting in midair and diving over the frantic men surrounding Corbet to finish the job. Chaos broke out around her. Her vision narrowed, focusing on one thing: killing Corbet.

Leaping into the circle, she watched with satisfaction as a wide-eyed and staggering Corbet pulled the arrow from his neck. Snarling, Falon leapt toward him. Just as she sunk her fangs into Corbet's chest, he thrust the bloody arrow into her chest. Liquid fire, his

Slayer blood seared her flesh, stopping her cold. Wild, chaotic visions crashed through her. Screams, flames, the death of hundreds.

A mother protecting her child as a savage black wolf tore it apart. *Lucien!*

Falon squeezed her eyes shut, blotting out the terrible vision. The screams. The scent of blood. A mother's desperation to save her child, but knowing she would die, too.

Falon screamed. It was too much.

Of its own volition, her body shifted to human.

Grabbing her by the shoulders, Corbet violently shook her. "He killed my sisters!" Corbet screamed, blood bubbling out of his mouth. "He killed my mother!"

His pain infused her. She understood. She wanted to mourn with him but he was her enemy. She tried to raise her arms to fight him off, but they hung heavy at her sides.

"Corbet drew first blood!" Falon shouted, justifying Lucien's actions. Though in her gut it sickened her. It all sickened her. The destruction of families, for what? Because of a dead king's hatred for wolves.

It was senseless.

Through the blood and grime on his face, Corbet's lips twisted in an evil smile. "And I will draw last blood. An eye for an eye. Now you die!" In powerless horror, Falon watched Corbet open his mouth. Sharp yellow teeth elongated before her eyes just like master Slayer Viktor Salene's had when he tried to claim her. But this time Rafael was not there to save her. Corbet bit her.

Falon screamed. Violent pain sunk deep into her. She screamed again, deeper, agonizing as lightning bolts of power struck through her body. Her strength soared. Grabbing a hank of Corbet's hair, Falon yanked his head back, pulling his vicious teeth from her shoulder. Her eyes met his onyx-colored ones, and in them she saw the horrors of ten lifetimes. He deserved to die more than once.

"Say hello to your uncle for me," Falon whispered in his ear before she snapped his neck. Kicking his body away from her, she grabbed Corbet's sword from its scabbard, and with one vicious thrust, separated his head from his shoulders.

Her heart pounded as adrenaline and power pumped through her.

Sword raised, Falon turned, crying out triumphantly to Lucien and Rafael.

Lucien ran toward her shifting to human just as Rafael shifted behind him.

"Falon!" he screamed, reaching out to her just as a Slayer's blade impaled her from behind. Her body jerked in horrendous pain. Stunned, she caught Lucien's horrified gaze from across the fray. She blinked as blood blurred her vision. In slow motion, she looked down to see the bloody blade of the sword protruding from her belly, then back up into Lucien's terrified eyes.

He got me.

Taking a deep, excruciating breath, she reached around to her back and grasped the hilt, then pulled it free from her body. As her crippled body dropped to its knees, Falon called upon her last bit of strength. She reversed the direction of the blade, and thrust it backward into the gut of the Slayer it belonged to.

As her power dwindled, she dropped the sword and hung her head.

Lucien's furious roar tore through the remaining Slayers, scattering them out of his path.

"Falon!" he roared, leaping across the decapitated bodies that separated them.

With her last bit of strength, she reached out to him. *Luca.*

He caught her in his arms as she collapsed onto the bloody ground.

Twelve

"FALON!" LUCIEN SCREAMED again, catching her as she crumbled to the ground. Rafael snarled viciously behind him even as he and the others fought off the remaining Slayers.

Terror corded in Lucien's belly. "Falon, speak to me!" he shouted, shaking her.

In answer, her heart shuddered violently against her chest, then stumbled to a halt.

"No!" Lucien howled. "No!" Frantic, he looked up to his brother.

Covered in Slayer blood, Rafael dropped to his knees and grabbed one of Falon's hands. "Take the other, Lucien."

As they had moments before, the brothers connected through her. Warmth infused their bodies, but Falon's body did not respond. They squeezed tighter. "Save her!" Rafael shouted at the Eye of Fenrir. It remained cool and quiet. "Traitor!" he hissed. "You will pay for this, mark my words!"

Lucien bit his free arm, severing a vein. Blood spurted in an arch, running down his arm. "Open her mouth," he directed Rafael. As Rafe opened her mouth with his free hand, Lucien pressed his open vein to her lips. Her heart shuddered again, then picked up a shallow, erratic rhythm.

"Falon," Lucien begged. "Please, wake up."

Releasing his hand from hers, he gently rubbed her throat, helping her ingest his blood. But she did not respond. Her heartbeat grew fainter. "Don't you die on me!" Lucien shouted, emotion choking in his words.

Rafael bit his wrist and looked to Lucien, who nodded vigorously. Rafael pressed his wrist to Falon's lips.

The combined bloods of the brothers mingled and dripped down Falon's cheek to the Slayer bite on her shoulder. When the bloods met, her skin flared with heat. Sweat erupted along her skin, slickening it. Her lips paled to white before their eyes and her breathing turned forced and shallow.

"There is something else wrong," Rafael said. Leaning closer, he lifted her eyelid. Falon's deep blue eye had turned nearly black.

"Slayer black magic!" Rafe hissed releasing her. "Corbet's blood is poisoned!"

Chilling dread filled Lucien. This was not happening! His hands shook as he gathered her into his arms. "I need to get her to Talia." He stood and turned toward the Slayer camp. "There were trucks at the Slayer camp. I'm going to take one; it'll be faster."

"I'm right behind you."

With Falon held tightly to his chest, Lucien ran for her life, eating up the few miles between him and a means to get Falon to safety in minutes. The first truck he tried had keys in the ignition.

"I'm going with you," Rafe said opening the passenger door, helping Lucien lay Falon down.

"Stay with the pack," Lucien commanded, shutting the door.

Rafe's hand stayed it. "I love her, too," he said, leaving no room for argument.

Lucien felt his brother's pain, but— "She is mine now. See to the pack." He slammed the door shut, then hopped into the driver's seat and turned the key. He jammed the gas pedal to the floor. As he fishtailed out of the dirt lot, he looked in the review mirror to see his brother watching them drive away.

Falon didn't need Rafe's help. What she needed was Talia. "How the fuck did this happen?" he shouted, banging his fists on the steering wheel. Why? *Why?*

Guilt ate away at him.

It was his fault Falon was on her deathbed. *His fucking fault!* He never should have let her walk out to Corbet like that! She would have beaten the living snot out of him, but he should have insisted. Lucien careened around a corner on two tires, then gunned the engine as the truck came down on all four wheels, and drove like a madman toward the only person he knew who could help him save the woman he loved.

And he did love her. Gods, he loved her! Fiercely. Passionately. Possessively. He loved her in a way he never expected to love a woman. Not just any woman. The most amazing woman he had ever met. That any of his kind had met. She was pure of heart. She was powerful. She was beautiful and brave. And damn it, it was his fault she was dying! His fear that Corbet would reveal his secret had spurned him to shoot before Rafe was ready. Their combined shots would have dropped the bastard! Corbet would not have bitten her, and she would not have been vulnerable to the other Slayer's blade.

He looked down at her pale face. He drove with his left hand; with his right, he stroked Falon's cheek. "I swear to you, Falon, if you survive, I will let you go. I will not stand between you and Rafe if that is what you want." As he said the words, his heart constricted so severely he could not breathe. Life without Falon would be no life at all.

Lucien made it back to Mondragon in record time. He crashed through the gates, grinding to a stop just before the warehouse doors. He grabbed Falon and nearly collided with Talia as she came running outside. "She's been poisoned with Slayer blood! She's dying, Talia! Save her!" he pleaded.

Talia's violet eyes sparked with fear. The pack gathered as Lucien hurried inside with her. "Set her down on the sofa," Talia said quietly.

Lucien did as he was told. Talia knelt beside Falon and felt her brow, then placed her ear to her chest. She touched the ragged bite on her shoulder, then lifted Falon's eyelid. The gathered pack hissed a collective breath. Talia lifted the other lid. The pack stepped back shaking their heads. Just like the right, Falon's left eye was onyx black.

"She is not a Slayer!" Lucien shouted at his pack. "She killed Ian Corbet! It's poison." He dropped to his knees beside Falon and smoothed her damp hair back from her face. He looked expectantly up to Talia's frowning face. "I command you to save her."

"Lucien, it's Corbet blood, the most powerful of all Slayer blood. I don't know—"

"No!" Lucien roared. "I will not hear what you cannot do. Only what you *can* do!"

"She needs a transfusion. From a compatible blood."

"She is not resistant to mine! Take it all! Take my heart if it will save her!"

"Your blood is strong, Lucien, and while it infuses Falon's with power, only her true blood can clear the Slayer poison from her body."

"What the fuck is true blood?"

"True blood comes from her parents or a sibling."

Lucien threw his head back and howled. This could not be! There must be another way!

"Sharia knows!" he said desperately. "She knows everything!"

Talia shook her head. "Sharia has gone north. She cannot help you."

Lucien leaned over Falon's struggling body. Her skin flushed bright red and was hot to the touch. As she continued to struggle for each breath, he moved to the sofa and drew her into his arms. Gently he began to rock her, feeling as helpless as the day his parents were killed. Tears stung his eyes. He buried his face in Falon's damp tangled hair. "Falon," he said hoarsely. "Don't leave me," he begged. "Tell me what to do. I will do anything."

Her heartbeat slowed to barely a blip. Desperate, willing to make the ultimate sacrifice for her if it would save her life, Lucien stood with Falon in his arms and carried her outside to the front of the building. Raising her in his arms toward the half-moon, he begged for her life. "Great Spirit Mother, I have never asked anything of you." Tears blinded him, the words choked in his throat. "I know you can restore life." Lucien dropped to his knees, still holding Falon's dying body toward the sky. "I beg you, take my life for hers. I give it freely!"

Lucien begged repeatedly, promising the Great Spirit Mother anything and everything if she would just grant him this one request. His powerful arms began to shake, but he would not lower Falon. He would not lower her until his prayers were answered.

A warm hand touched his arm. A soothing familiar scent wrapped around Lucien's head. Warmth skittered through his body. Lucien's arms trembled but he kept Falon raised to the Great Spirit Mother. A soft familiar voice spoke from behind him.

"I am Layla, great-great-great-granddaughter of the Great Spirit Mother Singarti. You hold my child in your arms."

Lucien's heart dropped to his gut. Dear Gods!

Half turning, he stared in amazement at the familiar face. "How?" he croaked, not believing she was here or the miracle of her words.

"There is no time to explain, Lucien. We must hurry."

Emotion he could not describe filled his heart. He lowered his arms, and through his tears, he turned fully to the small Lycan. Layla was as beautiful and serene as the day Thomas Corbet took her from Vulkasin. He saw so much of Falon in the stubborn set of her jaw and the confidence that radiated from her. But what touched him most was the hope in Layla's warm brown eyes. Gently he handed Falon to her mother. She cradled Falon to her chest, turned, and limped into the building. Lucien stood and followed close behind.

Talia ran to Layla, choking back sobs of joy, through her tears. The pack closed around her, making welcoming sounds of happiness. Lucien steadied the medicine woman. She walked on a raw stump of a leg. The price for her freedom that day.

Helping her carry Falon up the three flights of stairs to his bedroom, they placed Falon down on the bed. Layla spoke to Talia in a language Lucien partly understood, giving Talia a list of herbs and such to gather.

Layla pointed to Lucien's sword on the wall. "Take it down."

Lucien grabbed it and handed it to her, hilt first. She shook her head and held out her arm. "You make the first cut, Lucien." He did not hesitate.

Layla winced but squeezed the gaping slash on her wrist urging the blood to flow freely. She began to chant a low soothing healing prayer. Instead of giving Falon her blood by mouth, as he expected, Layla dripped her blood into the bite on Falon's shoulder. Falon's skin sizzled on contact, the fumes creating a putrid death scent. Layla's chant changed cadence. It became louder, more powerful, demanding the blood poison to leave her daughter's body. Then Layla dripped a line of blood from the bite wound along Falon's chest down her belly to the sword wound there. As before, on contact, Falon's skin sizzled. Layla's chants heightened in fervor and pitch.

Talia entered the room with a boiling pot of water effusing aromatic scents. Layla's chanting rose in volume as she pressed her wrist to Falon's white lips. Talia sprinkled herbs on Falon's body as she chanted a different prayer. For hours, the two women chanted, cleansing Falon with herbs and repeating the blood ceremony. Helplessly, Lucien watched Layla's skin slowly pale with each blood transfer. When her knees gave way, Lucien caught her.

"Layla, you have lost too much blood."

She shook her head. "As you, I would give Falon my last drop." She pushed off Lucien and continued to chant and transfuse her blood.

"Luca," Rafael's deep voice softly said from the doorway.

Wearily, Lucien raised his eyes to his bother's. They mirrored Lucien's fear and his love for the woman dying on his bed.

"Get some rest. I'll stay with Falon while you do."

Lucien shook his head and looked back at Falon's struggling body. He was not going anywhere. Nor did he raise opposition when Rafe pulled up a chair on the opposite side of the bed and took Falon's other hand. He would not begrudge his brother his place here if it would help Falon.

Lucien never once pulled his gaze from Falon's still body. Waiting, praying to her God and to his for just the slightest sign of improvement. Her breathing was so ragged, and her skin so pale that he thought each breath she took would be her last. Just when he thought he had lost her, she fought for another. He squeezed her hand in his, wishing he could infuse her with his strength.

Hours passed. Dawn's gray fingers parted over the eastern foothills announcing a new day. Though exhaustion claimed them all, neither brother left Falon's side, as Layla vigilantly continued to chant and give Falon her blood.

When the sun was high in the sky, Lucien's heart fluttered. Was that— He looked expectantly at Falon's hand in his. Did her fingers just move? He looked to Rafe's alerted face. Had he felt it, too?

"Angel face," Lucien said softy. "Can you hear me?"

FALON'S BLOOD RAGED with fire. Thousands of sharp molten blades tore into her. Her bones ached, her innards boiled, the pain so excruciating, she prayed for death.

Rafael's warmth and Lucien's voice echoed far away, hidden behind a soft chanting that took her back to her childhood. She wanted to call out to it, to tell it she was here! Not to let her go.

But she was locked inside a terrible jail cell, suspended in the black abyss of her nightmares. The same gray souls that followed her in her real world and dream world cried outside of her cell, no longer aimless but loud and demanding, begging for release. Who were they? Why did they follow her into her dreams and even her consciousness? They were there the night she met Rafael, looking sadly at her for help. But the sinister energy she realized was that of the Slayer Viktor Salene chased them away. Forbidding them to contact her. Why? When they wanted her help? Who were they?

Flames licked at her belly and her neck. Wild, wicked laughter pierced her ears.

"You are one of us, Falon Corbet!" Ian Corbet's decapitated head shouted for the entire world to hear.

His uncle, Edward, whom she had killed when he would have killed Rafael, held his own severed head in his arms, pointing at her.

"I lied! You are Slayer! Mondragon and Vulkasin will skin you alive
when they learn the truth!"

Hundreds of severed Slayer heads laughed at her. *We will meet
again at the rising! And you will fight with us. Not against us!*

"No!" she screamed.

She was Lycan! Not Slayer. *Never* Slayer.

"*Buniq,*" a soft familiar voice said. "You are safe."

Mama?

"Yes, my love, I am here. Shhh, sleep."

Falon fell back into the black hole of unconsciousness only to be
shaken awake by the shrill cries of the gray souls. They swarmed
around her barred cell, crying for release.

What do you want? she shouted at them.

Release us! they begged. *Release us from this purgatory. Release
us and we will stand beside you and fight.*

Fight?

*Slayers. We are thousands strong. Release us and we will die again
for you.*

I don't know how! she screamed, covering her ears and closing her
eyes.

Fire burned her shoulder. It stung her belly. The stench of burned
flesh assaulted her nostrils.

Lucien!

Warm hands stroked her cheek.

I'm here, love.

Her heart swelled. He had not abandoned her. What of Rafa?

I am here, too, her first love's deep voice soothed from the left.

I love you both. She sobbed.

More fire flared in her wounds.

She screamed.

"Steady, love," Lucien whispered against her cheek. "The last of the poison is being extracted."

Falon fell back to that place that was neither consciousness nor the dream world but somewhere in between.

"Her blood is clean," the soft voice said. "She needs your strength now, Mondragon."

A drop of warm blood touched her lips. Falon licked it. *Lucien.*

Take my blood, Falon. It will give you strength.

He slipped his big hand behind her head and lifted it slightly to his wrist, pressing it to her lips. She drank eagerly from him.

Liquid energy, it infused her body with warmth and vitality.

The ache in her blood began to subside. Her body began to cool and the gray souls evaporated, but the longing in their eyes would haunt her forever. Satiated, Falon released him. Lucien lowered her head and caressed her cheek with his fingers. Falon exhaled deeply. As she did, she reached up to his hand and pressed it against her cheek.

Now Vulkasin, the soft voice said.

Lucien's anger flittered through Falon. *No!*

You do her an injustice for refusing.

What injustice? She is better now, Lucien argued.

Had she not had the blood of Vulkasin and Mondragon in her veins she would have died where she fell.

Falon moaned. Her head hurt.

Make the cut, Rafael, the soft voice commanded.

Warm drops of blood plopped on her lips.

Rafa.

Take my blood, Falon, he softly said, touching her cheek. *Take it all.*

Her veins warmed as Rafa's blood infused hers with its strength. Her headache vanished. The shimmer of the three bloods fusing, then recirculating, infused her cells with vitality.

An incredible sense of contentment shimmered through her. Knowing she was safe, Falon allowed exhaustion to claim her.

FALON'S EYES FLUTTERED open. The steady thud of a heart beat beneath her cheek. She realized she lay on a bare chest. Lucien's clean woodsy scent cradled her. The room was dark, save for the soft glow cast by a few candles burning on the nightstand.

Her stomach growled. Strong arms tightened around her. She looked up into two fiery gold eyes. Slowly she smiled. Shocked, Falon watched those fierce golden eyes fill with tears.

"No, Luca," she whispered reaching toward his lips. "Don't cry."

When their lips met, lightning struck. The shock was so extreme, Falon cried out, pulling away from Lucien. Wide-eyed, she stared at him. He reached out a hand and cupped the back of her head, bringing her lips to his again. She stiffened, anticipating the shock of the contact again, but this time, warmth infused her.

She melted into his kiss as his fingers clasped her head, and his other arm tightened around her. She felt the wild staccato of his heartbeat pulse through her. Tears stung her eyes.

"Falon," he said hoarsely. "I can feel your heartbeat running through me."

"That's because you have stolen my heart."

He grinned. "It's about damn time."

She clung tightly to him as her weird dreams surfaced and prayed that they were just that, dreams.

Thirteen

"HOW DO YOU feel?" Lucien asked, tracing his fingers across her lips.

Falon closed hers eyes, pushing her dreams aside. She was alive and would rejoice in that. And the man who saved her. "Like I've been run over by a train. What happened?"

His darkened eyes caught hers. "What do you remember?"

Falon closed her eyes and slowly exhaled. "The last thing I remember was holding hands with you and Rafael." Her eyes flashed open with a sudden sense of dread. "Rafael? Did I dream he was here?"

Lucien's lips tightened but he nodded. "He was here."

Falon exhaled. "And you permitted that?"

"I would have done anything to save you, Falon."

Her tension loosened. "Something happened to change your feelings about Rafe. Tell me."

He shrugged, looking over her shoulder. "Your words are beginning to sink in."

He smiled when she gasped and looked at her. "I'm tired of the hatred that has been eating at me all of these years. It's time to put it aside, prepare for the rising, and focus on Slayer annihilation."

Speechless, Falon's jaw hung open. Lucien slipped two fingers beneath it and gently shut it. "Don't get me wrong, Falon. I will never welcome Rafe with open arms. But he is my brother and the fact that he has chosen another mate, and will honor that choice or die, gives me confidence he will not try to come between us." His eyes narrowed. "Because if he does, I will kill him."

The reminder that Rafael would soon belong to another gut-punched her.

Lucien's lips tightened. "I know how you feel about him, Falon. I wished you didn't. But as he is making a life with another, so, too, will we make a life together."

She willed the tears to go away. Her love for Rafael would never die—that Lucien accepted that gave her hope. But hope of what? Struggling to make him understand what she didn't even understand herself, she licked her dry lips. "I know it must be hard for you, Lucien. It would be hard for me. But there is something about the three of us. Back there, with the Slayers, touching you and touching Rafa at the same time, it was amazing. Power infused me, Luca. Power like I have never felt before. After that bullet came out of me, I felt invincible—"

He shook her slightly, his features fierce. "But you weren't invincible, Falon! How could you go after Corbet like that?"

She closed her eyes as it all came flooding back. In hindsight she had been foolish to risk her life and the lives of Vulkasin. But at the time she truly felt she was bulletproof. "Corbet stabbed me with your arrow. That's the last thing I remember."

"He stabbed you, then bit you. Then you were stabbed by another Slayer." His voice wavered with emotion. "The stab wounds weren't

the problem; it was Corbet's poisoned blood that nearly killed you."
He lowered his voice. "Falon, I almost lost you."

The naked fear in his voice moved her. Was there hope for them
after all? "I'm sorry," she said softly.

She rubbed her forehead with the palm of her hand as she tried
to muddle through what had happened to her. "I had really weird
dreams. I dreamt of Layla. That she was my mother."

Lucien sat up and scooted against the headboard, bringing Falon
with him. His arms cradled her as she would their babe. "I couldn't
save you, Falon. I tried. Talia tried." His voice choked with emotion.
"But there was nothing we could do. The poison in your blood was
killing you. The only way to cure you was to replace your blood with
true blood."

"True blood?"

"Blood of your parents or a sibling. I begged the Great Spirit
Mother to intervene. She sent me Layla. Who miraculously *is* your
mother."

Dumbfounded, Falon stared at Lucien. "How can that be?" As
the questions piled up in her head, emotion overloaded her. She had
a mother and she was alive! Love and wonder sprang into her heart
but riding its heels was more than a flicker of resentment. Why had
she abandoned her? What kind of mother would do that? "Where is
she?" Falon made to move from Lucien. Gently he pulled her back
into his arms.

"She nearly died from her blood loss, Falon. She's been in a deep
sleep since last night. Talia's with her."

"I want to see her." She wanted answers.

"As she does you, but first—" Lucien kissed her nose then slid
from the bed. "I have something for you." He moved from the bed
and walked over to his desk.

As Falon waited for him, conflicting emotions crashed together inside her. While she gloried in the news her mother was not only alive but a revered Lycan, she could not shake the anger that bubbled just beneath the surface of her happiness. She had been abandoned as a young child. Left to the broken-down foster system, never knowing who her parents were. It messed with Falon, as it messed with a lot of kids. What was she supposed to do now? Welcome her mother with open arms? Let bygones be bygones?

Oddly, a part of her wanted to do just that. But the suspicious Lycan part cautioned her to take it one step at a time. "How is she, Lucien? I mean, dear God, she cut off her foot to get out of that trap. Did she say anything about Thomas Corbet?"

"Her leg is healing, and she spoke only of her love for you."

For the moment, Falon chose to be cautiously optimistic. She would set aside her resentment for now. Maybe she wasn't abandoned. Maybe she had been kidnapped and Layla had been searching for her all these years. She allowed a small part of her heart to hope, and with that hope, a profound sense of belonging filled her. It was as deep as the feeling she had when she discovered she was Lycan. Of finally fitting in, no longer an orphan. She had a mother! Who despite her past, loved her enough to reveal herself and save her. Urgency filled her. So many questions only her mother could answer.

Quietly she watched Lucien in all of his naked glory open the top drawer of his desk and remove a long, carved wooden box. A new urgency filled her. To reunite with the man her body craved above all others.

When he turned, her gaze slid down the hard planes of his chest to the defined muscles of his abdomen, then lower. Slowly she raised her eyes to his. Their gazes caught and held. Falon's breathing hitched up several notches. Her breasts grew heavy and her nipples tightened. Lucien's dragon was on the rise. Her blood warmed exponentially, as did the sensitive folds between her thighs. "I—my body craves you, Lucien. Will it ever stop?" she asked breathlessly as he moved effortlessly around the foot of the bed and back to her.

When he sat down on the edge of the bed, his eyes continued to hold hers. Slowly he shook his head. "We are blood bound, Falon."

"It's more than that, Lucien. This feeling is more like lust on steroids. I can't stop wanting you."

"Whatever it is, it can never be severed."

She leaned up to his lips. "I never want it to be." Before the Slayer attack, the realization may have shocked her. Now? Anything less seemed wrong.

He smiled against her lips then cleared his throat. "Pay attention before I forget what I want to say."

Reluctantly Falon moved away from his lips. But she set her hand high on his warm thigh, and Lucien groaned. "Falon," he said sternly.

"You would think since a girl almost died she could get a little sympathy!"

He grinned and shook his head. "I'm the one who needs a little sympathy," he complained, looking down at his thickening erection.

Falon crossed her arms and flounced back into the pillows.

Lucien laughed at her pouty face and set the box down on her belly. "That's beautiful," she said, admiring the intricate carvings on the smooth ebony wood lid. "What do those symbols mean?"

"This one," Lucien said, pointing to the intricate swirling dragon-head design, the same symbol carved into the hilt of Lucien's sword, "is the insignia of my mother's people, Mondragon. This one"—he pointed to an abstract carving of a snarling wolf—"is the insignia of my father's people. Vulkasin."

"Rafe has that in the tattoo on his shoulder." Warmth surged through her when she thought back to the first time she had seen

Rafe's tattoo. He had been bloody and half-naked. Her eyes rose to Lucien's when she remembered the first time she had gotten a good look at his dragon.

"As I bear the dragon." Lucien smiled slyly.

Heat shimmered through her. "Yes, you certainly do."

"When my mother gifted Vulkasin with twin sons, my father had Hector fashion a gift for her." He opened the box and withdrew an intricately woven brushed gold band. In the center, a dragon and a wolf were artistically smelted facing each other, and joined by a heart-shaped blood ruby. It was stunning in its primal simplicity.

Lucien took Falon's left hand and placed the ring on her ring finger. He held it there and looked deeply into her eyes. He cleared his throat and huskily said, "Lycan do not marry as humans do, our marks are our vow, our bond. Many Lycan choose a mate, but very few find their true mate, Falon. In my mother, my father found his true mate as she found him to be hers. They shared a great love." His voice caught but he continued, "My mother cherished this ring. She was wearing it the day she died. On our tenth birthday, Rafe got the ring my father gave her the day they exchanged marks and she left me this one, on the condition that should I be so fortunate to find my true mate, I give it to her as a testament of my love. I have waited for thirty-four years to give this to the woman I love." His eyes held hers. "We have been through more in the last weeks than most people go through in a lifetime. Each hurdle we encountered, we jumped together. Each time we landed our bond forged stronger. Almost losing you made me realize, despite the circumstances that brought you to me, you are the only one for me." He paused, then said, "I would be honored if you would wear it, as a symbol of my love for you, *espejo de mi alma.*" He smiled. "You are much more than the woman I love; you are the mirror of my soul. We are one. The same."

Falon could not utter a word. Lucien's words stunned her. Never in her wildest dreams did she expect such a profound declaration. Yes, Lucien was passionate. But love? He had told her he was not capable of such an emotion. But she knew he was capable of deep feelings. Anger. Vengeance. Certainly lust. But also loyalty. Her heart hammered painfully against her rib cage. And love. Despite his denials, he loved fiercely. It showed in everything he did. He was fiercely devoted to his pack. He had loved his parents, and she knew despite his resentment, he loved his brother. But after all that his heart had endured, did he truly have the capacity to love her? Love her the way she loved his brother? Love her the way she—loved him? Her body trembled violently with her realization. God help her, she loved everything about him.

Falon did not have words to express the depth of her emotion. Even if she could express to him in words how she felt, her throat was so clogged with emotion, she could not speak. Big, fat tears plopped down her cheeks. All she could do was nod.

He slid the ring down her finger. He brought her hand to his lips and kissed the ring and her finger. "Whatever you want," he said huskily, "I'll give it to you. There is nothing I would not do for you. Nothing." He brushed his lips across hers. "You hold my life in your hands, angel face. Treat me gently."

"Luca," she breathed, slipping her arms around his neck. "I will never hurt you. I will never betray you. I love you."

Smiling tenderly, he said softly, "I make the same promise to you, Falon."

Their lips met in a slow, soul-searing kiss. A kiss that promised. A kiss that gave. A kiss that took. The kiss of true mates.

Falon lost herself in the kiss. Reveled in it, wanted it to last forever.

But Lucien gently ended it.

"You need to eat, Falon."

"Later," she breathed tightening her arms around his neck.

He smiled against her lips. "And you need a bath."

She stiffened and pulled away from him.

His eyes shone brightly. "You haven't had a bath in three days."

"Are you saying I stink?"

"Like a rotten egg."

He swooped her up into his arms and set her on one of the chairs at the table. He uncovered a tray with several bowls of aromatic stew, bread, and fresh fruit.

"Eat, and I'll start your bath."

Fifteen minutes later, her belly full, Falon sat chin deep in a velvety warm bubble bath. She had brushed her teeth but was too lazy to wash her hair. She just wanted to soak in her food-induced coma. She had not realized she was so hungry until she finished the second bowl of stew. The warm water and soothing bath salts were so relaxing she just wanted to slip beneath the bubbles and sleep for a week until her strength was fully restored.

Water sluiced against her chest in slow waves. Opening her eyes, Falon watched Lucien step naked into the tub. His bright eyes caught hers. "No monkey business until you've had a few days' rest."

He moved behind her and pulled her between his thighs. Mercilessly, she leaned into him, smiling as his cock came alive against her back. "No monkey business?"

"Falon," he said hoarsely. "Don't move."

She rubbed slightly against him. "Don't move like that?"

"Like that," he ground out.

He reached to the side of the tub and turned the faucet on. Warm water poured from the spout. He maneuvered her toward it and pulled the handheld piece out. "Put your head back," he softly commanded. She obeyed, and he soaked her hair with warm water. Pushing the hand faucet aside, Lucien grabbed the bottle of shampoo and squeezed a glob onto his hands. Working it into a thick lather, he dug his fingers into her scalp, and slowly began to massage her.

"Ohh, Lucien," she purred, closing her eyes. "That feels so good." The sensation of his fingers against her scalp sent tingles along her skin. Her nipples tightened. Arching, Falon dug her fingers into Lucien's hard thighs. His cock thickened behind her.

"Falon," he warned.

"I'm trying to relax."

"Try harder."

And she did, try harder. To relax. And finally loosened completely against him, enjoying his attention and the sensation of his hard warmth surrounding her. As intent as she was on the sensuality of having her hair washed by one of the two men she loved, Lucien had a purpose. He scrubbed her head until her scalp tingled.

As he began to rinse her hair, Falon thought of Rafael. The other man she loved. The man who had saved her life twice, just as Lucien had. She owed them both much more than she could ever repay. Not only for her life, but for their love. For giving her a home, whether Vulkasin or Mondragon, where she felt welcome. A place she belonged.

Her body shimmered with excitement as she remembered the infusion of power when she was connected to both men. How could she forget? Was that what Sharia had meant by the power of the three?

Were the three of them to join forces at the dawn of the rising to defeat the Slayers? She had felt invincible. Like she could take on all of clan Corbet and prevail. But that wasn't the case. Ian Corbet had poisoned her. She was strong, but not invincible. But that did not mean she could not learn from her experience. Next time she'd wear armor.

Lucien's big hands sluiced along her shoulders to her arms. The velvety warm slickness of the water sensualizing his touch. "Mmm," she moaned, arching toward him, wanting his hands in other places. Ignoring his own rule, Lucien lowered his lips to her ear and ran his tongue around the outer shell. "Falon, you are a shameless hussy."

"You make me that way," she panted, tilting her head, offering her neck. He took the bait, sliding his lips and teeth along her sultry skin, before settling at the juncture of her neck and shoulder. He kissed her, then sucked at her vital vein. His cock thickened behind her, digging into her spine.

As Lucien's hand slid up her belly to cup her rosy breasts, Falon pressed her head into his shoulder, giving herself to him. Her thighs parted as warm water swirled around her sensitive lips. Her beast roared to life. "Luca," she panted. "Make the ache go away."

He growled and nipped her neck.

"Please."

He stood lifting her with him. Dripping wet he carried her from the bathroom to the bed. He tossed her onto the linens. The clean scent of fresh sheets tickled her nose. She smiled and moved back into them. "Did you change the sheets yourself, Luca?"

His eyes blazed. "Maybe."

Falon laughed and backed away from him as he crawled on all fours toward her. His glistening cock and balls had swollen to gigantic. The heady scent of his lust swirled wickedly around her. "Lucien," she breathed, licking her lips.

His blazing eyes devoured her. "Falon," he said huskily, stalking her.

"Make it stop."

He grabbed her foot, slowly wrapping his fingers around her ankle, and pulled. She swallowed hard. Her musky sex scent was so pungent, she did not doubt the men downstairs were probably nailing anything that moved. She pressed her hand between her thighs

and cupped herself. The touch was too much. She gasped, shocked
at the depth of the sensation. Her fingers were wet with her honey.
Opening her eyes, she stared into Lucien's deep, passionate ones.

His breathing escalated. A thin sheen of perspiration glossed her
flushed skin. Bringing her foot to his lips, he licked her instep. Sensation riveted up her leg, spearing her womb. Her eyelids became
heavy. "Touch yourself again," Lucien commanded.

Sliding her fingers down her belly to her smooth mons, Falon
moaned as delicious prickles of sensation swept along the path of her
fingertips.

"Show me your secrets," he growled.

Swallowing hard, she nodded, and slipped her fingers between
her swollen lips, then slowly spread them in offering.

"God, Falon," he groaned. "Your cunt is so pink and so damn
wet, I can't wait to taste it." He licked her instep, then her ankle. His
eyes never left hers. She moaned loudly as he slid his tongue along
the sensitive skin behind her knee, then along the inside of her thigh.
Her body quivered when he blew hot breath across her sensitive lips.
His hands pushed hers away, his thumbs sliding up her seam opening her succulent flesh. "Baby," he moaned, "I'm going to make you
ache until you can't stand it." He pressed his lips to hers and licked a
deep swath into her.

The ache was already too much. Like a stack of cards, she folded.

"Lucien," she moaned, digging her fingers into his hair. "Make it
stop." She pushed into his face. He nipped at her clit, gently licking
the sting away. It drove her crazy. His feral tongue swirled around her
lips, suckling them. His thumb pushed back the sensitive hood of her
clit, gently brushing it, stimulating it to erect.

She moaned and purred, growled and screamed. All while he
slowly took his time, piling one ache on top of another, until her
body was one pulsating, aching mess.

"Lucien! Please," she begged, pulling his hair.

He licked a long swath along her aching pussy to her clit. As he suckled her sensitive nub, he slid a thick finger into her. "Lu-ci-en," she keened. The tension so intense tears burned her eyes. The lining of her pussy clenched so tightly around his finger, he moaned against her, the vibration sending shock waves to her core.

Wildly, her body bucked and twisted against his lethal lips. With agonizing slowness, his thick finger sluiced in and out of her in a sensual cadence. He was driving her mad. Pushing her to the edge. And just as she was about to take flight, he withdrew from her.

"Lucien!" she cried, sitting up and grabbing his shoulders. The smoldering heat in his eyes answered hers. "Don't stop!"

He growled, his wild, feral scent as intoxicating as his touch. His body shook with passionate rage. His dark fallen-angel face, tightened in sexual tension, stared at her with such intense need, she was afraid of disappointing him. She never wanted to hurt this man.

"I love you," she breathed.

His eyes flared, showing her a glimpse into his battered soul. Rising above her, cupping her head in his big hands, he brought her lips to his. "We are one," he said roughly, then filled her with his velvet-sheathed steel.

She hung suspended in that one perfect moment of poignant awareness, caught up in a perfect storm of sensation, unable to move, unable to speak, unable to express in words what she felt.

So, she showed him.

Fourteen

FALON'S BODY WAS wild, erotic, giving. Lucien's head and heart spun out of control. Selflessly she gave herself to him. Selfishly he took all that she offered, and then demanded more. She was everything to him. The sun, the moon, the stars, and beyond. Her low, throaty cries of pleasure each time he sunk into her inspired him to go deeper.

Her silky smooth skin sweltered beneath his touch. Her tight sheath possessively fisted him. Her heartbeat mirrored the chaotic rhythm of his. He wanted deeper into her, so deep he touched her soul as she had touched his.

"Luca," she reverently gasped, as if she were paying homage to him. In truth, it was he who worshipped her. Her hands slid up his arms before they locked around his neck, pulling his heart to hers.

"Falon," he said hoarsely just as his lips captured hers in a deep, spiraling kiss. He loved kissing her. Her lips were lush, soft, and always receptive to his. His tongue caressed hers in the same slow cadence his hips rocked into hers. Her body trembled violently beneath his. He swept the tears from her cheeks with his fingertips.

"No tears, angel face," he shushed against her lips. But he understood the overwhelming onslaught of emotion. He felt it himself. It terrified him. But he was in too deep to retreat now. Falon was his. She had accepted his mother's ring. Sworn her love and loyalty to him. His beast snarled possessively. Falon's answered. He felt it, there, just beneath the surface, lurking just as his was.

Electricity thrummed through her body, straight to his cock. He was close. Falon's body trembled. Her liquid muscles quivered like live conduits around him. He groaned as his balls tightened. She arched into him. "Luca," she cried, emotion clogging her throat. "I can't—do this—" She gasped. "It's too much."

He swirled his hips into hers, reveling in the way her body responded as if he worked her from a remote control. She choked back another sob, her head thrashing back and forth.

"You can," he encouraged her. "You are the bravest person I know." He kissed her, silencing her sobs.

Her body met his with equal fervor. Wrapping her legs around his waist, she dug her nails into his shoulders and held on for dear life. He was on the verge of total destruction when he felt the first waves of her orgasm tear through her and into him. He threw his head back, baring his teeth, waiting, until—she arched into him again as a feral cry ripped from her lips and she bit him. The pain and pleasure of her bite shimmered into his blood with blinding intensity. He let go and, as his body released into her, he sunk his teeth into her vital vein. Her low primal growls of pained pleasure matched his own. Completely connected, they crashed against each other in a euphoric explosion of love and lust.

Long moments later, still connected, Lucien held Falon's convulsing body in his arms. She had not stopped crying since they came so violently together. Her tears stymied him. These weren't tears of joy; they were desperate, sad tears.

He held her tightly to him, smoothing her damp hair back from her face, kissing her tears away, softly crooning to her as he would a baby. It only seemed to upset her more. He was unequipped in this area. But even if he were versed in what went on in a woman's head, he was afraid to go there. Afraid she had changed her mind and was now feeling sorry for the killing blow she was about to land him.

He sneered at himself. He was a great alpha. He had slain hundreds of Slayers, yet he feared Falon's tears.

He exhaled and gently began to pull away from her.

"No!" she cried, grabbing his shoulders.

"Did I hurt you?"

She cried harder, shaking her head, rubbing her face into the crook of his neck. He closed his eyes and pulled her into his arms.

"Did I say something wrong?"

She shook her head.

Lucien slowly exhaled, silently counted to ten, then said, "Throw me a bone here, woman."

"You'll be mad."

"We just made the most incredible love, and you're crying your eyes out. Either way, I'm not feeling so hot."

She sniffed back her tears, wiping her nose on his biceps.

"Thank you for that," he said grimly.

She started crying again.

"Falon! I was kidding. Blow your nose all over me if you want. Just for the love of Singarti, tell me why you're crying." His tone lowered to gentle. "Please, baby, tell me what's upsetting you."

She nodded and sniffed back the new tears. "I'm afraid."

"Not of the big bad wolf. You have him eating out of your hand."

She managed a ghost of a smile. "Lucien, the Slayers, they are so hell-bent on destroying us. I can't stop thinking of what will happen if we can't defeat them. My heart has been irreparably broken as it is, I could not bear losing you, too. And now that my mother is here, what if she abandons me again? I love Mondragon and Vulkasin. I just can't bear to lose anyone else. I don't know what to do."

Guilt assailed him. How much of her pain was he responsible for? Most of it. It made him feel like shit. He would move heaven to undo the heartache she had suffered because of him. Had he known about Mara before the council meeting, he would have walked away, never forcing Rafe's hand. Falon loved him. He loved her. Did that not count for something? Did it matter that Mara was a Slayer? Lucien told himself it didn't. What was done was done. To go back would cause more pain and heartache. He would let it lie.

But as far as the rising? He smiled. "There is only one thing we can do."

Her moist blue eyes looked trustingly up at him. It broke his heart to see such trust in them. He didn't deserve it. "What is that?"

"Win."

"Lucien, it will take all of us coming together to fight as one."

"And so we shall."

Her heart thumped against his chest. "Will you stand beside your brother?"

Lucien's temper flared. It always came back to Rafe with her!

He could not help the jealousy that sprang up every time Falon mentioned his name. Brother or not, he knew she loved him, and that her heart had been "irreparably damaged" from losing him.

God, how he hated that Rafe stood between them. He would give his right arm to possess the power to erase Rafe from her heart, but not even Rafe's death would keep his brother's shadow from their bed.

Still, he'd been a fool to think he couldn't love Falon so long as she loved his brother. Little had he known the depths his emotions would go for her. Or her for him. She loved him. He felt it in every-thing she did. She loved him completely, and unless he wanted to throw away the best thing that had ever happened to him, be the fool he was damn good at being, he would accept her feelings for his brother, and accept that she loved him, too.

It was enough. More than enough. He had her physical heart, and he owned her soul.

"I will do whatever is necessary to live to see the rising of the sun the day after the Blood Moon rising."

"I hope I do not have to remind you of your vow."

Lucien's resolve solidified. "I told you earlier, your words are sink-ing in. I'm trying hard to move forward but that part of me will take time. I know what must be done. I will see it done." He kissed the tip of her nose. "I won't let you down."

"I believe you."

"Good. Now go wash your face and get dressed. Mondragon demands their alpha show herself."

"I want to see them, too, but I hope they understand I must speak to my mother first."

"Of course they will. They were excited though cautious when she revealed herself. When she saved your life, her stock went way up. She is as wise a healer as Sharia, and an asset to any pack. For your sake, I hope she stays. But if you find you don't want her here, I will demand she leave."

"That's good to know because I have a lot of questions only she can answer. Plus I've had some crazy dreams, I know they have some-thing to do with the rising. I hope she can tell me what it all means."

The hair on his arms spiked. "What kind of dreams?"

Falon ran her fingers through her damp, mussed hair, twirling a strand around her index finger and thumb. Her arched brows butted together in consternation. "Of aimless gray souls following me." She raised her beautiful blue eyes to him. "I even see them in real life. The night I met Rafe they were everywhere, begging me for something. They scare me."

Lucien stilled. Could it be she spoke of the ghost walkers? Those Lycan souls who had not crossed over?

He rubbed his hands up and down her cold arms. "Do they speak to you?"

"No, well, not really, they just kind of exude sad energy. But I know they want something from me. Not the dark energy that scares them away, but from me specifically."

"How many are there?"

"Hundreds. Maybe a thousand." She looked at him. "Do you know what they are?"

He nodded. "Humans have urban legends, Lycan have them, too. In this case, what you are describing are mythical ghost walkers."

He felt the hair rise on Falon's arms. "Mythical as in not real?"

"No one really knows. Supposedly they're harmless as they are, but the myth says they can be restored to life by the blood that slew them."

"Who are they?"

"Lycan slain by the Corbet bloodline."

Falon gasped.

Lucien shook his head. "It's a myth, Falon. There is no way to raise the dead. If there were, my parents would be standing beside me right this minute."

Her eyes glittered with unshed tears. "Luca," she said softly, and rising up on her knees, she slipped a hand around his neck. "I wish I had known them." She brushed her lips gently across his.

"They would have welcomed you with open arms." Lucien grasped her chin with his hand and pulled away just enough to look her in the eye. "My greatest regret was not fighting past Rafe to protect my mother that day."

"Had you made it out there, Lucien, you would have died with your parents."

"At least I would have died trying. I live with that guilt every day."

"Set it down, Luca. It's what your mother and father wanted." She brushed her fingertips across his lips. "It is what I would want of our sons if that situation ever presented itself."

Emotion kicked him in the gut. "Ours sons?" He nipped at her finger. "I will protect them with my life."

"As will I. As did your parents."

With her words and his realization, a little more of Lucien's guilt and anger washed away. "You're going to turn me into a girl with all of your love talk."

Falon laughed. "I seriously doubt that. You are a deeply emotional man, Lucien. Your anger has been the smoke screen for how deeply you truly feel, how much you truly love. It makes you stronger in my eyes. Not weaker."

He growled low, liking her praise, and moved off the bed. "Get dressed. Mondragon awaits."

FALON SLOWLY DRESSED. Lucien watched with hungry eyes as she decided on a black cotton dress that laced up the front. As she was tying the laces into a bow, Lucien cleared his throat. She looked up at him and smiled. He handed her a pair of doeskin knee-high moccasins. They were beaded around the sewn edges with two feathers, one gold and one black, hanging from a beaded-leather strap at the back of the top seam.

"They're gorgeous."

Lucien grinned as she took them. "I thought you might like them."

Falon hurried and slipped them on. They fit perfectly. "Where did you get them?"

"Mondragon has many talents. They are a combined effort of many, all made with you in mind."

Falon shook her head, looped her arms around his neck, and kissed him long and hard. He had not dressed and his dragon was not above getting another workout. Falon stroked him. He hissed in a breath pulling away from her. She laughed and moved to a safe place in the bathroom. "I'm going to freshen up while you put that bad boy away."

Within minutes, Falon and Lucien made their way downstairs. Halfway down, Falon felt the excited happiness of the pack. Men's voices discussing the merits of one weapon over another, women chattering away about babies and recipes. Joachim's deep laughter filtered up to Falon. "Joachim is better?" she asked Lucien.

"Talia is an amazing healer. But just as amazing is the fact that Hector has fashioned him a most unique prosthetic. Wait until you see it."

As they descended the last few steps, Mondragon cheered loudly as Falon made her first appearance in three days. Those pesky tears threatened to spill again. Damn, her emotions were off-the-chart crazy. The full moon was not for another two weeks. But she wondered, despite the emotional upheaval, if her period was coming. She had noticed earlier the essence of her scent was stronger. Her breasts were more sensitive than usual and felt heavier. When Lucien touched them, she didn't know whether to demand he suck them or leave them alone. It hurt so good when he touched them. Maybe it was just a Lycan thing. Or maybe since she had put on a few pounds, her body was coming around.

Falon shivered in realization. If her cycle was beginning to recover from her unintentional starvation diet, then she would be able to conceive . . . She looked up at Lucien's smiling face. He grinned happily down at her. Her heart ached with emotion. Lucien would make a good father. She knew it intuitively. He had lit up when she talked of their sons. But how odd it felt to think of Lucien as the father of her child when she had known with a certainty Rafael would be the one to sire all of her children.

Her heart squeezed with bittersweet pain. Oh, Rafa. Even now you court your chosen one. I have felt your distance. And while I understand it, I will not lie and say it doesn't pain me to envision you with another.

She bit her lip. She could not bear to think of her beloved Rafa making love to another woman. Her gaze rose to Lucien's to find the light had gone out of his smile. Guilt swept through her.

He knew where her thoughts had gone. "I'll leave you to your thoughts."

She reached a hand out to him. "Lucien." The last thing she wanted to do was hurt this man. But she could not help where her thoughts strayed.

But he stalked away from her.

Surrounded by Mondragon, Falon felt lost.

"Falon!" Talia cried, hugging her. "You look amazing! The picture of health." Her violet gaze swept Falon's attire. "Your moccasins are gorgeous."

Falon smiled, looking down at them. "They are. I never knew Mondragon was so crafty."

Talia smiled a knowing smile. "There is only one Mondragon with the skill and patience to create such a treasure."

"Lucien said it was a pack effort."

"Really? Ask your alpha; he may rethink his answer and let you in on his secret." She grabbed Falon's hand and worked her way toward the back rooms. "I'm sure you want to see Layla. She has not been well, her recovery has been slow, but she is holding her own, so I'm not overly worried."

"Wait—" Falon said as they stopped outside the room next to the one Joachim was staying in. Suddenly she felt angry and insecure. "I—I don't know what to say to her. What if she did abandon me and only saved me out of guilt?"

Talia's eyes widened to the size of saucers. "No, Falon, she has spoken of nothing else but you."

Falon inhaled deeply and then slowly exhaled. In the end, it did not matter why Layla stayed away, because at the very least, for saving Falon's life, Layla deserved her thanks. "Okay."

Talia opened the door. As Falon walked through the threshold she stopped. Not fifteen feet from her, still and pale as death, lay the woman who'd delivered her into this world. "Mama," Falon breathed, going to her side. She clutched her cool hands into her warmer ones as she sat down on the edge of the bed. The instant Falon touched her mother's hands, she felt her heartache, and the pain of a woman who had lost not only the man she loved but her child. Falon's suppressed pain and anger over losing both parents surfaced with a vengeance. Layla's eyelids fluttered, but she did not open them.

"It's Falon," she said softly, emotion choking on her words. "Your daughter." Layla's heart rate flickered like a butterfly taking flight, then quieted.

Worried, Falon looked toward Talia.

"She's lost a lot of blood, Falon," Talia said. "She would not take any from Lucien or me. She's as stubborn as she always was."

"I'm going to stay here awhile, if it's okay."

"Of course it is."

When the door closed behind Talia, Layla's dark eyes fluttered open.

"*Falon*," she whispered squeezing Falon's hand. A hot rush of tears blurred Falon's vision. She didn't want to cry. Not for this woman—not yet. Not until she knew the truth. But her heart didn't care about the truth at the moment; it swelled with love and hope.

"I'm here."

"You have your father's eyes."

Falon longed to know everything about him. "Will you tell me about him, tell me everything when you're stronger?"

"One day . . ." Layla closed her eyes.

Falon let out another long breath. She should not have pushed. What if discussing her father was a sore subject? She looked down at Layla's smooth caramel-colored skin against her own alabaster skin. Because Falon was light-skinned and blue-eyed, she knew her father was also blue-eyed and light-skinned, the opposite of her mother's darker Mondragon coloring. Layla looked petite in the big bed. Falon was tall for a woman, with an athletic build, so she surmised she also inherited her height and body type from her sire. From Layla, she got the black hair, the Lycan, and the healing; where did her other powers come from? Perhaps her father wasn't even mortal. Then what was she?

Falon sighed and looked down at the woman who had given her life. She wondered if she would ever know who her father was or what had happened to him.

Was he alive? Did he search for her as she had searched for her parents all those years?

The hair on the back of Falon's neck spiked when she remembered she had seen the Eye of Fenrir on a man's hand when she was a child. Had it been Thomas Corbet? Had he come back into her mother's life after Falon's father had left? Had that been why her mother had given her away? To hide her from the Slayers?

It made sense. Hatred swelled within her. If Layla didn't want to talk about the horrors she suffered at Corbet's hand, she would not push her. Nor would she blame her for not wanting to relive that terrible time of her life. But if she did talk about Corbet, Falon would listen carefully, taking mental notes, and if he was still alive, hunt him down and skin the bastard alive.

LUCIEN COULD NOT shake his mood. He'd felt Falon's thoughts turn to his brother when she thought of children. How could he rejoice when the woman he loved thought of another man? And right after they had made love? He fisted and unfisted his hands, wondering how he was going to live with Rafe sharing his true mate's heart, mind, and their bed.

He swiped his hand across his face. His earlier peace had unraveled. He was torn about what he knew he had to do and what he had done. He had started to tell Rafe and Falon about Mara, but got sidetracked by the Slayers.

And then everything changed when Falon had lain at death's door. All that mattered was that she live. And when she came out of it, all that mattered was that he loved her. And by the grace of all the gods, she loved him in return. Why would he jeopardize his and Falon's chance of happiness when Rafe was honor bound to take the Siberian Lycan as his mate? By telling her about Mara they would all lose. It was his secret alone to keep. Not only was it a moot point, he told himself, but if the truth came out, he would be signing his death sentence.

Fuck it! None of it mattered, because he could not live with the lie. He would tell Falon the truth about Mara, and give her the choice: him or Rafe.

He strode into the spacious office off the common room. As he flicked on the light switch, a small box sitting on his desk caught his eye. It was a U.S. postal box with no postage, just his name scrawled in big, bold black letters on the top flap. He brought the box to his nose and inhaled deeply. It smelled burned. Like ash.

Intrigued, he opened the box and peered at the gray matter within. Definitely ash.

He sniffed again. Human ash. He recognized the scent. Furious, Lucien flung the box away from him.

The ash was what was left of Mara. Someone knew he had killed her, and had sent him a warning. Or was it a threat?

He had lain with a Slayer, then killed her and covered it up.

Turning toward the open door, Lucien stared out at his happy pack. Everything was coming together. They were strong, productive, and focused. Without Lucien, Mondragon would falter, then collapse like a row of dominoes. And with their collapse, others would follow.

He was between a boulder and the edge of a cliff.

Fifteen

FALON FELT LUCIEN'S presence behind her long before his scent reached her. His energy was dark, angry, and sad, but interspersed was a soul-tapping love she could not deny. She did not want to deny it. Denying him and what they shared would be like denying her right to breathe.

Slowly she exhaled and turned to him. Her heart caught high in her throat. Devastation etched deep lines in his tragically handsome face. She rose from the chair beside her mother's bed, extending her arms. "What is it, Lucien?"

He shook his head, looking past her to Layla. *Not here.*

Falon turned back to her mother's sleeping form, reached down to squeeze her hand, then slipped from the room with Lucien.

"Falon!" Joachim shouted jovially as he stepped from his room with Lise wrapped inside his good arm. Musky sex scents swirled around the couple. Combined with Lucien's nearness, Falon's body warmed. She felt the flash of Lucien's answering warmth. She groaned, wondering if she was becoming fertile. She and Lucien could not keep their hands off each other on a normal day, but now the air seemed punctuated with sex pheromones. All she could think about was Lucien and how fast they could get naked.

Joachim grinned and hugged Lise closer.

"I see you have recovered and then some," Falon said, looking at the small female Lycan accompanying him then at the metal contraption attached to his arm. "My God, Joachim, you're a one-man arsenal."

He raised the contraption. With a flick of his elbow, five sharp switchblades popped out where his fingers would have been. "I'm deadlier than any Slayer and five times as sharp."

"Put that away, Joachim!" Lise cried as she flinched away from the glinting blades.

Joachim snapped his elbow and the blades withdrew, leaving only metal digits.

"He can cut a Slayer's head off in less time than it takes to draw his sword," Lucien said.

"I can see that," Falon said.

"Did you tell her about that mongrel out back?" Joachim asked Lucien.

Falon looked to Lucien's scowling face. "What mongrel?"

"Angor."

"Angor is here?" she asked excitedly. That meant Rafael would be near, as well. Didn't it? "Why?"

Lucien let out a long, exhaling breath and ran his fingers roughly through his hair. "In light of what happened, Vulkasin insisted that mutant mutt shadow you. And since I value your health above everything, I agreed. What I failed to do was make Rafe responsible for that beast's appetite. He's eating us out of house and home."

Falon smiled at Rafael's thoughtfulness and Lucien's ever-evolving acceptance of his brother.

Lucien's scowl deepened. Falon pressed a comforting hand to his chest. "Thank you for allowing him here. I saved Angor's life. He has a special place in my heart."

"Just another way for my brother to push himself on Mondragon."

Falon bit her bottom lip to keep from scolding the petulant Lucien. "If you don't want Angor here, I will send him back."

Lucien took the hand on his chest and brought it to his lips. "I told you, I don't begrudge you the added protection of that beast. I only begrudge my brother his continued involvement in your life."

Falon's smile waned. "He will mark his mate soon enough, Luca, and then you will have nothing to worry about."

Joachim and Lise quietly slipped away, leaving them to their privacy. Falon watched the storm gather in Lucien's golden eyes. "As long as he lives, I will worry. Even if he were dead his ghost would haunt us."

Falon's back stiffened. "Are you saying you don't trust me?"

"I don't trust—" Lucien dropped her hand and swiped his hand over his face. "I don't trust myself; how can I trust you or my brother when I saw how he looked at you when we didn't know if you were going to live or die? He was dying himself, just as I was! I know you feel the same for him, and it tears me up inside each time I think about it."

"We have exchanged marks!" she cried, angry that he would think she would run to Rafe if he would have her. Maybe she would have before the Slayer attack, but not now. Lucien was her chosen one. And Rafe was promised to another.

"But you still yearn for Rafe!"

It was Falon's turn to swipe her hand across her face in frustration. How could she make this proud, stubborn man see that while she loved his brother she loved him, too? "Lucien," she said slowly. "I will not lie to you. I have never lied to you about my feelings for Rafael. I love him. But I also love you."

Her heart blanched when Lucien flinched. "Would you rather I lie to you about it? Or would you want me to not love him? Because if I stopped loving him, what kind of person would that make me?"

"All mine!"

"Perhaps, but also a shallow, fickle mate not worthy of you or Mondragon."

Lucien rubbed his temples. "Falon. I understand your feelings for my brother. I even admire your loyalty to him. But you must understand what it does to me every time I know you're thinking of him with love and lust in your heart."

It would hurt the same if she thought of Lucien in the arms of another woman. "It would tear me up inside thinking of you loving another woman. You loved Mara. Because of that love, an entire pack has been split in half. Two brothers who loved each other became mortal enemies. Don't think that her impact on your heart doesn't affect me. Because it does."

He hissed in a breath.

"The difference between you and me is, despite all that threw us together, I stand here with you because I choose to be here. I know you love me. And that is enough." Lucien scowled, not buying what she was selling. "Lucien, we cannot change what is. We can only make the best of it."

He looked away from her. Stubborn man! She grabbed his chin and forced him to look at her. "I love *you*. I accepted your mark, your seed, and your ring! I may at this very moment carry your child. Accept that I am here because I choose to be here."

"What if you were given the choice to return to Rafe?"

His words hit her like a hammer. Her jaw dropped. "I—"

His eyes darkened dangerously. "By your hesitation, your answer is clear." He stalked away from her.

"Lucien!" she cried, running after him. "I love you, damn it!"

He turned vicious eyes on her. "But not enough to forsake Rafe for me."

She grabbed his hand and pulled him so hard toward her, he flew backward into her. Despite the pain of his body smashing into hers, her rage mushroomed. "Stop this now! If I leave here it will be because of your hand on my back pushing me out!"

The color drained from his face.

"Your pride is going to destroy everything you hold dear, Lucien Mondragon! *Including me.*" Falon stepped away from him as she tried to calm the tempest in her heart. She loved Lucien. With every part of her that loved Rafe. But damn if he didn't drive her crazy! She calmed more, trying to put herself in his shoes. It would eat her alive as it ate at him if she had to share his heart, his thoughts, his soul with another woman. That Mara was not the love of his life was a blessing of immeasurable wealth. She doubted she could live with her ghost standing between them, a constant reminder of a love torn from his arms. If Mara had lived, it would be virtually impossible.

"For all my talk, I cannot say I would be able to handle it if Mara suddenly materialized."

His golden eyes glittered with moisture. "The difference is, I never gave her all of my heart. She was not my other half. She was an infatuation at best. I know that now. I know it because I know what it is to love completely." He exhaled. "Falon," he said softly. "I thought I could handle this. I thought your love for me would be enough. I thought I could make love to you and ignore that you were thinking it was Rafael who touched you."

"I have never thought of him while I was with you that way!"

"Maybe not now, but later, especially when you know he is forever lost to you once he marks the Ivanov girl."

"I cannot predict the future, Lucien! Don't force me into a corner! I don't deserve this. And neither do you. It will tear us apart. And I don't want that." She grabbed his hands. "Luca, this is an impossible situation. But we are strong enough to see it through."

She looked up to his raging eyes. He loved her. But that damned devil, his pride, was doing its best to tear them apart. He removed her hands from his and stepped away. "I don't want you to hate me. I don't want to destroy the best thing that has happened to me. I need to find a way to come to terms with my jealousy, Falon. Until I do, I think it would be better if we don't share the same room."

Her stomach pitched and heaved. "What are you saying?" she whispered, afraid of the answer.

"I need some time. I'll sleep down here for a few nights."

"Is that what you do? After everything we have been through, run away when you can't have your way?"

"I gave you all of my heart!" he ground out. "Every piece of it, despite the fact that half of yours still belongs to my brother!"

While she understood his need for space and his hurt feelings, she was angry. This was not her fault. "I guess, Lucien, you should have thought of the repercussions of your actions before you took me from Rafael! Your failure to deal with this situation has nothing to do with me. I did not create it. *I* did not ask for it. I sure as hell would never have agreed to accept the council's verdict had I known the end result!"

Lucien's body jerked as if he had been gut punched. The color drained from his face.

"I didn't mean it that way, Lucien. I meant—"

"I know exactly what you meant," he snarled and stalked away.

Falon slumped against the wall as her world came crumbling down around her. She hadn't meant she regretted being with Lucien. She wanted to be with him! With all her heart. Had not the events of the last month and a half played out as they had, she would never have known she was capable of such profound feelings for not one man but two. Lucien brought out the primal in her. He strengthened her. He infused her with passion. He made her better. Stronger. He was as much a part of her as Rafael. She would never trade her love for him away. And she knew in her heart, she could not live without Lucien.

But she could not tell him that. He had to discover that, lingering feelings for Rafe aside, he could not live without her. Only then could he return to her. Only then could they mend this chasm between them. Only then could they begin anew and hopefully build on that foundation. She closed her eyes and leaned her head back against the wall. When had her life become so complicated? Why couldn't they all just live happily ever after, together?

Until the rising had passed and the Lycan nation stood victorious, there was not going to be a happy ever after for anyone.

Falon pushed off the wall and slipped back into her mother's room and sat down beside her sleeping form. Taking her hands into hers, she said softly, "Tell me what to do."

Layla's soft, even breath was her answer.

Falon spent the night in a large overstuffed chair beside her mother, drifting in and out of troubled sleep. Each time she woke, she resisted the urge to go to Lucien. She felt his turmoil. She felt his anguish. It mirrored her own. Desperately she wanted him to take her into his arms and promise her it was going to work out. But until he believed that, they could not be together.

Finally, as dawn's fingers cast a gray shadow on the new day, she fell into a fitful slumber.

"Falon!" Talia's worried voice woke her from a deep sleep. "Layla has gone!"

Falon's eyes popped open to find her mother's bed empty. "Where did she go?"

Talia shook her head. "I don't know."

Falon stood and sniffed the air. Her mother's scent was still fresh. "I must find her."

She moved past Talia, who caught her hand. The petite healer's gaze was sincere but at the same time, Falon felt her compassion. "Falon, for twenty-four years she has stayed away. She returned to save her child. That she left without saying good-bye means she does not want to be found."

"But I need her!" Falon cried, moving past Talia. She needed answers. She would track Layla down to get them, too. Falon hurried from the room and grabbed an empty satchel from the kitchen, then ran to the back of the compound. As she opened the back doors, Angor's deep red eyes met hers. He growled a welcome. She rubbed the three-hundred-pound mutant wolf's head.

"Come, my friend. We have work to do." Quickly Falon undressed and stuffed her clothes and moccasins into the small bag, then shifted. She snatched the bag up in her jaws and turned toward her mother's scent. With Angor at her back, they took off like lightning in an electrical storm.

LUCIEN STOOD AT the open doors at the front of the warehouse and watched Falon and Angor leap over the high fence and disappear into the morning mist. Every instinct told him to go after her and beg for forgiveness. But he hesitated. He wasn't there yet.

Lucien snarled. Last night he had gone to Layla's room with the intention of telling Falon the truth about Mara, of setting her free, but when faced with the cost of doing so, he could not bring himself to do it. He could not bear the thought of losing her. But what he'd done was worse. He'd questioned her loyalty, her love, and her integrity. He had pushed her away anyway. He scoffed at his pathetic attempt to be the one to walk away. If he walked away, then it could not be said she left him for Rafe. If he walked away, his secret would die with him. If he walked away, his life would not be in jeopardy for what he had done.

It didn't matter how he spun it in his mind. He was a fool on every level. A weak, dishonorable fool. He was not worthy of a woman like Falon. Maybe he always knew it, and because his beast knew the truth, he found a way to push her away without telling the truth.

He shoved his hands into his jeans pockets. He strode to the gates and peered out at the human world. His gut, his heart, his soul cried out for Falon. But his damn pride held him in lockdown. Falon had told him once it would eat him up and kill him. Right now death seemed the better bargain. Because he did not want to live if Falon was not standing beside him.

He exhaled a long breath. He despised his weakness. He was not fit to lead even a fly into battle.

Raising his head, he stared at the fading half-moon still lingering in the morning sky. In less than six weeks, the fight for their lives would commence. Lucien threw his head back and howled. It was time he kicked the sleeping dogs awake.

FALON FOUND HERSELF standing at the edge of the deserted Amorak camp. Clinging scents still swirled about the place. The Amorak had begun their journey north to the battleground of the first Blood Moon rising. It would be where the final battle would be fought. She shifted to human and pulled her clothes out of the satchel and dressed. Then she followed her mother's scent to a small cabin at the end of the dirt road.

Cautiously, she pushed open the door and caught her breath. Her mother sat on a threadbare mattress, wrapped in an Indian blanket, her deep brown eyes peering intently at Falon. She smiled a ghost of a smile and patted the space beside her. "Come, daughter, and sit with me awhile."

Falon left Angor to guard the door and slowly sat down beside the mysterious woman who had given birth to her. "Why did you leave without saying good-bye?" Falon softly asked.

"Because I wanted you to follow me."

"All you had to do was ask."

Layla smiled serenely. "I needed to know you would come of your own volition. I also needed you outside of Mondragon and Vulkasin."

Though years and questions separated them, Falon felt an affinity for the woman who was her mother. Her blood flowed warm and vibrant in her veins. Layla had given her life not once but twice. And because she felt such a deep bond and trust, Falon let what was prominently on her mind gush out.

"Mama, I don't know what to do! I love them both! But even though I've chosen to stay with Lucien because I truly want to, he's driving me crazy with his jealousy because I will never stop loving Rafe." She dropped her head into her open hands and groaned. "I feel like a soap opera diva, torn between two lovers." She lifted her head and looked to her mother for council. "My heart is a shredded, tattered mess that doesn't know what to do for Lucien."

"Lucien must find his own way."

Falon threw her hands up in frustration. "But what if he doesn't? I *love* him."

"I understand. But in the end, *buniq*, all three of you must follow your hearts."

"How can we? It's an impossible situation. I love two men! I can have only one even though they both love me. One lives and dies by his honor and is promised to another. He gave his word he would not interfere in exchange for my life." She swiped her hand across her face in the same fashion Lucien did when he was frustrated. "The other's pride will not allow him to see he spites his face by cutting off his nose."

Layla's smile widened. Oddly, Falon found great comfort in it. "Rafael and Lucien have always battled for supremacy," Layla began. "They battled the day they were born. Rafael's head emerged with Lucien's arm wrapped around his throat as if trying to pull him back so that he could be first."

Falon smiled despite the gravity of the topic. "It's still that way."

"The brothers share a deep love, Falon. It was torn apart by a treacherous woman, it can only be repaired by one with a true heart for them both." Layla looked at Falon with deep affection. She touched her cheek. "By a woman who would die for them both."

Falon swallowed hard. "I love them both. I would die for them both."

"I know that, you know that, the entire world knows it. But—until the brothers can come to terms with what must be, then you, my love, will pay the price."

Falon smiled at her mom. Layla was wise, she was beautiful, and she had missed her comforting warmth terribly. But caution held her heart at bay. "Why did you stay away so long?"

The light went out of Layla's eyes. "I could not return. Not after—Corbet."

"I've heard the terrible story of how Corbet and his brothers came in and destroyed Vulkasin. How so many died that day. But, Mama, those who survived would have understood. It was not your fault Corbet took you away from your family."

Layla smiled a ghost of a smile. "Part of me did not want to return. Part of me still doesn't."

Shocked by her words, Falon asked, "Why not? I would think you would find comfort with your own kind."

The pain on her mother's beautiful face was tragic. She could not imagine living through the horror of that infamous day. "The memories of that day still haunt me. It was terrible what they did. I have never witnessed such cruelty. When I see or smell a Lycan that day comes back to me as vividly as the day I lived through it. I feel guilty for surviving when so many I loved did not."

"It's not your fault. You need to forgive yourself for surviving."

She sighed, shaking her head. "It's not possible."

"Hey, you ended up with me," Falon said, grinning, trying to lighten the grave mood.

Layla made a sound halfway between a choke and a sob. When Falon looked closer, she saw the well of tears in her mother's eyes. She squeezed her hand.

Layla smiled through the tears. "You were my blessing, Falon. My gift."

"Did you love my father?"

Her smile waned. "Very much."

"Tell me about him. Is he still alive?"

"It seems like a lifetime ago when last I saw him. I don't know if he's dead or alive." Her eyes dimmed as she turned to Falon. "He was a troubled man, much like Lucien. His demons were not of his own making, but despite them, he tried to love me as he wanted to love me. But in the end, he could not let go of his past."

"Did he love me?"

Layla smoothed Falon's hair from her cheeks. "He loved you with all his heart. But he knew the darkness in him would harm you. To protect us both, he walked out of our lives."

Falon grasped her mother's hand and pressed it to her cheek. "Did—did Thomas Corbet hurt you?"

Layla squeezed her hand and pushed it away. "I can't discuss him."

Falon felt her mother's pain as if she was the one who had been struck by it. "Did my father know about Corbet?"

Layla's hands trembled. "Please, Falon, I can't."

Falon tamped down her frustration. She wanted to know everything about her father. If he was alive, she wanted to find him. Meet him, understand that part of herself that came from him. And she wanted to kill Corbet for all the imagined vileness she was sure he inflicted on her mother. But she would not push Layla. Not today. "If you ever want to talk about the Slayer, I will listen and make no judgments."

"You're a good daughter."

For a long time, Falon sat quietly, trying to find a tactful way to ask her mother how they had become separated.

As if reading her thoughts, Layla explained, "Because of the Slayers, Falon, I had to hide you. I was afraid they would find you and harm you."

"But Corbet is my last name."

"I hid you in plain sight. When they searched for you, I knew they wouldn't give the name Corbet a second thought. It worked."

Falon's temples began a slow dull throb. She closed her eyes, trying to steer the headache away, but every time she concentrated on her childhood memories, the pounding started up. "I remember the ring. The Eye of Fenrir on a man's hand. Was it Thomas Corbet's hand?" She opened her eyes to see Layla nod.

"I was there the day he resurrected it. It was why he took me from Vulkasin. Without my blood as sacrifice the ring would not reveal itself."

"My God! Did he try to kill you?"

"Nothing so graphic or painful. But the entire episode was terrifying. Fenrir revealed himself to us before Thomas forced him back into the ring. He was ferocious and hideous to look upon."

"How did he force Fenrir back?"

"The bearer of the ring holds all the power over the wolf. Rafael has no comprehension of the true power he holds on his hand. Sharia will reveal the powers once the packs are gathered."

"Rafe has made sure it never leaves his body as wolf or human. But it has been messing with his head, too. I think the wolf is restless."

"Rafe must understand that despite what Fenrir wants, Rafe has the final word. He cannot be forced to do anything he does not naturally want to do, and his word is final over Fenrir's."

Falon let out a long, exhausted breath. Her temples pounded. But she would have her answers. "The night I met Rafael, a man named Viktor Salene approached me." Falon watched her mother's face for any clue that she knew the man. The flare of her nostrils was her only tell. "Did you know him?"

"Yes," Layla whispered.

"He knew my name. Told me he was taking me to my people. Slayer people."

"Viktor Salene was a crazy Corbet wannabe."

"What's so great about the Corbets? They are bloodthirsty murderers!"

"That fact is inarguable. But amongst Slayers, the eldest son of the eldest son of Peter Corbet are born with innate powers no other Slayer possesses. They are revered among all Slayers."

"How do you know this?"

"I was a captive of one of those eldest sons. I heard and saw more about the life of a Slayer than any Lycan before me."

"Why did Salene insist I was a Slayer?"

"I don't know. Maybe he sensed your innate power, not realizing you were Lycan."

"How did he get the ring from Corbet?"

Layla shook her head. "My gut tells me he slew Thomas for it. He would never have handed it over of his own free will."

"Rafe killed Salene and took the ring."

"The ring is where it should be. For now anyway."

Falon's eyes narrowed. A hunch niggled at her. "Did you—have affection for Corbet?"

Falon hissed in a breath when she caught the softening in her mother's eyes before she could hide it with indifference. "How could you?" she demanded, horrified by the thought. "After what he did? Is that why you refuse to talk about him? Is that the real reason you could not face your pack?"

Layla's eyes filled with tears. "You were not there, Falon. You did not see the side of him I saw."

Falon fought hard to keep her emotions under control. No, she had not walked a mile in her mother's shoes, but even so, she could not fathom how *any* Lycan could feel compassion for such a heinous individual. Falon despised Thomas Corbet on principal alone for what he had done to Rafe and Lucien. So, too, should Layla.

"He's a murderer."

"What are Rafe and Lucien?"

Falon's jaw dropped. Never would she expect her mother or any Lycan to defend a Slayer against a Lycan. "How can you ask such a thing when you were there! When you witnessed firsthand their cruelty? What would you expect any Lycan to do to the people who destroyed their family? Hug them and hang out? The Slayers started this fight centuries ago. As you know Lycans have only one natural enemy: Slayers. Lycans fight for survival not because of hatred or because some douche-bag king didn't like wolves but because they have been singularly persecuted for almost a thousand years!"

Falon shook she was so angry. But more than that, disappointed that her mother would sympathize with their mortal enemy.

"Falon, I have slain my share of Slayers. If any one of them walked into this cabin, I would tear their heart out. What I am saying is, there are two sides to every man. And not all men who are born into hatred embrace it."

"Are you saying Thomas Corbet didn't get off killing Lycan?"

"No, I'm just saying perhaps if he had a choice he would not have."

"We all have choices, Mother." Falon sat back against the wall, crossing her arms over her chest. This was not how she wanted to get to know her mother. It was not what she expected. But now that the cards were on the table she would have all her answers. But Layla blindsided her with a question.

"Did you ever expect to soften toward Lucien?"

Falon hissed in a deep breath. "He is not a Slayer!"

"But he wanted to kill Rafe, the man you loved, and he would have slain you had the council's verdict upheld the Blood Law to the letter."

"No, he would not have!"

"You are a hypocrite, Falon. You despised Lucien. You knew if you were to mark him it would destroy Rafael. Yet you did it anyway with no regard to Rafe's feelings."

"I did not despise Lucien! I despised what he did." And she did care about Rafa's feelings. Had she not marked Lucien neither of them could move on. And to survive they had no choice but to do so.

"As I despised what Thomas did."

"Did my father know of your affection for that horrible man? Is that what really drove him away?"

Layla's lips thinned into a grim line. "As you, I was torn between two men, Falon, and because I was a coward, I have neither. Do not make the mistake I made. Find a way to love them both."

"They will not allow me to openly love them both."

Layla smoothed Falon's furrowed brows with cool, soothing fingertips. "You have just not found a way to convince them yet."

Falon's brain throbbed inside of her skull. She wanted to shift and run. Run away from her questions, the answers she did not want to hear, and the turmoil in her heart and soul. But she didn't. She stood and dug her heels in deeper.

"Why did you abandon me?"

Layla's cheeks darkened but she looked Falon in the eyes. "I am sorry for that, Falon. But it was the only way to keep the Slayers off your scent. You had to be away from me. Completely. I *chose* to give you up so that you would survive."

"I was miserable. All I had was my name, and after I ran away at fourteen from my foster home, I changed even that."

"I regret your misery, Falon. There was never a minute of any hour that I did not think of you. But in my heart, I know what I did was right. That you are here with me today, alive, is proof."

Hot tears stung Falon's eyes. In her heart, she wanted to justify the decision her mother made, but in her soul, Falon knew she would never give up her child. She would fight to the death to protect her. She would have swallowed her pride and her fear and returned to her people for love and protection.

Falon had one more question and though she dreaded the answer, she knew she must ask it. "I see spirits. Lucien called them ghost walkers. He said you would explain."

Layla hissed in a sharp breath. Her deep brown eyes widened with wonder and fear.

The hair on Falon's arms crawled like caterpillars across her skin.

"You're going to drop another bomb on me, aren't you?" she asked, not wanting the answer.

"You have your father's gift of the sight, Falon."

"What does that mean?"

"It means you possess the power to restore life."

Sixteen

"THAT'S IMPOSSIBLE!"

Layla shook her head and scooted closer to Falon. "Ghost walkers are restless spirits, Falon. Lycan spirits that have fallen by a Corbet sword. Their life forces were so strong when they were alive that although their bodies dissolved upon their deaths, their energy remained. All they need is a conduit to return to their earthly forms."

Falon sat stunned, her stomach a nervous flutter of disbelief. "What kind of conduit?"

"A vessel with the gift of the sight, of seeing and hearing the lost souls who walk the earth around us."

"I can't help them!"

"Alone you can't. For there to be any hope of their resurrection, you must control Fenrir's magic. It's powerful. While that deformed wolf has used his power to kill his own kind, he also possesses the power to restore those lives."

"How?"

"That is a mystery. But I do know from the whispers of the northern elders that there must be blood for blood."

"Like how Corbet needed your blood to resurrect the ring?"

"Yes. I am a direct descendant of Singarti, the Great Spirit Mother who cast Fenrir into the ring. Only the combination of my blood and the blood of the eldest son of the Corbet bloodline could call it out. Thomas knew what to do, too, and it worked."

"Would Sharia know what to do?"

Layla chuckled. "That old witch knows everything. I swear she has a crystal ball."

"She said for the Lycan nation to prevail, the power of the three must unite."

Layla's eyes darkened but she nodded. "It has always been foretold."

Falon swallowed hard. "She seems to think the three in question are me, Lucien, and Rafe."

Layla nodded. "I always assumed the power of the three would be a Vulkasin, a Corbet, and Fenrir. But I understand now. The power of the three is the only power to defeat Fenrir."

Falon's temples began to throb again. None of this made sense. It was like chasing your tail. "But what of Rafael's chosen one?"

Layla cocked an arched brow. "He has not marked her yet."

"But he has vowed to do so. He would never go back on his word."

Her mother shrugged. "Perhaps he doesn't have to."

Falon's brows wrinkled. "What do you mean?"

"Rafael made his vow based on information he had at the time. If that information should change, then he would have an out."

"I don't know what you mean by that."

"I just mean with the entire nation at stake, nothing is carved in stone, *buniq*. Not even the Blood Law."

Falon rubbed her head as the migraine erupted full force between her temples. "I don't understand any of this. I don't *want* to understand any of this! It's too hard and makes no sense to me."

"What *do* you want, Falon?"

"I want Lucien *and* Rafael."

"But if you can have only one, which would it be?"

"That is like asking me whether I would choose my heart or my soul."

"To live a full life, you must possess both."

Falon lay back on the thin mattress and clamped her hand across her eyes. She would sell her soul to Thomas Corbet for both men. "Try telling them that."

"Perhaps you should."

Falon lifted her hand and peered at her mother. "What are you saying?"

"Have them both. Tell them that is what you want. Accept nothing less."

Falon jackknifed up; her cheeks flamed red-hot. "Are you kidding me? They would tear each other apart!"

"If they love you, they will share you. If they want to see the morning after the rising they will have no choice but to come to terms with it."

"I—ah, I don't think Sharia meant it like that, Mother. She meant united in spirit and power." Warmth fizzled through Falon's veins. Oh, dear Lord, in her perfect world she *would* have them both. But she lived in reality. "Rafael is honor bound to Anja, and I am soul bound to Lucien."

Layla smiled and lay back onto the mattress, pulling Falon into the security of her arms. "To be united in spirit, one must be united in heart, body, and soul. From there comes the power."

"Mother!" Falon cried, embarrassed that she was talking about, well, alluding to living with two men in a sexual relationship. Her skin shivered with warmth. Lord, it would be a wild ride. "Lucien and Rafe would never co-alpha, and they would *never* share me that way. And honestly? I would go crazy trying to make them both not be jealous of the other. It would be impossible."

"If you say so, Daughter."

"I say so because it is so."

But when she closed her eyes, Falon could not help but think of the two men she loved and what it would mean to belong to them both.

SHAMELESSLY, FALON RAN naked through the timber. Her path up the steep mountain ran parallel to the road to Vulkasin. When Rafe's scent became too strong to ignore, she banked away, backtracking, looking for a calm place where she could lay beneath the moon's soft glow and call upon her imagination to make her dreams come true. She shifted, increasing her speed. Her long, lean body stretched; her taut muscles loosened. The wind brushed across her face through her silky fur. She was free. Free to love whom she wanted, when she wanted. Free of Slayers, free of the impending doom. In her dream she could do anything, be with anyone.

Feeling a presensce nearby, she looked to her left and gasped. Lucien's black wolf ran beside her. His golden eyes glowed brightly, his wolf grin holding happy promise.

A nose nudged her right flank. Startled, Falon looked back. Her heart stumbled in her chest. Rafa's deep aqua-colored eyes glittered beneath the moonlight. He moved up and in perfect step, the three of them raced across the mountain.

Her heart sang with joy. There was no hostility, no snarling or posturing, just peaceful synchronicity.

As they came back around and down the mountain, Falon came

to an abrupt stop at the edge of the small pond nestled peacefully behind the Amorak encampment. Both alphas stopped beside her. For long minutes, they stood blowing, catching their breath. Lucien stepped past her into the quiet pond and drank. Falon threw her head back and growled happily, running into the water and splashing him playfully. He grinned and dove in after her. She shifted and came up for air. Naked in his human body, Lucien laughed and swooped her into his arms. She looped her arms around his neck, feeling loved and carefree. His hard muscles felt good on her soft skin.

"I love you," she happily cried. His hands cupped her tender breasts. She arched against him, as his lips possessively claimed hers in a deep breath-stealing kiss.

Firm fingers traced along her spine. Tearing her lips from Lucien's, she quarter turned and gasped. Rafael smiled down at her. Wide-eyed, she turned to him, lacing an arm around his neck while she kept the other possessively wrapped around Lucien. "Rafa," she breathed. His lips dropped to hers, still warm and damp from Lucien's lips, in a long, passionate kiss. She turned fully into him, missing the protective warmth of him. His erection stabbed her in the belly. Of their own volition, her legs lifted and locked around his hips.

"I have missed you," she crooned to Rafael.

"No more than I have missed you, my love."

Falon's heart overflowed with emotion. He still loved her, despite everything, he still loved her.

Lucien growled softly behind her, reminding her he was there. She laughed and turned to him. Stroking his cheek, she looked up into his darkened eyes. "My proud Luca, I miss you even in my sleep."

Lucien's erection swelled between her buttocks. Rafael's between her thighs. Her entire body shimmered with arousal and awe. There was no growling or snarling. No fighting over her as if she were a bone. They were there, united, for her.

If only it were not a dream.

Falon leaned back against Lucien's strong chest and wrapped an arm around his neck. Snaking her fingers into his hair, she rose to his lips as she turned more fully toward him. As his lips captured hers in a deep spiraling kiss, Rafael's lips imprisoned a sensitive nipple, suckling her tenderly. Falon moaned, reveling in the wondrous touch of both men.

Lucien's hand snaked around her waist to her other breast. When his fingers plucked her sensitive nipple, she cried out in pleasure. Her damp skin steamed beneath their touch. Her heart pounded against her rib cage. Her womb clenched, hungering for each of them in turn. Rafa's big hand slid down her belly, to her mons. She gasped in Luca's mouth and his tongue swirled against hers, silencing her cries of pleasure, when Rafael slid his fingertips across her hard clit, then between her swollen lips. She jerked against him, moaning louder, arching into Rafa's sweet assault, as Lucien's lips held hers captive.

She dug her fingers into Rafael's leg, spreading her thighs in unabashed offering.

Sliding a thick finger into her, he took her offer. She cried out, pressing her head back against Luca's strong shoulder. The need to mate was strong. Her body was on fire, her essence heady. Both men's nostrils flared, recognizing she was ripe to conceive.

Falon closed her eyes, absorbing the fact that, dream or not, she was in the middle of a perfect storm. Never in her wildest fantasies had she imagined how blissfully insane it would feel to be loved by both brothers at the same time.

Rafa moved his finger slowly in and out of her. Lucien's finger gently slid along her anus, gently probing, carefully stretching her. Falon bit her lip, drawing blood. The sensation of what Lucien did to her was odd but exhilarating. She wanted to experience more. And as she was wont to do with Lucien, Falon faithfully followed where he led her, trusting and excited, knowing he would take her to a place she had never been.

The scent of her blood stirred both men's bodies. Rafa growled low, grazing his teeth along a turgid nipple. He nipped her, then licked away the sting. Luca slid a finger into her anus. One slow inch at a time. Her vaginal walls clamped around Rafa's finger as she tried to loosen for Luca's.

Rafa slipped his finger from her. Falon cried out, digging her nails deeper into his thigh. His blazing eyes caught and held hers as he lifted her hips and steered his warm cock into her waiting wetness.

"Rafe," she sobbed against Lucien's lips as his brother slowly filled her. Her eyes rolled back into her head, the feeling so mouthwatering she could not form a word to describe it.

"Easy, angel face," Lucien said as he, too, slipped his finger from her. Impaled on Rafa's swollen cock, she shuddered when Lucien spread her cheeks and slowly probed her with his.

Anticipation sizzled along every nerve ending in her body.

Falon moaned when he entered her inch by incremental inch from behind. "Luca," she breathed as the new scintillating sensation took hold.

"Relax," he said softly. "I would never hurt you." When he slowly pressed deeper into her, Falon loosened, not realizing she had been tense. There was no pain, only a pleasure that she could not define heightened by the extra stimulant of his cock ring.

He was gentle and slow, easing his way into her. Rafael held her steady, not moving in her as Lucien filled her. "You okay, love?" Rafa asked, stroking her cheek. She was so overcome with emotion and sensation, she was unable to speak at the moment, Falon nodded. Rafa smiled and brushed his lips across hers. "I love you."

"I love you, too," she managed before an avalanche of tears flooded her eyes. They were so gentle, so patient, so caring.

"Thank you, Luca," she breathlessly moaned. "Thank you, Rafa."

She closed her eyes, blinking away the tears, wanting to revel in this new and astonishing emotional and physical sensory overload. Of being filled by them both. Of them giving themselves to her unselfishly.

She hung suspended for an eternity as her body adapted to them. Energy sparked and snapped inside of her. Her womb clenched like a fist around Rafael, and her bottom hugged Lucien. Three hearts beat to the same chaotic cadence. Three bodies as one. Three souls as one. Lucien's heart thudded against her back, Rafe's against her chest. Their bodies thrummed with her energy. It was magical, omnipotent, and sublime. The power of three.

When Rafael moved deeper into her, Falon gasped, the sensation of his potent energy sparking like a match to gasoline. As he pulled away, Lucien rocked into her from behind. Falon's body shimmered with sensation, then melted around him like warm honey on a hot biscuit. A deep moan began in her belly and worked its way up her throat, sloughing from her lips in a long, satisfied sound. It was too much, but not enough. In a slow, succulent cadence, they moved in and out of her. Taking her to a place she never imagined existed. A place dreams were made of.

Heat, lips, hands, and cock worked her body into such a fevered pitch, Falon feared she would come apart at the seams. Her body was on fire with wild electrical sensation. Every part of her, every cell, every molecule sizzled with unleashed desire. Her heart sang with emotion overload. Her pussy clenched Rafe as her anus fisted Lucien. Her body arched, drawing so tight she was sure she would snap in half. The energy inside of her built to a towering crescendo. And just as she came apart, bursting into a million tiny pieces, Rafael bit her neck on one side from in front, and Lucien bit her neck on the other side from behind. They exploded within her, their seed hot and thick.

Hers.

She screamed as a devastating orgasm slammed into her.

FALON WOKE WITH a start. Sitting up, she gasped for air, her body trembling violently as energy snapped in microbursts around her. Wildly, she looked around. Her mother's calming scent reminded her she had fallen asleep at the Amorak camp.

Angor's low growl from outside the door soothed her. "It's okay," she whispered. Though her body still shimmered with the remnants of her orgasm. "It was just a dream." One hell of a dream!

Falon shook her head, running her fingers through her damp, tangled hair. She sucked in a huge breath of air and exhaled loudly. My God, that had been so real. Her heart still pounded like a sledge-hammer against her breastbone. Licking her dry lips, she stood. She needed air. As she stumbled from the cabin, she pressed her hand to her chest and caught her breath. She was naked! Her vaginal muscles clenched. Her bottom was sore. Her hands went to her neck. She flinched as her fingertips brushed tender flesh.

Her heartbeat spiked. Not possible. *It had been a dream!*

Her nipples strained against the sultry night air. She moaned, sliding her hand down between her thighs. She was soaking wet and on fire.

She ran toward the small pond at the back of the camp. Her dress and moccasins lay scattered as if she had taken them off in a hurry among the soft moss bank. Her heart thundered, the percussion choking off her breath.

"It was a dream!" she shouted at the night.

She did not wade into the cool water; instead, she dove in head-first, gasping as the cold mountain water sluiced against her sultry skin. When she broke the water, her fevered body shivered.

Standing, she smoothed her hair back from her face, then gasped. Her hard nipples tightened. Not from the cool air wafting across them, but from the penetrating gaze of the very naked and very aroused man standing at the water's edge.

Emotion infused her. Her body trembled so violently she could barely stand as he walked toward her and into the water, stopping only a few feet from her.

"Rafa," she breathed. It took every ounce of control she possessed not to reach out to him. To touch his handsome face and smooth away the deep stress lines that etched him.

"Falon," he said huskily. "It's not safe out here. Vipers and Slayers wander the forest looking for souls to claim."

"I had a dream about you."

His eyes blazed. "I know."

"You know?" Her cheeks flared with heat.

He took a step closer to her. "I heard you call my name. I could not help myself, Falon." His voice cracked under the pressure. His big hand slid behind her neck to cup her head. He drew her to him. A violent storm raged across his features. "I came to you even though I swore on your life I would shun you. Even though I swore I would mark another by the next full moon." His voice was rough, cruel almost, as if he despised himself. "But I never swore I would stop loving you."

"My dream was so real." She brushed her fingertips across his lips. "Are you real? Or am I dreaming again?" Closing her eyes, she inhaled his deep earthy scent. Her eyes flew open. Intermingled with his scent was her essence and—her heart pounded—Lucien's . . .

She trembled violently. It wasn't possible. *It was a dream.* Because only in her dreams could she have the two men she loved.

They stood so close their warm breaths mingled.

"I am real, Falon. I have always been real."

"Oh, Rafa," she cried. "How I wish things could be different." She leaned her head back into his hand, letting him do the work. She was weary of this struggle between the two men she loved. "I dreamed of you inside me. It was so real, I had to come out here to cool off, but then I found my clothes here, and you are here, and you smell like me." She lifted her head and faced him almost eye to eye. "What happened?" she demanded, suddenly feeling ashamed. She would never betray Lucien, not even with the other man she loved.

He growled low. "Do not tempt me to show you—again."

Falon slapped her hands over her mouth to keep from crying out. Dear God! Had she allowed Rafael into her dream only for it to become a reality? "How could you do that to me? To Lucien?"

"How could I do *what*? Make love to my chosen one? My chosen one that was stolen from me? The one that for the first time since she was marked by another called out to me?" He shook her. "Do you have any idea what it does to me knowing you are fucking my brother and liking it?"

"Rafa, please, don't do this."

"I'm not sorry for coming to you, Falon. Call me again and I will come to you before you finish your thought."

"Rafe, stop it! This is not who you are!"

"It *is* who I have become. I'm done making it easy for you, Falon. I want you, and damn it, I'll have you when you call me."

Rafael's passionate words stunned her. It was because of her, dreaming of what could never be that he had broken his vow and come to her. Furious with herself for her weakness, Falon realized, though there had been progress with the brothers since she had accepted Lucien, she didn't fool herself into thinking that, given the chance, Lucien and Rafael would kill each other over her.

Sadly, she shook her head. "I would not dishonor you or Lucien that way again." She looked regretfully into his eyes but stepped back. "It was just a dream, Rafa, nothing more." She sucked in a long breath.

He reached out to her but pulled back. She smiled and took his hand and placed it against her heart. Her breasts trembled in remembered passion. Rafe hissed in a long breath. "I will always love you." She moved into him and on her tiptoes, kissed his lips. "Good-bye, Rafe," she said softly.

He groaned and slipped his arm around her waist, pulling her into his lips. Deepening the kiss. Her body washed warm with passion. With love. With more regret than most people lived with, in ten lifetimes. Tears stung her eyes as she pulled away from him. "I am Lucien's now. I will not betray him with more than a farewell kiss, Rafa." She moved past him, but he caught her hand and pulled her back into his arms.

"I have lived my entire life by a self-imposed honor code. It has brought me nothing but heartache." He grit his teeth, pressing her tighter to him. "I vowed on your life, Falon, not to touch you again." He closed his eyes, and she could see him fighting his desire to say fuck it all again. "And I failed us both. For that I am deeply sorry."

Gently but firmly she unwrapped his arms from around her. "Rafa, I wish with all my heart things could be different. But a wish is just that, a wish." She moved past him and looked to the edge of the tree line to see a snowy white she-wolf waiting in the mist. And behind her, Lucien's flashing golden eyes.

Falon scooped up her dress and quickly donned it, then grabbed her moccasins. She did not look back at Rafa. If she did, she would fall apart, and she would not do that to him. But mostly she would not do it to Lucien. He deserved more from her. Much more. And she would give it.

But her chosen one was not going to make it easy for her. His fury reverberated off the trees like harnessed lightning bolts in a jar.

She watched the she-wolf shift into a beautiful woman. Proudly she walked past Falon to Rafael.

She spoke to him in a low husky voice in a language Falon did not understand. When Rafe answered in the same language, in an equally husky voice, she felt as if she had just been kicked in the solar plexus. She froze, unable to take another step. When she turned, they disappeared into the mist. Her eyes rose to Lucien's.

Angrily he strode toward her.

Anger and hurt rose up in her chest. Anger that Lucien followed her, and hurt that Rafa had so obviously moved on. But there was also guilt. She took it out on the one she loved. "Did you follow me?" she accused.

"Yes."

"Do you think so little of me that you have to skulk around in the night and spy on me?"

"I came after you out of concern for your safety, but it seems there was another reason for me to skulk about. I find you naked in my brother's arms!"

Falon flung her arms in the air. "It wasn't what it seemed."

"Do I look like a fool, Falon?" he yelled, getting in her face. "I saw it with my own eyes. You were kissing him! You told him you wished things were different!" He jammed his fingers through his hair, and then shook his long mane. His eyes narrowed dangerously. "You want things different?"

"I wish—"

"Consider them different, Falon!" He flung his hands in the air. "I release you!" He lowered his head and said it again, "I release you! You are free to go after my brother. Hurry before he marks the beautiful Anja! Lord only knows you would never stand down if Rafe loved another!"

"You are an ass, Lucien!" she screamed. "By wanting things different, I meant that I wished no one would be hurt!"

His teeth flashed in the moonlight. "Are you hurt?"

"Yes! Are you?"

He swiped his hand across his face. "I am hurt every time I imagine you with Rafael! I had visions of the two of you fucking! So you're damn straight I came looking for you. And what do I find? You naked and in his arms just now!"

"I told him good-bye, Luca. I told him I would not disrespect you by being with him."

He shook his head, blowing hot, frustrated breaths. "I love you above my life, Falon. I could not stand it if you were unhappy with me. I meant what I said."

"What?" she asked, fearing the answer.

His smoldering eyes caught and held hers. "I release you." His voice cracked with emotion, but he stood unwavering. His simple declaration despite his anger and his palpable pain shut her down. She didn't want to fight with him anymore.

Her heart shuddered in her chest. Suddenly she was very cold. And afraid. "Where would I go if I were not with you?"

"To Rafe," he said stiffly.

"Then I would long to be with you."

"I don't want to be your default chosen one," he said roughly, turning away from her.

She grabbed his shoulder, turning him back to face her, then took his hands into hers and pressed one between her breasts, while she pressed her hand to his heart. "Don't you feel it, Luca? This is no ordinary love we share." She kissed his fingers. "I want *you*. I *choose* you. I cannot say it any plainer."

His body was tight. Everything about him was tight. Controlled. Protective. Every part of him screamed that his pride would not love a woman who loved another man. Most especially his brother. That realization terrified her. The sudden real possibility of losing Lucien pounded into her reality.

She would not let Lucien go. She could not live without him.

Her fingers tightened around his. "Luca," she quietly pleaded. "Do not cast me aside. I could not bear it."

He closed his eyes. When he opened them, she gasped. They glowed a preternatural red. Barely controlled, his beast lurked just beneath the surface. Frightened, she moved away from him. He snarled and yanked her to him.

For the first time, Falon feared Lucien's beast would hurt her. Her beast rose in her defense. Lucien snarled again. "Do you acknowledge I am your one and only alpha?"

"Yes," she said with no hesitation.

"Will you submit all to me, Falon?" he roughly demanded.

She swallowed. "Yes."

"Do you swear on my brother's life you will never lay with him again?"

"Yes." Falon squeezed her eyes shut. Her body trembled violently as she prayed she would never have a dream like she just had.

Lucien pushed away from her and stripped off his clothes, then shifted. His big, black wolf circled her as if she were a snared rabbit and he was deciding what part of her he would tear off and eat first.

Falon stood rigid but ready to shift if he made a move to hurt her. He walked behind her and pressed his warm nose to the back of her knees and sniffed. She shivered as his nose moved up her thigh to her buttocks. Falon stiffened. Guilt over her dream infected her. She swallowed hard in response to his low snarls. He moved around to the front of her and snapped at the hem of her dress, ripping it from her. She cried out, shielding herself from his blazing wolf eyes. He sniffed her feet, then her calves. As his nose rose, he snarled as he sensed where Rafe had been. His nose pressed against her fingers, she used them to shield her core from him.

She was still wet and warm. Getting wetter, warmer. He pawed her hands away. Her thighs trembled. What was he doing? Why was he doing this? Was it some form of primal reaffirmation? Would they have to start over? Part of her wanted to walk away from his bullying tactics, but the calm part of her realized that whatever he was doing, he had to do it. For him. For her. To prove something she was unsure of. And she had to allow him that.

No longer afraid, she raised her chin, straightening her back. Her breasts rose, her aching nipples speared the cool night air. Lucien's wolf licked her thigh. Then her hip, her belly, just below her breasts. Her body thrummed with heat. Her primal core had never been hungrier for him as it was now. Was it because she was fertile? Was it because of how tender and giving he had been with her in her dream? Was it because the primal part of her longed to submit completely to his alpha?

Whatever the reasons, she did not move one muscle. He would do what he would do. And she would let him. From there, they would rebuild.

He growled low as he came around to her back. He rose on his haunches and with his great paws forced her down on all fours. Falon closed her eyes. When she opened them, she stared into Lucien's golden wolf eyes. His wolf grin was not laughing and playful. It was hungry. Primal.

"Lucien," she whispered. "Tell me what you want."

He snarled and shook his head.

Falon swallowed hard, unsure what to do. They stood at the edge of an emotional precipice. He was pushing her to the edge on purpose. To see if she would take the leap of faith with him. Proof that she trusted him. Closing her eyes, Falon held her breath for a long moment. She trusted Lucien with her life. How could she not? He was the other half of her soul.

He sniffed her neck, where Rafe had marked her. Guilt caused her to tremble. He sniffed the breast Rafa had suckled. He snarled. She gasped for air. He knew his vision had been the truth! But did he not see himself there, too?

"Lu—"

He snarled viciously and moved around to her backside. He nipped her right butt cheek. She yelped in surprised pain. But following hard on its heels was spearing pleasure. She moaned and rocked her hips toward him. She was dripping wet. And on fire.

How dare you fuck my brother behind my back!

It was a dream!

Fucking is fucking.

Luca! You were there, too! Both of you.

You're fertile, Falon. I can smell your essence for miles. No alpha can resist it. That is why, despite his vow, Rafe came to you. I will kill him for that.

"No, Lucien! It was a dream!" she screamed.

He snarled and nipped her again. Instead of soothing the pain, he nipped her a third time. His rage was surpassed only by his lust. He panted heavily, his musky wolven scent strong. Dominant. Dangerous. Electrical currents shivered through her body, sparking every erogenous zone she possessed. Her nipples hurt they were so tight. Her womb clenched and unclenched; thick moistness slickened her thighs.

Falon arched her back and made a low keening sound. Her body had caught Lucien's fire. She wanted to shift and feel his wolf inside of her. He growled, pressing his head against her bottom as if he struggled for control. She moved against him. "Take me," she begged. Great wracking sobs of emotion clogged her chest making it difficult to breathe. "Take me, damn it! Mark me, Lucien. Mark me for the last time," she pleaded.

He growled again and pushed her until she rocked back and forth, begging him with her body.

He mounted her. Falon caught her breath. "Lucien," she cried in shock. He would not. It was— With his nose, he swept the hair from her neck. He licked her jugular where Rafael had bit her. His sharp teeth nipped at her tender skin. She yipped in pain. His long, soothing tongue took the sting away.

He growled, his big, warm body possessively covering hers. Her knees and elbows trembled.

You will accept my wolf.

Lucien!

Will you?

Yes. God help her. *I will!*

He entered her. Not giving her a second to change her mind. The shock of what he did registered at the same time the taboo pleasure hit her, gut deep.

Seventeen

LUCIEN LOST CONTROL of his beast. Anger, frustration, and pain tore through him, the hurt no less than if Falon had reached into his chest and ripped out his beating heart. It had reduced him to his most primal self. He'd seen them together in his visions. Felt the love between them. The energy. His heart took a devastating blow. But when he'd seen with his own eyes, her naked in Rafe's arms, smelled their sex scent wafting throughout the forest, shouting to the world she was fertile, he saw only red. Bloodred. He still did not understand how he prevented his beast from tearing them both apart.

Maybe, just maybe it was the part of him that understood just how torn Falon was. That same wicked, jealous, dishonorable part of him that had gone uninvited into her and Rafe's bed and tormented her with lascivious thoughts and caresses, even when she'd begged him to stop.

Even now, as she accepted his beast's body inside her. Because she said she loved him. She. Loved. Him. She might love Rafe, but she chose to stay with him.

Why couldn't he accept her love for him? Was he that much of a coward? She was his, damn it! In all the ways that mattered. In body, heart, and soul. She proved that now. She accepted all of him. Even now, his beast at its most volatile. Her body trembled beneath his. But not in fear . . . His body trembled in response. Gods, she was amazing. But this was not the circumstance he wanted his wolf to meet her woman. He was behaving like an animal.

He snarled, snapping the air, furious with his behavior. Furious he had sunk to such a dastardly low, when all he wanted was her love. The red haze of his beast receded. He shifted to human and abruptly withdrew from her.

Falon's sweaty, writhing body collapsed beneath his. Still on all fours, Lucien's body jerked and twitched, his passion far from subsiding. His fury and self-hatred barely under control, he sucked in deep gulps of air, wanting to take her into his arms, beg for her forgiveness, and swear he would never question her love for him again.

Reaching out, he touched her hip with a trembling hand. Her body flinched. She turned tear-swollen eyes toward him. Her dark hair was a wild mess around her beautiful face. He had caused her so much pain and heartache with his jealousy and hatred. He did not deserve her. Someone like his brother did.

"Falon," he breathed, afraid to touch her. Afraid she would reject him. Afraid it would do him in.

Like a child who had cried too hard for too long, her chest vibrated with emotion. Her lips parted, she struggled to speak, but only a hoarse whisper emerged. Slowly she rose to her knees. Childlike, she swiped at her tears with the back of her hand. His heart melted as all of the love he had hoarded poured out of it.

"I am a colossal ass, Falon. I don't deserve you. I don't deserve anything but your contempt." He swallowed hard, reaching out, catching her teardrops on his fingertips. "I'm sorry for hurting you just now. I'm sorry for taking you from Rafe." He dropped his hand from her and moved back from her. "I love you too much to force you to stay with me." The hot sting of his own tears pricked his eyes. "I truly release you, Falon. You are free to return to Rafe. I will not stand in your way."

Unable to bear to see the joy in her eyes when it finally registered she was free to go, Lucien hung his head in humble submission, offering all of himself to her if by some miracle she would choose to stay with him, but refusing to make it more difficult for her to walk out of his life if she chose to.

Time stood still. His heart stopped beating; his breath stilled in his lungs.

Soft fingers slid through his hair. His heart lurched. Warm hands cupped his face, tilting it upward. Breath rushed from his chest. Deep blue eyes glistening with tears caught and held his. He swallowed hard, afraid to move, waiting for her to say good-bye. She moved closer. So close her sweet, warm breath puffed against his lips. Her hands tightened as she brought his lips to hers.

He wanted to melt into her lips, to gently lay her back on the soft loamy ground and make love to her. But he held back. Afraid he was misreading her signals. Because how could she love him after all he had done to her?

"You are a cad. A bully and a beast. You are jealous and vengeful. Impatient and petulant." She inhaled softly, then exhaled. "But you are my choice, Lucien. Not by default. Not by chance. And not by anyone's mandate except my own." She brushed her lips across his. "You are my alpha, Lucien Mondragon. I am yours. I submit to you as you submit to me now. In all things we are equal." She pulled him to her as she lay back onto the moss. "Except one."

His body trembled as he followed hers to the ground. He swallowed hard before he asked, "What exception is that?"

A ghost of a smile tugged her lips. "That you never deny me."

He smiled widely. "I live to serve you, oh, great and beautiful alpha."

As his hips pressed to hers, she raised her legs and wrapped them around his hips. "My time is at hand," she breathed. "I can feel it. Tonight we begin the next generation."

He trembled above her, afraid *he* was dreaming. Afraid he would wake up and it would all be gone.

"Now, Luca. My body is on fire for you."

Her wild, feral scent was intoxicating. Her sensuality simmered hotly, on the verge of boiling over. He slid into her slick heat, not stopping until he touched the tip of her womb. She moaned, arching into him. Her deep blue eyes softened with emotion. Bracing over her on his elbows and knees, he cupped her face in his hands.

The velvet lining of her vagina hugged him tightly, lovingly, wantonly. He felt her heartbeat thrum through her, to his cock, to his balls, to his own frantic heartbeat. "I love you," he whispered. "With all my heart, I love you."

It began slow and unhurried. Two bodies reverently worshipping the other. But the flame burned too hotly within them for slow. Their tempo increased. Their breaths shortened, as their bodies struggled with a wild, roller-coaster give and take.

Lucien's lips claimed hers in a wild, deep, soul-stealing kiss. His heart, body, and soul reached for hers. And hers answered without hesitation.

As the sun broke through the sleepy haze of night, they made love. They mated as nature intended. They became one, and then shattered into thousands of tiny pieces of love, hope, and renewal.

* * *

FROM THE EDGE of the Amorak camp, Rafael stood unmoving as he watched his brother make love to the only woman Rafe would ever love. Rage. Fear. Lust. And a deep abiding love for the woman who called his brother's name as she climaxed mixed in a deadly cocktail.

His beast snarled for release. The Eye of Fenrir flared with vengeful heat on his hand.

What Rafe had done earlier was underhanded, it was cowardly, it was wrong on every level imaginable, and he would not undo it. Fuck his honor. Fuck his pride. Fuck his damn vow!

All he wanted, *needed*, was Falon in his arms. She had scared ten years off his life when she lay dying from the infected Slayer blood. He had felt as helpless as he felt the day his parents were slain before his eyes.

He growled low. He had chosen to stay behind locked doors that terrible day. Had forced Lucien to as well, saying that they gave their word to their mother and should honor it no matter what. Honor. What had it gotten him but heartache? He lived with the guilt of the fallout of doing the honorable thing every day of his life.

Tonight he had thrown his honor and all the bullshit strings that went with it out the door. He wanted to see Falon. Needed her as he needed air to breathe.

When he went to her earlier, he had gone only with the intention of slipping into her subconscious to hold her. One last time. Before— he snarled—before he marked another. But what he found was her running, dreaming, wishing that he and Lucien would stop fighting and become one with her.

He hadn't had the willpower to stop himself from following her. He had not planned to do anything more than hold her. But when her dream took off in that wild direction, he knew it would be his only chance to connect with her one more time. Before, honor bound, he marked the noble Siberian she-wolf. He looked over his shoulder making sure Anja had not followed him. She was a worthy mate, but not the one Rafe wanted.

But what he didn't expect when he found himself buried balls deep in Falon was to experience the love she felt for his brother. It was as much a part of her as her love was for him. It was strong. Undeniable. He hated that she loved Lucien. Hated that she found comfort in his brother's arms when all Rafe wanted to do was love her. But despite his jealousy over Falon's feelings for Lucien, it was Rafe's reluctant love for his brother that made making love to Falon as she also made love to Lucien bearable. It had been damn sexy watching her body morph into that hyper-sexually-aware state she was in when she came undone around him. The energy from her orgasm had shot straight to his cock and balls, infusing him with vitality. She did that to him. He was omnipotent. The king of the world. And she belonged to his brother.

He scowled, looking back at the couple lying entwined on the ground. Their bodies finally parted. Falon's breasts rose and fell in short shallow heaves as she caught her breath. Lucien, he silently snarled. Lucien, the ladies' man of all ladies men, kissed each nipple, then worked his way down her smooth belly.

Accepting Lucien with Falon in his dreams was one thing; reality was altogether different. Jealousy tore through him.

He could not bear to watch as Falon parted her thighs for Lucien's mouth. Her sweetness was still on Rafe's own tongue. Oh, how she had clung to him, taking all of him into her, her velvet lining fisting him possessively. He didn't care that Lucien was there. Didn't care that she was the happiest that he had ever seen her with the two of them. All he cared about was being inside her. Filling her with his unrequited need. Marking her with his seed.

Rafe smiled.

Falon's essence screamed fertility. He had caught her irresistible scent miles away. He could not have stayed away. Not even for honor's sake. Her blood coursed through his veins and his in hers. Their bond was too strong to break, despite what the Blood Law decreed.

Had his seed struck home tonight? He scowled. Or would Lucien's? Time would tell if her womb bore the fruit of his seed or his brother's. What would Lucien do if Falon gave birth to a golden-haired babe?

Rafe growled possessively. Brother or no, Rafe would raise his child as Vulkasin.

And it would tear Falon in half if he took their child from her. Rafe could not bear to hurt her like that. What would Lucien do? Shun the child? Refuse to raise his brother's get? Rafe exhaled as he reluctantly looked back at the happy couple. Lucien was a bastard to be sure, but he was not a monster. He'd proven over the last few days what had come to be more important to him than revenge. When he had arrived with Falon to save Lucien, he sensed then that much of his brother's vengeance had left him.

Rafe smiled bitterly. Falon had a way of making a man realize what wasn't important. Who knew angry, vengeful Lucien had the capacity to love as deeply as Rafe did? Because Mara was not love. It was black magic–induced lust. He'd go to his grave knowing she was a Slayer and he had done the righteous thing.

But none of that mattered. Lucien was making a life with Falon because he loved her. Not because he wanted to piss Rafe off. Could Rafe ask anything less of him? No, but it would never change Rafe's love for Falon. Or his desire to have her back in his arms, as his chosen one.

He knew Lucien would raise Rafe's child as his own if Rafe did not stake his claim. How could he rip his child from Falon's arms? But how could he allow him to be raised Mondragon?

There was no answer that would not destroy the other. And he did not want to destroy even as he watched her make love to his brother. Rafe realized the last thing he wanted to do was cause Falon more heartache than she had already suffered. But he so desperately wanted to be a part of her life. To touch her. To make her laugh. To make her sigh with contentment. Father her children.

He wanted all of that and more. He moved back into the tree line. But he could not have Falon, not without killing his brother. And for that, she would never forgive him. He would not be able to forgive himself, either. For all that Lucien was, he was his brother, and he loved him.

So, he was back to square one. The woman he loved was lost to him forever.

He looked back toward Vulkasin where Anja waited. Where his pack waited. Willing him to mark the white wolf so that she could return the mark. But—he could not bring himself to do it. Not yet. He had until the full moon.

He swiped his hand across his face and stepped farther back into the trees. His pack had waited sixteen years for him to mark a mate. When he had marked Falon, they'd rejoiced. When she'd been stolen from them, they'd fallen into despair. Anja gave them hope that they would soon be able to conceive.

"Rafael," a softly accented feminine voice called to him.

He turned to Anja's smooth alabaster body glowing amongst the trees. She was naked, except for the small dream-weaver necklace she wore. A welcome gift from him. As stealthy as the wolf she was, she approached him. Her gaze followed his to where Falon and Lucien lay joined together.

"She is beautiful," Anja said.

"She is."

"She is fertile."

"She is."

"She loves your brother."

Rafe nodded, hating the truth of her words. "She does."

Anja turned to him. Her crystal-clear eyes burned hot with desire. Like a gossamer butterfly, she lowered herself to her knees before him. He hissed a long breath, touching her silky soft platinum-colored hair as she smoothed her palm up his erection, rubbing her thumb across the thick bead of moisture crowning his cock head.

"Is this for her?"

Rafe grit his teeth. "It is."

With a slow wide swath of her tongue, Anja licked the pre-come from his cock. "Then you are wasting it."

She rose and stood almost eye to eye with him. She was tall, graceful, intelligent, and powerful. "When you are ready to rise like that for me, Rafael Vulkasin, you know where to find me."

She stalked off, leaving Rafe with a raging hard-on, not for her, but for the one woman he could never have again.

Eighteen

THE GROUND RUMBLED beneath her. Falon's first coherent thought was an earthquake. Not giving it much mind, she snuggled deeper into the strong arms that held her. She'd slept through worse.

"Slayers on horseback," Lucien whispered urgently, grabbing her naked body from her resting place. "We need to go!"

Falon's heart rate leapt as all of her senses fired up. *Slayers!*

"My mother!"

But Lucien was already running toward her little cabin. As they approached, Layla stumbled from the doorway. Angor growled viciously from behind them.

"It's a hunting party," Layla choked out. The horror in her eyes terrified Falon. She knew her mother was reliving the last time she'd come face-to-face with a Slayer hunting party.

Lucien hoisted the healer onto Angor's back. "Take her to Vulkasin," Lucien commanded the Berserker. The great mutant wolf growled in understanding, but did not move. His piercing red eyes focused on Falon. "Go, Angor. Take my mother to Vulkasin."

The great beast leapt past them into the forest. Some of the fear in Falon subsided. Her immediate worry, her mother's safety, was no longer a concern. From the direction of the wind and the intensity of their scent, she knew the Slayers traveled toward them from the south. And while horses traveled at a good clip, Angor was strong and twice as fast as any Lycan in full wolf. He could navigate the abundant pine and unruly terrain much easier than a mountain goat much less an equine. Layla was safe. For now.

"Lucien," Falon said, her blood warming for a fight. "I can taste their blood."

Lucien grinned down at her. "I appreciate your bloodlust, love, but we're running."

Shocked he would turn tail, Falon demanded, "Since when does Mondragon run from a Slayer?"

He grabbed her hand and pulled her toward the pond. "Never has a Mondragon run from a single Slayer, not even a handful, but that is a hunting party heading our way, and while our combined power and skill is formidable, we don't stand a chance against what's coming."

Lucien shifted and Falon followed suit. *We're going to give them the run around until Layla and Angor are safely at Vulkasin, then we'll head south to Mondragon.*

Falon growled, not liking the passive action but understanding the reasons for it. They took off due west, allowing the snarling pack of dogs leading the horde to get a glimpse of them. Fear shimmered along her spine at the brief but powerful sight. At least two dozen mailed and weaponed Slayers astride thundering black-leather-studded horses.

As wolves, Falon and Lucien had the tactical edge over the horses.

They could easily maneuver beneath the thick pine forest and rocky terrain. But the mastiffs that were barking and snarling less than one hundred yards behind them were in excellent shape and, though heavier, possessed stamina.

Sensing her concern, Lucien soothed her. *We have the edge, just stay beside me.*

For nearly an hour she did. Though they kept a comfortable lead, each time Lucien turned southward, the Slayers fanned out behind them preventing them from making the turn. Falon was beginning to get winded.

Ride my draft, Falon.

Falon slowed to step in behind Lucien.

The mastiffs behind them didn't have a fatigue problem.

Dogs of war, they had the benefit of their masters' black magic.

I cannot continue this pace, Lucien.

Make it over the next ridge, angel, and we'll be two miles from Vulkasin.

Vulkasin would be a welcome respite but were they leading death to their doorstep?

I would not bring harm to my brother or his pack. The compound walls will hold the Slayers at bay.

But as they crested the ridge, a gauntlet of Slayers awaited them at the bottom. In their hurry, they hadn't noticed the wind shift or the scents that went with it.

Falon skidded to a halt in the damp loamy earth halfway down the hill. Lucien's strong body kept her from tumbling into the waiting thugs. They turned to go back up the ridge but the blazing eyes of a dozen possessed dogs formed a wall preventing their escape.

Stay calm, Lucien said.

If we shift and combine forces, I can push the dogs back.

Are you strong enough?

Yes!

Simultaneously they shifted then grabbed hands. Falon faced the dogs and with every bit of mind power she possessed, she raised her hands and shoved them backward. As the dogs went tumbling backward over the ridge, the Slayers thundered up the hill behind them.

Falon whirled around with Lucien and just as she shoved her hands palms out toward the two dozen Slayers, her jaw dropped in shocked awe.

Standing behind the Slayers were Rafael's six gigantic mutant wolves, their fanged jaws flashing in the morning sunlight. Behind them, all of Vulkasin stood in full battle gear, and behind them, the Russian packs.

The Slayers reined their horses around and faced the deadly threat. The horses pawed the soft ground nervously. Snarling behind them, the dogs regrouped along the ridge, catching Falon and Lucien between the bad guys.

Rafael drew his double swords and sneered. "Today is your day to die, Slayers!"

A sword, Rafe! Lucien called.

In a lightning quick move, Rafael hurled one of his swords to Lucien. He leapt high into the air to grab it. As he came down, he kicked dirt into the closest Slayer's horse's face. The steed snorted and reared and as he came down, Lucien leapt into the air again and decapitated the Slayer. As his body fell to the ground, Lucien grabbed his sword and tossed it to Falon.

Momentary confusion rippled through the Slayers. Vulkasin and the Russian packs took advantage of it. As if they had been practicing the tactic for ages, they circled the demons on horseback.

The dogs on the ridge snarled and snapped, rushing them. Falon raised her sword pointing at the pack. "Down!" she commanded. No one was more surprised than the Slayers when they obeyed.

"Attack!" the Slayer leader commanded from behind Falon.

Their haunches bunched up to leap. Falon stepped boldly toward them. "Down!" Her voice boomed through the pines, forbidding everything but obedience. The savage hellhounds whimpered like pups and lay down again.

With her free hand she raised her hand in the stop position and said firmly, "Stay!"

She turned to the furious Slayer and smirked. "Even your black magic cannot trump a true bitch's power."

Nearly two dozen pairs of eyes glittered malevolently at her from behind dull black, split-nose helms. The Slayers were furious, but she also sensed their apprehension of her. Word had begun to circulate. It was well known she had destroyed Edward, second most powerful Slayer only to his brother Balor. She was sure these guys, though not the same scent as clan Corbet, knew she'd had a hand in Ian Corbet's death, not to mention the hash she and Lucien made out of the Vipers last week. It was established she had powers a normal Lycan did not, and that she was not shy about using them on Slayers. But what most likely gave them the most cause for concern was the fact that the two most powerful alphas on earth coveted her above all other women, Lycan and mortal. She was special. And she owned it.

I'll handle them, she said to Lucien and Rafe. It wasn't a request, but a command. As the hellhounds obeyed so did her alphas. But unlike the hounds, Lucien and Rafe were highly alert and prepared to assist.

"Who are you? And what is your status amongst your clan?" Falon demanded of the first in command. "And who"—she pointed to the pile of ash at her feet—"was he?"

"I am Eric Warner, nephew of Balor and sergeant at arms for clan Corbet." He looked absently down at the bloody corpse. "That was my brother Jonas, the former captain of my uncle's guard."

Falon raised her sword to Warner. For a brother, he didn't seem overly sad. His lack of emotion solidified for Falon the coldhearted contempt she had of the Slayers. They were an evil bunch bent on simple destruction. Not because of the lore, but because they were simply terrorists who enjoyed, no, *lived* to kill. "He wasn't very good at his job." She narrowed her eyes and asked, "How would you like to die today?"

His horse pawed the ground as if he were asked the question. "I would ask the same question of you." Warner sneered.

His band of Slayers had slowly drawn into a tight circle, much as Ian's men had when they were under attack. The only difference being they did not form a protective circle around Warner, though they were tightly woven into an impenetrable wall of horseflesh, chain mail, and weaponry. The Slayers may be outnumbered twelve to one, but they were better armed and— Falon's gaze swept the leather-wrapped spiked forelegs of the sturdy horses. Those razorsharp spikes could shred a human or wolf in half with one move. If they attacked, they were going to lose Lycans in the process. Sparing even one Lycan life was paramount not only to Falon emotionally, but to the eventual rising.

Her bloodlust for a fight warred with her need to be diplomatic. She was feeling cocksure of her rising power. So she flexed her muscles. "I'll give you the first shot, Eric. If you miss or if I deflect your effort, then you dismount and give me the same opportunity. If I hit my mark, you all die."

A collective gasp went up from both factions.

Falon! Lucien and Rafael said at the same time, stepping forward.

Stand back! By your actions you show your lack of confidence in me!

But it was exactly those actions that gave Warner the notion she was not as powerful as rumored.

"I'll take that offer and up you one," Warner said confidently.

Falon nodded.

"I hit you, even a nick, my men are to remain unharmed and you return to clan Corbet with me."

The silence was so deafening you could hear a pine needle drop onto the soft ground.

"I agree." She stood where she was, only ten feet from the mounted Slayer, and raised her arms with the sword clasped in her right hand. "Take your best shot."

Warner raised his sword high over his head, and just as he was about to hurl it, he tossed it to his left hand and pulled a nasty looking dagger from a short sheath on his belt. As it touched the air, it glowed white-hot. In a low throaty drone, he chanted a spell. The blade hummed to life in his hand.

She'd been duped! Falon steeled herself as the heat of the conjuring spell gripped her. Invisible hands grasped hers, squeezing her sword hand until the weapon dropped from her numb fingers. Her legs wobbled unsteadily beneath her. Wide-eyed, she stared, unable to speak as Warner's incantation gripped her.

The only thing unparalyzed was Falon's mind. She was as clear and coherent as a full moon on an endless night. Wary and powerless to stop it, she watched the dagger rise above Warner's head, the glinting tip of the blade pointing directly at her heart. With the speed and heat of a laser it burned into her chest. The velocity of the hit forced her backward several feet.

She heard Lucien's calls to her, but her anger was so thorough, she had eyes and ears only for Warner. Her anger was not at the Slayer, it was at herself for underestimating the Slayer's power. And overestimating hers.

Her body was numb, no longer in her control. The dagger burrowed deep into her. Twisting and turning, tearing her flesh and bones. Tunneling for her heart.

In her peripheral vision, the thud of hooves on the ground, the clash of steel, snarls, and screams reverberated in her head. The warm spray of Lycan blood spattered her face.

Her knees buckled, her vision clouded. She collapsed to the ground. Falon fought to stay conscious, not to succumb to the cold grayness that engulfed her. What had she done?

Luca . . .

A strong hand clasped her right hand. Another her left.

The power of three, angel face.

Luca. Rafe.

Focus, Falon! Rafael commanded. *Focus.*

The power of the alphas infused her with energy. Her eyes flew open. *No,* she cried out as she watched one Lycan after another fall beneath Slayer swords. The pain of watching them fall was more than the pain of the dagger in her chest. It was her fault they fell.

Lucien and Rafael pulled her to standing as they fought off Slayers. Falon dug deep, knowing the combined power they possessed.

As she had Ian Corbet's bullets, she forced the dagger from her chest. Mesmerized, she watched it rise above her then turn traitor to its master.

"You swore to accept the outcome of the challenge!" Warner screeched.

Falon shrugged. "I lied." And she'd do it again. Wasn't all fair in love and war? Fascinated, she watched the dagger. Like a flash of lightning it flew at Warner just as he wielded his sword above his head to separate Lucien's head from his shoulders.

Wide-eyed, the Slayer screamed as the blade sliced into the tightly welded metal links of his mail, then found its way home, deep in his chest. Breaking her hold with Rafael, Falon reached for Warner's sword. Amazingly, it cleaved to her hand as if it recognized her as its new mistress. With power beyond her measure, Falon swung

the great weapon high over her head and brought it down on Warner's neck as he fell from his horse. He hit the ground in two pieces.

Falon cried a feral battle cry when the remaining Slayers turned
their horses, spurring them to safety.

"After them!" Lucien cried. As one, the packs shifted and like a
nightmare they took off after the Slayers. The Berserkers took the lead,
and as they came up over the ridge, they leapt into the air and down
upon the remaining horsemen as they hit the bottom of the crevice.

Their powerful jaws bit off several Slayers' hands, disarming
them. Falon grabbed a sword in her jaws from the ground and in full
gallop, she flung it at a fleeing Slayer. It sunk deep between the
shoulders. As he hit the ground, she pounced on him, tearing him
into unrecognizable pieces. The balance of the packs swarmed
behind her and soon, every horse was riderless. Quickly, Falon
shifted, as did Lucien and Rafe. Along with the others, they made
quick permanent work of the remaining Slayers. For long moments
Falon stood naked between Rafe and Lucien, blood spattered, chest
heaving, her heart rate frantic, and watched in fascinated excitement
as each Slayer turned to ash.

Euphoria infused her. She looked up into Lucien's sparkling eyes
and heat swept the length of her. Her nipples tightened and her
breathing labored intensely as she sensed his heightened sexual
awareness. She could not have turned off the thing between them if
she wanted to. There was something about the heat of the battle with
Lucien that brought out the most primal part of her. She growled
softly, wanting him with an intensity neither one of them could deny.

He slipped his bloody arm around her waist and pulled her tightly
against his chest. "I swear by all that is sacred, Falon, if you ever pull
another fool stunt like that again, I'll kill you myself!" His lips
crushed against hers. Falon moaned, leaning into him. His skin
burned against hers. His cock lengthened against her belly.

Rafael's possessive growl behind her stoked her primal fire to inferno-grade heat. Lucien's arm tightened around her waist, his kiss deepened. When Rafe touched the small of her back, Falon cried out. His added touch sent shock waves through the three of them. Lucien snarled and pulled her away, like a dog with his bone, unwilling to share. She understood. She belonged to Lucien.

"Rafael—" a deep accented voice called from several feet away. Instinctually, Falon knew it belonged to Anja's sire.

Lucien pulled her away from the fray and into the thick grouping of trees nearby. "Lucien, we can't—" Falon protested despite her yearning for him.

"As much as I want to lay you down and make love to you right this minute, Falon, I pulled you away so that Rafe could save face with his future in-law."

Shocked, Falon looked up at him. His passion was still thick and hot against her, but his eyes looked past her to the heated discussion going on between the two alphas. "Why?"

His bright golden eyes turned from the animated conversation going on in the clearing to her. They softened when they rested on her. He raised his hand and gently swept the blood and grime from her cheeks. "Because, once again he came to our aide. I owe him my respect for that if nothing else."

Falon smiled and pressed her hand to his. Bringing it to her lips, she kissed it. "You never cease to amaze me."

Lucien smiled and looked past her to the alphas. Falon followed his gaze. They stood toe to toe, nose to nose, their voices low and furious.

"He has called Rafe out," Lucien said softly.

"What does that mean?"

Lucien's arm tightened around her possessively. "Rafe either marks the old man's daughter tonight or fights the old wolf to one of their deaths to preserve her honor."

Nineteen

LUCIEN TILTED FALON'S head up. Dreading the truth, he asked the question burning his tongue. "Does your heart still long for what you can never have again?"

The tension in Falon's body tightened. He fought the urge to pull away. He was a fool to have asked, but he would hear her out. He had after all asked the question. Slowly she shook her head, but the glitter of tears in her eyes belied what he knew was in her heart. "I will always love Rafael, and if I said the thought of him making love to Anja would not hurt me, I would be a liar." She smiled softly and gently touched his fingers on her chin. "But my love for you has filled my heart to full. You have revealed your true self to me, Lucien. You've trusted me with your heart. I have entrusted mine to you. That bond cannot be broken. Not by my feelings for Rafe, not by anything."

Lucien swallowed hard as the truth about Mara surfaced. His gut did a slow, unsteady roll. "Falon, I—I am not the man you think I am."

She rose on her toes and kissed his lips. "You are much more."

He gathered her tightly in his arms. Her sweet essence filled his nostrils. "I need to tell you the truth about Mara."

Falon shook her head and nipped at his shoulder. Heat flared hotter in his loins. She laughed and rubbed her belly against his erection. "If you told me she was the love of your life, it wouldn't matter. So long as I am the chosen one of your heart, her ghost will never come between us."

She pulled back just enough to gaze up into his eyes. The truth tasted sour in his mouth. But to cleanse his palate, he needed to tell her. "There is more to it than that."

Falon's brows wrinkled. "Is she alive?"

"No!" he hurried to assure her.

"Then there is nothing to discuss." She looked past his shoulder to the clearing. "The alphas have come to an agreement."

Lucien turned to see Rafe and the elder alpha begin to address the packs. Falon slid her palm down Lucien's burgeoning cock and squeezed him, then looked longingly down at the wide bulging head. "The dragon is going to have to wait. The last thing I want to do is to walk out there amongst battle-excited males smelling like the one thing on all of their minds."

Lucien growled softly and nuzzled his cock deeper into her hand. "I would kill any one of them who so much as sniffed you."

"After the rising, beat your chest to your heart's content; until then, behave yourself."

Falon released him. He hissed in a deep breath, resisting the urge to press her up against the tree and sink balls deep into her. It would always be so with her. The hunger for her body. The need for her heart. The fear of losing her . . .

Falon grasped his hand and walked with him to the gathered packs. As soon as she was within scent, the males turned hungry eyes on her. She was the only female present, and though walking amongst them naked was commonplace, at that moment, she felt exposed under their hungry eyes. She met their stares with her chin high, refusing to be ashamed of her body. Deep in the combined packs, a wolf snarled and snapped his jaws. A sharp command in Russian squelched it. Rafe dragged reluctant eyes from her and turned away, growling low.

"Mount our wounded on the horses," Rafe ordered. "Then collect the Slayer swords."

"What of their dogs?" Falon asked.

Rafe turned stormy eyes on her. "They will be destroyed."

"No!" she said, striding toward him.

"Their fate is not up for debate."

"Rafe, please, they're victims of their masters. You saw how they responded to me. Give them to me. I'll take full responsibility for them."

He growled low, shook his head, and turned away from her.

She grabbed his arm to stay him and plead her case. He hissed and jerked away from her. "Don't touch me," he ground out.

Falon opened her mouth to tell him to go to hell. To tell him if she could control herself then damn it so could he! But she didn't. She would not disrespect him that way.

"They're possessed, Falon," Lucien said, coming up behind her. "There's no telling what spells inhabit them."

"But they are innocent creatures!"

"For all we know they may be Slayers in the guise of hounds. One minute they can be curled up in front of the fireplace and the next slitting our throats."

"But what if they are what they appear to be? It would be inhumane to destroy them!"

"Would it have been any less inhumane to have been torn apart by them?"

She shook her head, not wanting to agree with Lucien's rational. In her gut she knew he was right, but they had responded to her! She looked up to the ridge to see them in the exact position as when she commanded them to stay. "Come!" she called.

Rafael snarled, drawing his sword. The packs responded in kind. As the massive dogs charged down the hill their auras flickered black and red. Falon's heart thundered in her chest. Black auras always meant the same thing: evil. It was the aura of every Slayer she had encountered. Red equaled passion. Whether anger or love was hard to tell, but in this case she could guess. She stepped aside and closed her eyes, allowing Rafe and Lucien to do what they needed to do. She covered her ears until it was over. She turned to see the mutilated dogs materialize into human form, their tattoos identifying them as Vipers.

Dark foreboding stole over her. She had been so easily duped. Not once but several times by Slayer magic. How far would they go? How powerful were their spells?

"Why did they obey me if they were Vipers?" she asked mystified.

"They knew what you were capable of and valued their lives," Rafael said simply. As he strode angrily past her, he said for her ears only, "Never defy me again." His tone left no room for rebuttal. Her female wanted to tell his male to go to hell, but she understood his anger. Once again she had challenged him in front of his pack and this time before the visiting packs. It made him look weak, when he was anything but.

Once the horses were collected and the wounded mounted on them, the packs shifted and ran for home. Falon was glad to be gone from the battlefield and the foreboding that haunted her since she was so abruptly awoken that morning. She wanted the sanctity of her and Lucien's room where she could relax and feel safe. She had mixed feelings about returning to Vulkasin. Anja would be there, and so would her family. She would always consider Vulkasin her family. And in fact, by way of both alphas, they were. Falon shifted with her mate. Side by side they ran with the wind, the day's victory sending their spirits soaring, but even, Falon thought, if the day had not started so exciting, so long as Lucien ran beside her, even the most mundane of days would be exhilarating.

As they broke through the forest edge into a wide clearing, Vulkasin loomed dark and powerful ahead. The three-story block walls stood like silent sentinels, protecting the pack within. Emotion flooded Falon. So much had happened behind those fortress walls . . .

Just before the massive gates opened, Falon and Lucien shifted. As they strode hand in hand into the compound yard, they were enthusiastically welcomed by the females of all three packs. Anja, beautiful and ethereal stood center stage, smiling as she caught sight of Rafael. But her smile waned when she saw Falon behind him. It didn't matter that she was with Lucien—her mere presence was enough to cause distress. Falon understood. She would feel no different, and if truth be told, she had her own demons to deal with each time she encountered the lovely Anja. Jealousy, anger, and oddly enough, pity. While Anja would have most of Rafael, the artic beauty would never have his most cherished part: his heart.

As they made their way into the large log structure that was their main living space, they settled in the large common room. The Vulkasin females swarmed Falon, touching her, stoking her hair and smiling. Their mood shifted from excited welcome to highly-charged fervor once they caught a good whiff of her. They didn't stop touching Falon. Indeed they touched her more. Guarded but inquisitive.

They sniffed her hair, her skin, her breasts. Their attention made her uncomfortable. She looked to Lucien for answers but caught Rafael's scowl instead.

"Why are they acting like this?" she asked him.

Before Rafe opened his mouth to answer, the males began to circle the group of gathered females. Musk-scented pheromones flew around the room. Clothes were coming off as their musky scents intensified. Rafael's scowl deepened. Falon moved back from the rutting pack, afraid one of the males would grab her in his lust-induced state. And that's exactly what it was. The pack was acting just like it had the night Rafael marked her; and the way Mondragon acted when Lucien marked her. The packs had gone into full-blown orgy mode. Except now there was a fierce urgent undertone that had been absent before.

"Cease this now!" Rafael roared above the grunting, moaning packs.

"Ask the sun not to rise, Rafael," Layla said, pushing her way through the horny throng. "You will have better luck."

"Why are they in full rut?" Rafael demanded. "I have not marked my chosen one."

Layla's dark eyes danced merrily. "Indeed you have and she is fertile. Your pack recognizes what you do not."

"That's impossible!" he said, looking at Anja, whose cheeks reddened.

"Not her," Layla said softly. She turned to gaze at her daughter. "Vulkasin recognizes Falon as your true mate."

Falon stood stunned by her mother's words. Her gaze lifted to Rafael's and saw hope flicker in his deep aqua eyes. Her heart hammered against her chest. It was impossible!

"Then I suggest," Lucien said tightly to Layla, "that you explain to them that's not possible."

Layla shook her head. "Mother nature does not recognize the Blood Law."

"This is an outrage!" Anja's sire bellowed, shoving past the half-naked pack. The thick grizzled alpha grabbed his daughter by the arm and thrust her into Rafael's. "Take her now and mark her!"

"Father!" Anja gasped.

His thick bushy eyebrows slammed together. "Return the mark, daughter!"

Falon stood in shocked silence. She thanked all the gods that Lucien, who stood beside her, save for his one comment, kept his seething rage leashed.

When Rafael hesitated, Sasha erupted. The Siberian alpha turned raging eyes on Falon. "How dare you entice one who is promised to another?"

"I—" Falon began indignantly.

The old alpha reached for her.

Growls erupted from Lucien and Rafe. Lucien stepped in front of her just as Rafael set Anja from him.

Vehemently, Falon shook her head and held up her hands. "It's true!" she admitted. She looked the old man straight in the eye. "Though unintentional." She bowed her head as a sign of respect to the old alpha, then turned to his daughter. "My apologies, Anja; it has not been my intention to dishonor you or Rafa—er, Rafael."

She stepped back and looked into her first love's tortured eyes. It took everything she had not to tell him she loved him.

But what she did next was harder. She had to do what she knew she should have done before now. Taking Anja's hand, Falon placed it in Rafael's. "I relinquish all claim on you, Rafe.

"Take her to your bed and mark her. Be content to pair with such a noble woman who loves you." Falon stepped back, fighting back the tears. "Find love with Anja as I have found love with Lucien."

Her heart wrenched unbearably even though she knew releasing Rafa face-to-face and in public was the right thing to do. And yet, it felt all wrong.

Rafael stood still as stone, his disbelieving eyes locked on Falon's. There was no chance for them now. It was as it had to be. Time for them both to move forward with their separate lives.

Go, Rafa, be happy.

I will never be happy with another.

Try.

Try, as I try, she thought. Lucien made her happy. But part of her heart would always mourn for Rafe.

When Rafe turned and led Anja up the same stairway he had carried Falon up many times, Falon reached for Lucien's hand. She smiled when his big, warm fingers entwined with hers and he gently squeezed them. This was as difficult for Lucien in some ways as it was for her. Despite the emotions, the wants, and the longing, this was the right thing for Rafa. It was right for her and for Lucien. It was right for the packs. The discord needed to end for the packs to unite as one and build a new future. One without fear of Slayers. One where they were no longer persecuted.

While she, Lucien, and Rafe were meant to be together as the power of three to defeat the Slayers, it was nothing more than that. Because once they survived the rising, each pack would concentrate on rebuilding. Each pack with one male alpha and his chosen one.

It was the way of the packs. As it always had been and would forever be. She turned to Lucien whose golden eyes bore hotly into her. "Make love to me, Luca."

He took her hand and led her from the thick, humid air of the great room out into the morning breeze. Silently she followed him to the back of the main building to a small cabin. He opened the door for her and followed her in, shutting the door behind him. "This was Talia's cabin before she came to Mondragon."

It was, Falon surmised, just as Talia left it. The full-size bed neatly made with a multicolored Indian blanket draped across it, a rustic dresser with a colored-glass lamp, and a small glass-faced cabinet with jars of herbs and balms. The only other piece of furniture was a straight-back chair at the foot of the bed. Lucien pulled Falon into the tiny bathroom with the most basic of amenities. A commode, small sink, and a single stand-up shower. Lucien reached past her and turned the water on. "The stink of Slayer blood is not conducive to what I'm going to do to you." Gently he nudged her under the cold water. She gasped. He was too big to get even half of himself into the shower with her, so he did the next best thing. He lathered up the soap and as the water thankfully warmed, he washed the blood and grime from her.

"Why hasn't anyone else used this room?" she asked.

"The women keep it clean in anticipation of Talia's return."

"Don't they know she isn't coming back?"

"She may, one day."

"Why does she stay with you?"

He chuckled as he lathered her sensitive breasts. "For the same reason you do. I'm irresistible."

Falon gasped as his fingers gently plucked the aching tips of her breasts.

God, she would never tire of this man's hands on her. "Lucien," she purred. "Harder." Over the last few days there was a heightened sense of awareness of Lucien. A heightened sense of sensitivity, both physical and emotional. The urgency to mate was strong. And not just in human form, but in full wolf. It was part of the quickening, the fusing of each part of her, the primal and human to complete her evolution as a true Lycan alpha.

"Your body is changing," Lucien said softly. His hands stroked her full breasts. They were heavier, more tender, and more sensitive. "I wasn't aware perfection could be improved upon." He dropped his lips to an aching nipple and suckled her deeply.

Falon rose on her toes, digging her fingers into Lucien's long hair, pressing him harder against her. He tugged the nipple with his teeth and slowly shook his head. "Ah, God, that feels so good." Her body lit up like a Roman candle. Her slick skin slid up and down his firm muscles. The confines of the small shower heightened her urgency. She rinsed off and pushed Lucien away from the shower toward the bed.

He laughed and grabbed a towel and wrapped it around her wet body. "Give me two minutes, angel face, and I'm all yours."

Falon wanted to stay and lather him up as he had her, but knew if she did she would end up on her knees with his cock in her mouth, and while the thought of that whet her appetite, selfishly, she wanted all of him.

LUCIEN WASHED HIMSELF in record time. Every part of his body was rock hard with anticipation. Every part of him wanted to touch every part of Falon. To imprint his skin on hers. Mark his scent on every inch of her.

As Lucien felt the quickening in Falon, so, too, did he detect a change in himself. He was a wolf of the highest order. Strong. Intelligent. And sexual. But the primal part of him, the beast was always lurking now just beneath the surface of his skin. It prowled restlessly beneath his skin, fusing with his human. Demanding. Possessive. Dangerously unpredictable. It was wild, wanton, and had eyes for only one woman.

He didn't bother drying off. Instead, he strode dripping wet into the small bedroom and stopped at the magnificent sight on the bed. Falon's hair lay in a wild wet web around her glowing face. Her blue eyes blazed with passionate anticipation. Her tits were full and rosy, their peaks luscious and hard. His gaze swept down the smooth creamy plane of her belly to her hips. Then to the gentle rise of her mons. She was free of hair, smooth, and—he swallowed hard. Her glistening pink lips peeked coyly from between her thighs.

Falon slid her hand down her belly and slightly parted her thighs giving him a more intimate peek at her creamy wetness. "Lucien," she moaned. Blood shot straight to his dick. He loved the way his name rolled off her lips, like an erotic gasp. His cock throbbed. He fisted his hands, setting his jaw as she slipped a finger into her dewy cunt.

"You're beautiful, Falon."

She arched her back and pressed her finger deeper into herself. A low moan escaped her lips. "I feel as if every nerve ending in my body is raw and tied to every erogenous zone. I want to fuck. I want to mate. I want to make love." She gasped. "I can't help touching myself the way you do."

Lucien's knees buckled as she slowly fingered herself. He sat down on the straight-back chair at the end of the bed and watched as she brought herself to the edge of an orgasm. He grasped his cock and began to slowly pump himself. His balls tightened as a smooth sheen of sweat erupted along her flushed skin.

"Falon," he said roughly, afraid if he stood, his legs wouldn't support him. "Come here."

Twenty

HER BODY STILLED. As her slick fingers slid from her body, her enticing essence filled the air. Lucien's cock swelled to painful in his hand. Slowly, Falon rolled from the bed and sauntered toward him. Her scent wrapped around him, taunting and tempting him with erotic promise. When she stopped between his knees, her warmth infiltrated his skin like steam. He closed his eyes and inhaled deeply, savoring the moment. She was fertile. Perhaps she already carried his child. The prospect thrilled him with such euphoria it terrified him.

Slowly he opened his eyes and caught his breath. Her skin glistened in the afternoon sunlight, like sunshine on the beach. He reached out and touched the smooth, dewy skin between her breasts. Her chest rose as she inhaled a small gasp. He slid his finger sensually down her belly, into her belly button, then over the smooth rise of her mons.

Her body trembled when he slid his finger around her slick little clit. It was as hard as he was. "Falon," he breathed against her belly.

"You are the most amazing woman I have ever met." He pressed his lips to her warm skin just above her navel. Her fingers slid down into his hair holding him there.

Emotion swelled in his chest. He wanted to make slow, sweet love to her. He wanted to slam her against the wall and take her in one fell violent thrust. He wanted to shift and take her that way. He wanted her every way, everywhere, every minute of every hour of every day. He had lost himself completely to her and would change no part of it, not for anything.

His lips trailed a languorous path down her belly. He kissed the cradle of her left hip, then lower to the sweet swell of her pubis. He pulled back just a few inches and slid his thumbs down her slick seam, and then slipped them beneath her succulent folds. Slowly, as if revealing the eighth wonder of the world, he revealed the innermost pink of her.

Her sweet cream glistened, dripping onto his finger, one thick drop after another. "Beautiful," he whispered, pressing his lips to her. Falon moaned deeply, digging her nails into his scalp. She trembled under his touch.

"Lucien . . ."

Catching her hard nub around his tongue, Lucien swirled it, lapped it, then dug his tongue deep into her honey and licked the sweetness from her.

Her body shook violently, the electric shock of her orgasm reverberated against his lips and tongue, followed by a moist rush of female come. His fingers tightened around the cradle of her hips. He burrowed deeper into her, sucking her in a slow, erotic cadence as the waves of her orgasm subsided.

Her skin flushed warm and wet with sweat. "Luca," she moaned, sliding down to her knees between his. He lost himself in her deep sapphire-colored eyes. He cupped her face in his hands and lowered his lips to hers, kissing her deeply, reverently, honestly.

The salty taste of her tears touched his lips. "Don't cry, angel," he soothed.

She shook her head, wrapping her arms around his neck. "I feel so much. So deeply. It terrifies me."

He smiled, smoothing her damp hair from her cheek. "I feel the same, but know that I will always protect you, us, what we have." His hand lowered to her belly. He splayed his fingers across her womb. "I will never allow our children to be hurt."

She shook her head again as a fresh flow of tears erupted. "I have a bad feeling."

His eyes narrowed. "About what?"

"About everything. That hunting party today. The one last week. The Vipers. Where has Balor been through all of this? I feel as if he is slowly chipping away at us while he plots and plans our demise."

Lucien smiled tightly. "It's what he does. It's what we do."

She shook her head and laid it against his shoulder. "I feel like we're always on the defensive, Luca. Always on the lookout, never knowing what lurks around the next corner."

"It has always been so, Falon. After the rising, we will never have to look over our shoulders again." He stood, bringing her up with him. "Tomorrow afternoon, at the latest, the swords I commissioned months ago will arrive. Not only are they made of the finest Spanish steel, but they are hewn with toxic amounts of thallium and cinnabar. One nick and the Slayers will instantly become too ill to continue to fight. A downed Slayer is a dead Slayer."

He watched the light flare in her beautiful eyes before it dulled. "But what about between now and then?"

He tightened his arms around her waist, then picked her up. Kissing her, he took the two steps to the bed and laid her down on the Indian throw. "Between now and then, I'm going to discover a dozen new ways to make love to you."

Falon sighed and pulled him to her. His big, warm body protectively covered hers. She knew as long as she was in Lucien's arms she would be safe—but what of the times she was not? The dark foreboding that stole over her that morning when the hellhounds turned to Vipers had only intensified. She trembled violently, knowing something dark and dangerous lurked just outside, patiently waiting for the witching hour.

"Turn your brain off, angel face, you're giving me a complex," Lucien teased. His lips blazed a searing trail from her lips, down her throat to her aching nipples.

Falon let out a long, surrendering sigh and luxuriated in his touch. Who knew the arrogant, selfish bad boy of the Lycan nation was such a sensitive, considerate lover? His teeth nipped and tugged at a nipple. She closed her eyes and arched into him. It hurt so good. Everything he did to her felt good.

Until . . .

The sudden vision of Rafael thrusting between Anja's alabaster thighs caught her off guard. She gasped, the vision shocking her in its vividness.

Unwilling to release the image, she watched it unfold. "Rafe," Anja cried when he withdrew from her. "Do I not please you?"

"You please me fine," he growled and turned her over, pulling her up on all fours.

Falon moaned, and rolled over. Lifting up on her hands and knees, she swept her bottom against Lucien, wanting his thick heat inside of her. Lucien entered her at the same moment Rafe entered Anja. Falon cried out in pleasure, the feeling of Lucien filling her bordering on sublime. She closed her eyes and watched the image of

Rafael's thrust and retreat into Anja. In some selfish, primal corner of her mind, what should have upset her thrilled her.

The tightness of Rafe's jaw, the intensity of his eyes as he concentrated on what he was doing. He did not want Anja. Not the way he'd wanted Falon. Not the way she wanted Lucien. But his desire for the pale Lycan was enough. Rafael's long, lean golden body was as magnificent as Lucien's.

Anja cried out as Rafe drove hard into her. When he lowered his lips to the nape of her neck and bit her, Falon cried out at the same time as Anja. Whether she cried out in sadness that Rafe was lost to her now or because of the sublimity of Lucien, she didn't dare explore. Lucien's fangs sunk into her neck. His thrusts urgent, bordering on violent. His fingers clasped hers, pushing her arms over her head so that only her bottom remained in the air.

Wild and rough, he pumped into her. Falon snarled, the beast in her rising to the surface. It was answered by Lucien's. Fierce, raw, and frantic, they fucked. They snarled and bit, licking the blood from the inflicted wounds, each fighting for dominance over the other. They rolled from the bed.

On all fours, Falon turned on Lucien. His golden-colored eyes blazed fire. She tossed her hair over her shoulder and lowered her head. Lucien grabbed her around the waist and turned her around. Pushing her thighs apart with his knee he took her. Falon shifted to wolf, the shock of Lucien inside her as a human sublime. He fucked her rough, he fucked her long, and he fucked her hard. Just as she was about to come, he shifted to wolf, nipping her shoulder as a sign of his dominance over her.

She threw her head back and snarled, snapping at the air. And just as abruptly as their wild manic mating began, Lucien pulled out of her, shifting back to human. Breathless and confused, Falon shifted, too. She turned to look at him, questioning his actions with her eyes. On all fours he moved into her, pushing her onto her back.

"I love fucking you. I love your ferocity, your passion, your adventurous spirit, but right now, before we rejoin the packs"—he dropped his lips to her trembling breasts and kissed them as if he were saying good-bye forever—"I want to make slow, sweet love to you."

Falon let out a long, relieved sigh. He smiled against a nipple as he licked it to stiff. "What did you think?"

Parting her thighs, she wrapped her arms around his neck and drew his lips to hers. "That you didn't want me like that."

He shook his dark head, his eyes darkening to molten gold. "I love you that way. I love you every way. But, right now, this minute, I want to love you this way."

Hot tears stung her eyes. What was it about this man that touched her so deeply? Was it his pain? The terrible scars he bore like a battle flag, or was it the depth of his feelings? They ran deeper than the darkest depths of the ocean. He gave her all of him. And she felt guilty because she held a part of her heart safely tucked away for his brother and she knew it tore Lucien up inside.

Deliberately she had stayed out of Lucien's thoughts, not wanting to know if he was wondering if she were thinking of Rafe and Anja. Because she had, but not like he would think, she wouldn't touch on the subject.

"No one loves me like you do, Luca." And it was true. Though she had spent more time with Rafe, they had not reached the emotional depths she and Lucien had. That wasn't to say they wouldn't have, but Lucien tugged at a part of her heart that Rafe never had. The protective part of it. The beast in her would die rather than hurt this man.

"No one ever will," he said huskily, sliding into her.

More tears leaked from her eyes. Emotion swelled painfully in her heart. She didn't deserve Lucien's love. But she would not refuse it. It gave her a reason to open her eyes each morning. It was what infused her with power. It was what drove her passion.

Slowly, tenderly, as if she were a rare, fragile, priceless piece of art, he made love to her. Falon sobbed harder with each deep thrust, each reverent touch, each gentle caress, each cherished word.

No one else occupied her mind, body, or heart at that perfect moment when her body shattered around his. "Lucien!" she cried, grasping him tighter to her. He smoothed her damp hair from her eyes and kissed her as his body exploded inside of hers.

Clinging to each other like lifelines, Falon and Lucien lay in silent awe of what had just happened. It was beyond making love. It was too emotional, the word *love* too simple to describe what had transpired between them.

Falon knew if she were not already carrying Lucien's child, she was now. The emotionality of their connection was too strong for nature to deny. She took Lucien's hand and slid it down to her belly. "I think we just made a baby."

His chest constricted against hers. Pulling back, Falon looked up at Lucien. He turned away from her. "Lucien, are you crying?"

"Alphas don't cry," he rumbled.

She smiled and grasped his chin in her hand and gently turned his face to her. The sparkle of moisture glittered in his golden eyes. Her smile widened. "You are such a big, bad wolf."

She kissed him and pushed him from her and leapt to the floor, not wanting to embarrass him. "I need another shower! And clothes! I don't like walking naked around all those horny dogs out there."

Lucien lay back on the bed and stretched out, folding his arms behind his head. "I can't say that I blame any of them."

"How would you like to feel like a bone tossed into a hungry pack of mongrels?"

He laughed and said, "I used to be one of those hungry mongrels lusting after you."

She stepped into the bathroom and turned on the shower. "Yeah, and see what it got you? Misery!"

As she stepped into the shower, Lucien came into the small bathroom and leaned against the shower jamb. He crossed his arms over his chest and gave her a long, appreciative once-over. When his eyes rose to hers, she knew he had something on his mind he didn't want to discuss.

Grabbing the bar of soap she began to lather her chest. She smiled as his gaze dropped to her hands sliding across her tender breasts. "Luca!"

His lips split into a wide grin and he shrugged. "Once a dog always a dog."

She slapped the bar of soap into his hand and turned around. "Please wash my back."

When he obliged she said quietly, "Tell me what's on your mind."

"Nothing more than everything."

"Specifically, right this moment."

His hand stopped and she heard him sigh. She turned and took the soap from him and demanded pointedly, "Tell me."

"I need Rafe's help getting the swords to the northern hunting grounds."

Falon raised a brow. "And while you don't have a problem asking him for help, you're worried about how I'm going to be around him and his chosen one?"

He nodded. Falon handed Lucien the bar of soap again and turned around. When he ran it across her shoulders, she said, "It will be awkward for all of us. In the beginning at least, but we're all adults, Lucien. I accept Rafe has taken a mate. I'm even—I'm happy for him—" She turned and said honestly, "I'm glad that with his marking Anja, the pressure is off me."

"If you would return to him, he would have you."

"Well, I'm not, so he can't." Falon knew she hadn't given Lucien the answer he wanted by the tightening of his lips. But she didn't want to talk about her feelings for Rafe or choices that would never have to be made. She was weary of the stress of it all. She was focused and ready to move forward.

She reached up and turned the shower nozzle on him. "Let me rinse off, then you can have your turn."

When Falon emerged clean and dry from the bathroom she was happy to see a stack of her own clothes neatly folded on the dresser. Hers from when she lived here. Anja would have had them immediately removed from Rafe's room.

"Anja didn't waste a second, did she?" she asked as she pulled on a pair of black leather pants.

Lucien ruffled her hair as he strode past her. "Can't say that I blame her."

"Whatever."

She finished dressing as Lucien showered. As she did, she noticed a neat stack of what she knew by scent were Rafe's clothes on the chair. It hit her how ironic it was, the brothers reconciled and mated because of the one woman they nearly fought to the death to possess. Who'da thunk?

As Falon brushed her damp hair dry, Lucien dressed. He stepped around her and stared at the sheer white gauze shirt she had put on. His dark brows scrunched together as he slowly shook his head. She wasn't wearing a bra and felt more than a little like a hussy in the sheer, formfitting fabric, but it was the only shirt in the stack.

"It's all I have!"

He reached over to the dresser and opened the top drawer and pulled out a red-and-white checkered flannel nightshirt. "Wear this."

"I'm not wearing that!"

He dug deeper and found a skin-tone bra. "Then wear this."

Falon snatched it from his hand and knew it would be too tight. Talia was petite to Falon's tall, and though just as endowed as Falon, the bra would be snug. She snatched the shirt off and hurried to put the bra on. Her breasts were tender and when her hand swept across a nipple as she clasped the front clasp she hissed in a breath. Her eyes rose to Lucien's. Her skin immediately warmed. But she shook her head and backed away. He moved toward her, his laconic eyes burning with heat. His nostrils flared as he sniffed the air between them.

"By all that is holy, Falon, I don't know if I can control the beast in me anymore when it comes to you."

She hurried and pulled the shirt on and buttoned it as she tossed her hair over her shoulder. "What's wrong with us? I feel the same way. I have for several days now."

"It's the quickening of your body. It happens to females when they become fertile."

"God, let's hope it doesn't last long. I don't know how long I can go on like this."

He scooped her in to the circle of his arms. "So long as your body is only slaked by mine, I don't care how long you're like this."

Not daring to kiss him lest she start what she could not finish, Falon touched his chin and gently pushed him away to a safer distance.

A hard, rapid knock on the door startled her. "It's Joachim," Lucien said, clearly surprised.

And the foreboding she had finally been able to file away reemerged with a vengeance.

Twenty-one

"THE SWORDS ARE here, Boss," Joachim announced, stepping through the door to the small cabin. He smiled and nodded respectfully to Falon before continuing. "But we have a problem."

"What kind of problem."

The foreboding howled louder.

"The longshoremen decided to strike at midnight. We can't get to the container."

Lucien's eyes glittered. He slapped Joachim on the back. "When have we ever let a little thing like that stand in our way?"

"There's been violence. The picket line is ten men deep, and the docks are crawling with cops. Getting in and out of there is going to be like trying to break in and out of Fort Knox."

"Who says we have to break in or out?"

"Do you know someone who can help us?" Falon asked Lucien, hoping that was the case. Because she wasn't keen on dodging Oakland cops or angry truckers.

Lucien's eyes glowed preternaturally. "I have markers everywhere, including Oakland."

Joachim scratched his jaw with his metal fingers. Falon cringed, thinking if he wasn't careful he was going to rip his face off. Joachim stopped and grinned. "Oh, yeah, I forgot about that dude, what was his name? The one with the crazy kid strung out on meth—"

"Captain Tucker, OPD."

"Yeah, that's him. He owes you big-time."

Lucien smiled. "Indeed he does."

Her interest piqued, Falon asked the begging question. "How does he owe you?"

"Balor Corbet needed a high-ranking cop in his pocket. He approached Tucker and was told to beat it or he'd arrest him for bribing a police officer." Lucien shrugged. "Balor set Tucker's son up in a crack house with a naked underage girl in his arms, took pictures, and blackmailed the good captain instead."

"That's terrible!"

"It was a means to an end and not an uncommon one at that. But, as fate would have it, I'd been tracking Corbet that day. I took advantage of the fact that his posse of goons wasn't shadowing him. I was three steps away from cutting that bastard's head off when I overheard the exchange between him and Tucker. I went wolf on Corbet. Destroyed his camera with the pics and would have destroyed that bastard, too, but his thugs showed up. I knew if we went to blows I'd come out on the short end. I took the captain aside and told him one day he would have to pay for my intervention. Tonight he pays."

Falon inhaled deeply, then slowly exhaled. "Once the swords are unloaded, then what?"

Lucien smiled his wolf smile and extended his hand to her. When she slipped her small hand into his big, warm one he said, "That, my love, is the question of the hour." Joachim opened the door for them.

Lucien guided Falon out the door ahead of him, a sign of his respect, and said, "Let's go grab some chow and see what resources Rafe has at his disposal and go from there."

Falon's empty belly growled, but she was too nervous to eat.

As they crossed the compound yard, Falon looked up at the sinking sun. It was late into the afternoon. The sun would be setting soon and with that realization nervous gooseflesh erupted along her arms. She could not shake the feeling that something terrible was waiting for them on that dock.

"Lucien," she said, pulling his hand, stopping his forward motion. "I have a bad feeling about tonight."

He smiled and touched her cheek with a soft caress. "I have a bad feeling each time I leave the compound. Such is our life. But soon that will all change."

Falon pressed his hand more firmly to her. "I hope you're right."

He smiled and said, "I'm never wrong."

AS THEY STEPPED through the threshold of the clubhouse they entered into a wild, raucous party. Rafe sat with his mate at the head of the long dining table, while most of the pack cavorted shamelessly around them. It was like a Roman orgy *sans* the hard-core sex. Falon sniffed the air. From the smell of it, the hard-core sex had already taken place. Now they were celebrating Rafe's new mate.

Immediately, Falon caught his stare. He scowled, holding her gaze. Her heart somersaulted in her chest. Anja's mark was visible on his neck. Her stomach roiled nervously. She felt terrible. Not just heartsick, but guilty. Not only that Rafe was saddled with a woman he didn't love, but that the one he did love was standing in front of him, untouchable and with another man. Sharp pangs of jealousy she could not will away needled her. She knew if the positions were reversed she would be unable to control her emotions. That she had Lucien made this impossible situation bearable.

Rafe's nostrils flared as he caught her scent. His scowl deepened. Heat rose in Falon's cheeks. Had he watched her and Lucien as she watched him and Anja? Suddenly she felt ashamed for her voyeurism.

She looked away from Rafe and straight into Anja's arctic blue eyes. White-hot fire sparked in their depths. Rafe's mark was as clearly visible on Anja's creamy white neck as hers was on Rafe's.

Only by death could either one of the marked pair choose another. The mark was more binding than any human contract. It could not be undone. Except in Falon's very unusual case.

Falon swallowed hard, fighting the chaotic feelings swirling inside of her. She understood the unspoken words Anja directed at her. Rafe belonged to Anja now and she would stand for no interference from Falon. Falon nodded so subtly only Anja recognized it for what it was—an olive branch. She would not interfere.

"Falon," Lucien said, clearing his throat, "can you do this?"

She looked up into his concerned eyes and smiled, squeezing his hand. "I am alpha, I can do anything."

He returned the squeeze and called out to his brother. "Rafael, your council." It wasn't a question, but rather a respectful invitation to parley.

Rafe stood and nodded. He took a step from the table, then paused and, as if it was an afterthought, turned and extended his hand to Anja. As his mate, she had the right to be as much a part of pack business as Falon did. Regally, she slipped her hand into his and stood, her chin high, her eyes bright and sure of her place.

Falon and Lucien, with Joachim trailing behind, followed Rafe and Anja into his office. As the door closed behind them, Falon's eyes swept the room before landing on Rafe's large desk. Instantly, she remembered the last time she was in Rafe's office and how passionately Rafael had taken her there on his desk. Not once but twice.

Obviously, Rafe remembered as well, because he looked neither at the desk nor at her.

Lucien pulled a chair out for Falon as Rafe pulled one out for Anja.

"My shipment of swords is sitting on a dock at the Port of Oakland," Lucien said. "I need to get them off and to the northern hunting grounds as soon as possible."

"Why not arm our men here and travel north with them?" Rafe countered.

"If they were normal swords and the nation was here as one, I would, but neither happens to be the case."

"What is abnormal about the swords?"

"They are hewn with toxic properties; one prick by the blade and it will be a matter of minutes before the toxins infiltrate the bloodstream and render the victim paralyzed. A paralyzed Slayer is a dead Slayer. I don't want to take the chances that any one of our people will have an accident. We need every man and woman for the rising."

Rafe nodded, impressed. "How can you be so sure it will work on Slayers? Their black magic is strong and getting stronger."

"They won't be prepared for what's coming at them, and by the time they figure out what's going on it will be too late to counter the poison with magic."

Anja nodded. "We have used similar methods in Siberia against the thugs who hunt us there. But they were able to easily conjure a spell to counter the effects."

"What properties did you use?" Falon asked, trying not to sound confrontational.

Anja swept her long platinum hair from her shoulder and speared Falon with a cold glare. "Organic."

"Organic is good, but as you have said, it's easy to counter," Lucien said evenly. "Since Slayer magic works best against organic properties, I sought the expertise of a chemist. He created a synthetic alloy that if exposed to the bloodstream is lethal. It's what coats the blades."

Rafe nodded. "Then the safest, most expedient way to get them north is to fly them."

"My thoughts as well. We'll need a pilot. Under normal circumstances, a private charter would work, but in this case I don't want to take any chances of the authorities nosing around." He looked pointedly at Rafe. "Do you have access to a privately owned aircraft that can haul several tons of payload?"

He nodded. "I do." And Falon knew exactly who he was thinking of. Mr. Taylor, whose daughter Rafe had rescued last month. Mr. Taylor's gratitude was without boundaries. And he had the capital to deliver anything Rafe requested.

"I'd prefer not to fly out of a commercial airport for obvious reasons. There's a private airstrip in Galt that can accommodate larger aircraft than the weekend Cessna fliers I have access to. Can you arrange for your contact to meet us there tomorrow afternoon?"

"I can. I'm going to assume the swords will be transported via tractor trailer?"

"As soon as we can move them, that's my plan, but we have a hiccough."

Rafe cocked an eyebrow.

"The docks are shut down at the moment due to a strike. If it were something else, I'd wait it out, but every damn local union is sympathizing with the longshoremen and there's no telling how long it's going to take for them to get back to work."

"We can cross the picket line. It's legal but dangerous," Falon suggested.

"With a little help from OPD, that's exactly what we're going to do. We'll take two trailers in: one empty for the swords, the other loaded with armed Lycan."

"Does Corbet know about the shipment?" Rafe asked.

"Not that I know of, but that doesn't mean he won't catch scent of us once we cross into his territory. If they follow us or wait for us to come out, I want to be prepared."

"Use the swords then and destroy them all," Anja said, the bloodlust in her eyes flashing dangerously. Falon felt an answering heat in her own blood but she took an extra beat to consider the ramifications of their actions.

"If one of them survives they will have time to conjure a counterspell," Falon said dryly.

"Not if we kill them all," Anja argued, obviously not wanting to be thwarted by her mate's former lover.

Falon felt Rafe's body tense across the desk. Lucien on the other hand remained casual more than willing to allow Falon to flex her intellectual muscles and show up the Vulkasin alpha. He was vindictive that way, and though she didn't want to cause Rafe undue stress, she was not about to let this woman think she had one-upped Falon. Call her trite, spiteful, or vindictive in her own way, but Falon pushed back harder than she had to to make her point.

"I'm sure in your remote part of the world, the Slayers you encounter are formidable, but I surmise they are nothing compared to clan Corbet Slayers. Clan Corbet is the breeding ground of highly intelligent, bloodthirsty bastards who have mastered the art of black magic to such a level, they can blink and Lycan will drop dead. Here in the civilized world, what we have is two world powers at war, not the Hatfields and McCoys shooting buckshot across the fence at each other. So, with all due respect, when you have actually experienced what we face daily and understand their cunning and determination, you will discover it's best not to assume anything when it comes to clan Corbet Slayers."

High color stained Anja's cheeks. "My chosen one bears the Eye of Fenrir! His power supersedes every Lycan, alpha or not, including yours!"

Falon inhaled slowly and deeply, and then exhaled. "I will not dispute the power of the ring, but until Rafael understands how to wield that power it's of no use to any of us."

Anja's hands fisted at her sides; anger seethed in hot malicious waves from her. Falon leaned in and said softly, "Raise a hand against me and it will be the last thing you do."

"Cease this now!" Rafael bellowed coming to his feet. "The swords will not be unveiled until the day of the rising. Once we are north, the power of the ring will be revealed to me. Until then, both subjects are closed for discussion."

Falon sat back in her chair. Lucien's comforting hand touched her shoulder. With it, her frustration ebbed. The situation was impossible. While she could not blame Anja for her hostility, Falon didn't have to take it. She would not. She was alpha.

"Rafe, considering the emotional and physical state our packs are in, I think our combined forces will serve us better than if Mondragon takes this on alone."

Rafe nodded. "We'll be ready to leave in an hour." He walked around his desk and extended his hand to Anja. As she took it, Rafe said, "Make your preparations."

"Mondragon is ready," Joachim said. "They await only their alpha's word."

"Have them meet us at Twin Cities. I need to make a call to arrange the trucks," Lucien said as he helped Falon up. As was protocol, the hosting alpha and his mate departed first, followed by the visiting alphas. As Falon and Lucien walked back into the great room she was glad to see the activity level had calmed some. The men waited with eager faces, knowing a hunt was at hand. The females bustled around the room and kitchen, making their own preparations.

"Joachim," Lucien said to his sergeant at arms, "call Naz and have him trailer my bike to our rendezvous—"

Joachim grinned and shook his head. "I trailered both our bikes up here when I found out you were here. Your sword is in the truck, and Talia packed you both fresh clothes."

Lucien smacked him on the back. "Well done, my friend."

"How did you know we were here?" Falon asked.

"Because Lucien is my alpha and I his sergeant at arms, we share thoughts," Joachim explained. "Not to the extent that you and he do, but I get snippets of his thoughts when he opens them up to me."

Falon nodded, digesting that information. Would she still be able to reach Rafe the same way, now that the marks had been exchanged?

She wrestled with the urge to find out. She could simply wish him well and know for sure . . .

"I need to make a call, angel face," Lucien said, his voice light and chipper. She didn't want to contemplate how much he seemed to be enjoying Rafe's discomfort. Or if he was gloating. She glanced at him, and he laughed and said, "I am not such a prick as that, Falon. I know any unhappiness Rafe bears, you must in some way bear as well. I'm just happy to be here amongst my family again. It has been too long."

She smiled brightly, his joy contagious. "I'm happy you are happy."

He kissed her soundly on the lips and said, "Get something to eat, you'll need your strength," then strode back to the office.

Twenty-two

FALON GRABBED A sandwich from a laden tray nearby and ate quietly. It went down like a rock. Her stomach was still nervous.

"Falon, a word with you in private," Rafael said flatly as he approached her, at the same time indicating they should go outside.

Falon swallowed the last of her sandwich and looked past his shoulder to see Anja watching them with the intensity of a hawk.

What of your chosen one?

She does not control me.

Untold relief flooded Falon. Her connection to Rafe was not lost.

You can still hear me?

I will always hear you.

Rafael extended his arm ahead of him, and Falon moved past him to the bustling compound yard. Rafe touched her elbow and guided her to a quiet place on the side of the large log structure that housed the pack. He did not remove his hand until she stopped and turned to face him. Guilt washed through her. His touch still stirred her. She acknowledged that it always would.

He cleared his throat and took a safe step away from her. He locked his hands behind his back as if he was afraid he would touch her.

"I won't bite you," she teased, trying to lighten the tension between them.

His aqua-colored eyes blazed fiercely. "I don't know how to do this, Falon!"

A different tension filled her. "Rafa," she said, wanting to reach out and soothe his hurt but knowing she could not. "Neither do I, but it must be what it is."

"*Why* must it be?"

Shocked by his words, she stared at him. "You of all people understand the whys better than anyone."

"I have lived my entire life by the letter of the Blood Law. I have sacrificed everything. What has it gotten me?"

"Rafael, this—what's happened between us—it has united the nation. Without you, there would be no hope for a future."

"I don't want a future without you in it."

Her heart broke for the hundredth time into as many pieces. "I will always be with you in your heart."

"That's not enough, damn it," he snarled. "I want all of you!"

Falon shook her head, wanting what he wanted but not at the cost of losing Lucien. She was torn between two men she loved equally but differently. She had one, but the other? He belonged to Anja.

"Rafael, you need to stop thinking of what you have lost and instead rejoice in what you have gained. Anja is beautiful and strong, and she loves you. I can see it in the way she looks at you. Give her a chance, as I gave Lucien a chance."

"Was I that easy to replace?" he sneered.

Rafe's words stung. But before the pain could overpower her, Falon pushed it back with anger. Everything she'd done had been for the greater good and he thought it was easy? Easy to let him go? Easy to watch him with Anja? Easy to know that a part of her would always yearn for him, even as she luxuriated in Lucien's arms?

"Don't do this! I loved you with all my heart. It nearly killed me to lose you!" she shouted. Lowering her voice, she said, "My heart still aches for what we shared, but I love Lucien, too. If it were he who I lost to be given to you, I would feel the same."

Rafael stilled at her words. He looked past her to the sinking sun then focused his gaze on her. He took a deep breath, then slowly exhaled. "I have been selfless all my life. I have always put the pack first; it is what a true alpha does." His eyes blazed passionately. "It doesn't mean that I like it or that if I could change it, I wouldn't!"

"Rafael, if there was a way none of us would lose, I would move heaven and hell to get it. But you have exchanged marks with Anja, as I have with Lucien. It cannot be undone. I would not have it undone even if there was a way. I won't hurt Lucien. I don't want to hurt him. I am sorry that you are the one suffering the most. I don't know how to fix it. I don't want to hurt you or myself any more than we already hurt."

His mouth twisted bitterly. "Lucien was Mother's favorite. The one she doted upon. I was jealous of that for so long. When she died, the last word she breathed was not my father's name nor mine, it was Lucien's. I hated him for that, for having that piece of her heart I did not. I feel the same way now with you."

Falon smiled sadly. "It's funny how things reveal themselves. Lucien has always been jealous of you. The golden son, your father's heir apparent. Don't you see how your jealousies have driven you apart? He is your only living blood. He loves you! He's floating on clouds right now being here with his family. Let the shit clogging up your heart go. Let the past go so that you can rebuild a golden future."

His eyes flared, he opened his mouth to argue. She put her hand up in a stop position. "Don't say it, Rafe. What is, is. I want no part in hurting your brother or the packs."

For several long minutes, she watched Rafael wrestle silently with his heart and his honor.

"You are a true alpha, Falon," he whispered. "Your loyalty is admirable, your integrity above reproach. I will take that lesson from you." He nodded and stepped farther away from her. "But know that if you need me, for anything, I will be there for you."

"As I you."

He nodded again, his arms still locked behind his back. Slowly he turned and walked briskly back into the clubhouse. Falon stood staring at the closed door for long minutes. Her heart hurt. Her head ached. Her soul cried out for fairness. But she didn't know what fair was anymore.

Her only constant was the knowledge that she would never forsake Lucien or stop loving his brother.

The door opened and she watched her mother limp out, searching for someone. When Layla's eyes found Falon's they smiled at the same time. Falon hurried to her mother so that she didn't have to take the cumbersome steps toward her.

"How is your leg?" she asked.

"Still a little tender but better." As she spoke, Layla reached up around her neck and lifted the multicolored amulet necklace from her neck then reached up and placed it over Falon's head, settling it down around her neck. "This was your father's. He swore it gave him clarity and protection. I want you to have it."

It warmed on her skin content with its new owner. "Mother, you don't have to—"

"I want to. You'll need it tonight and every night until the one after the rising. Call upon it for strength, Falon. I have many times over the years and it has never forsaken me."

Falon caught the smooth stone in her hand and rubbed it. It pulsed in her hand. Or was that her own pulse she felt against it?

Falon drew her mother into her arms and kissed the top of her head. "Thank you."

"Let's go!" Rafe shouted, striding from the clubhouse in full leathers and swords. Similarly dressed, Lucien strode beside him.

They were heart-stoppingly handsome. One dark, the other light. Powerful, skilled and revered among their kind, the twin alphas, Mondragon and Vulkasin, the last hope for the entire nation.

Rafael's deep green eyes caught hers before quickly moving on. When Lucien's gold eyes caught hers and held her gaze, she smiled. Quickly she hugged her mother good-bye, then ran to her alpha.

Lucien's bike was warmed up. As he mounted, he stood forward to steady the machine as she hopped on. Falon saw Anja doing the same thing on Rafe's bike. She didn't think of the last time she rode like that with Rafe. She focused on the man with eyes only for her, making sure she was safely seated.

Falon smiled and put on the helmet Lucien handed her. As she buckled the strap, he gave the bike some gas and pulled up beside Rafe.

"The trucks are waiting in Hayward," Lucien shouted over the roar of engines. "We'll pick up Mondragon in Twin Cities, then take the back roads into Stockton, then work our way over to 680 and head south, then west through the canyon, steering clear of Oakland. Once we load the trailers, we'll go straight up 880 into Oakland."

Rafe nodded. The gates opened and the packs roared off. Almost seventy-five on bikes followed by several panel vans carrying more. Despite the magnificent showing of might, the pall of foreboding settled around Falon once again. But as they made their way down the Sierras and into the flatlands without incident, she thought maybe she was being overly dramatic.

When they picked up Mondragon along the delta roads, she felt better. Their numbers swelled. Once the long drive into Hayward was finally over, they loaded several bikes into the back of one trailer along with dozens of armed Lycans. The others would follow farther back but with eyes, ears, and noses alert.

As Lucien started the big Mack truck's twin diesels, Falon was grateful for the opportunity to stretch. She loved riding behind Lucien but doing so for hours on end was uncomfortable. She hoisted herself up to the driver window and said, "Don't you think it's odd that we have not caught the scent of one Viper or Slayer since we left Vulkasin?"

Lucien nodded. "It occurred to me, and there is one of two reasons for it. They are in hiding after we took care of so many of them this week, and preparing for their next attack, or they are waiting on the fringes where we can't detect them and watching our every move. I prefer the first but suspect the latter."

Falon's skin chilled. "How many are there?"

"On any given day in Nor Cal, a few hundred, but with the rising looming and Corbet recruiting like he has been, there could be three times that."

"How many worldwide?"

"Over a thousand."

"What are our numbers?"

"A little less."

Falon mulled the numbers over in her head. "If we take out Balor Corbet before the rising, what will that do to the Slayers as a whole?"

"Throw them into a tailspin. Balor Corbet is the only surviving son of the original bloodline of Peter Corbet. We take him out, the remaining Slayers' magic wanes, as does their will. The Corbets have driven this feud since it began. With that bloodline extinct, eradicating the rest will simply be sport."

"That was why it was so important to kill Edward? He was a Corbet son? And his son?"

"Yes, and Ian last week. The entire male line with the exception of Balor is gone. Only he can perpetuate it."

Excitement trilled through Falon. Meeting Balor Corbet would be a good day. It would be a better day when he lay in two pieces at her feet.

When Lucien indicated Rafe and Anja ride with them in the semi, Falon almost asked him to rescind the offer. She didn't want to be that close to Rafael in the small confines of the cab for so long. And she sure as hell didn't want to sit anywhere near his imperious mate! But that would make her look weak. She was anything but.

Once the second trailer was loaded, the four alphas climbed into the cab and headed north. As Lucien expertly maneuvered the huge semi onto the freeway, his throwaway cell phone chirped.

"Yeah," he answered.

The deep drone of a man's voice spoke for several minutes before Lucien said, "Got it." He snapped the phone shut and said, "That was my OPD contact. He's made arrangements for us to enter the dock from a closed road. His boys will be waiting to let us in."

Falon's nerves tingled along her spine as they drove north. Downshifting, Lucien took the exit ramp and turned west. The streets were quiet and dark. Ominously so.

As they approached the designated gate, Lucien flashed his headlights. A single flash of light acknowledged him, and the gates rumbled open. As they drove through, several uniformed policemen stood on either side of them and waved them toward the numbered rows of containers.

"It's too easy," Falon said. "I think we should turn around, Lucien."

He reached over and squeezed her damp hands. "No sign or scent of a Slayer. We're good."

As they pulled up to the designated container, Falon's skin chilled. This wasn't right. Something was terribly wrong.

"Lu—" Falon was about to tell him of her foreboding again but she stopped herself. She didn't want to freak him out when he was confident all was as it should be. Absently, she stroked the amulet her mother had given her and prayed to a higher power that she was wrong.

She jumped in her seat when the air brakes hissed when Lucien put the truck in park. The second trailer pulled up alongside them. Joachim gave Lucien the thumbs-up from the cab.

Lucien hopped out, followed by Rafe and Anja. Falon sat quietly in the cab, her eyes searching the darkness for any sign of danger. It was there, she could feel it, dark and menacing, but she could not put her finger on any one thing to explain her trepidation.

The passenger door opened. "C'mon, Falon," Lucien said, extending his hand. "I want you to see these before we load them."

Not wanting to but having no alternative, Falon took his hand and hopped down into his arms. He pulled her tightly against him and kissed the top of her head. "I love you."

She trembled at his words. "I love you, too," she whispered and hugged him tighter to her.

"Calm down, angel," Lucien soothed. "You're starting to make me jumpy."

Before Falon could beg him to leave, Joachim handed Lucien a large pair of bolt cutters. He returned to the container, and in one snap, the lock fell to the ground with a dull thud. Lucien grinned and looked at her, then at Rafe and Anja.

"Come see." He pulled the heavy container doors back and stepped into the dark hull. He pulled a flashlight he had taken from the truck from his back pocket and turned it on. And there, at the end of the large container, were stacks of large wooden crates.

Falon scanned the abyss and hurried in behind Lucien. She turned to make sure Rafe was close by. She caught Anja's nervous glance. It wasn't just Falon; Anja felt it, too.

As they approached the crates Lucien yelled over his shoulder to Joachim, "I need a crowbar."

They were answered with the loud boom of the doors slamming shut behind them. And then the light went out.

Twenty-three

DEEP MANIACAL LAUGHER reverberated around them. Terrified, Falon reached for Lucien in the darkness. It took her keen wolf vision just a few seconds to adjust to her blacked-out surroundings. As Lucien's fingers wrapped around hers, they backed toward Rafe and Anja. Together they might stand a chance against what lurked there in the darkness.

"Balor Corbet!" Lucien shouted. "Show yourself, you spineless coward!"

More laughter mocked them. "Is the life of your beloved whore worth the Eye of Fenrir, Mondragon?"

"I do not possess the ring."

Falon moved closer to Rafe, and with her free hand she grasped his with the ring. It surged with heat against her skin, the red glow lighting up the room. Falon caught her breath when she looked up. There, perched atop the highest crate, sat a man dressed like he had just stepped out of the thirteenth century, one who looked remarkably similar to his brother, Edward. The Corbet brand was strong.

Rafael's fingers closed tightly around Falon's hand. Connected to both brothers, their power thrummed through them with the intensity of an electrical current.

Balor threw his head back and laughed. "Ah, yes, the fabled power of the three." He stood and pointed a condemning finger at Lucien. "Your power is useless against my magic."

"Come try us on for size," Falon challenged. With her mind, she lifted one of Rafael's swords from his back, and with a sharp flick of her head she flung it at the Slayer. Like a lightning bolt it flashed past them, stabbing him in the shoulder.

He laughed. "Impressive, but hardly superior to my power." Balor pulled the sword from his shoulder and hurled it back. With a sickening thud, it struck Anja in the chest.

Her scream combined with Rafe's roar of anger reverberated inside the container. Air hissed from Anja's punctured lung, her muffled sobs heartbreaking to hear. Gently, Rafe laid her down and pressed his hand to the wound to stem the blood flow. Not waiting for an invitation, Falon struck again, and this time it hit Balor closer to home. Furiously, he hurled it back, hitting Anja again, this time impaling her thigh to the plywood container floor.

Lucien snarled and moved toward the Slayer but Falon held him back.

"Go ahead; let the slayer of my daughter come forward to pay the price for her life."

"She deserved to die, just as you deserve to die, Corbet." Lucien sneered.

Balor laughed demonically. "My Mara was a beauty. She deserved more than what you gave her."

Falon's head snapped back at Balor's words. "Mara was your daughter?"

Balor's cold eyes glittered in the darkness. "She was my eldest. My most cunning. The future of clan Corbet! Mondragon killed her!" he shrieked.

Falon shouldn't have been shocked hearing that Mara had indeed been a Slayer, but a Corbet?

How had Rafe seen what Lucien could not? How—? And then it dawned on her as all of the pieces fell into place. "She used black magic to beguile him, just as the Slayers used magic to change the Vipers into those dogs!"

"She would have bred Slayers into the pack and through them destroyed the entire line!" Corbet chortled.

"She would have, had not Rafael seen through her guise and killed her," Falon said. She looked down at the hemorrhaging Anja. Corbet's magic impeded Rafe's healing powers. The lovely Lycan was bleeding out.

Realizing any efforts were a lost cause, Rafe stood and faced Corbet, genuine grief etched on his face as his gaze kept flickering to Anja. "You've got your facts wrong, Corbet. Lucien didn't kill Mara. I did. I tore that whore's heart out of her chest. I watched her bleed out. I would do it again if she were alive," he spat.

Balor laughed uproariously, as if he knew a secret that would destroy them all.

"You crow what you cannot claim, Vulkasin. She survived your pathetic attempt to kill her!"

When Rafael opened his mouth to argue, Lucien stepped forward. "And there has been no greater satisfaction in my life, Corbet," Lucien said as he sneered, "than the night I cut that treacherous bitch's head off!"

Falon gasped. "Lucien?"

He gazed at her then nodded to Rafe before turning back to Corbet. He laughed caustically. "The only thing that will top her death is yours."

"She survived my attack?" Rafael asked in disbelief, looking at Balor, then to his brother.

Lucien nodded.

"That's not possible; she was bleeding out, she— Why didn't you tell me?" Rafe demanded, taking an adversarial step toward Lucien.

The same shock that reverberated through Rafe now rocked through Falon. Mara had been alive and— She gasped, horrified at the repercussions of Lucien's deceit. He'd lied to have her! But at what price?

"All along you have known the truth?" Falon echoed Rafael's demand. The gravity of his secret stupefied her. He had lied to her! Lied, when he swore he never would. He lied to them all! And because of it, not only had they each suffered immeasurable pain, but the entire nation would now suffer.

Lucien turned contrite eyes on her. "I didn't know she was alive. All this time I believed as we all did, that Rafe killed her that night. It wasn't until that day I was caught in the Slayer net that I learned the truth." He begged her with his eyes to stand true beside him, but no matter what he said now, she could not forgive him this ultimate betrayal. "She came to me that night, Falon, while I was chained and caged. I was shocked, disbelieving that it was her, that she was alive. But it *was* her. And at first I believed her lies. She told me she had been held captive by the Slayers all these years, and that she had snuck away from them when she learned I was being held captive. She promised to help me escape, that she wanted to return to Mondragon with me as my chosen one." He raked his fingers through his hair. "But I didn't want her. When she sensed it, even her magic couldn't hide what she truly was when I refused her. I saw her as Rafe saw her the night he thought he killed her. I did what I should have done all those years ago. She died a true death."

Enraged, Rafael took another step closer to his brother. "Yet you kept the truth to yourself and allowed me to mark—" His gaze dropped to the mortally wounded Anja.

Despite her shock, and Rafael's rage, Falon maneuvered herself between the brothers. They had completely lost focus on Balor and if they killed each other now, they were screwed. They owed their packs more than that.

"By Blood Law you should have confessed what you had done!" Rafe shouted. "You have no right to Falon!"

Rafael reached out to grab her, but Lucien snatched her to him. His grip was hard and unrelenting. He would never let her go.

"I tried to, Rafe. My intention was to tell you both that night. But Ian attacked before I could. Then Falon was at death's door." Lucien shook his head, holding her tighter against his chest. "I tried to right the wrong by releasing Falon. I gave her the choice to stay with me or return to you."

"But you knew I could not return to Rafael when he'd given his oath to Anja!" Falon broke free of Lucien's grip and whirled around to face them both—and was hit with the inescapable truth that she loved these men. Both of them. Equally.

Despite the pain and suffering Lucien's lies had created, she could not bear to see him so heartbroken. She could never bear to see him face a death sentence for laying with a Slayer. Ironically, even now, she could not bear even the thought of losing him that way, so part of her was glad for his deception.

Yet the other part of her . . .

She looked Lucien deep in the eyes. "You didn't tell me Mara was a Slayer," Falon said quietly. "You didn't tell me there was no

Blood Law to be avenged. I thought, by choosing you, I was doing right by all of us."

Lucien's golden eyes flared angrily, and then dimmed. "Would your choice have been different, Falon, had you known the truth? Because I, who fear so little, feared that the most. What little honor I possessed, I gave up to keep you. Was I right to fear your choice?" He reached out to her. "Would you have left me?"

Falon bit her lip until she drew blood. She was torn straight down the middle. There was no way she could answer that question. If she answered that her choice would have been the same then, she would destroy Rafe. If she answered differently, she would destroy Lucien.

She looked at Rafe. Anja's blood glistened on his neck and hands. She turned to Lucien and saw the same blood on his hands. It was Anja's blood, though he had not touched her. If he had told the truth, she would not be lying at death's door.

Yet despite reasons beyond the lies, the truths, and everything in between, there was only one answer that was the honest answer. "I would have chosen you both." There. She'd finally said it.

Anja gasped from where she lay dying on the floor. Dark clouds of anger gathered forcefully on Lucien's and Rafe's faces. It was not the answer either wanted or expected. But at least it was the truth. And with it, despite the perilous position she was currently in, she felt a profound sense of relief.

"How sweet," Balor said snidely, rising in the air above them. "The Lycan whore would have had her cake and eat it, too." He flung his hands downward, one at Lucien the other at Rafael, snaring them with invisible ropes, immobilizing them. Balor smiled malevolently and floated down toward the floor. Hand extended to Falon, he said, "Take it, and come with me now or they both die here tonight."

Fixing her glare on Balor's onyx eyes, Falon's mind reeled with scenarios as she probed into the Slayers' aura to gauge his power.

Without the power of the three, she was on her own. While her power was strong, building daily, she knew Balor was not only physically stronger but emotionally he had the warmth of a shark, and that was his greatest weapon of all. She touched her father's amulet. *Give me clarity, Father, give me your strength. Show me the way.*

It warmed in her hand, sending vibrations through her body. Holding the amulet in her left hand, Falon extended her right to Balor.

She was going to backdoor him by shocking him with half-truths. As he took her hand, wrapping his long, cool fingers around her, Falon said simply, "Did you know that your brother Thomas loved my mother?"

Balor hissed in shock. It was preposterous what she suggested, but she had heard the partial truth from her own mother's lips. Why not embellish for the sake of their lives?

"Did you know that he took her north with him?"

Balor was predictable. He could no longer stand to touch her. He moved to fling her hand from his, but Falon tightened her grip. "Did you know that together they raised the Eye of Fenrir?" Pulling him toward her, her grip tightened painfully. "Did you know he shared his secrets with her, just as she shared them with me?"

His eyes widened in disbelief. Falon yanked him hard toward her, and just as he would have crashed into her, she flung him to the ground. When he hit with a resounding thud, Falon leapt up into the air just as he had done, and found herself floating above his stunned body.

"You see, Corbet?" she taunted spreading her arms wide. "I can do what you can do, only better." She slammed her open palms toward him; the force of the energy shoved him halfway across the container toward Anja, who moaned painfully beside the stunned Slayer. Balor's onyx eyes narrowed as he gathered himself up. His deadly black aura flared ominously in the stuffy container.

Slowly, Falon backed away from him, positioning herself between Rafe and Lucien.

Rafa, Falon said, as she moved around the container, inching closer to her men, *tell your woman to grab your sword lying beside her and to take her best shot on Balor. Any distraction will help.*

Just as Falon was close enough to Rafe to reach for him, Balor conjured a fireball and hurled it at her. Falon somersaulted out of its path, and turned in anticipation of another one but stopped all movement.

Incredulous, Corbet looked down at the sword tip protruding from his belly and bellowed in rage. Anja had managed to get up on her knees and, with Rafael's sword, she had impaled the Slayer. For her deed, Balor snatched Anja by the throat and viciously hurled her across the small space. She hit the inner metal wall with a sickening thud. Falon cringed, feeling terrible for her and Rafe. But it gave her the distraction they needed.

Falon grabbed Rafe's hand then Lucien's, breaking the holding spell. The Eye of Fenrir glowed hot on Rafael's hand. *Demand that it help us, Rafe, or we will die!* Falon cried.

Blood dripped from Balor's mouth to the spreading crimson mass on his torso. He pulled the sword, tip first, from his belly. He grunted when the bloody hilt emerged. He sneered, turning his cold black eyes on them.

"My magic is as ancient as Fenrir but stronger. Mondragon, you will die here for your trespass on my family. Rafael for the same crime. But before I kill you, you will watch me skin your whore alive just like I did your parents."

"You have it wrong, Balor," Falon countered. "Rafael has but to call upon Fenrir for aide."

Balor laughed. "If he understood the power of Fenrir, he would have called upon him long before now. That he hasn't tells me he doesn't know how!" His eyes narrowed. "Perhaps I should let you live, Mondragon. It will give me great pleasure to watch your own kind destroy you for breaking the cardinal Blood Law."

"No one here will bear witness to your trickery, Corbet," Falon defended Lucien. She squeezed his hand.

Balor shook his head and looked at Rafael. "What of you, Vulkasin? Will you bear witness that your brother lay with a Slayer? Was about to mark her and set her above all Lycans?" Balor laughed when Rafe didn't rise to the bait. "That he stole what was rightfully yours from right under your nose?!"

Rafael's hand shook with rage. The tension in his body was so acute, Falon was sure he would snap in half. But despite the demons he wrestled with, he did not make a move toward Lucien.

"He *fucks your* chosen one!" Balor railed. "She screams his name, not yours! And yet you do nothing but stand there. You are no alpha!" he spat. Balor looked over to Anja's broken, bloody body, pointing to it. His voice lowered conspiratorially. "She bears your mark but not your heart. She is at death's door and will no longer stand in the way of your honor. Call out the wolf, Fenrir! Demand that he destroy Lucien, and with your brother's death, you and your slut can rule the entire Lycan nation!"

Falon squeezed Rafael's hand. "Rafa, he seeks to destroy us all."

But in the end, it was Rafe's honor not his vengeance that swayed him. When Anja moaned softly, calling to Rafael, he went to her, breaking his contact with Falon.

Balor dove at Falon, snatching her up into his arms, breaking her connection with Lucien. She twisted out of his grip, shoving him hard against the metal wall, but he didn't let go. He grabbed her by the hair and swung her around with such force she was horizontal to the floor. Lucien snarled, leaping up to grab her, but she crashed into him, the velocity of the hit slamming him against the wall. He slid down beside Anja.

Unable to stop Balor's blinding assault, Falon screamed out for Lucien. In a blur, the Slayer grabbed one of Rafael's swords from the floor and, with a quick jerk of his wrist, he grabbed Falon by a hank of her hair, pulled her head back against his chest, and slit her throat.

Twenty-four

ENRAGED, LUCIEN ROARED as he watched Balor slit his beloved's throat. Rafael's war cry behind him was deafening. Together they lunged at the Slayer. With Falon hanging from his hand by one arm, Balor slammed through the closed container doors. He launched himself high above them onto a huge hook, hanging from a two-story-tall crane.

"Come an inch closer and I'll cut off her head," Corbet threatened.

Lucien slowed his approach, though he stayed within striking distance. Rafael landed on the edge of a stacked container beside him.

I swear on our mother's heart, I will kill him before he kills her, Lucien swore to his brother.

Get in line.

With Rafe's sword pressed to her neck, Balor hung Falon out over the Lycan packs, who were just coming out of some kind of spell. Groggily they looked to Lucien for direction. "Behold, you curs," the

Slayer shouted. Over two hundred eyes stared upward. "I hold not only the life of one alpha in my hand but the life of two!" He pulled Falon's limp body against this chest and spread his hand across her belly. He laughed uproariously. "Her womb bears the fruit of an alpha! But which one?"

Balor glared at Rafael. "Is the life of your child worth the Eye of Fenrir?"

Lucien snarled low. That Corbet would even suggest Falon carried Rafael's child was ludicrous. She belonged to him! Only his seed could strike home. Though emotions fought over each other in his heart, Lucien's gaze had not wavered once from Falon's dying body. Nothing mattered to him more than her life.

Rafael raised his left hand to the heavens; the stone flared red-hot in the night. "I command you, Fenrir, to save the life of my chosen one! I command you now!"

"Rafe, no!" Lucien cried. In his grief, Rafe hadn't thought through his command.

But it was too late.

Lucien watched as all eyes locked on Falon, waiting to see that vital spark of her life force restored. But the howling winds that suddenly kicked up did not return Falon to either brother.

Instead, Fenrir did what Rafe had commanded.

"Rafe?" Anja softly called, stumbling in a daze from the container.

Horrified, Rafe turned away from his unintended one and back to the woman he loved.

Lucien howled at the waxing moon. Falon's heartbeat slowed to a stutter.

"Name your price, Balor. I will give you anything for her life," Lucien pleaded.

"I want the ring."

"I do not possess it!" But even if he did, the ring in the hands of Corbet, or any Slayer, was certain death for the entire Lycan nation. It was not negotiable. "I will make the trade," Rafael said, stepping forward holding the ring in his hand. "But only with your oath that you will never slay another Lycan or pay someone to do it for you."

Are you mad?! Rafe? Hand over the ring and we all die!

I only bait him with it.

Lucien felt no relief; he could not when Falon was on the edge of death and he was powerless to help her. The combined packs, all two hundred of them, were still groggy like drunken puppies and no help. Balor's spells were strong; it was why the arrogant bastard had showed up alone. Falon's heart stuttered again. But after a long-drawn-out minute, when it did not beat again, Lucien's beast reared its vicious head. He charged the Slayer, knocking him backward, the velocity loosening his grip on Falon. Lucien swung round and caught her in his arms. Rafael leapt up, and with both booted feet he kicked Balor so hard, the Slayer flew backward. He hit his head on a steel beam so hard, he could hear the sharp crack of his skull before he bounced off and fell onto a container. If Corbet wasn't dead from the impact, Lucien would finish him off. Gently, Lucien landed on the dock and lay Falon down on the ground. He worked frantically to save her. He pressed his fingers into the severed vein to plug the blood flow. Rafe dropped beside him and pressed his fingers alongside his brother's. The packs pressed close to witness or aide the brothers who desperately tried to save this most special Lycan's life.

"Corbet's magic impedes our healing skills," Rafe said furiously. "I don't know how to break the spell."

"She needs blood." At the same moment, the brothers bit their arms, then forced their blood into Falon's mouth. Each took turns rubbing her throat, helping it down. When her lips darkened to blue, Rafael shook his head.

"You stay here, damn it!"

Desperately Lucien put his ear to her chest, listening, begging for the slightest hint of a heartbeat. But there was none.

"I will not let you die!" he shouted, starting chest compressions with his free hand. Her skin cooled beneath his warm skin. "Angel," he cried. "Please, baby, stay with me. *Stay with me!*"

Frantic, Lucien looked to the one person he had always looked to for answers since he was a boy. The person he trusted above all others. But when he looked across Falon to his brother for help, and saw that Rafe's rage, horror, and despair mirrored in his own, Lucien broke down.

"This isn't happening!" Rafael shouted to the gods. "It's not her time! She's too strong! Too brave!" Deep, anguished sobs clogged his chest. "Too special . . ." His voice trailed off, as his tears fell onto her pale cheek.

"She's not gone, Rafa. She's getting back at us for our fighting," Lucien said, trying hard to believe it. But when Rafe raised his red, watery eyes to his, in their hearts, the brothers knew she was truly lost to them this time.

Gut-wrenching grief coupled with a profound sense of loss—not only of what he would never experience again, but the impact of Falon's death on the entire nation—shook Lucien to his foundation.

Rafael stood and roared curses at the gods. When they refused to answer, he raised his fists toward the fickle heavens. "Restore her life, and I will selflessly serve you!"

The gods ignored his plea.

"Deny my love her life, I will deny you my homage."

Realization struck them all that the gods were not going to come to Falon's aide that day. "You forsake me when I need you most? So be it! I don't need you. I possess the ring, and he who possesses it possesses all of the power!"

Rafael held his hand up to the midnight sky and commanded Fenrir, "Save Falon! Restore her life and I will set you free!"

Flames flared from the ring in answer.

Rafe dropped to his knees beside Falon, anxious for her to draw her next breath. But when she did not, Rafe cursed the wolf.

"Restore her life, and I will release you! I swear it on my own life!"

The ring spewed flames again. And still, Falon's heart did not beat.

"Release him first so that he can save her!" Lucien shouted across Falon's lifeless body. "Release him now before it's too late!"

Rafael raised his hand to the heavens again. "I release you, Fenrir!" he shouted, setting the terrible but mighty beast free after three hundred long years locked in the ring.

Winds kicked up across the cold bay, swirling around them with the force of a mini tornado. The clouds darkened as the ring burned furiously into Rafael's finger. It glowed, white, crimson, and onyx. Sparks shot high into the night air. A sudden explosion shattered it off Rafael's hand. When the dock cleared, Lucien nearly gagged at the horrific sight before them.

Dear gods. What had they done?

It, Fenrir, was twice the size of Angor. Most of his bulbous, deformed body smooth, shiny red skin with tufts of black wiry hair sticking out. His muzzle was too big for his small head, his fangs crooked and yellow, his beady eyes, bloodred.

He snarled, daring any one of them to voice the disgust their faces conveyed at the sight of him. Fenrir leapt straight up to where Balor had fallen and snatched the groggy Slayer by the scruff of his neck, then dropped back to the crowded dock. They parted for him.

Snarling low, breathing heavy, his drool soaking Corbet, Fenrir dragged the now fully conscious Slayer toward where Falon lay.

"Fenrir!" Balor cajoled the wolf as he tried to stand. "At last you are free! I am your humble servant!"

The wolf snapped the last surviving male Corbet's neck in half, then sunk his fangs deep into it drawing blood. When he'd had his fill, Fenrir dropped the Slayer's body to the ground, then moved to Lucien, who held Falon in a death grip.

Fenrir snarled, indicating that Lucien should lay her down. "Do it," Rafael said. "We have nothing to lose."

Reluctantly, Lucien lay Falon down on the cold dock. Fenrir snarled him back several feet, then opened his jaws and copious amounts of Corbet's blood spilled onto Falon's neck and chest seeping into her wound.

Lucien watched, horrified, unable to stop it. He would get them all killed if he even looked as if he were interfering, but more than that, if this was how that damn wolf was going to save Falon, he would not stand in his way. He glanced at Rafe, who stood as tense and anxious as Lucien.

The instant the wolf licked the blood-soaked wound on Falon's neck, her heart beat. With each lick the wound healed, and her heart grew stronger. When her beautiful blue eyes fluttered open, Lucien could scarce draw a breath he was so overwhelmed with joy. He felt at that perfect second in time as if the woes of the world had been lifted from his shoulders. Dizzy with joy, he bumped into Rafe, as he moved toward Falon. Rafe moved step for step with him, as intent on getting to Falon as Lucien was.

But it was not to be for either of them. Falon screamed in horrified shock as she realized what was touching her. Fenrir snarled and stood up on his haunches and shifted into a giant, deformed half-man, half-wolf hybrid.

"Holy mother of all the gods!" Lucien hissed.

For one so large and grotesque, Fenrir gently picked up Falon in his arms and carefully raised her to the heavens. "I have found the one, Gilda!" he called to the mysterious druid witch of lore. His excited voice was deep with an odd old-world accent. "The one true of heart and of both bloods!"

"No!" Lucien said, striding toward the creature. "She is Mondragon, *my* chosen one. She bears my child!"

Fenrir threw his head back and laughed as lightning flashed around them. In the calm that followed an old crone of a woman appeared. Long gray hair framed a deeply lined but wise face. She was dressed in a dark woolen gown of old. The weathered leather belt hanging low on her thick waist hung heavy with leather pouches and assorted bones and teeth. Lucien looked to Rafe. Most of them, he recognized as wolf teeth and jaws.

Fenrir's eyes glowed molten. "For you, Gilda, I give you your twin souls in payment for your benevolence." He swept his hand toward Rafe and Lucien.

No fucking way, Lucien said to his brother.

Gilda cackled as one would expect an old witch to cackle but instead of accepting what Fenrir offered, she shook her head. "You owe me for three centuries, wolf, not just one."

"I have been imprisoned for the last three hundred years! I do not owe for the centuries I was a prisoner!"

Gilda wasn't having any of it. Which meant Lucien and Rafe were about to go up in a puff of smoke.

Let it play out between them, Lucien cautioned his brother when he picked up his swords. *Maybe they'll kill each other.* But they couldn't retreat and leave Falon with Fenrir.

"Pay now, you monstrosity," Gilda demanded. "Or die with the twin souls."

"You would cheat me?" Fenrir accused. His rage roiled around them with the intensity of an electrical storm. His power was ominous and otherworldly. Beyond anything Lucien imagined existed. Knowing that, Lucien knew there was nothing they had, nothing they could do that would make a dent against the terrible wolf.

"Be gone, hag, your usefulness is no longer needed," Fenrir said and sneered. He turned his blazing eyes on her and, as if they were lasers, zapped her. The old woman screamed, rending her hair, kicking in a circle as the heat bore into her and through her. The putrid smell of burning flesh clogged the air. Lucien moved closer to Fenrir while everyone's attention was on the witch.

He caught sight of Falon's terrified eyes. It nearly did him in. *Stay calm, baby. Rafe and I are going to get you out of this mess.*

He focused on her as he spoke to her, unclear as to why she didn't acknowledge him. It was as if she could no longer hear him. "Falon, blink if you can hear me." When she didn't blink coldness filled his veins. Was Fenrir so powerful he could come between a marked pair like this?

In a puff of sulfur-colored smoke, the shrieking witch disappeared.

Holy fuck. We need the treated swords, Rafe! They are our only hope, Lucien called to his brother, who was closer to the container than he was.

Fenrir roared furiously; drool dripped down his fangs, pooling at his feet.

We're going to have to wing it, Rafe said.

He grabbed swords from his surrounding men; tossing two to Lucien and taking two for himself.

Fenrir turned to Rafael and Lucien, who moved together, swords in each hand, ready to fight for Falon's life. Fenrir scoffed as he looked piteously at the weapons. "Those cannot harm me."

Lucien's heart rate shot up one hundred points when he saw Falon pick up Balor's dagger from his ashes. Her eyes met his, then

Rafe's. She nodded and plunged it upward, deep into Fenrir's heart. The wolf screamed as his grip loosened. Falon shoved the blade deeper, twisting it and stirring it. Fenrir's agonizing screams were so shrill they covered their ears to prevent their eardrums from rupturing. But Rafe and Lucien rushed the beast, slashing his vital veins and stabbing his vital organs, careful not to cut Falon. He kicked them away. Both men tumbled backward into the wall of Lycans.

Blood poured from Fenrir's distorted chest, but despite what Falon had done and the damage they had inflicted, Fenrir appeared no worse for the wear. He was a damn cyborg.

Lucien motioned his men to spread out. Vulkasin backed them as did the Russian packs. And while a full-on assault would be their only chance to slay the wolf, Falon was in the way. Lucien would not take a chance of losing her again.

"What do you want, Fenrir?" Lucien demanded, stepping forward. Rafael stepped up beside him. "I will hand you the world for the return of my chosen one."

Fenrir looked up from his wounds to Lucien as if he were nothing more than an annoying fly.

"Release me, now!" Falon commanded the wolf. His distorted face softened despite the dagger lodged in his chest. He grabbed the hilt and yanked it free, sending his blood spewing in a high arch across them all.

Fenrir flung the dagger to the ground and snatched Falon tightly into his arms. His lips twisted in what Lucien was sure Fenrir constituted as a smile. Awkwardly he stroked Falon's shoulder and said, "I cannot. I have waited almost one thousand years for you. You are my chosen one. My true mate."

Falon screamed, horrified, struggling in his arms. Her powers had no effect on the beast. "She belongs to Mondragon!" Lucien shouted, knowing the wolf who had been scorned since his birth by his own kind gave no credence to Lycan law. "She carries my child! Return her to me!"

Fenrir speared them both with a harsh glare, and then said to them not nearly as gently as he had spoken to Falon, "She belongs to me now."

And then to the brothers' horror, Fenrir absconded with her into the night.